# THE
# SATTERFIELD
# INCIDENTS

### A Sailor's Odyssey in the Vietnam War

## JAMES LAYTON

# DEDICATION

This book is dedicated to God who gave me the gift of writing. To my wife, daughters, grandchildren and family; my deceased parents who served as members of *The Greatest Generation*.

To all who served in America's conflicts living and dead including the Vietnam War; to seafarers everywhere who have and continue to sail in harm's way through the world's oceans.

# TABLE OF CONTENTS

# CHRONOLOGICAL LIST OF PHOTOS AND MAPS FOR SATTERFIELD INCIDENTS

1. MAP OF PUGET SOUND SHOWING BREMERTON AND SEATTLE
2. PHOTO—DESTROYER IN DRYDOCK
3. PHOTO—ENLISTED BERTHING AREA
4. PHOTO—PETTY OFFICER DRESS BLUE/DRESS WHITE UNIFORMS
5. PHOTO—ENLISTED MESS DECK
6. PHOTO—MANNING THE BRIDGE
7. PHOTO—GEARING CLASS DESTROYER IN THE PACIFIC
8. MAP—SAN DIEGO
9. PHOTO—SAN DIEGO
10. MAP—PACIFIC OCEAN
11. MAP—PHILIPPINES
12. PHOTOS—WHITE ROCK BEACH IN SUBIC BAY
13. THE EASTER OFFENSIVE, 1972
14. MAP—SUBIC BAY
15. PHOTO—US NAVAL BASE, SUBIC BAY
16. PHOTO—BRIDGE CONNECTING SUBIC BASE AND OLONGAPO CITY
17. MAP—DA NANG HARBOR
18. MAP—SATTERFIELD AREAS OF OPERATIONS
19. PHOTO—FORWARD MOUNT GUNS FIRING ON

# FOREWORD

In his very first book, *The Satterfield Incidents*, author and Vietnam-era Navy veteran James Layton takes the reader on a most descriptive and action-packed adventure on the *USS Satterfield*, a World War II destroyer, now employed during the era of the Vietnam conflict. Donning the pseudonym of James Hickey, Layton, the oldest of twelve children from an Irish Catholic family, brings you into his world—the world of a principled, yet impressionable 21 year-old as he becomes a member of the *USS Satterfield*, bound for the South China Sea.

On board are a host of colorful and unforgettable characters: from equipment maintenance man Ralph "Buddha" Duff, to damage control man Tom "Flames" Alden, to radio first class petty officer Walter "Badass" Bearden, Layton is able to paint vivid physical and psychological portraits of these and many more shipmates. What the reader will find equally amazing is the high level of brief, yet complete detail which Layton provides throughout the novel. It is as if these events just took place, as opposed to the actual setting of a generation ago.

In closing, whether you are a seasoned Vietnam era Navy veteran, or a landlubber looking for an action-packed narrative, Jim Layton's *The Satterfield Incidents* is guaranteed not to disappoint. Here you will find the real drama within the ranks of Uncle Sam's Navy.

Samuel Plaza, American History Professor

# PREFACE

Each ship that has ever been built has a rudder which steers her. The wake is the trail she leaves behind her stern while moving. The width and length of the wake is dependent simply upon the size and speed of a vessel, for it can extend hundreds of yards astern and then suddenly vanish as waves or currents engulf it.

A ship's character and soul is her crew, for she responds to the actions and behaviors of those that man her. Likewise, sailors reflect the ship and its history, becoming one unique entity, embarking on far-flung journeys, their destiny unknown.

Those who never served aboard naval or merchant vessels can barely conceive or understand the psychological ramifications and shock surviving sailors endure after their ship sinks into a black sea and dies.

A vessel is a home and feeder, like a mother hen protecting her own. This is the reason that men, for thousands of years, have referred to her as she and why it is devastating to abandoned sailors to see her plunge beneath the surface into the abyss.

There are psychological man-made wakes which never cease but have profound and lasting effects on crew that remain in their souls until death. During trauma in combat, men have risen above their finite capabilities, driven by the human spirit to save both vessel and shipmates, thus attaining victory.

This is an account of sailors with mixed personalities and their joys, sorrows, and ordeals at sea during the Vietnam War. It is about sailors willingness to sacrifice their lives on a sinking ship despite overwhelming odds. The internal conflicts which ensued were but a prelude to a unique event in Naval history unprecedented since World War Two.

All of the characters are fictitious. The narrative combines human interest, conspiracy and adventure interwoven with historical facts.

Like main character James Hickey's odyssey, I was on a retrospective journey remembering experiences aboard ships during the controversial war. Though difficult and mind wrenching at times while recollecting certain personalities and incidents, it was nonetheless cathartic and therapeutic.

The work takes the reader on a historic flashback into the souls of the main participants. To be sure, there are poignant spiritual and psychological elements that have a direct bearing on their experiences, conflicts and plot.

I conducted extensive research to ensure historical accuracy, including interviews with former crew members of the USS *Higbee*, upon which the novel is based.

I am indebted to Cecilia Kawolek, caretaker of former commading officer, Ronald Zuilkowski, who graciously provided official naval photographs; to my friend and hero, the late John Thomas Allardyce, with whom I had the pleasure of spending several hours via phone gathering relevant information; to former ship's company personnel E.S. Kerr III, Gil Rodello, Marlowe Ng, and Gene Thompson, who provided significant data; to my wife Barbara, who was patient and had confidence in me; to my friend American History Professor, Samuel Plaza, who encouraged me to write; finally, this book wouldn't have been completed without the assistance and thorough editing of my friend Kay Keysaer, the expert design of computer graphic specialist Michael Andolaro and Great Lakes Maritime artist David Grose for the novel's cover.

It would benefit the reader to familiarize oneself in understanding nautical terminology on the following page to avoid confusion and/or misunderstandings since these terms are used intermittently throughout the book.

The reader will glean the reality of life at sea and of the internal and external struggles of sailors during the war. I attempted to include humor and character development as well.

Finally, I trust the reader will understand what I am attempting to accomplish: the willingness of men to sacrifice for others, and despite an intense storm, internal conflict and combat, overcoming adversity, and Hickey's sojourn and struggles in conquering fear. Embark with me aboard the *Satterfield*. You will never forget the voyage.

James Layton
San Diego, California
October 2016

# GLOSSARY

**ABANDON SHIP** Order/announcement from living ship's commanding officer in charge for crew to leave the ship due to inability to save it from sinking

**ABYSS** Depth of 1,800 feet (300 fathoms) or greater beneath the sea surface

**AFT** Area on main deck between the middle and stern or rear of ship

**ALOFT** Any area above the main deck

**AMIDSHIPS** Indefinite area between the bow and stern (or rear) of ship

**ASROC** Anti- submarine rocket launched from amidships mount

**AYE, AYE** Response by an enlisted crew member to an officer, understanding that an order or command is received and will be obeyed

**BERTHING** Area (s) where officers and crew sleep

**BOW** The exact front of a ship or boat just below the main deck

**BRIDGE** Command space one or two decks above main deck primarily used for ship's navigation and operational control

**BULKHEAD** The walls inside a ship

**CHOW** Military term for food

**C.O.** Commanding officer, Commander rank normally aboard destroyers equal to Lieutenant Colonel in other military branches

**DAVIT** A steel device used to hold, raise and lower small boats aboard ship

**DC** Damage Control man rank in U.S. Navy responsible for ship repair and fighting fires

**DD** U.S. Naval designation for destroyer

**DECK** Floor

**DUNGAREES** Blue working uniform for enlisted sailors

**FATHOM** Six feet

**FORCASTLE (focsle)** Area aboard ship between the bridge and bow used for storage machinery and crews quarters.

**FREEBOARD** Outboard areas between main deck and the sea

**GALLEY** Location where meals are prepared and cooked

**GENERAL QUARTERS** Announcement aboard ship calling crew to battle stations

**HALYARD** Ropes extending from main deck up to ship's mast used for raising and lowering flags

**HATCH** Round or oval steel door with flanges for securing spaces

**HEAD** Bathroom

**HELMSMAN** A sailor positioned on a ship's bridge manning the wheel for steering

**HULL** A ships bottom

**KNOT** A ship's speed at sea, each knot equals 1.15 m.p.h.

**MESS DECK** Crew's dining area normally comprised of long steel tables

**O.O.D.** Officer Of the Deck—Officer in charge in absence of the Captain

**PORT** The left side of a ship

**QUARTER DECK** Area just behind the bridge on the main deck

**RACK** Bed or bunk

**RUDDER** Large steel square located at stern hull below waterline for steering

**STANCHION** Vertical beam supporting spaces or frames on ships

**STARBOARD** The right side of a ship

**TBS** Talk between ships—short range communications between vessels

**TOPSIDE** The deck above a space, normally the main deck

**WATCH** Assigned duty based on specific billet or job classification

**X.O.** Executive Officer, second in command under the commanding officer

# PART I

## EDGE OF CONFLICT

# 1

# "DESTROYER"

Men at times are masters of their own fates.
The fault dear Brutus lies not in our stars,
but within ourselves that we are underlings.

Julius Caesar, William Shakespeare

Man is a microcosm on God's eternal seas. Since the creation, there have been intermittent storms on oceans resulting in deaths, but also turmoil within men who've sailed through them. Like the precarious sea, man's intrinsic being is a restless spirit, struggling between good and evil, rushing like waves toward unknown shoals.

Fear knew him as a boy. It functions as an insidious lurking beast, originating in youth, and like a minute cancer grows and spreads throughout the psyche. Alone, it sits in the subconscious, resurfacing in adulthood, and flight is impossible. Still present, it worms its length, enveloping like an invisible serpent, subjugating the capitulating man, but then releases its grip and frees his soul after confrontation and fight. Fear overwhelms many, but some struggle against almost impossible odds overcoming it. One man choose the latter.

The silver-haired sixty-five year old man slowly walked up to the long, dark edifice on a sunny day in the nation's capital. Large bags under his eyes, stress lines on the face and turkey neck reflected years of hard labor supporting his family. His brown-complected, petite spouse with jet black hair, two daughters and four small grandchildren stood twenty feet behind.

Painful arthritis shot up his spine as he slowly moved toward the dark wall. He scanned the 58,000 names of those who paid the supreme sacrifice in a controversial war, long before. The senior wondered, and asked himself, where is he? He searched five minutes, then his eyes widened, focusing on a name. It was painful. Evident stress lines appeared on his forehead while he carefully moved his hand over the name. Tears swelled and flowed down his tanned cheeks as his fingers touched, then moved across each letter.

His right hand rested over a friend's name while he closed his eyes. The man thought, "It's been a long journey, but I had to come and honor you. You were my strength and inspiration." He reflected, "My God! It seems like yesterday this all happened. I was young."

In the dark reaches of the soul, his mind quickly flashed, forty-three years through him like a video in reverse. What happened to all those years? His memory was still sharp.

The senior closed his eyes, thinking on the scenes of his life. Suddenly, a starlit moonless night came into view as a huge mist rose over a mountain range and descended, almost blanketing Seattle. He thought, "I'm not hallucinating. What was it? Fog! Yes, I remember it well." Fog is quiet. It creeps in silently "on little cat feet", then covers the land and slowly moves on in the night as the poet Robert Frost aptly stated.

It was April 1971 when Navy petty officer James Hickey boarded the last car ferry, making the one hour trip from the city to Bremerton, Washington. While the boat chugged, he stood outside, gazing at the mist wondering what lay beyond. A chill crawled up his back. Fear entered briefly.

He thought, "Push it out, forget it." Fear knew him since boyhood because of an abusive father. Two years before, a crusty drill instructor put the fear of God through him and seventy other recruits of Honor Company 117 during twelve weeks of basic training in San Diego

An eerie silence engulfed the massive old Puget Sound Naval shipyard. He was alone. Rows of docked vessels sat like gray sentinels with guns on superstructures, protecting sleeping civilians and sailors. The sun would rise in five hours.

Tired from carrying a 50-pound sea bag three hundred yards over his slender, five foot seven 150-pound frame, the 21-year old auburn-haired sailor now stopped, and gazed at his new home a few yards away.

The ship was asleep, surrounded in cement dry dock, away from the sea. She was built for speed, carrying men, roaming free on oceans, but now immobile; confined like a convict, alone in a walled cell. Sophocles appropriately stated that "ships are only hulls when no life moves in the empty passageways."

Massive lights on forty-foot poles illuminated her. Securing her fore, amidships and aft below the dock were six huge, square boulders. The Navy classified her USS *Satterfield* as DD 816, a Gearing class destroyer. The bow number signified the sequence of such vessels built. She was 3,300 tons with a forty-foot beam, a half-inch hull and measured ninety feet longer than a football field. The hull slanted toward aft with only ten feet from stern deck to water line, while her bow rose twenty feet above normal water level. Bright lights surrounded the vessel.

"Well, the yard birds must have been real busy today, working on this old tub," he thought. An enclosed gun mount with dual barrels sat between the bridge and the angled bow. On both sides of her sleek superstructure were two twin forty millimeter anti-aircraft gun mounts amidships, a deck below two stacks where black smoke ascended while at sea. Three torpedo tubes sat port and starboard slightly above the main deck between the bridge and forward mount.

All receiving and transmitting radio antennas were down. Messages were retrieved at the base communication building. A second dual rifle mount rested on the fantail between a small helicopter deck and the stern. Along starboard, hundreds of yards of cable wiring and extension cords spread into various compartments like the tentacles of an octopus. It was her first overhaul and renovation in twenty years.

Since the early 20th century, sailors nicknamed these vessels "tin cans" because of quarter- inch armor side plating, making them susceptible to enemy shells. Initially, their purpose was attacking and destroying enemy submarines. Ton for ton, the destroyer is the most versatile, efficient, maneuverable and fastest ship ever devised by man.

Unlike all other military forces, a ship is most vulnerable to destruction: susceptible to air, surface or underwater attack. She can't hide in foxholes, behind barriers or hills, escape in jungles or wait beneath the surface; she only steam on water, a virtual sitting duck.

Yet, destroyer men are unique and in a class by themselves. They are the first to absorb shellfire in battle hence summoning an intense feeling of pride in those who sail on them. Sailors and ship function together as one, in teamwork fashion, producing a strong spirit de corps among crew.

Destroyers, escorts and frigates were named after important, famous Naval and Marine Corps personnel and heroes.

In 1944, *Satterfield* was born as her keel was laid. She was launched, christened and commissioned a United States ship six years before Hickey first breathed air.

The ship's history was noteworthy. In 1945, she participated in battles against Japanese naval forces in the Pacific, shooting down six suicide planes and earning two battle stars. During the Korean War, she provided gunfire support and carrier escort duties winning another six stars. The first years of the Vietnam War saw the ship engaged in several gunfire support missions against the Communists.

He thought, "It's unusually quiet, too quiet. What am I getting into? May as well go aboard and find out." After taking out his orders, he lifted the brown sea bag over his left shoulder and strolled to the wooden forward brow. Cautiously walking across from pier to ship over the narrow structure he felt uneasy looking down thirty feet and seeing the ship's hull where several torch welds were evident.

A lone enlisted man in an undress blue jumper and bell bottom trousers wearing a white duty belt and .45 caliber pistol stood on the quarterdeck like a protective sentinel. They were asleep inside the old sea warrior. As customary, he turned and saluted the small American flag hanging above the stern, looked at him and stated, "Request permission to come aboard, sir."

"Granted and ya don't have to call me sir, but now my head's inflated pal." Extending his right hand, the man smiled. "I'm Tom Alden Damage Controlman Second Class." The grip was firm and non-threatening and the Eastern accent tone soft, comforting Jim. "What's yours buddy?"

"James Hickey, Radioman Third Class. Here's my orders."

Alden stared and grinned. "Welcome aboard. They call me ' flames' cause I train guys ta fight fires." He was medium built, two inches less than six feet with brown hair above an oval, tanned face on a 180-pound frame.

They instantly jelled. Jim gazed into his eyes. What struck him was the broad smile and his light green eyes that conveyed genuine sincerity.

His demeanor echoed a soul who would sacrifice himself to protect both vessel and shipmates.

In brief minutes, he encountered the vitality of a man possessing selfless character, as if he would do anything for you -- an adventurous spirit, rarely found in men.

Alone, the two discussed their backgrounds. Alden was 24, born an orphan in New Jersey, shuttled from one foster home to another. He found school uninteresting. Sitting at his desk as a teen, numerous times he gazed at blue skies, yearning for excitement and unknown challenges. It was as if his innermost self was being suppressed. A voice cried within: seek the unknown, beyond the horizon.

Later, with the help of social services, united with his real father in Pennsylvania, yet insecurity remained. He longed for the sea. That is where his destiny lay. When he was seventeen, after pleading several times his reluctant father had agreed and signed required enlistment papers.

Alden spent the first few years learning damage control and fire-fighting aboard a Landing Ship Dock vessel, home ported in Norfolk, Virginia. The adventure he sought came to fruition during sightseeing excursions in four countries when the ship called at various Mediterranean ports. Shortly before twenty-two, he re-enlisted, bought a car with the bonus, courted and married Janet, an attractive local girl.

Hickey, the oldest of twelve, grew up in Michigan. His parents served in the Navy stateside during World War Two. At times his father was overbearing; hence he'd developed a closer relationship with his mother. Most of the family was educated in Catholic schools, while dad worked hard, sometimes at two jobs, to provide basic necessities. Despite the son's shoveling snow and caddying for affluent golfers as teen, money was tight.

The family was relatively happy. However, intermittent conflicts with his father prohibited a consistent and harmonious relationship. He relaxed by escaping outdoors or sitting alone at a nearby creek, day-dreaming and losing himself reading famous sea novels, *Moby Dick and Two Years Before the Mast*. He also enjoyed watching the Emmy-winning *Victory At Sea* on an old black and white television. He bought and assembled plastic model ships.

Like Thomas Alden, James Hickey had a restless spirit. He enlisted at nineteen and was luckily sent to San Diego for basic training because a few relatives had relocated there ten years prior. Broad shouldered, he had a smooth light tan complexion with medium brown eyes below conspicuous, bushy eyebrows; he had a confident swagger and radiated a slight grin.

Alden listened, shook his hand again and smiled, "Hey buddy, sounds like you and I got something' in common. Let's get together again, okay?"

Hickey smiled and nodded. "It was nice meetin' ya, but I've got to get below, store my uniforms and hit the rack cause reveille's in a few hours. See ya later." It was a good beginning for Hickey.

Two decks below the quarterdeck behind the forward mount was the berthing area. A square glass-enclosed battle lantern, hanging on a bulkhead, emitted a dim red beam for limited vision.

He cautiously walked down the silver ladder, hearing snores as men slept, but suddenly stopped halfway. A strange feeling of impending malevolence rushed into his being. He thought. "There it is again, fear. For some mysterious reason, I'm uncomfortable and have an eerie premonition something isn't right, but I'm not worrying. Force it out. There's a lower empty bunk in the corner. Get to bed." Sleep was easy.

At 0:600, four distinct bells sounded on *Satterfield*, and then the unmistakable twirling sound of a boatswain's pipe blared over the loudspeaker. A Southern voice sternly announced, "Reveille, reveille, all hands heave out and trice up. Sweepers, sweepers, man your brooms get a clean sweep down fore and aft. The smoking lamp is lit." Jim thought, "I wish I could sleep another hour."

Sailors in white skivvies jumped out of rows of bunks to the deck, put on working blue dungarees and shot the bull. Each row contained twelve racks, lower, middle and high on three inch mattresses above canvas bottoms, supported by metal frames. At the end of each bunk was a hook. Before leaving, a man raised his bunk (trice up) on an angle and secured it to a flange on a steel pole.

Still groggy, Hickey sat on the edge of the bed, gathering his thoughts. Metal lockers were located under the bunks where only necessary skivvies, socks and uniforms were neatly stored, the remainder left in sea bags.

A man slowly approached, stopped and grinned, "Morning, pal, my name's Don Gates from Alabama. You must be the new guy, right?" Jim nodded. "Welcome to CR Division. I think you'll like it aboard. Where

**Above: U.S. enlisted Navy Dress Blues and Dress Whites Uniforms**

**Enlisted Berthing Area**
*Used by Permission, Tin Can Sailors Association*

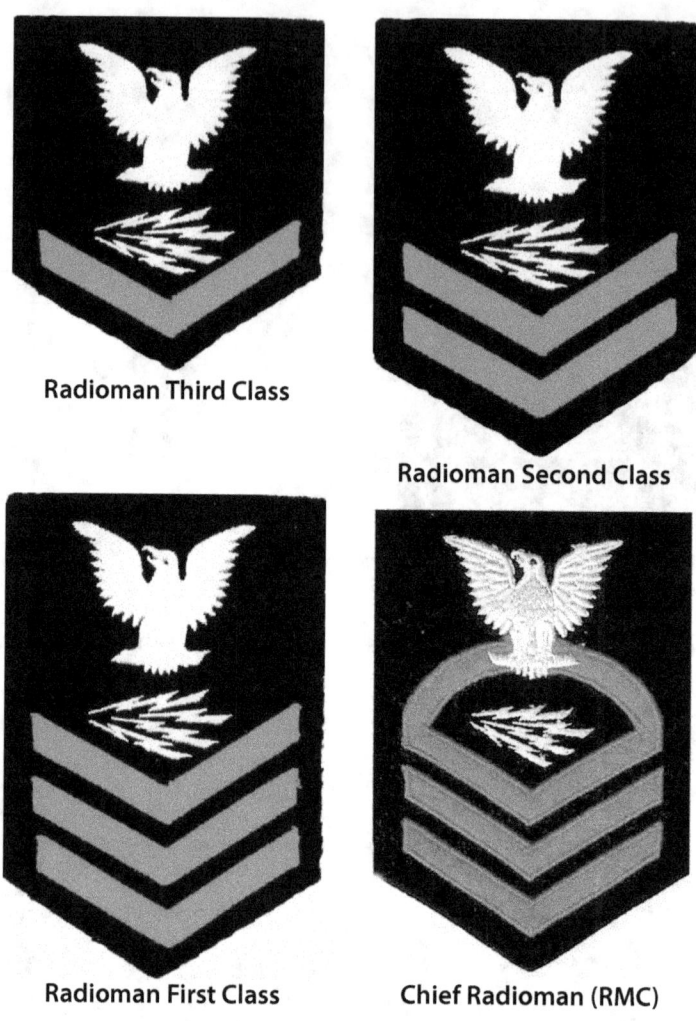

**Radioman Third Class**

**Radioman Second Class**

**Radioman First Class**       **Chief Radioman (RMC)**

**Radioman Ranks**

did ya serve?" His inquisitive nature was unnerving. A stocky man of twenty, he had a deep Southern accent.

Careful about responding to a relative stranger, he looked and asked, "Why do you want to know? What difference does it make, huh?"

Gates snapped, "Man, I guess nothin', just curious, that's all."

"Well, if it's that important to ya, I was at a communications base on Guam, eighteen months, but glad I'm off that rock."

"Man, you can have that piece of shit island for all I care. We travel fast here on this ship and came back from Vietnam four months ago." He smiled. "We saw some cool places in good liberty ports."

Radioman Seaman Gates had an unusually large head on a five eight 190-pound frame, with chubby cheeks and a pug nose. He relished attempting to know everything about a man's personal life.

Hickey dressed and walked forward of sleeping quarters into the mess area for breakfast.

The Navy prided itself in having good chow for morale. While eating, he listened to small talk among the communicators. Hickey was one of the few short men in the department. Repetitious four-letter words from some were unnerving. He thought, "I guess this is the real Navy."

Others finished quickly, leaving him alone. After devouring ham and eggs, Jim walked toward radio central, but Sidney Reemer caught up with him, put a hand on his shoulder and looked into his eyes. Reemer from Oregon was a tall, muscular and a tanned twenty-one year old. A unique feature was a Roman nose and piercing brown eyes. Though witty and calculating, his deep baritone voice caught your attention. A pugnacious chap, he'd challenge or fight at any incitement. Sidney was compatible with most and loyal to a few close mates. He advised, "Listen, Hickey, if ya got any sense, put in for a transfer now because there's a jerk lifer in the division. Stay clear of Bearden and give him a wide berth, cause he's trouble."

The words sent a chill up his spine. Though second in rank behind Chief Larson, Radioman First Class Walter Bearden practically ran the division. Because of his cavalier attitude toward new men, they secretly nicknamed him "Badass." He was the worst kind of superviser, with a habit of mocking and harassing subordinates while on duty.

Was Badass the evil presence he felt? He thought, "I don't need any more stress." His mind flashed back to adolescent years. At times, he underwent anxiety caused by an alcoholic father, who desired higher expectations beyond Hickey's capabilities, yet intermittently, his dad was empathetic and understanding. Because of the tremendous pressure being sole provider, working hard at an auto company, he expected his son to "set an example for your brothers and sisters."

Despite efforts in school, chores, watching siblings, he couldn't fulfill his father's demands and tired of hearing lecture after lecture, coupled with verbal abuse after drinking bouts. Apprehension enveloped the youth. He longed to escape, seeking new challenges and adventure in finding his real purpose in life by conquering the yoke of fear.

The evil he innately felt soon was manifested in a man unsuited for supervising or leading others. He didn't have long to wait.

There's an old saying in the U.S. Navy. Rank has its privileges. Essentially, the difference between a lifer and career sailor is one of behavior, respect, and how respect is earned. The lifer's ego inflates. He is consumed with power, some in particular relishing and thriving upon harassing weak or vulnerable lower enlisted men.

Many years ago, historian and philosopher Lord Acton observed, "Power tends to corrupt and absolute power corrupts absolutely." In contrast, a senior career petty officer recalls that a few years before, he too was a lower ranked man. He strives to know subordinates, earning respect by rational methods, patience, guidance and training with the goal of functioning as a cohesive unit as opposed to intimidation tactics, employed by some lifers consumed with power for its own sake.

He must speak with Alden with whom he felt comfortable. Tom worked in Repair Two in the Damage Control Division. He thought, "The first chance I get, I'll find him."

Hickey looked in vain among the 300 aboard the vessel. Government civilian workers blazed away with torches repairing the hull and renovating spaces. The screeching noise was deafening.

Communications division had four spaces located one deck up from the main, not far and aft of the bridge. Transmitters and the AC unit were across a narrow passageway from Radio Central, both secured by a gym lock set into the hatch with the combination changed weekly for security purposes.

To the left in R.C. sat two typewriters for code work and racks of UHF (ultra high frequency) black painted receivers for fleet broadcasts and two teletype machines. Three teletype units, a cryptographic safe and boxes with classified data were located in a small rear area. The most significant gear was the Navy cryptographic device, Fleet Broadcasting System (Orestes KW7) monitored by the NSA.

In her Master's thesis, Army Major Laura J. Heath poignantly stated.

The FBS (KW7) transmitted all US Navy operational orders to ships at sea. It was designed in such a way that it was effectively impossible to detect or prevent rogue insiders from compromising the system, and was the most widely used encryption device used in the Western world.

**Destroyer in Dry Dock Repair**
**Official U.S. Navy Photograph**

Cryptographic codes were changed daily, and only personnel holding top secret clearances had access to these spaces.

He stood near the hatch, gazed and grinned at the words on a small sign "CITY ZOO" above the opening. Not knowing the combination, he knocked on the metal door. A loud voice bellowed, "Who the hell is it"? Momentarily stunned, he replied. "It's Hickey, the new guy."

A short, barrel chested man in dungarees and skivvy shirt opened the door, laughing, "Scared the shit out of ya, didn't I?"

"Yeah, almost."

"My name's Ralph Duff. The guys call me 'Buddha' round here cause of my big gut. I'm the equipment maintenance guy and got this little shop in the rear. No one bugs me. It's my own little world." Ralph smiled and extended a hand, "I'm glad to meet ya." Duff had a large pink face, a beak like nose and gleaming blue eyes below light brown hair.

After entering, he put his hands over both ears as screeching sounds pierced the air, echoing off bulkheads. Men in dungarees knelt down chipping away old paint with tools, each identified by last name stenciled in black, just above their right chest pockets.

The four walls were painted battleship gray, common on all naval ships. In the center, was a large desk with twin phones where the watch leader sat. Behind, were two three-inch wide metal, pneumatic tubes extending up the bulkhead and through the overhead. Called the rabbit, they were used for rapidly sending messages via compressed air to the bridge and C.I.C. or combat information center.

To the left were a six-foot long counter with mimeograph copy machine and a wooden message distribution box with slits denoting major shipboard divisions. Six-feet to the right of the desk was a bulkhead dividing a narrow area. Various communications equipment lined the bulkhead including cryptographic, code and extra teletype machines.

"Here, Hickey, take this chipper and join the guys wearing goggles. I'm trying to help ya before Bearden gets here." He liked 'Buddha.'

Jim walked around and knelt next to an eighteen year old seaman badly perspiring. After depressing a button, the foot long ten pound caterpillar began rapidly digging into old deck paint while hundreds of small chips shot into the air. He wondered,"Why am I doing this tedious work? It should be assigned to lower ranked guys." On Guam, his duties were operating cryptographic equipment and teletype machines and processing messages. He thought, "This is demeaning. Hell, I'm not a deck ape."

Shortly thereafter, a man silently walked behind the laboring sailors, observing like a stalking panther. Jim slowly turned around, glancing up at a slender figure hovering above him as an overseer. He deliberately focused eyes on Hickey, frightening him. The man shouted, "What the hell ya looking at, squirrel? Don't ever stare at me, ya hear? Now get to work." The man mumbled incoherently, laughed to himself, grabbed a cup of coffee and left.

Gates, working a few feet away, and shouted, "Hey, ya really got balls challenging Badass. He's leading first class petty officer. Are ya crazy or something'? Shit, he's like a shark, looking' for new meat and bad news, Hickey. Ya better stay clear of 'em if ya know what's goods for ya." Jim's body momentarily shook like it did as a youth. Cocky Gates had been aboard a year. Similar to a quiet serpent, and with ears like a sonar system, he relished slithering in and out of conversations listening to shipmates.

After working a few hours, Jim's arms ached as sweat poured down his cheeks. His new mates exchanged one dirty joke after another, mentally sickening him after an hour.

Twenty men comprised Communications division including six signalmen led by forty year old Chief Petty Officer William Larson. He had salt and pepper like hair above a five ten slender frame and had an easy-going type personality. In addition to standing watch super-viser duty, Larson relegated much of the department's responsibility to his friend Bearden and spent extra time in the chief's lounge gambling playing poker. His attitude toward subordinates and work could be construed as passive since he had eighteen months remaining before retirement. He thought, "I'm just biding my time on this old ship. Why sweat it?" A few men were unique.

Ron "Smitty" Smith was a lanky, intelligent 20-year old Black from St. Louis with a good sense of humor who loved jazz. Jim and Smitty quickly bonded.

Diminutive and scrawny Gary "mouse" Warden, was a fair com-plected and taciturn lad you hardly knew was around because of his quiet demeanor.

Hickey hadn't met the other first class petty officer Timothy Loggins or third class Mark McGovern, both of whom were on two week leaves.

Red-haired, twenty-one year old lean Seaman Barry Carter had to be restrained by sailors overseas for uncontrolled drinking and fighting ashore. Because of a Boston accent, men referred to him as 'Caaaada."

At sea, watches were eight hours, twenty-four seven, supervised by Larson, Bearden and Loggins respectively. Three to four men stood each watch in main radio including one in the transmitter space.

Larson and Bearden were close. Bearden, the lifer, choose the watches he desired since he had a year more time in rank than Loggins. Most of the lower ranked men enjoyed Loggins or "Log" and his jolly behavior. He was patient, easygoing, and understanding when train-ing subordinates. In all, they seemed like a good bunch of guys except for Bearden. In the ensuing weeks, Hickey would keenly observe Log's behavior and his interpersonal relations.

Hickey's seventy-three year old grandfather Harold served in the First World War as a private and was wounded in France. Jim sought his advice in dealing with others in the military. "Son, be careful out there and don't trust everyone cause there's a lot of back stabbers. I don't want to see you get hurt. Be wise choosing a few close friends because you got to trust and depend on 'em." The wise words echoed in his soul.

While eating noon chow, second class petty officer Michael Thomas sat across and looked at Jim. "Ya know somethin' Hickey, I think you're going to be all right here. Obey the lifer's orders and don't let 'em get to ya. See, that's what he wants, and he really gets his jollies off by controlling guys. He's got a big ego and I think his whole purpose is breaking guys like he did last year over in WESTPAC." Reemer, Smith, Carter and Gates turned their heads, nodded and listened.

"What happened?" asked Jim.

After finishing eating, Thomas paused, looked at them and ordered, "Listen up." Thomas, twenty-four, from Minnesota, wore glasses above a square-jawed, tanned face. At six one on a stocky frame, men respected the dry humored sailor. His mellow tone was reminiscent of that of a D.J. on a classical or easy listening FM radio station. An astute listener, he was intelligent and sedate.

Mike related that while the ship was at Subic Bay, Philippines, nineteen year old Fred Cortland had a medical emergency while on liberty forty-five miles away in Manila. He collapsed and fell to the floor shortly after eating dinner at a restaurant. After being rushed to nearby Sangley Point Naval Air Station Hospital, he was diagnosed having a nervous breakdown. The sailor was unconscious for two days, but no one contacted Subic or the ship about his predicament.

The day after he entered the emergency room, the destroyer left for South Vietnam, and he was declared A. W. O .L. Bearden was elated, writing him up since he harassed the poor youth for months at sea. After being hospitalized a week, Cortland was driven to Clark Air Base north of Manila, flown to Da Nang, Vietnam and shortly after, returned aboard *Satterfield*.

The following day, he appeared at Captain's Mast (a non judicial hearing) before the vessels' skipper Commander Harrison as Bearden stood nearby at attention. Later, Cortland had told Thomas that the lifer lied about his duty performance to the captain. Harrison believed Bearden because the experienced petty officer outranked him by two stripes. Unfortunately, there were no further inquiries into the matter.

Despite Harrison's understanding of the medical condition and extenuating circumstances, including hospitalization, Cortland was reduced a rank to Seaman for failure to contact the duty officer aboard after regaining consciousness. He was ordered to perform additional duties which further exacerbated his mental state.

Psychologically, he was devastated because of a pay decrease that lowered his monthly allotment for his needy family back home. Extremely distraught because of the injustice displayed, he lapsed into depression, going so far as attempting suicide by slicing his wrists before Thomas quickly grabbed the knife, tossed it aside and stopped the bleeding.

After the incident, disgruntled sailors were heard whispering and asking, "I wonder when Captain Bligh's (of *Mutiny on the Bounty* fame) leaving?"

Aboard ship, the captain (highest ranking officer) is God with complete authority. The tanned and stocky 39-year old Theodore Harrison had a muscular neck and his six two body and reeked of arrogance.

Four years after an unsuccessful admittance to the Naval Academy at Annapolis, he graduated from college, was commissioned and spent years aboard vessels in various capacities. *Satterfield* was his third command of a U.S. ship.

He was focused more with the mission and relations with senior petty officers than on improving morale. Desiring a better command, and promotion to the coveted Captain rank, he drove the crew relentlessly. He continued his apathetic behavior among most of the lower ranked men.

The unfortunate Cortland, was a clear victim of circumstances and mental torment by the lifer, which resulted in a drastic plunge in morale aboard. The men despised the self-absorbed Bearden and Harrison. Additionally, a few higher ranked petty officers with inflated egos, bided their time in other areas and also contributed to low morale rather than supporting the crew.

Recently promoted executive officer (second in command) Lieutenant Commander Chadsworth Pursell performed duties well, yet his Achilles heel was in his relationships with lower ranked men. The 33-year old mirrored Harrison, displaying aloofness among younger enlisted with a habit of unexpectedly showing up in departments only addressing senior NCO's and junior officers. Several enlisted loathed seeing him slowly meandering around, and then cringed as he drew near. His snide remarks in wardroom meetings about young enlisted being "useful pawns" unnerved other officers.

He stood six feet, was medium built and fair-complected with a ski sloop like nose and trimmed mustache below blue eyes and brown hair. Born with a silver spoon in his mouth to affluent New York parents, Pursell spent the majority of twelve years stationed at shore bases. Aboard a year on this, his first ship, *Satterfield* became a stumbling block in a career path he found difficult tolerating, never feeling comfortable at sea living with hundreds of others. He longed to return to a large base with day duties and extra time pursuing his real passion, tennis.

On the one hand, Pursell's behavior around Harrison could be described as reticent. Conversely, during Harrison's absence on the bridge or elsewhere, he was precarious and unstable, reverting to nervous behavior, at times followed by emotional outbursts at junior officers and enlisted.

Pursell reported directly to the Captain. He was responsible for coordinating departments, keeping records, maintaining discipline, as well as for the welfare and morale of the crew. Successful with the first two, he failed with the last three.

Jim inquired, "Hey Mike, what became of the guy?"

Thomas continued. The busted sailor wrote a few letters to Congressmen detailing what occurred and requested an inquiry. Shortly afterward, the Navy had enough, choose not to pursue it, but instead washed their hands of the affair. He requested a transfer desiring to complete his four-year hitch, but the Navy, fearing an inquiry, authorized an early General Discharge for the youth.

The news spread like wildfire throughout the ship. Many of the crew hated Bearden, Purcell and Harrison. Within a week, fifty men requested transfers.

"That's an outrage," Jim exclaimed. "I feel sorry for that guy."

Just then, Douglas Kennel showed up with a cup of coffee and stared at Hickey. "Shit, man, wait till ya hear about the other kid Badass done in." Kennel was a scruffy fellow who wore glasses on his partially ruddy face. Men called him "dog" out of a habit of loud barking after seeing an attractive woman. A few mistrusted him because of spreading rumors.

Thomas took a long sip of coffee, lowered his head thinking, and related about short stature Seaman McGuire. Aboard a few months, he was frustrated by Communications Officer Stewart refusing to listen to complaints about Bearden, informing the sailor that he had to channel through the chain of command. Speaking with Bearden was a waste of time. McGuire complained to Chief Larson who assured him he would confer with Badass, yet nothing changed.

*Satterfield* was Lt.jg. (junior grade) Robert Stewart's second duty station after graduating from Officer's Candidate School. He was twenty-seven and stood five-eight with hazel eyes and curly blond hair on a slender build. Most of the men had little respect because of his superficial character, cynical mannerisms, apathetic behavior, aloofness and consistent support of Larson and Bearden. The were a triumvirate. On several occasions Stewart became unnerved when enlisted addressed him as "mister", opposed to "lieutenant" which everyone knew he preferred.

He rarely smiled or showed emotion among men, yet was somewhat gregarious and himself in the presence of Larson, Bearden and Loggins. Most of the men disrespected and mentally divorced him after his half dozen major decision blunders in the radio shack.

They began surreptitiously gravitating to "Log" for guidance and support. Tim was pensive. He intently listened and observed, but initially repressed thoughts regarding these problems.

Thomas shook his head frustrated and said, "Heck, what did Stewart expect the kid to do, put in a chit (request) or write a letter to Bearden and then Larson, asking permission to speak him? That would be crazy. He knew it was futile."

He continued. "Well, the kid got frustrated, went down to berthing and wrote a letter to the X.O. detailing Bearden's harassing tactics, verbal abuse and slipped it under the door of Pursell's stateroom. Ya know what happened?" They shook their heads and stared. "Nothing. Would you believe it? Shit, no action was taken against the lifer. Matter of fact, harassment actually increased. The kid was scared shitless and had trouble doing his job with Badass jumping on him practically every time he turned around."

Thomas lowered his head a few seconds and then looked at each of them. He was somber as his expression quickly changed. "They broke him. He was deeply upset by Larson and Stewarts' passive attitudes and daily abuse from Badass. One dark night, the kid walked out and jumped into the South China Sea. After muster the next morning, they declared him missing. We joined another ship and spent a day vainly searching and never saw him again."

Sid turned, looked at Jim and exclaimed, "Now ya see what I was talking about when I suggested ya put in for a transfer? This guy's a real asshole."

"Didn't the Navy do anything?" Jim asked incredulously.

Thomas related. "The Navy convened a brief inquiry for a couple hours in Da Nang. A few lower ranked guys no longer aboard, were called to testify in front of a review board comprised of Commanders and Captains, but fearing retribution from Bearden not a word was uttered against them. I shut my mouth too." His jaw dropped as he cupped his hand. "Now, I feel like crap thinking about it."

Afterward, men in communications knew of a cover up, based on outright lies and deceptions. One man even wrote an anonymous letter to the Navy Department, describing what occurred including Harrison and Pursell's intransigence, but due to their exemplary records the Navy protected the officers and no action was taken.

The lifer acted like nothing serious happened, further alienating the men. In his demented mind, he sought new prey. A few sailors hatched a plan to catch him alone on deck some dark night, and toss him over the side for the sharks to feed. There was a huge drop in re enlistments. Because of pride and arrogance, sin permeated the souls of those responsible, deteriorating morale among a plethora of sailors. It was the antithesis of harmony aboard ship.

Thomas paused, swallowed, glared at him and concluded. "This is all true Jim. I just wanted ya to know what happened. We hated seeing them go especially Cortland who we knew longer.

They both tried doing well. Now, be real careful, all right?"

"Ok, thanks."

"Scuttlebutt has it we may get a new captain after returning overseas and it can't come too soon."

The others nodded as Carter bellowed, "Yeah, like right now."

Gates chimed in, saying, "Ya know, Hickey. It was kind a weird when we were on liberty in the Far East after both guys were gone. Bearden would come into a bar where we were, sit down and buy us all a beer. He'd smile, laugh, tell a few jokes and act like nothin' happened. Man, a real Jeykll and Hyde."

Thomas concluded. "Some of the crew started believing the ship was jinxed or something. Just watch your stern, pal."

Hickey replied, "Well, I'll do the best I can."

At 1600, the sailors finished duties and walked down to the berthing area to grab a brief rest before chow. He lay on the three tier lower bunk thinking about Thomas' words. What had he gotten into? He decided avoiding the lifer if possible. Tom would be his support vehicle.

The evening pork chop meal was delicious as usual. Throughout U.S. military history the Navy was renowned having the best chow.

After leaving the mess deck, he walked down toward berthing, carrying a newspaper. Another man walking opposite rudely brushed him,

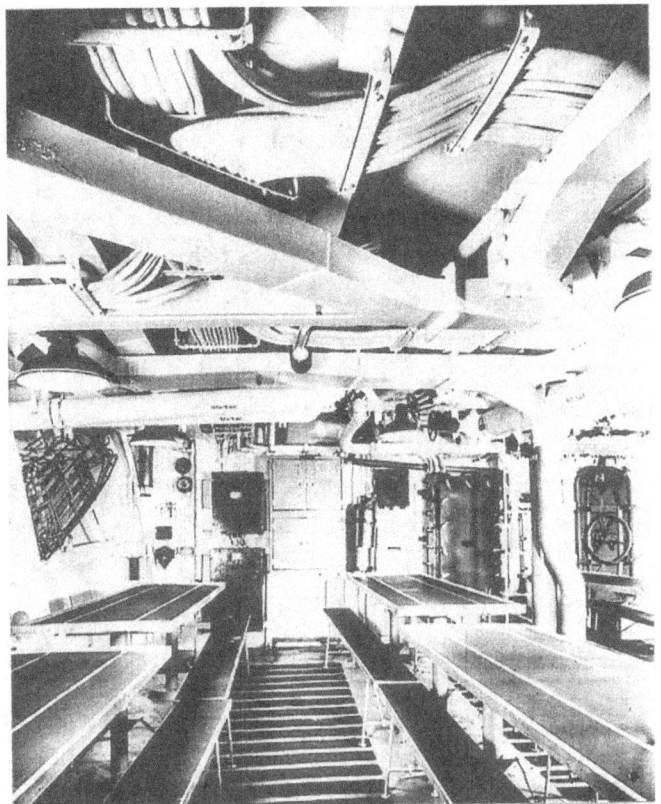

**Enlisted Mess Deck**
*Used by Permission, Tin Can Sailors Association*

sending the paper flying to the deck. Jim bent down to grab it, but a shiny black shoe quickly stomped over the folded object.

Jim looked up at his countenance. The eyes were lifeless! His lean hatchet face was somewhat shriveled, like a prune. A conspicuous tack-sized wart protruded on the lower right cheek. At 180 pounds, he stood just over six feet with a neatly trimmed rectangular mustache and dark brown hair combed straight back above a slender frame. His pointed jaw, piercing, slanted eyes and long wavy nose reminded him of Hollywood bad guy actor Lee Van Cleef in the Western *The Good, The Bad, And The Ugly.*

A chill ran up his spine as their eyes locked. A cynical grin suddenly appeared as he picked up the paper and handed it to him. "I didn't want ya losing this."

"Ah, thanks." Jim turned and started walking away.

The man shouted, "Just a minute sailor. Are you the new guy in my division?" The tone was hoarse and irritating. Jim stopped and looked at him. "I'm Bearden." The lifer quickly reached, grabbed Hickey's right hand applying an intimidating and crushing grip.

The eyes and devilish sneer caught Jim's attention. The pupils were dark brown, almost black. It wasn't the eyes, but the power behind the muscles that penetrated deep into Hickey's being. Scared and nervous, he felt like prey being observed by a jungle cat waiting to spring.

Bearden stared at him and exclaimed, "You know Hickey. My aim here is having everyone toe the mark to make CR division the best unit aboard this old ship. Do you understand?"

"Ah, yes I do."

The lifer turned around and departed, emitting a low, sickening chuckle from his throat, unnerving Jim. Badass' gait was unlike most: seeming to slowly oscillate, almost glide as his eyes quickly shifted port and starboard seeking prey like a hungry tiger shark.

Jim thought, "My, God, this guy's on a power kick. What have I gotten into?" He returned to berthing, attempting to relax after the tension, thinking about Bearden, a few past clashes with his dad and an encounter with a recruit while in basic training where an altercation ensued in the barrack's head in San Diego. The kid snapped a disparaging comment about his mother and laughed. Jim quickly swung, landing a strong punch on the instigator's cheek, knocking him against a sink before two others broke up the fight.

Intrinsically, not a violent man, Jim lost more fights as a youth becoming at times reticent and docile. His lack of confidence as a teen originated from clashes with a father he feared.

At six feet 200 pounds, his father an intimidating presence. His dad loved him and tried being understanding while guiding his son, but conversely, his authoritarian nature, coupled with the stress of providing for a large family, resulted in inconsistent behavior.

He found solace in a kind, humble mother. She took initiative, defending him when aware of her husband's erratic attitude due to excessive alcohol consumption.

Jim's insecurity led to conformity, the antithesis of leadership. He desired acceptance from others. Innately, he loathed dirty language, pedestrian among sailors, but did condone the verberge through fear of ridicule, yet remained a non-conformist and wisely choose a few men he was compatible with. He was uncomfortable, intimidated by large macho types, but relaxed with those who were kind and understanding. Though normally sanguine, insecurity, inner rage and fears had to be rectified before peace was restored in his soul.

The two leading first class petty officers, Bearden and Loggins, were studies in contrasts. Three distinct elements set them apart: upbringing, ego and dispositions toward subordinates. Like Hickey, Bearden grew up in a dysfunctional home. Raised in Ohio, small for his age, teased and ridiculed in school, he was a stool pigeon and the brunt of numerous pranks, which lowered his self-esteem.

In early adolescence, the family moved to a small town in Alabama. His alcoholic father refused to address him by name. It was 'Hey boy, come over here' or 'Boy, do this'.

In 1954, Bearden joined the Navy after graduating high school, desiring success in a self-fulfilling career position, and consequently fleeing prior abuse. After service at two shore bases stateside, gaining proficiency in the billet, he was sent to the Atlantic Fleet and promoted to non-commissioned officer. He had found a home and security.

Bearden reenlisted in 1960 and was ordered to a cruiser home ported in Long Beach. There he met a local woman and married. They had no children. Three years later, he was elated after being promoted to the rank of First Class Petty Officer while his wife worked as a beautician.

He became an expert in all phases of naval communications, attaining consistent 4.0's on quarterly evaluations. Shortly thereafter, vindictiveness slowly emerged within him, smoldering, like hot lava rising beneath a volcanic mountain.

It was and is the goal for all lifers and career enlisted to earn and attain the coveted rank of Chief Petty Officer. In effect, although obeying orders from officers, they manage the U.S. Navy.

A few years after promotion, Walt was frustrated after failing the Navy wide exams for the rank, and two years later was chagrined after not passing another CPO test.

Stuck in paygrade and rank quicksand, he became increasingly despondent, taking his anger out on subordinates. Initially an enigma, his precarious and inconsistent behavior kept men on edge. A bitter individual, on numerous occasions he'd erupt without cause. He brooded and thought. *I took crap as a kid, but not anymore, and now that I've got rank, I'm gonna dish it out.* Negative conditioning manifested erratic behavior. Encouraging and positive reinforcement disposition toward sailors didn't exist in his repertoire. What counted was results and production, regardless of a persons' self esteem.

Because of superior intelligence, his ego inflated. Cold, innately calculating, Bearden was cynical, impatient and emotional during stressful situations.

The two leaders had divirgent methodologies in communicating and training. While instructing, Bearden's rapid machine gun-like deliveries obfuscated, resulting at times in confusion among subordinates. If the individual immediately failed grasping the message, he'd lash and berate the man like a stern school master.

He desired power for its own sake, manipulating others to psychologically fill a void resulting from an insecure past. In company with Larson and officers, he had a predilection for sycophants heaping praises on his expertise in communications yet loathed anyone having the temerity to challenge him. Inflated hubris (pride) was his Achilles heel.

Conversely, Loggins was the youngest of four siblings raised on a farm by ethical parents a few miles from a small town in southern Iowa. He enjoyed playing harmless pranks on buddies, but excelled in scholastic and sports, particularly football.

Parents taught him the value of hard work. They emphasized. "Timmy, success isn't your state in life or wealth, you achieve it the way you treat others." He never forgot those words of wisdom.

After the two sailor's unfortunate incidents, his behavior increasingly became antithetical against any attempts at undermining the men's morale or dignity. He valued each person and had a unique aura or presence about him.

Aside from a magnetic personality, and confident swagger, a salient feature was a bright smile and demeanor upon entering a space, turning heads, captivating others, reminiscent of Hollywood legends Clark Gable, Cary Grant, Steve McQueen and Robert De Nero. His stocky frame and disposition reminded many of renowned comedian Jackie Gleason. Tim's contagious haw, haw, haw roaring type laughter resounded throughout a space. Though not extremely ostentatious, he was fortuitous and humble. An erudite individual and voracious reader, he'd enthusiastically plunge into a variety of classical literature off duty, and on various occasions during watches intermittently quoted Socrates, Augustine, Aquinas, Shakespeare, and Lincoln to his men.

Proud of his naval record, he was value oriented, patiently instructing subordinates. He'd sit alongside a man commenting in a relaxed tone, "You see, this is the reason the equipment functions this way, understand?"

He desired a harmonious team environment through guidance, focusing on attaining the best performance, but sympathetic toward those grappling with problems. Conversely, if a man loafed or had a lackadaisical attitude, a stern expression brought the subordinate back to even keel.

Aside from mild gregarious behavior, he was reliant and reassuring during stressful situations, embodying the true example of a leader by employing equanimity in relations and life.

For two weeks, Bearden studied Hickey's performance and training. After a few mistakes on teletype equipment he'd shout, "Hey boy, watch it now, watch it. Now, damn it, can't you go faster. Come on, come on." He'd ask and then chuckle. "Ya know what I like about ya Hickey? Absolutely nothing." He relished nettling and found a new victim, a person he could torment, short, like the others.

After another week of the lifer's haranguing and outbursts, anxiety and fear increased in Jim. He became obsessed with conquering it. In the eventuality of vitriolic outbursts, he initiated a regimen of deep breathing and physical exercises before standing watches under Bearden.

Apprehension increased in radio due to Bearden's irascible behavior, keeping the men on edge. Word spread as the spirit in the department slowly deteriorated. While on duty with Jim, a couple murmured in hushed tones, "Oh, oh, there goes Badass again, laying on Jim." The lifer's attitude and demeanor was like an invisible python, gradually squeezing, choking Hickey's soul.

Alone, thinking of his dilemma, Jim thanked the Almighty for meeting Tom, a trusted confidant. After three weeks, liberty call again would be announced. He'd enjoy a beer with his his new friend and head to Seattle, hopefully meeting a decent lady to pick up his spirits. It was an escape. This was the situation in May 1971.

# 2

# "SEATTLE, A SOOTHSAYER AND A GIRL"

Most of the men looked forward traveling to Seattle for liberty with a skeleton crew standing watch aboard. Late on one sunny afternoon, Hickey showered, put on dress blues and walked toward the after brow. As several men waited debarking, he saw Loggins twenty feet away. Half a dozen sailors surrounded the barrel chested, animated veteran waving his arms telling a joke. Laughter filled the air as they lined up producing required yellow liberty cards.

The impeccably attired five-foot nine, 200-pound man wore spit shined black shoes and squared Dixie cup hat. He was broad shouldered, the epitome of a fleet sailor. Four rows of various colored ribbons adorned his right chest below a square jawed, round face, wide nostrils, and round nose. A large white petty officer crow was on the upper left arm above four small white jagged lightning bolt symbols, signifying his trade. Just below were three gold v shaped stripes denoting first class petty officer rank. Four evenly-spaced golden hash marks were sewn across the lower left arm identifying at least sixteen years honorable service.

Timothy Loggins toward the heavens, turned and looked, making eye contact with Jim. Loggins grinned, nodded and bounded off the ship as Jim stood in line and thought. "My gut feeling he's an inspiring leader and good man. I think we'll get along fine." Time would tell.

At the base entrance Hickey produced his I.D. to a Marine gate guard and hurried into Bremerton. Old three and four story buildings lined the main street in the city of 35,000 as several sailors happily cavorted about entering and leaving bars and restaurants. He searched a half dozen bars before entering The Voyagers Nest.

It was an inconspicuous old tavern built before the last Great War. Several round wooden tables were scattered about left of a long bar. Nineteenth-century sailing ship photos, a large anchor and a three-inch wide brown figure eight rope near a marlinspike adorned the walls.

The bar was crowded with seamen, a few dancing with local girls as rock music blared from a corner juke box. He scanned, finding Alden sitting alone at the end of the bar, reading a newspaper and holding a bottle of Ranier beer.

He walked in and tapped him on the shoulder. "Tom, how are ya buddy?"

Alden turned around, smiled. "Jim, it's been a while since I saw ya. Listen, I've got an extra stripe and make a few more bucks, let me buy ya a beer."

The bartender, a stocky 50ish retired chief petty officer with large handle bar mustache gave a stern look. "Let's see some I.D., sailor." It bothered Hickey looking a few years younger than twenty-one.

"What will it be?"

"Give me an Olympia."

"Here's looking at you shipmate," Tom said. He thanked him as they toasted. The cold suds were refreshing. "Jim, ya been aboard now for a few weeks. I'm sorry I haven't had a chance to run into you because I've been real busy training new guys firefighting tactics on the base. How's it going?"

Jim related about the routine drudgery, chipping paint, and getting acclimated with new equipment. He frowned, mentioning apprehensions about Bearden despite being comfortable with most shipmates.

"Yeah, I know about that lifer and wish they'd transfer him. He's bad news. I feel sorry for the two guys he screwed, especially the one who jumped overboard."

Jim stared a few seconds at a couple attractive girls. "I've got to find some kind of escape or therapy to get my mind off that guy and relax."

Alden took a long swig, downing the remainder, folded the newspaper, moved closer and gave Jim a serious look. Listen, "Your buddies are right. Avoid him if ya can. I've seen his kind. I think after they make first class or chief something snaps in them. They get power hungry and some carry the rank too far. You see, career guys get better results from their men and there's harmony. I've been in a couple years longer and have more responsibility. I try to educate and guide my men, refusing pulling rank unless necessary, unlike others sitting on their own little thrones."

He smiled and put his hand on Jim's shoulder. "Listen, see Seattle. Try meeting a nice girl and occupy your mind with someone or something positive. Don't dwell on the asshole. That's what I'd do."

"Thanks buddy. "When I first met you I knew I'd feel relaxed speaking with ya about anything. What you said is right on the money. I'll take your advice."

A well-endowed, mini-skirted young brunette in heavy makeup walked and nuzzled behind Alden. "Hey, good lookin', wanna dance and buy me a drink?"

He turned around, grinned and extended his left hand. "Nah, not interested, honey." Ya see this ring? I'm happily married with a great wife and little girl. Go lure some other fish around here." He quickly lit a Marlboro and exhaled. She scowled and left. "Jimmy, they're all alike around here. This one's just another gold digger. Did you notice she didn't hit up on you? It's cause I've got an extra stripe. Hey, wait till we get over to WestPac: it's worse with all those Oriental hookers in bars, especially at Subic in the P.I. He smiled. "I can't wait till we hit San Diego. It'll be great seeing Janet and Shannon. I love them so much, and sometimes it grinds me missing them. You know, God's great. He gave me a wonderful lady and a beautiful daughter, and they get most of my pay. Earlier this year, they drove all the way to California from upstate Pennsylvania. I'm sure they'll be waiting on the pier when we arrive."

"You're a blessed man Tom. I'd like to meet them. When do you think we'll leave?"

"I believe in a couple months, after the contractors finish. First, we're heading out for sea trials and have to pass various inspections." His eyes flashed. "Oh, I almost forgot, you've never been ta sea, have you?" Alden smiled while gazing into his eyes. "Man, there's nothing like being on the water. I love the sea except when it's rough. Hopefully, we'll have favorable weather. Listen. Don't let those guys in radio get to you when they start razzing about not having sea legs yet, cause it's only a traditional thing. You see? I think you'll be fine. Hang in there."

"Jim, you're a good guy and I know you'll make a fine sailor aboard."

Jim patted his back. "Thanks for being my friend. I've got to shove off now and catch the ferry. Hey, want to come with me?"

"Nah, I'm heading back to study some manuals. You be good, Jimmy, and hope ya find a pretty girl over there."

After running a few blocks, he paid two bucks and went aboard as the last car entered a large holding area below the main deck. The 300 foot white boat was packed with sailor's and civilians. Inside was a large area with long pew like wooden seats in the middle. Single long benches below large windows ran port and starboard. A few feet in front of restrooms were three vending machines. A stairway led to a sun deck where a four-foot high viewing rail sat.

The boat got underway, and the sun would set in two hours. He bought a Coke and ran up to the top deck. It was the first time he viewed some of the vast expanse of Puget Sound. He marveled, gazing at scattered small and large inhabited, heavily forested islands, surrounded by deep black water.

As passengers idly chatted, he looked down behind the stern at the wake while the vessel churned steadily in calm water toward the city.

The day slowly faded as the sun set beneath the western firmament. After an hour, several lights from city skyscrapers glimmered in the distance. Seattle.

The vessel tied up at a downtown pier and passengers disembarked as vehicles drove off a ramp on to pavement. He gingerly scampered down the brow and headed for Pike Street, the main drag. After walking a few blocks, the aroma of fish from markets greeted him, permeating the night air as several automobiles motored about.

Gazing skyward, he saw the monorail speeding on an elevated track above, carrying occupants to the 1961 World's Fair, still on display in the near distance. He between buildings, viewing the majestically lit 600 foot high white Space Needle with its windowed elevator bringing patrons to the top of a fine dining restaurant. He thought. "It's too rich for my blood. Pay days a week away and money's tight. I'll find a reasonable place to eat."

In the Pacific Northwest, stars gleamed while the moon provided light as he walked up inclining Pike street passing closed businesses and entered a little restaurant. Four wooden booths lined the windows. In front of a long counter were circular stools and above a grill was a large menu. He liked the quiet, well lit environment where four couples dined.

He stood at the counter and ordered, then turned around and quickly scoped the place, but suddenly stopped as if transfixed. She sat alone in a corner booth, reading a book. The girl, attired in a royal blue dress was slender, almost petite. The face was lean. She was beautiful.

Jim sat near a front window eating fresh shrimp and occasionally looking at passersby.

Shortly thereafter, he a few seconds toward her. She paused, sipped a Coke, quickly turned her head and smiled. He, grinned, turned and gazed out at the street.

Having butterflies in his stomach, he wondered if he had gumption to walk over and meet her. He thought about some of the times striking out while playing baseball as a boy. Well, at least I tried; as they say, no guts, no glory.

Jim rose, walked over, looked down and smiled. "Hi, I'm Jim Hickey. What's yours?

Would you mind if I sat here?"

She looked up and smiled. "No, go right ahead. I'm Ann Kelly."

After putting the book aside, there was initial silence after he sat as both studied each other a few seconds. Ann was twenty-one, five foot five with medium blond hair which fell a few inches above the upper neck. He was awed by her gleaming, light blue eyes above high cheek bones on her smooth fair countenance. The sailor stared and thought. "Wow, it's just my luck meeting a gorgeous Irish lady."

They conversed for two hours and got acquainted, feeling compatible with each other. He walked, escorting her a mile and ascended Pike to an apartment she shared with another woman.

He asked, "Why don't we get together tomorrow, head over and see the World's Fair?"

"Oh, I've been there many times, but I can show you around since you've never been there. Yes, it sounds good. I'll look forward to it. Good night, Jim."

It was getting late as he walked back down and reflected. I have gotta find a cheap hotel room. After walking several blocks, he turned on a side street and as a few cars sped by. The city began to sleep.

He saw a dilapidated three-story brown building with a sign on the front door. "Rooms for rent, 12 bucks per night", and entered.

An old man with snowy hair wearing suspenders sat behind a little wooden counter. A three row rack of small wooden square slots for room keys sat behind on a table. "Hi, sailor, suppose ya wanna a room, eh?" The man's eyes peered above silver rimmed glasses while looking up and staring at Jim. "Now, I don't allow any hookers or girls with guys in here, understand? He whipped out twelve singles from his bell-bottom blues.

"Ah, sir, don't sweat it. Ya won't haveany problem with me. I just walked my new girlfriend home.

He smiled, "You seem like a decent young man. You know, we get a lot of transients around here, but I had to check just to be sure. The room's down the corridor."

Jim was glad the quarters were on the main floor. The ten-by-ten room was shabby. Light yellow paint on walls peeled, like strips of shredded tape. Aside an end table, a queen size bed lay near a window overlooking an alley. Facing was a dresser, with a large square mirror a few feet away. The building and bed had existed since the Roaring 20's.

He struggled pulling down a resisting shade, then turned and opened the single end table drawer, seeing a dusty Gideon Bible. After taking off his uniform, he flicked on a small lamp, lit a cigarette, lay in bed, thought about the girl and extinguished the butt. The supporting mattress was comforting and sleep came quickly.

The morning sun flashed brightly among majestic skyscrapers overlooking the sound as imposing Mt. Rainer stood, like a watchful guard miles in the background. He rose early, showered, dressed and walked outside. Fresh air from Puget Sound blew striking his face as he walked to a nearby diner for breakfast. The city woke as a few people emerged from dwellings.

The locals said Herb's Place opened during the Great War and was still a gathering spot for retired mariners and naval men. It wasn't fancy. A long counter greeted the customer, and a half dozen tables guarded windows. Hickey was surprised looking at battleship gray walls where several framed black and white photos of merchant marine and World War Two American naval ships adorned the walls. Little five-by-seven plastic menus sat on the counter. Near the restrooms, stood an old juke box. Five gray-haired men chatted idly in a corner as he walked over and scanned selections.

Jim liked nostalgic songs from the 30's; 40's and 50's, and then eyed one, distinct from the rest, *The Navy Hymn*. He thought, "I haven't heard that in years."

After inserting a quarter and selecting a half dozen, he sat at the counter then ordered a three dollar breakfast. Baritone voices began to sing. "*Eternal Father strong to save whose arm hath bound the restless wave, who bid'st the mighty ocean deep it's own appointed limits keep; O hear us when we cry to thee, for those in peril on the sea."*

Suddenly, a booming voice pierced the air, stunning the sailor and patrons, "Now, why in the hell did ya have ta play that damn song, - sailor?" An elderly man, sitting twenty feet down the counter glared at him, lowered his head and wept.

A stocky cook with bubble like cheeks wearing a white apron, quickly turned from the grill leaned over the counter, looked at him and whispered, "Hey kid, we never play that song when Sam's here. You see, he lost buddies after his ship was hit and sunk in the Pacific. Ya sure have guts, but ya probably didn't know."

"Yeah, you're right. I'll talk to him"

"No, let it play out. I think he'll be all right." Jim felt for the man as he quickly devoured scrambled eggs, bacon and toast, then gazed at Sam drinking black coffee, "Hey, mister, I'm real sorry. I didn't know about your misfortune."

"Misfortune my ass, shit, it was war, kid", he snapped. The tanned fifty-five year old had an unusually large, square face with receding gray hair and a protruding stomach on a short frame.He looked older than his years. He stared, sizing the young sailor, eyed the ship's patch on his right shoulder a few seconds, and shouted, "Hey kid, come over here. I wanna talk with ya."

Jim felt uneasy. "Would he chew me out?"

"Come over, I'm not gonna bite your head off."

He moved down the counter and sat near him. Deep in thought, the pensive man looked at his steaming coffee then raised his head and stared at him. "Don't worry, kid." The man expanded his chest, took a deep breath and said, "Listen, I'm over it. Ya didn't know, and I under-stand. No hard feeling?"

"Yeah, sure." He was relieved.

Large biceps protruded under his blue, short sleeve shirt. They shook hands. Despite his age, the grip was strong and firm. A conspic-uous six-inch long girl in one-piece bathing suit was tattooed on his right forearm. On the left, were bold letters USN below a three-inch wide anchor. "I'm Sam Mallos and I retired a few years ago as a Chief Boatswain's Mate after thirty years."

His low pitched baritone voice immediately captured Jim's atten-tion. "Don't talk about what happened before out there." Ya seem like a good kid."

Mallos stared, focusing on the small three-inch long, dark blue patch with white letters signifying his ships' name sewn on the right shoulder. "You're on the *Satterfield* and she's a tin can, right?" Jim looked at him and nodded.

The old sea dog's face brightened into a smile. "Yeah, I remember her. I was a twenty-four year old kid on another destroyer, the *Walker*, in the same task force before we got hit by two Jap suicide planes off Okinawa." His forehead wrinkled as stress lines appeared. He paused, looked down at his drink, thought and gathered his recollections. "Man, *Satterfield* did good knocking down some planes. I'll tell ya somethin', kid. Ya never saw anything like that in your life. It was the loudest sounds ya ever heard with all those guns firing at those bastards who were tryin' ta sink us."

"If ya don't mind me asking, how did it happen?"

His expression quickly became teary eyed as he looked down and took a deep breath. He closed his eyes a minute as the left hand suddenly quivered a few seconds next to his cup, and then Mallos stared at him. "Ya see, I was helping load four-round clips into one of our forty millimeter twin guns blasting away when the first plane hit our bridge, killing the captain and ten other guys. We blasted four out of the sky that morning, and then another one came in real low, surprising us, hit the stern five-inch gun mount, blew up ammunition and killed a lot of guys. Shit, there were body parts and blood all over. The explosion sent me flying over the side into the sea. I was lucky I didn't get sucked under, and caught in our screws. I must have been in the water for an hour or so after I saw her go down with some of my buddies still aboard."

A tear formed in an eye as he pressed his lips together and continued. "It's kind of hard saying this, but I cried like a baby after that. Later, a ship came by, picked me and a few others up." He wiped his eye, leaned within inches of Jim, raised a forefinger and remarked, "Let me tell you somethin', Jim that was the saddest day of my life losin' my ship."

Mallos stopped, looked down, took a long sip, then a deep breath and was relieved after alleviating years of repression. He ordered another cup, moved within a foot of Hickey and raised his voice. "You fellas on *Satterfield* better take care of her. She's a good old ship and if somethin' happens over there, ya better work yer asses off, fight tooth and nail saving her cause she's all ya got, see? Now, kid, ya remember what I told ya, all right?" Jim nodded.

For three minutes, silence permeated the restaurant as he thought about his words. Mallos eyes filled with tears as he looked up at a photo of an old destroyer steaming in an ocean.

Jim lowered his head, feeling sympathetic and thought, "It's gotta be painful for him even talking about his terrible experience, but perhaps it was for the best getting it off his chest."

The cook motioned him away and whispered, "You know, sailor, I've been here for years and never heard him talk much about it before. Maybe it's good he finally got it out of his head."

"Yeah, I was just thinking the same thing. I hope he'll be ok. I like the guy."

Mallos lowered his head again, stared at the drink, then ordered, "Hey, come back here. I gotta talk to ya." Jim walked back and sat on the circular stool next to him. "Hickey, ya should thank the Navy for sending you to her. Ya see, a destroyer's the real navy cause their the fastest and first ta fight. Shit, I'm still a destroyer sailor at heart." Jim took a deep breath, then told him about Bearden and some of the men's frustrations.

"Let me tell ya something.. I saw those kinds of jerks for years on shore duty and ships. I was never that way with my guys because I guided them. I was like their daddy. Ya see, when men you're responsible for respect, look up to ya, then ya get better results and you shouldn't make em' fear ya. They do their duties well and are happy. You don't demand respect like that guy on your ship, you earn it. I'm proud I trained and helped a lot of guys just like you."

"Yeah, I see what you mean. It makes sense." He felt comfortable with Sam.

The cook, leaning on the counter listening,remarked. "I did my twenty as a Commissary Man aboard ships and know exactly what he's talkin' about. Ya got career guys and asshole lifers."

Hickey thought and gazed at Mallos. "What if the situation becomes unbearable, even if the chief and lieutenant won't take action against him?"

Mallos gazed up, moving his eyes across various ships on the wall and thought. "Well, if that happens ya need to have a secret meeting with guys ya can trust." He raised his forefinger close to the sailors face. "Listen, be real careful though, only trust a few close mates and choose 'em well because before ya know it, someone will back stab ya."

"I see what ya mean Sam. Ah, what should we do if it gets out of hand?"

Mallos scanned the walls again, thinking. "Now, I don't suggest ya do this, but historically, men have mysteriously disappeared over the side, and gone missing. On a few occasions, I've read in *Navy Times* that so and so got killed on leave, or in the war; you see a few notes where some guy got lost at such and such latitude and longitude. It tells me he either died aboard, fell, or was thrown over the side." Hickey's eyes expanded, almost in disbelief.

"Surprised eh? Hell, in all my years I've seen a lot, and kid, it's all true." Mallos leaned and rested a hand on Jim's shoulder. "Listen, I'm not advising ya do it, but if you've exhausted all yer efforts and the situation warrants, then wait for a moonless night. If he walks aft, get a couple mates and be careful none of the deck sentries see ya. Grab and toss him over. If he's not sucked under the ship and chewed by the screws, the sharks will finish the job. The problem will be solved. Ya see? Trust me, I've seen it happen."

"Yeah, I hope it doesn't happen because I wouldn't want it on my conscience the rest of my life."

"There's another way Jimmy. You and a couple a guys could pick 'em up near the stern, hold him over the lifelines some night and scare the shit out of 'em. He'll get the message. The problem is, he'll run to his Chief or some officer and sing, then your all gonna get screwed, probably kicked out of the Navy, and maybe even wind up in Leavenworth Prison."

"Thanks for the advice. Let me buy ya another cup." He sat for an hour, fascinated while listening to some of the old salt's adventures in foreign lands.

"Jimmy, watch out for those hookers in the Far East. All they want is money and marriage cause it's a free ticket to the USA. Be careful, a lot of em' carry venereal disease, and ya don't wanna get that do ya?"

"Nah, no way", he replied, shaking his head.

They shook hands and said goodbye. Jim walked, but as he grabbed the door handle Mallos turned around, and shouted, "Hey kid, come back here. I got something ta tell ya. Sit next to me once more, will ya?" A strange expression suddenly appeared on Mallos' weather-beaten face. He looked worried.

The man leaned over and whispered, "Listen, I don't know how ta say this, but I just got a weird thought in my head. I get these sometimes, where, I don't know. Now, don't think I'm crazy or somethin', cause I'm not." He took a deep breath, and stared at him. "I got a bad feeling bout something."

"What are ya talking about?" Sam gazed at the coffee without blinking for almost minute, unnerving Jim. "Sam, com on, get it off your chest. What's bugging you?"

Mallos took a long swig, turned and looked at him. Standing ten feet away, the cook leaned against the counter, listening. With a right forefinger, the veteran motioned Jim closer. Sam looked frightened and murmured, "Son, I was searching for the right words." He thought, "Ah, let's see. What is it? Ah, I know. Ya, see, I have this feeling inside something bad's gonna happen to her."

"To whom, Sam?"

"Why to your ship lad, to your ship. Some call it a, a premonition. Yeah, that's what it is. I've had a few of these feelings before and always somethin' bad happens. I can't explain it, but my wife can vouch for it. Now, don't get me wrong, I hope it doesn't for your sake and I'm not trying to scare ya. You're a good lad and will make a fine sailor." Mallos' eyes squinted. "I had to tell ya because in a way, ya remind me of myself when I was your age, full of adventure."

"What do ya mean?" Fear rushed into his soul as his face turned red. "Are we gonna get sunk or something?"

Mallos finished his drink, got up and put a hand on his shoulder. "Listen, Jim. A few words quickly entered my mind. Honest, I don't know where they came from. I've rarely shared these feelings with others, except my wife. I had to tell ya because I'd feel guilty if didn't, understand?"

"What words, Sam?"

His body quickly shook a few seconds while he mumbled to himself, then turned, looked at him and whispered, "I only heard these four words, 'five hurt, two overboard.'" Sam closed his eyes.

"Oh my, God, are we gonna get hit by a typhoon or something?"

The veteran's tone rose as he gazed into his eyes and said, "I don't think so, but I do know this. I believe you're gonna be okay. That's it. I'm sorry. It was on my conscience, see?"

Jim lowered his head thinking, then turned and looked at him. "Maybe I should keep this to myself, otherwise guys might think I'm crazy, right?" He took a deep breath and looked at him. "Wow Sam, this has really got me thinking and worried now. I hope your wrong about it though."

Sam retrieved his hand and stared, "You know if I were you and wanted to tell somebody, I'd pick one trusted mate aboard. Ya got it Jimmy?"

"Do you know something Sam? I wish you could go with us when we sail, but hell, that's wishful thinking."

He reached out his hand; clasped Jim's, smiled. "Yeah, thanks shipmate. I'd love to go pal, but know this much; my hearts' with you and all those others aboard her. When I kneel down for prayers at night to the big man up there, I'll say one for you and your old ship. Jimmy, take care of her and she'll get all of ya back home safely."

He turned, took a few steps, looked back, waved, smiled and said, "Thanks, Sam. You're a class guy and I'll never forget you." Mallos and the cook stood, grinned and waved goodbye.

The gait was slower than normal as he lowered his head, reflecting on the words. He thought. Sam wasn't a fortune teller nor was he hallucinating, that's for sure. The sincerity and words of the stranger captivated him. He would remember Sam Mallos who made an indelible mark on his soul.

The words "five hurt, two overboard" rang in his head as he walked a block. He thought. Damn it, I've gotta think of something else. He called Ann and arranged to meet later at the monorail loading dock.

She wore green slacks and a yellow sweater. His heart warmed seeing her approach him smiling. The monorail was a long white passenger vehicle on a track about eighty feet above the street. They boarded and swiftly moved to a large park late that morning. Site of the 1961 World's Fair, it was a carnival atmosphere. Several amusement booths and rides entertained families. Acres of beautiful green lawns with flanking shrubs and flowers surrounded thousands, congregating there. The most imposing tourist attraction was the 600 foot ivory white Space Needle. An elevator took hungry individuals and on lookers to a rotating windowed, circular restaurant on top. Groups of sailors walked around, while children scampered about laughing and playing on swings and slides.

After debarking, he quickly grabbed her smooth hand, and strolled around seeing various sites. He decided trying to impress her at an arcade with sharpshooting skills, though having none. He grabbed a short pellet gun rifle, and fired, surprised at getting two bull's eyes. She smiled and yelped, "Wow, Jimmy, good shooting." Few called him that, but he didn't mind. She was tickled when he gave her a foot long prize doll.

They walked around, people watching and conversing. He told her about encountering the old veteran, rambled about the ship and his duty on Guam. She was patient, yet felt a little uncomfortable not knowing what to expect with a man she hardly knew, but was innately pleased being with a gentleman.

By afternoon, crowds increased and spread throughout the expansive area. They enjoyed Ferris wheel and carousel rides, then stopped and had lunch. He wished the day wouldn't end. The fresh spring air from the nearby sound was refreshing as they passed an open bar. He thought; I'm not drinking because a dignified lady is with me.

As evening arrived, they returned downtown and walked. He asked, "Do you wanna see a flick?"

"What's a flick?"

"Oh, sorry, that's what we call a movie in the navy. She smiled and nodded.

During the Steve McQueen film *The Sand Pebbles* about a gunboat sailor, he placed an arm around her tender shoulder and nuzzled close. Afterward, they walked back to the apartment. He gazed into her eyes, planting a brief kiss on her lips. She responded, then grinned, "Thank you for a wonderful day, Jim. You're a good man"

He gazed into her eyes. "I like you, Ann." She smiled. He left, thinking and walking a few miles within the city, oblivious of distance, time, or space. The day faded as darkness enveloped the area. After boarding the ferry, he stretched on a long wooden bench and thought about the girl. The man had no desire for carnal relations. She was decent, kind, gentle and pleasant company. The liberty was therapeutic, an antidote to the specter of Bearden, but now, he dreaded returning.

After debarking, he phoned her, and they spoke for twenty minutes. He enjoyed listening as her soft, kind sounding voice, pleasantly rang in his ears. "Jimmy, are you coming back over?"

"Well, honey, if I don't have watch next weekend, I'll be back, but I promise I'll call you. Listen, I'd love to go back and see ya right now, but gotta leave. I'll miss you, honey, until I see you again."

She struggled saying the words. "That was sweet of you to say that. Listen, don't worry about anything all right? Remember, I'll pray for you. Goodbye." His heart sank. At 2200, he went aboard, clambered down into berthing and retired. What lay ahead?

# 3

# "SEA LEGS"

The next morning started well as Chief Larson trained Hickey and a few others on new communications gear. On Guam, he learned to operate the KW26 cryptographic equipment, teletype machines and processing messages, but had to master R390 receivers. He was assigned to process messages and send messages via teletype. Bearden wasn't around, which was fine with most of the men.

On the weather decks, the long extension cords were removed, halyards and antennas were re-installed. A few civilian contractors finished welding tasks on her old hull. She would soon put to sea.

After four hours indoctrination and testing equipment, the radio gang had lunch. Later, Hickey and Thomas, wearing dungarees, walked out on a weather deck. On the pier, a large mobile crane removed both port and starboard old, forty millimeter gun mounts to Thomas' consternation.

Thomas' eyes widened in surprise. He then turned and asked, "What the hell's the navy trying to do to us?"

Hickey looked down where a large, square steel box sat on wooden pallets and inquired, "What's that, Mike?"

"Oh man, I saw a picture of it in *All Hands* magazine a few years ago. I think it's an ASROC mount and looks like we're getting it." The unique weapon was an eight-cell anti-submarine rocket system, with the capability of firing nuclear rockets deep into the sea, destroying subs, the Navy instituted the Fleet Rehabilitation and Modernization or FRAM program.

Several destroyers, including *Satterfield* underwent extensive overhauls and renovations including the installation of the DASH (Drone

Anti-Submarine Helicopter) system. The chopper's maximum range was twenty-two miles. After sonar detection, a small unmanned chopper, carrying a homing torpedo, would lift off, remotely controlled by three men, operating the system.

In retrospect, depth charges were removed years before, hence the necessity for the ASROC and DASH installations. Some ships, including *Satterfield*, had one aft gun mount removed to accommodate installation of a small chopper platform and hangar, leaving one double five inch mount remaining on the fantail. The result was a substantial decrease in anti-aircraft defensive capability, consequently, guided missile destroyers and frigates carrying surface to air missiles would accompany older destroyers in overseas task forces.

The crane slowly lowered the remaining mount on to the pier where sailor's unhooked steel wire clamps after placing it on a large flatbed truck. Shortly thereafter, the ASROC was carefully lifted and positioned behind the forward stack where yard birds welded it to the deck. *Satterfield* was the last destroyer receiving the FRAM system.

Thomas bellowed, "Damn it!"

"Hey, what's wrong?"

"Listen, I know our purpose is destroying subs and the ASROC will help, but now they've left us practically defenseless against air attack. We have old World War Two five-inch guns that aren't rapid firing, and besides I heard the Commies in North Vietnam only have a few subs." He listened intently to the veteran. "Man, Jim, if we're ever attacked by aircraft, all we'll have are a few fifty caliber machine guns. Let me tell ya something, I'm worried."

Five days swiftly flew by as Bearden walked in and out of spaces eyeballing men, but to their surprise, didn't bother anyone. Friday liberty was announced at 1700. Hickey couldn't find Alden, but ran down the after brow, then raced to a nearby enclosed phone booth and dialed Ann. Her soft voice warmed his heart.

"Are you gonna be busy Sunday?"

"No, but why can't you come Saturday?" she asked.

"I've gotta study some manuals after watch and can't make it. Where can I meet you?"

"I'll be at the ferry pier at noon, ok?"

"Sounds great, honey. I can't wait to see you. The last Sunday in May was bright and cloudless. There was a local Memorial Day activity scheduled in Bremerton.

He showered, donned seasonal dress whites and put twenty bucks in his jumper. As he approached the quarterdeck to show the liberty card to the officer of the deck, an uneasy notion of someone staring, unnerved him. He looked at the forward mount.

Bearden leaned against the mount's hatch, took a drag on a cigarette and glared. While Jim advanced within a few feet of the officer, Badass shouted in a cynical tone, "Where ya goin', boy?" Momentarily ignoring him, he quickly looked away. "Hey boy, I asked you a question."

Taking a deep breath, he turned, at him saying, "I'm going on liberty, that's all."

He approached the O.O.D. standing on the quarterdeck and saluted. (A relic of Roman days when images of the gods were housed in that section of the ship and were paid homage by everyone as they came aboard. Traditions of the Navy) "Sir, request permission to leave the ship."

"Granted," came the reply.

The lifer started walking toward him. His heart raced as he asked, "Sir, is it any of his business where I'm going?" The lieutenant looked puzzled and scratched the back of his head.

"No, I guess not, sailor, unless you've been written up, restricted or are in trouble." The officer looked at Bearden who stopped fifty feet way. "Is he your supervisor?"

He pressed his lips together and responded, "Unfortunately, yes. "After producing the card, he saluted the lieutenant, turned, saluted the small American ensign flapping over the stern and ran down the brow to earth. Walking briskly, he refused looking back and was free of him, for now.

Moving past bows of ships, fear enveloped him. He stopped and thought, "My God, what if he heard every word? I'd really be in trouble, but I'm not worrying about it." His eyes closed a few seconds as he visualized her smile, flushing negative thoughts out of him. The temporary escape was necessary for his peace of mind.

Jim made the one-hour trip, arriving shortly before noon. From the top deck he saw her standing, gazing up and smiling. Elated, he ran off and embraced her.

After dinner, they sat in a corner booth, frequently kissing. Joy filled his heart. She slowly pulled away, stopping his affections. "Let's go to a coffee shop because I need to talk with you, Jim." They walked a few blocks to a small, dimly lit place and sat on a couch enjoying the quiet atmosphere, listening to piped-in easy listening FM music. She was quiet and pensive, surprising him. Something was troubling her.

"You know I really like you, but I don't want a serious relationship. You see, I have to find a job, and that's been on my mind. Besides, you haven't told me when you're leaving, and if we fall in love, I don't wanna be heartbroken when you leave. Please understand, Jimmy." Her sincerity caught him off guard.

He thought, took a sip of coffee, stared into her eyes and remarked, "You're right, Ann. I should have told you. We're leaving in a few weeks after sea trials. Disappointed, her lips pressed together, the eyes closed as she lowered her head in sadness. He paused and thought a few seconds. "Listen, why don't you look for work in Diego? I haven't been there since basic training, but it's a nice place, and I've got family there with connections. I'm sure they'd help you."

"That's thoughtful of you, but my family's here and I'm committed to staying." She extended both hands, touching his and gently pleaded. "Please understand, all right?"

Lowering his head, a sad expression came over him. "Well, what can I say? Listen, let's make the most of what little time we have, and enjoy each other's company." She nodded. They leaned back, closed their eyes and hugged, listening as Johnny Mathis sang *When Sunny Gets Blue*.

He placed a long, tender kiss on her sweet pink lips. She responded, but couldn't repress her sorrow as tears trickled down her cheeks. Their lips parted as he grabbed a Kleenex and gently wiped the drops. "Thanks, Jimmy, you're sweet. Let's pretend this is our last meeting, alright?" He was speechless. Passion took over both. Their lips joined, enrapturing each other for twenty minutes. She quickly pulled away, took a deep breath and stared. "I'm getting excited and don't want us going too far. We'd better leave, okay?"

Disappointed, he nodded, "Yeah, Ann, I think your right. I'll walk ya home."

After arriving, he reached and tried handing her a ten dollar bill, but refused, saying "Listen, Jimmy, that's thoughtful, but I have enough now. My folks help out. The Navy doesn't pay you much."

He placed both arms around and drew her near as they passionately kissed goodbye. Sadness crept over him as he walked back down Pike. He thought, "Damn, I wish was stationed here, get away from Bearden and be with her, but I've gotta be realistic about the whole affair.

The sun set as the ferry now pulled away from the dock. He climbed to a viewing deck and leaned against the safety bar, gazing as downtown buildings faded in the distance. He thought. I'll find a new girl in San Diego, but almost forgot. On Guam, a buddy had written to a Filipino girl from Manila. Jim received a letter from her friend with a nice photograph. Linda Chu Hernandez was beautiful. They'd exchanged letters a few times and desired meeting when *Satterfield* sailed to the Far East. This brought little solace and consolation, but now he would concentrate on upcoming duties and sea trials.

Memorial Day dawned partly cloudy and spring was in the air. After finding Alden, they walked to downtown Bremerton and watched an impressive parade with marching bands, floats, and VFW, American Legion veterans who fought in past wars.

Later, sitting in a restaurant, he told Tom about Ann and wanted a little advice. "Listen, shipmate. For many years sailors in different ports have fallen for local girls, and then shipped out. Man, the same things been repeated many times. Sailors are nomads. Now, I don't doubt ya like her and she's probably a decent young lady, but pal, we're shoving off soon. It's hard, but ya gotta accept the reality of what's goin' on."

"Yeah, you're right, gotta move on, but damn,it isn't easy."

Alden laid an arm around his shoulder. "I feel for you, buddy. Look at it this way. You'll always have the memory of her. Make the last couple times special. Now, that's the best advice I can give ya."

"Thanks, Tom. You're a true friend." After returning, He stopped him before going below. "Hey listen, I'm really concerned about Bearden. I hope you don't mind me leaning on ya if I gotta problem with him."

"Nah, come by anytime over in Repair Two, buddy, all right?" He turned, walked a few paces, back and smiled, "Until that time Jimmy, until that time." The words soothed him.

*Satterfield* quickly prepared for sea trials as various divisions completed training new men and senior NCO's continued making daily reports to their prospective department officers.

In communications, men were comfortable learning recently installed new equipment.

Shortly before taps, Hickey took Loomis aside and asked, "Listen, I heard you're getting out in few weeks, right?" Frank Loomis was a short, but cheerful, fair complected chap who wore black glasses. On occasion he would abruptly sing a few words from a song his mother taught him.

"Rock a my soul in the bosom of Abraham, rock a my soul in the bosom of Abraham, oh rock a my soul."

His face brightened into a smile. "Yup, Jim, I'm a short timer; only got twenty days and a wake up, then I'm outta here and looking forward to it. These four years have really gone fast. I think I'll hang around and look for work in Seattle."

Jim mused, "I'll introduce him to Ann and maybe they'll hit it off." He told him about their brief relationship, emphasizing her warm personality, lady-like demeanor, then grinned. "I know you'd like her. If you two mesh, at least she'll be in good hands after we leave, buddy. What do you think?"

"A couple weeks ago I ditched this gold digging, dumb blond after dating her for a few months. I was all gaga over her cause she's a knock out, but hell, I got tired of hearing her always talking about herself. Shit, every time I turned around I was spending money and broke before payday." He smiled. "Jim, the timing's perfect. I like the way you're playing matchmaker. Yeah, I'll meet her, why not?"

Jim smiled. "I'll see if she's open to meeting you buddy, all right?"

"Yeah, sounds good, thanks."

As Loomis departed, Hickey shouted, "Oh, I forgot to mention, there's a small fee involved for my matchmaking service, ha, ha." Frank turned around and chuckled.

The following Saturday, he returned across the sound on a bright day. Anticipating his arrival, she paced up and down the pier. Ann gazed up after the boat was secured. His somber, non-verbal demeanor caught her attention.

They embraced and quickly kissed, but it wasn't the same. He gently grasped her hand, escorting the lady toward a sidewalk running parallel along a main avenue. "Let's go back where we first met some weeks ago," he suggested. She grinned and nodded.

After dinner, he ordered two glasses of Merlot and proposed a toast. "Ann, here's to our future wherever we may be and may we meet a good partner for life."

She sipped, grinned and stared, "Jim, that was nice. I suppose this is goodbye, right?"

He shook his head with a blank expression, put both hands over hers and gazed. "No, not really. We're not leaving for another couple weeks." He told her about Frank and the possibility of being introduced to him. "Frank's a decent guy, and I trust him, Ann. Listen, I wouldn't recommend anyone. At least give him a chance and see if you'll be compatible. Does that make sense?"

She lowered her head, closed her eyes, thought a moment and responded. "Yes, Jim. If he's anything like you, I know I'll like him." His eyes quickly swelled. She grabbed a napkin and gently dabbed forming tears.

He rubbed his fingers over her soft hand and grinned, "God, Ann, you're gonna make a great wife someday for a lucky guy. I'm sure you'll like him. He's an outgoing and good natured guy who'll treat you well." She grinned, and consented meeting him. It was their last time alone.

By mid-June, the vessel was in shipshape condition. On an overcast morning, the huge cement barrier wall protecting her opened, and water from the sound rushed into the dry dock.

In radio, Gates overheard Jim complaining to Thomas about Bearden's harassing tactics after the lifer exited. He snapped, "Hey new boy, why don't ya call the base chaplain or some-one who gives a shit." As Thomas frowned after hearing the snide remark, Hickey quickly turned and stared at Gates as tension increased, initiating a growing rift between the two.

Within minutes, the vessel rose. She came alive. The boatswain's mate's pipe twirled, and the announcement came. "Make all preparations for getting underway. The smoking lamp is out." Three inch thick Manila hemp lines securing her were lifted off two bollards on the dock. Boilers were lit building up steam, and then black smoke rushed out of two stacks as the ship backed into the sound, carrying a dozen contractors, engineers and crew.

Jim and mates sat in the communications central space feeling the ship come alive. She was built and created for the ocean, but now had to prove her worth by passing several tests. The destroyer slowly made its journey north through one-foot waves in dark water passing small inhabited islands dotting Puget Sound. *Satterfield* slightly rocked like a baby cradle.

Thomas grabbed a cup of black coffee and slowly walked around the space observing the reactions of the few men who'd never been seaborne. He stopped, grinned, looked at Hickey and two eighteen year old's and asked, "Ya turning green yet, Hickey?" Jim shook his head. "Shit, this is nothing; wait till we get into the Pacific. That's when the fun starts and gets real interesting. Ha, ha. I can't wait to see your faces when we really start diving into waves."

The five-hour voyage took them past Bellingham, into the wide Strait of Juan de Fuca gateway to the Pacific. Throughout the vessel, tests

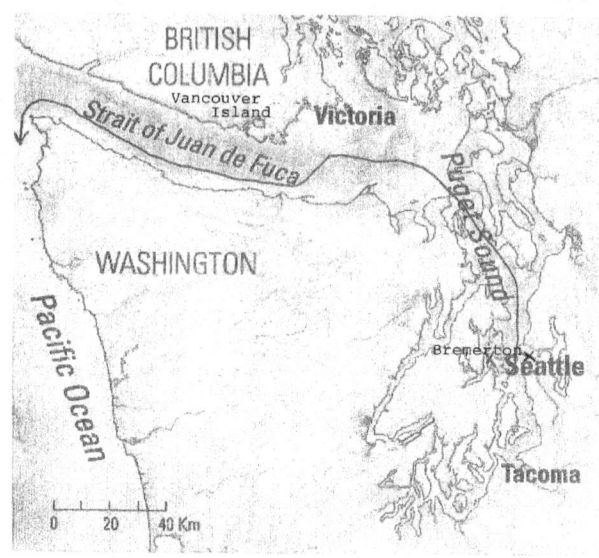

**Sea Trials Course, Spring 1971**

were run, particularly below in engineering spaces. Devices indicating the vessel's stability, boiler, steam, pressures and various tolerances were carefully measured by civilians and senior petty officers. Hull technicians using two foot flashlights checked each space at and below water level for any leaks. She was solid.

The ship maneuvered, performing a few brief turns; while a mile away small fishing boats sat idle. In the distance loomed the vast expanse of Canadian wilderness.

Men operated equipment, teletypes and ran several test messages. Receptions on teletypes were garbled. Bearden entered, ordering Reemer and Thomas to troubleshoot, identify and make corrections. Routine message transmissions performed well.

After changing frequencies, messages sent from the base were still being received without clarity. Jim sat in front of a teletype, quickly sending out a message as an inch wide perforated, yellow tape exited out of the machine's side.

Chief Larson ran out and gazed skyward viewing receiver antenna wires flapping in twenty knot winds. Shortly thereafter, Bearden grabbed Hickey's shoulder, surprising him. "Hey kid, I want ya to go aloft, climb the mast and tighten the antenna wires." He at Thomas. "I think that's the problem. Give 'em a safety harness and a pair of asbestos gloves so he doesn't slice his hands on the steel mesh antennas." Before the 20th Century, in British and American naval history, men were sent aloft as punishment for major infractions, a demeaning task, but he hadn't done anything wrong.

He rose and put a blue jacket over his dungaree shirt as Bearden gave a menacing stare, then quickly grinned as if achieving a small triumph. Before leaving, Thomas walked up and whispered in Jim's ear. "Hey, that lifer gave you a shit detail. Be real careful climbing the ladder and don't look down, all right? Obey his order and don't stare at him. Ya see, that's what he wants. Good luck."

"Thanks."

Jim put on large gray thick gloves and walked back toward the mast on the 01level, a deck above the main. Several dark clouds loomed ahead on a balmy morning as Canadian winds struck him. On the main deck, officers and contractors wearing hard hats and holding clipboards, scribbled notes while checking various compartments, relevant to Satterfield's performance.

After shutting down power in radio, Stewart sent word to the Combat Information Center to cease rotating radars before he went aloft. Hickey climbed a short flight onto the 02 level, and walked toward the two-foot wide steel ladder. A burly Chief Boatswain's Mate with a stern expression stopped him. "Sailor, where are you going?" He told him about the order. "Well, go slow, and I'll keep an eye out for ya, son."

"Thanks, I'm glad someone is."

As he began a slow ascent 40 feet to the tripod mast, as an audience of inspectors and a few officers congregated, gazing up from the main deck. His gloves gripped the ladders'sides as *Satterfield* swayed. He thought, "They're watching me; don't screw up Jim. God, let me hold on."

After reaching and shimming around a large square radar, he reached a little two by two platform. He thought, "Don't look down and be scared. Concentrate on your duty."

The highest object on the ship was the fore top, just above the yard arm. Extending down from the mast and yard arm, were four two-inch thick, reinforced ultra-high frequency (UHF) receive antenna wires, two of which were lazily flapping in the breeze. He figured this had to be the problem.

After attaching the harness around a pole, he pulled the wires down, tightly securing each around metal flanges protruding from the mainmast pole, completing the duty. He stared at a mountain chain starboard a few miles away seeing the vast forested Canadian wilderness on massive Vancouver Island.

Tranquility rushed through flooded his body and soul 80 feet above water. Bearden and others seemed distant. Despite the side to side swaying of the vessel, he thought. This must have been like ages past when men went aloft on wooden sailing ships. He was in another realm as a surge of freedom enveloped him. He smiled, scanning the beautiful topography a few minutes and breathed a sigh of relief, yearning to remain without inclination of returning below. It was peaceful. Succumbing to curiosity, he looked down. Dizziness rushed through him. Quickly, his head rose, again, staring toward land.

Suddenly, a booming voice from the Chief pierced his own little world, surprising him. "Hey, what are ya doing? Having a picnic up there? Maybe ya want me to even send ya up a couple sandwiches too, eh? Get your ass back down here." He nodded and waved. A few hard hats chuckled. He slowly descended, making sure his black work shoes touched each step as his eyes focused on each hand gripping the ladder's sides. He told himself. Don't look down. Upon reaching the deck, the contractors applauded. A lieutenant approached and shook his hand.

"Well done, sailor." Hickey smiled.

"Thank you, sir."

Shortly after returning, Bearden ordered tests run on receivers and teletype gear. He was pleased with results, but again glared at him, showing no sign of appreciation. Jim refused to lock eyes with him. Bearden quickly exited and went into a transmitter space. The radars were turned on and initiated their rotations.

Gates, Thomas and Loomis approached, patting him on the back. Loomis smiled. "Wow, man, we heard some guys clapping outside on deck and didn't know what it was. You're famous now."

"Ah, don't think so, just following orders from Badass."

Loomis stared and commented, "I've been aboard this tub two years and never heard or saw anyone go up and do that. Good job, buddy."

Thomas chimed, "Ya probably realize by now Hickey, the asshole has it in for ya, right? Just don't eyeball or challenge 'em. Don't show or let him know he's getting to ya, cause it turns him on for some sick reason, see?"

"I understand."

During the next few hours, the ship underwent several turns, reducing speeds amid several engineering modifications. Satterfield cleared Juan de Fuca then made a forty-five degree turn and entered the Pacific as white caps formed on three-foot swells. She plunged forward while spray surged over the top of her bow.

**Manning the Bridge aboard Destroyer at Sea**
*Used by Permission, Tin Can Sailors Association*

Jim and five others operated equipment, sending and receiving messages. Jim rose from a chair and strolled to grab a cup of coffee, but suddenly the ship heaved to starboard as he slid against a desk. Gates shouted, "Wow! Hey buddy, ya gotta know how ta walk like a penguin around here cause ya could get hurt." Standing nearby, a few veterans chuckled.

Thomas chirped, "Yup, I think Hickey's turning green, aren't you?" He shook his head, although feeling a little sick. After taking a swig of coffee, Thomas walked over. "Here, Jim, take a couple Dramamine, it'll help you."

"Thanks, I appreciate it."

On the bridge, Harrison gazed through binoculars against the large, rectangular bridge window observing the waves behind the forward gun mount. He was always thinking. He barked to the nearby helmsman, "Come to course 240, all ahead, flank speed."

The tall nineteen year old sailor responded, "Aye, aye, sir, course 240, flank." Boiler tenders and machinist mates sprang to life in *Satterfield's*

**Gearing Class Destroyer in the Pacific**
*Official US Navy Photograph*

bowels. The main throttle was turned on full. Men observed gauges, showing increased steam pressure as dual shafts turned twin screws under her stern to 391 R.P.M., resulting in a maximum thirty-five knot speed.

The bow rose, then plunged as saltwater swarmed over the bow and gun mount. The old old gal sliced through ocean, three miles off the coastline, while black smoke rushed out of her stacks. Harrison grinned and at Pursell standing nearby, "Well Chad, we're really bringing home the mail now, aren't we?" The X.O. nodded.

"Yeah, we certainly are."

Back in radio, men held on as the ship vibrated after hitting a swell. Chairs were secured with quarter inch rope. Two new men quickly raised their hands to faces, exited, ran and vomited in the head. After two hours of pushing the ship to its limits, Harrison ordered her back into the strait at half speed. Jim was glad he'd taken seasick pills and shortly after got accustomed to the up and down swaying motion of the ship.

She returned, tying up at pier two, not far from the main gate, pleasing everyone. On most naval bases, smaller ships, including destroyers, were normally docked at the first few piers; conversely, larger vessels were secured further because it took longer building enough steam for getting underway in case of an emergency or war.

A week later, final evaluations were presented to Harrison. The Captain, officers and contractors were pleased with the final sea trial results. *Satterfield* passed with flying colors. In two weeks she would depart Puget Sound.

# 4

# "SOUTH TO SAN DIEGO"

Ann arrived in Bremerton, meeting Hickey and Loomis at a cozy little restaurant. Within minutes after the introductions, it was obvious both were fixated on each other.

Hickey grinned and looked at them. "Listen, I'm odd man out and gotta run. You'll wanna get acquainted with each other. I'll see ya back aboard."

"Yeah, thanks, buddy."

She moved close, planting a brief kiss on Jim's lips then smiled, "Thanks, Jim for being who you are. I'm sure we'll get along fine here. Be careful out there. I'll pray for you every day. God bless you." He stood briefly, pressed his lips together attempting to stifle remorse.

A week later, Loomis was honorably discharged. He walked roamed, bidding farewell to everyone except Bearden. Carrying a sea bag on the weather deck, he looked at Thomas, Reemer, and Hickey standing on a deck above and bellowed, "So long guys. I'm a civilian now. I'll take care of all the round-eyed babes here, and you handle the ones over there." He walked down the after brow, turned and hollered, "Hey, don't volunteer for a damn thing over in the Nam because I don't wanna hear about any of you guys getting killed. I'll miss you, buddies." They waved as he jumped into a taxi.

The following Monday morning was beautiful as the sun's rays gleamed off the masts of gray painted ships in the old yard. Several crew brought provisions aboard as the ship prepared for getting underway.

Commander Harrison drove on to the dock, parked alongside his vessel, exited out of the shiny blue Ford and kissed his wife good bye. As he marched up the forward brow, the boatswain announced over the P.A. "*Satterfield*, arriving starboard." A ship's captain always went by the vessel's name. Men on deck stood at attention and saluted.

A loud boatswain's pipe twirled, then a deep Southern voiced barked, "Now make all preparations for getting underway. Set the special sea and anchor detail. The smoking lamp is out." A hundred people stood waving, among whom were Ann and Frank who had obtained visitors passes. Hickey and his mates, attired in dress whites, stood at parade rest gazing down. Loomis flung an arm around her shoulder as she nuzzled close. Hickey smiled.

Deck hands busied, making sure all halyards were secure before raising colored signal flags. Boilers were lit, valves were turned, steam shot into pipes and black smoke thrust out of her stacks.

The officer of the deck, standing outside the bridge, ordered, "Cast off all lines." Mooring lines were removed from three dock bollards and cleats by a few sailors standing on the pier. Frank and his new girl were somber, waving their last farewell as *Satterfield* moved from land. Loomis turned, looked at her and remarked, "Damn, I'm sure gonna miss those guys."

She slowly backed away into the sound, steamed northwest through the strait, entered the Pacific, and turned south steaming at twenty knots, a few miles off the coast. The ocean was smooth as glass. It was 1,253 miles to San Diego, but Harrison had a surprise when halfway to their destination.

Shortly after 0900 the following day, Harrison ordered general quarters. "This is a drill, this is a drill, general quarters, general quarters, now all hands man your battle stations." Three hundred men sprain to life and ran to battle stations, securing hatches and man holes. A sailor had to arrive at his station within three minutes before hatches were closed. Each man tucked the bottom of his dungarees or khakis into socks in case of fires.

Jim and others hurried up a ladder from berthing on to the mess deck and ran into radio spaces. Two donned headsets and sat at a table ready to send and receive Morse code. Hickey sat at a large teletype machine in the rear. Others wore life preservers as they rushed into the bridge, gun mounts, CIC (combat information center), and other spaces.

Harrison was relatively pleased with the results, but not entirely satisfied because of a few departments who reported late to the bridge. In the ensuing months, there would be more practices, including collision, fire and abandon ship drills.

Shortly after ten, the ship turned forty-five degrees to port sailing past the uninhabited Farallon Islands, the small land mass, playground of the great white shark and gateway to San Francisco Bay. After passing through the dangerous area, an announcement came over the public address system or 1MC. "Now make all preparations for entering port. Set the special sea and anchor detail. The smoking lamp is out."

That morning, she moved under the Golden Gate Bridge into the bay. The crew was delighted as she made a ninety-degree turn south. Thick fog covered the entire area as Hickey, Gates and Thomas stood on the quarterdeck while the ship steamed ten knots through choppy water. Before approaching Alcatraz Island, Harrison announced.

Now, hear this. This is the captain speaking. We'll be spending two days here. The Haight Ashbury area of the city is out of bounds and off limits for all personnel due to anti-war demonstrations and illegal drugs. Avoid the area. I expect you to conduct yourselves well as military men. Stay out of trouble, respect the local natives and enjoy your brief visit here. That is all.

The ship passed under the Oakland Bay Bridge and docked at a large commercial pier near the downtown area. McGovern, Duff, Reemer and Gates donned whites and went quickly ashore.

All petty officers including Duff and Reemer had the option of wearing civilian clothes ashore. A year before, the Navy desired to improve morale and retention authorizing men in pay grades E-4 (P. O. Third Class) and above to wear optional civilian clothing (stored aboard) on liberty. Many home ported sailors paid a small monthly fee, storing attire at locker clubs ashore.

Around noon, the fog lifted as bright sunlight enveloped the city. After chow, Jim went and leaned against the stern lifelines. Seattle was nice, but this city overwhelmed him.

Small fishing boats and hundreds of yachts roamed the bay. Row after row of merchant ships sat idle at piers. Numerous cars traversed over the San Francisco-Oakland Bay Bridge as thousands of gulls cried and soared above water. It was a site to behold.

He focused on a large vessel across the bay, south of Oakland, turtling from a distant pier, near the Alameda Naval Air Station. An aircraft carrier! He had never seen one this close.

The 1,000-foot long, 70,000-ton behemoth passed under the bridge as 2,000 sailors in whites, standing at parade rest, lined her sides. An unmistakable large, white 41 adorned the middle of the island and deck bow.

One of the chiefs strolled over near him, and pointed. "That's the *Midway*, sailor. She's a famous aircraft carrier. After she hits open water, the squadrons will land on her."

"Wow, that's some ship. She's isn't nuclear, but I wonder how old she is."

"Well, she was launched at the end of World War Two, and I served two years on her back in '65 when she first went over to Vietnam. We had some great pilots in those squadrons. All I know is she served in Korea, a few tours near Nam and even had the first naval ace of the war when I was aboard.

"She must be a floating city."

"That's right. I believe there's about 5,000 aboard. When we get overseas, she might refuel us, and we may have to do plane guard duties when she recovers her planes after combat missions." Back then it was common referring to these types of ships as "bird farms." They watched until the carrier sailed under the bridges and then faded into the Pacific.

Hickey's watch was uneventful and pleasant. Bearden was ashore. The local Herald Examiner had featured a full page spread about a charity pro football game that Sunday at Kezar Stadium. The hometown 49'rs were playing the New Orleans Saints. He thought, "I'll try and get a few buddies to go."

On Saturday morning after breakfast, he walked into comm central and grabbed a cup of coffee. Loggins supervised, while two others idly chatted. Initially unfamiliar with "Log", in the ensuing weeks he'd cautiously observe his behavior hoping Loggins could possibly be a mentor. From others, he learned Log was a career sailor, mellow, resilient, and a leader of men.

During mail call he'd receive letters, magazines, a farm report and newspapers. A Southpaw, he wrote numerous letters to friends, his wife in San Diego, parents and a son running a large Iowa farm.

Log stopped reading, smiled and looked at Hickey. "Hey, Jim, see if there's anything important coming over the order wire in the corner."

His low tone was comforting. Jim was glad being addressed by his nick-name and walked over, checking messages sent during the last half hour. If there was imminent danger of attack, a combat condition or a significant fleet situation, a repetitive bell would ring inside the teletype signifying an immediate flash or emergency message rapidly coming through the equipment, but that was rare when ships were in port.

There wasn't significant information, other than standard daily notices of vessels in port, weather reports, confidential data transmitted by the Twelfth Naval District, Alameda Naval Air station, the shipyard and nearby Presidio Army Base. Each message was extracted, logged by reception time, copied by a mimeograph machine and placed in various division slots according to priority.

On watch under Loggins, Jim learned of the man who significantly influenced his life. After being raised with five siblings in a laboring family, Loggins enlisted. He spent a few years in the Philippines, then was stationed at Pearl Harbor for six, after four in the Pacific Fleet. He came aboard a year ago and gained the men's respect.

Normally, first class petty officers chummed with their counter parts, but he didn't regularly socialize with Bearden; the two having diametrically different approaches toward subordinates and mores.

Loggins was cognizant of the two unfortunate sailors but didn't manifest sympathy for the men under him; instead, he choose a non-confrontational attitude—aware the lifer had a year longer in rank, coupled with the Chief and Lieutenant wrapped around Bearden's fingers because of past lies and deceptions. Although empathetic with the sailor's declining morale, he attempted adherence to the status quo, yet his intransigence during and after the incidents stupified most of the lower ranked men. Loggins would bide his time and observe, but his vacillation after the events haunted the sailor's consciences.

In the ensuing days, Loggins and Jim familiarized themselves with each other. Off watch, their discussions centered on philosophies of life. He'd found a mentor whose views mirrored his.

In hierarchical importance they were God, family, country and the uniqueness of every individual. Under Bearden's tutelage, anxiety and fear existed; in sharp contrast, under Loggins supervision, harmony prevailed. Behaviorally, men were relaxed and compatible as he patiently guided them, like an older brother.

Attempting better morale, Loggins would intermittently blurted hilarious sea stories and jokes as subordinates listened and chuckled.

His pot belly shook while laughter filled the space. With receding black hair, he looked older than his thirty-eight years while puffing on a cigar. Shortly, before an account of one adventure, he'd look at each man, pause and state, "Ya know, ol' dad here remembers."

Loggins magnetic personality attracted everyone's attention. He was rarely irate or let his emotions overcome rational behavior. A patient leader, he relished training young men.

Relatively sedate, he'd lose himself reflecting, and then turn moody after learning of his wife's infidelity while he was overseas.

Loggins slowly got up, walked to one of the receivers and tuned in a popular radio station. "Ya guys wanna hear some good music?" The response was unanimous. Traffic flow was minor as they listened to one hit after another from The Fifth Dimension, The Temptations, Chicago, and Stevie Wonder. Later on watch, Jim thought, "My gut feeling is I think I can trust this guy and will bend his ear if I need to."

That night around 2400, Jim was half asleep when a drunken Reemer, Gates and Mark McGovern staggered down the ladder, loudly boasting of their shore conquests with women."Wow, was she ever something, man", hollered Gates. Wearing white boxer skivvies, Jim rose and walked over while the two laughed as a few resting men grumbled.

"I'm in love again", hollered Mac. Mark McGovern from Virginia, was a five-foot-ten, slender, tanned and handsome Third Class Petty Officer who had come aboard right out of radioman school two years before. He was an excellent communicator, loved to party, but his goal was having a girl in every port and getting through his tour as quickly as possible.

Jim exclaimed, "Hey fellas, quiet down and hit your racks. We're trying to sleep. Ya got duty tomorrow and need some z's. Ya woke us up. Cool it, will ya? Ya can tell us all about those babes in the morning, but right now, we gotta sleep."

They stopped, surprised at his temerity challenging them. Reemer squinted while veins expanded down his neck and two piercing eyes moved within inches of Hickey sending a chill up Jim's spine. He blurted and slurred, "Ah, don't ever tell me what to do, ya hear me, new guy?" The three inebriated mumbled incoherently, took off uniforms and then retired.

The next morning after chow, Hickey searched, but couldn't find Alden. He grabbed coffee, went to the bow, lit a cigarette and watched as a huge commercial freighter tied up nearby.

Shortly after, he found Thomas, Warden and Kennel down in berthing preparing for liberty. He announced, "Hey mates, there's a charity football game this afternoon at Kezar Stadium, and they may give us a discount because we're military. Do you wanna go? " They agreed, but first desired a few beers downtown.

Before noon, the four ran down the after brow and jumped into a nearby cab. The city was alive as cars sped and thousands meandered on streets on a bright day. After downing beers and hot dogs, Thomas chirped, "Hey buddies, we better head over 'cause the game starts in about an hour. They walked several blocks, up near Knob Hill and in the distance saw the old brick arena. Alcohol kicked in as "Dog" began shouting and rooting for the opposing team irritating several civilians sitting nearby. Thomas leaned over and whispered, "Hey, asshole, shut up. Can't you see we're surrounded like Davey Crockett at the Alamo? Ya wanna get us killed or something?" The words sunk in, and he was suddenly mum.

Later, they took a cab and entered a dimly lit, inexpensive restaurant where a dozen patrons dined. A young, attractive ebony lady sat alone, writing a letter near the entrance. They sat at a corner table, forty-feet away, and ordered Cokes and cheeseburgers.

Kennel's eyes gleamed, staring at the woman. He whispered, "Do you guys see what I see? Wow! She's a doll. Sort of looks like Diana Ross of the Supremes, don't she?"

Thomas chewed his sandwich and , "Yeah, she does, come to think of it."

Dog murmured, "Hey, I feel like barking and howling, but this isn't a bar. Man, I'd sure like to go out with her." He looked at Hickey, sitting near Thomas. "Bet ya don't have a hair on yer ass to go over and talk with her."

The lady finished writing, looked over and smiled. They were enamored with her beauty.

She wore a beige dress and silver star shaped earrings dangled over a short, petite frame. The jet black hair hung over the middle of the neck.

Jim got up and looked down at his buddies. "Watch this." It was another adventure he craved. He walked over, leaned against the table and smiled, "God, you're beautiful. Mind if I sit down?"

She smiled. "Thank you. "Go right ahead sailor." He introduced himself, telling her about the ship and family as his three mates sat staring.

Laura and seven years older than Jim. Her sweet, melodic voice and lady-like demeanor attracted him. She had a unique proclivity, choosing her words.

For twenty minutes they conversed about families, hobbies, and the Vietnam War. She smiled and asked, "Want a Coke?" He nodded, then mentioned the "n" word was forbidden in his home growing up and he believed God made everyone equal. Jim related admiring brave individuals who traveled South on Freedom buses back in the early 60's to protest discrimination. Innately, he didn't view her as a Black woman, but rather a warm individual with whom he felt comfortable.

She carefully moved her right hand, placing it on his and smiled, "You seem like a nice guy, Jim. Do you want to come home with me?" The question caught him off guard. He wondered if she was a prostitute or trying to roll him; after all, they had just met. His three buddies rose from their table, walked over and stopped.

"Are you guys returning to the ship?"

Kennel replied, "Nah, we'll probably go steaming for a while before heading back. How about you? Comin' along?"

"Nah, I got a better offer. Laura here, wants to take me out, but money's tight."

She quickly interrupted. "Don't worry; I'll take care of everything." He smiled and looked at them.

Thomas exclaimed, "Wow, Jim, no decision here. Heck, go with her. She seems like a nice person." Kennel opened the door. As they waved and departed, Thomas quickly shouted, "Hey, don't forget, we sail at 0800 tomorrow. Don't be late because you don't want to piss Badass off, right?"

"Yeah, you know it." As he sat opposite, she looked at him with a puzzled expression.

"What's steaming and who's this guy Badass?"

"It's an old U.S. Navy term for bar hopping. They're a pretty good bunch of guys and I like the ship." He was hesitant answering the second question, but stared at his drink and thought as his jaw dropped. She knew he was troubled. Initially reluctant, he related about Bearden's behavior and history.

She looked, reached and touched his hand. "Look, don't think about him now, all right? You're with me." Laura rose and smiled. "Let's go." He worried. I only have three bucks left and hope she's treating as the thought of seeing Badass on liberty crept into his being, like a recurring specter.

As night approached, they departed and jumped into a taxi. Feeling uncomfortable sitting near a relative stranger, he inquired, "Hey, I forgot to ask you. Where do you work?"

Her face brightened into a smile."I'm an entertainer at a club."

"Oh, you're not a stripper or anything like that, are you?"

She laughed, "Listen, relax honey. I have honorable intentions, and you won't have any problems with me. You're a nice kid and I think you'll enjoy yourself tonight because I'll take care of everything, Jim." He worried about the mere three bucks left in his pocket, and the thought of seeing Bearden on liberty which crept into him like a recurring specter.

The cab pulled over near an old three story building. He was surprised she tipped five bucks. As he followed her to the top floor, she turned around near the entrance and smiled. "I think you'll like my place." He was cautious, but wondered. "What am I getting into?"

The spacious two-bedroom apartment had a huge living room, with an L-shaped leather couch and three rainbow decorated vases holding flowers on end tables below four large paintings of Venice, Rome, Greece and London. A large dining area was just off a small kitchen while nearby a hallway, lead to a bathroom and sleeping quarters. He gazed around and thought, "This is real class." He was comfortable.

She approached, took off his hat and black neckerchief, laying them on a nearby table. Her sincere eyes met his. She moved closer, planting a short kiss on his lips producing an instant,smile on him.

"Wow. That was nice Laura. I didn't expect that. Hope ya don't mind, but I'm tired and wanna rest cause the hops and barley's kicking in."

She grinned, "Here, follow me." The guest bedroom was small, compared to her large room with a queen-sized bed. After he stretched on the bed, she bent, took off his spit shined shoes and pulled a light blue blanket over him. "There, how do you feel?"

"Not too shabby. I feel good." She bent down, planting another kiss on his cheek.

"Now, you better get some rest, you're going to need it."

Four hours later, he awoke to boisterous talking and laughter, coming from the living room as six people, ranging from twenty-five to forty stood, congregating, partying and drinking. Laura announced, "Hey, gang; follow me, because I got a surprise for you." They entered the room, stood, grinned and looked down, unnerving him.

"Well, here's my sailor I brought home. Too many swabbies hit on me at work and I've never brought one home, but Jimmy's a gentleman and special." She jumped in beside him and kissed his cheek, to his embarrassment. Three mini-skirted women and two older men clad in suits laughed.

A tall, attractive Hispanic lady chirped. "Hey, Laura, you taking your sailor man out with us tonight?"

She put her arm around, hugged him and exclaimed, "Hell yes. It's my night off and I'm buying." She gently patted his chest. "Don't worry Jimmy because tonight your mine and we're going to have a blast."

He rose and dressed while she introduced each of her friends, yet was still uncomfortable with the strangers. They walked down and hailed two cabs. At ten, downtown buzzed with activity as bars and clubs rang with jazz, folk and rock n roll music. Thousands congregated, dined at restaurants, outside patios and people watched.

Laura and two older middle-aged women in back flanked him. He was surprised seeing various musicians sitting on every other corner, playing string and brass instruments for tips. Hippies in groups strolled along streets, some staggering because of drugs or excessive alcohol consumption. The cab turned on Mission Street, making a quick right, stopping in front of a club where colored lights circulated around a conspicuous sign above.

She smiled, "Well, here we are. This is where I work. Let's go." They exited while a second cab halted near the rear. Several people from the young to seniors entered and exited.

He looked up and saw the bold letters "The Pink Elephant" and underneath, Exclusive Club, Cover Charge $10.00, We Check I.D.'s. Rock n roll blared into the night from a six-piece band.

Five attractive mini-skirted women rushed, excitedly greeting her. Based on their enthusiastic behavior, he had the distinct feeling Laura was the club's headliner. The San Francisco Herald Examiner recently had an article about her philanthropy and numerous hours of volunteer work, helping orphans and the homeless.

After sitting in a large semi-circle leather booth, he inquired, "What kind of work do you do here, Laura?"

She nuzzled next to him, lit a cigarette and smiled. "I've been singing and dancing here for nine years. It's like my second home, but I'm off tonight."

His host bought round after round, as one toast followed another. He was a beer man, but she insisted, ordering Singapore Slings. He reflected, "Well, at least there's shrimp cocktail to eat on the table."

He knew Laura was special and trusted her. After two hours, her gregarious personality captivated the table. Intermittently, customers flocked around, like hovering bees saying hello, meeting her. He thought, "Damn, I sure lucked out. I'm with a V.I.P. Wait till the guys hear about this."

Within two hours, drinks were affecting him. At 1a.m, as the band took a short break, he leaned against her shoulder for comfort as she conversed with others. She turned, looking at each loving every minute while holding court. "Know something, I've got plenty of money, but I remember where I came from when my family struggled, surviving across the bridge in Oakland. Yup, my daddy always said 'Honey, you can't take it with you. Respect everyone and be kind.' I've never forgotten that. I'm buying another round while my sailor boy relaxes." She lifted his face and gently kissed his lips, sending a chill up his spine. He smiled.

By two, most were near inebriation. She rose, looked down and grinned, "Folks, we better leave cause the place closes soon, okay?"

Jim slept for over an hour, still resting on her shoulder. She helped him up, put his Dixie cup hat on, led him out and hailed a cab, after bidding everyone goodnight. He put an arm around her as she assisted him, slowly climbing three flights of stairs back to her apartment.

He sat on the bed slurring, reminding her to shake him at seven. She took off his hat, jumper and shoes, carefully moved his legs on to the mattress, covered him up, leaned over, kissed his cheek and in a sweet voice murmured, "Good night, Jimmy and God bless.

Five hours later, he was alarmed hearing Laura's panic, sounding voice. "Oh my God, Jimmy! The clock radio didn't go off and I must have over slept. I'm so sorry. You gotta get going now, honey."

She ran into the room, put the jumper over his head, arranged the black neckerchief as he quickly tied his shoe laces, and quickly made him instant black coffee, but he only drank half a cup.

He stood by the door and put his arms around her. "Thank you for last night. I had fun and I'll never forget you." Wearing a night gown, she looked up at him as a tiny tear formed in her eye.

"Listen, you take real good care of yourself overseas in that damn war, you hear?" He smiled and gently kissed her. As he walked down the first flight, she stood near the opened door and smiled. "Now, get going and catch your ship because you only have fifteen minutes."

For a moment, he felt like returning, asking for a few bucks for a taxi, but ran out into the bright sun. He waved his arms and a cab pulled up. "Hey buddy, get me to the commercial pier as fast as possible." Sitting in the rear, he eyed the meter just below the dash on the right wondering how far three bucks would take him.

After a mile, he shouted,"Stop here cause' I'm about broke." After the vehicle slowed to a stop, the meter read two fifty. He jumped out, paid the fare, and snapped. "Keep the change."

The short gray haired cabbie cringed."Oh gee, thanks sailor, you're the last of the great spenders, but I hope ya make it on time."

Hickey ran, crossing Market Street, then reached Mission, when suddenly, a car flashed around the corner, stopping two feet away, stunning him. The burly, irate driver leaned out of a window and shouted, "Are you crazy or something, sailor? Hell, I almost hit ya."

Ignoring him, he took off again running and thought, "I've gotta make it and can't slow down." Out of breath after a half mile, he staggered against a building and whispered to himself. "I've only got less than a mile left." He tucked the white hat into a pocket and galloped faster while his heart pounded. Because of his speed, it seemed like the buildings rushed toward him. The man slowed and looked up at an old clock atop of an eight-story structure. He thought, "Oh my God! I've only got five minutes before she leaves." He murmured a prayer, "God, help me get there."

After rounding another corner, he saw masts towering over nearby buildings. The ship billowed black smoke out of stacks as he sprinted on to the pier passing a large white merchant vessel. Astonished, he thought, "Shit, the lines have already been taken in."

He stopped across from the quarterdeck as the O. O. D. glared and shouted, "What's wrong sailor?"

"Ah, sir, this is my ship. I'm in CR division and need to board." He bent down, getting his breath back as his chest repeatedly heaved.

The officer's eyes widened in disbelief. "How do I know this is your ship?"

The sailor moved near the edge of the dock, and pointed to the small white capitol letters *USS SATTERFIELD* on a little three-inch long black strip on his right shoulder, which all uniformed fleet sailors wore for identification. The officer shouted, "Yeah, I see it sailor. Now, hurry up."

The lieutenant shook his head in disgust as three seamen laughed nearby. Seeing the problem, two civilian dock workers walked up, lifted, and then shimmied the wooden brow back on to the quarterdeck. After Hickey thanked them, one man exclaimed, "Better him, than me."

He boarded and saluted. "Request permission to come aboard, sir."

The officer stared as his voice rose, "Granted. You know something sailor. You'd better thank your lucky stars we were just getting up steam because we would have sailed without you, and you would have been in deep trouble. Do you hear me?

Embarrassed, he lowered his head and murmured, "Yes, sir."

"It's a good thing you're not in my division because I'd write you up. Now, get to your duty station."

"Thank you, sir."

Half the crew came out, lining port and starboard sides at parade rest, for standard departing quarters. While quietly returning to berthing he feared running into Bearden.

Gates sitting on his bunk looked up. "Hickey, where ya been? Badass has been lookin' for ya after we had muster a little while ago. Man, I think you're in a world a shit, and ya better hope he doesn't write ya up. Good luck. You're gonna need it."

"Thanks for the warning, Gates. Ya know I needed that like a hole in the head."

He hurried into the mess decks, wolfed down breakfast and worried. I've gotta get back into radio, but what will I say to Badass?

The vessel slowly backed into the bay as twenty knot winds struck halyards and whipped the hoisted American flag near the top of the mainmast. She moved past Treasure Island Naval Base, Alcatraz, under the Golden Gate and then turned south after hitting open water. Westward winds produced white caps above two-foot swells as Harrison ordered half speed, ten miles off the California landscape.

After disengaging the hatch lock, Jim entered communications. Three men were busy sending and receiving Morse code and teletype messages as Chief Larson stared at Hickey. Jim started pouring a cup of coffee when a man bellowed, "Hey, squirrel, who said ya could have one, eh?' It was the unmistakable voice of Badass. He put the cup down and turned, facing the lifer three feet away.

Bearden stood, placing his hands on his hips, cynically grinned and squinted. "Well, Hickey, ya finally got on my bad side, didn't ya? I feel real good now that ya screwed up." He moved closer as his expression turned angry. "Thought you'd play a fast one and sneak aboard, and then everything would be ok, didn't ya?" Tiny drops of sweat formed on Jim's head as he swallowed.

"Nope, that wasn't my plan."

"Well, you sure as hell embarrassed me. You should've been here for muster at 0:745. What took ya?" He quickly related about the lady and what occurred. Nearby, Gates and McDonald laughed.

Bearden quickly turned around and berated them. "Ya think that's funny or somethin'? It's not, so shut up." They continued working, but Thomas, sitting in a corner, shook his head.

The lifer snapped, "Let me tell ya something Hickey. She had better been worth it cause now you're at the top of my shit list, ya hear?" Jim slightly nodded.

Badass gave an evil look as his eyes bulged then remarked, "Ya know, tomorrow we hit San Diego, and the first few days there's port and starboard liberty. I heard ya got family down there. Well, I got good news for ya. You're restricted aboard for two days after we tie up. Do ya understand, twerp?" He hated being called that demeaning word and immediately clenched a right fist alongside his dungaree trousers. In the sixth grade, Hickey nailed a boy in the face for that remark.

Bearden noticed his momentary tension. He shouted, "Hey, idiot, ya got a brain? Answer me." Hickey didn't want others getting the impression the lifer was getting to him. He merely nodded, then turned, walked around a bulk-head and sat, looking at messages coming over a teletype machine. Bearden mumbled a few unintelligible words to himself, smiled and joined Larson for coffee.

Their sick laughter unnerved Mac and Thomas sitting ten feet away. Bearden took a sip, looked at the chief and murmured. "Ya know, I was trying to scare the shit outta him, but he didn't shake in his skivvies like the others. I'll break him though, if it's the last thing I do and give him a taste of what the old Navy was like." Larson grinned and nodded as Badass continued. "Shit, years ago, there was some hard ass on a cruiser that never stopped bothering me when I was a seaman. I got tired of being picked on when I was a kid in school, and then as a lower ranked guy. I've been First Class eight years, got some power now and don't have to take shit anymore, right Chief?"

Larson subtly pandered to Bearden's ego and quest for power. He smiled, but a few others within earshot, heard just about everything from the boastful lifer. Innately, he was a miserable man, unhappy with himself. His comments quickly spread in the division.

During noon chow, Thomas, Reemer, Carter, Kennel and two others were eager to learn what happened to Jim, who sat across at a long steel table eyeing his food.

"Dog" started it all. "Guys, you should have seen this guy in action yesterday after the game. He was something, boldly going over and yacking with that doll. Hey Jim, tell us. Did ya hit a home run and score?"

While eating ham and macaroni, he calmly looked up and over at Kennel. His snide comment, unnerved him. "Man, ya gotta one track mind, don't ya?" I guess that's why we call ya 'dog' and we all know what they like to do." Dog glared, embarrassed as the others chuckled.

Thomas remarked, "Hey, Jim, cool it, ok? Don't take your frustration with Badass out on Dog. Listen, all we wanna know is if ya scored, buddy." He liked Thomas, more rational than some of the others.

"Fellas, I'll just say this. She took me back to her place." They leaned and smiled like eager high school boys, desiring to hear more.

Gates chirped, "Come on now, give us all the details. What happened?"

"Well, it wasn't like you guys probably think. Don't get your jollies up."

Carter, sitting on the end snapped, "Listen, was she a hooker who suckered and rolled ya?"

He stopped eating and stared at him. "No, she was probably the classiest lady I've ever been with. I left the restaurant with three bucks, took a nap, then she took me out with a few of her friends and treated me at this swank club where she works." He paused, shook his head and grinned. "She got me bombed and all I remember is walking out and leaning on her as the place closed."

He continued as their eyes focused on him. "Laura put me to bed and tucked me in, but her alarm failed cause the next thing I knew she hollered it was seven-thirty. I'm telling you guys, she's well known in Frisco and helps a lot of people even though she's an entertainer. Listen, I didn't want to go to bed with her. She's a lady. I had fun, enjoyed her company and still had the three bucks this morning for cab fare. Believe it, or not."

They were speechless as their jaws dropped. Reemer quickly blurted, "Wow, that's really somethin'. How many times do you get a chance like that in life, eh?" He laughed at their blank expressions. "All you guys thought he scored or got hustled last night, eh? Well, ha, ha, the jokes on you guys. Ya know, Hickey, I guess ya handled it pretty cool. I'm glad ya had a good liberty."

"Thanks, Sid."

Sid quickly looked at each and raised his voice, "Ok mates, now how many of you guys got lucky, never spent a dime and were treated by a lady last night, huh?" There was silence. "Shit, I didn't think so. Let's get back ta duty." He found new admiration for Reemer.

That evening shortly after sundown, he walked, leaned against the port lifelines and lit a cigarette. In the far distance, lights from towns, homes and moving vehicles flickered in the moonless night. He thought about Bearden's words, but now, only desired focusing on seeing family and enjoying the next six months in San Diego.

It seemed like yesterday, that he went through twelve weeks of basic training there, over two years ago, then to Norfolk, Virginia for sixty-day schooling, before duty on Guam.

"Hey, Jim, what are ya doin' out here?" Alden's enthusiastic voice interrupted his thoughts.

"Man, you're a sight for sore eyes. It sure takes a while for your eyes to adjust out here with no moon, ya know."

"Yeah, know what ya mean, buddy. How's it going?"

He thought, "Be careful and choose the right words." He related what happened in Frisco and subsequent punishment from Bearden.

"You know something, Tom, those other guys were right about what they said about him after I first came aboard. The guy's strange and a little scary. He really enjoys intimidating others especially if he thinks they're weak. He's not a happy guy, and I wonder if he's got a family or any close friends. The chief and lieutenant cover for him. Personally, I believe they don't wanna make waves as long as the division performs well."

Alden listened, then looked at him intensely and responded, "First of all, buddy, you know ya screwed up missing muster, but I'm glad they let ya back on. Wow! That must have been a close one, and I bet you were real nervous, eh? Ya know something?' The correction or punishment must fit the infraction, but this guy went overboard. If it were me, I'd probably give ya extra duty for a few hours. Heck, it's not like ya went AWOL or something."

"Yeah, that makes sense."

Tom looked out toward land. "I enjoy coming out here sometimes to think. The salty air hitting me is refreshing. I can't wait to see Janet and Shannon when we get in tomorrow."

He thought a minute, then turned and looked at him. "I know about that jerk and heard what happened to those guys last year. Ya know aboard ship, there aren't too many secrets, especially if there's been a suicide. It pisses me off the Navy hasn't done something about him. Listen, Jim, this guy's really unstable, and I think he has a cold heart. There's some sort of emptiness inside the guy. It's almost like he doesn't have a conscience and he's evil, buddy. I also heard about a third of the guys in your division put in for transfers after those incidents. Doesn't that tell ya something? Do your duty and don't let him see any fear or anger because I think he thrives on it. Now, that's the best advice I can give you."

He put an arm around Alden's shoulder. "You're a true friend and shipmate,Tom, and I'm glad I've got someone ta lean on." Jim flicked the cigarette into the sea, bid him goodnight and went below to sleep.

The following morning, a jubilant mood ensued among everyone in the department, everyone, but Hickey. He went down to berthing and listened to boisterous chatter among some of the men while donning dress whites and civilian attire.

McGovern slipped on his jumper and stared at Hickey. "Look, Jim, we all know you're pissed at Badass and don't think it's right the way he's targeting ya, but look at the bright side. Shit, in two days, you'll be ashore with family. Don't sweat it. We'll drink a beer and maybe even a few for ya, downtown."

"Thanks, Mac."

He ached inside when the announcement came. "Now hear this. Make all preparations for entering port. Set the special sea and anchor detail. The smoking lamp is out. All personnel not on watch fall in near port and starboard lines."

Most of the division went topside, lining parallel to lifelines near the stern. Two hundred sailors faced outward at parade rest. Harrison ordered speed reduced to six knots as she passed between the harbor entrance buoys, a mile out. Thick fog lifted earlier, as the sun beat down on a cloudless morning.

Point Loma Peninsula greeted *Satterfield* off port as water splashed against rocks on the shore nearby. Four hundred feet above, stood imposing Cabrillo National Monument, named after the Spanish explorer who first made landfall there in the Sixteenth Century. With hands clasped behind his back, Jim looked up at diminuitive like tourists who gazed through binoculars at the ship.

Large, million dollar plus, white homes rested above a two-lane road that snaked along the hilly peninsula overlooking the ocean. Not far from the peak, thousands of veterans from three wars rested at the National Cemetary.

An F-4 Phantom jet capable of Mach two-plus speeds, roared, lifted from North Island Naval Air Station (birthplace of naval aviation) and soared into the California sky. After passing the sub base off port, a long row of high palm trees, exotic hotels and clubs welcomed tourists to Shelter Island.

Standing next to Loggins, Jim turned, smiled and whispered, "Hey Log, I feel good. It's been over two years since I was here. I have a godmother who works at a marine sales outlet on Shelter and it will be good seeing her and the rest of the family."

He nodded and grinned, "Yeah, I'll bet. Well, I'll be meeting my wife soon, and that'll certainly be interesting."

Just past the island's huge marina, the ship turned ninety degrees, heading south between Harbor Island and the air station. A small flotilla of yachts converged, within 20 yards from her, a few motoring behind the wake. Numerous cars sped along palm tree lined Harbor Drive, running parallel along the water during morning rush hour.

As she passed the Anti-Submarine Warfare School, the men viewed a succession of 707 Boeing passenger jets roaring down Lindbergh Field, then soaring over the Marine Recruit Depot and Naval Training Center.

To the left, downtown San Diego loomed, and off starboard the two giant carriers *Constellation* and *Ranger* rested, one behind the other next to a large pier at the air station across the harbor. They passed downtown, and then under the long, winding bridge connecting the city to the Coronado Peninsula as vehicles motored above the ship.

The ship steamed beyond the immense National Steel shipyards where commercial vessels were built, repaired and unloaded. Just beyond the shipyard was the huge Cruiser-Destroyer Force, U.S. Pacific Fleet Base. Locals and sailors called the spot Thirty-Second Street due to its location a few miles from downtown. There were numerous piers stretching south. The harbor ended miles from the base near the naval helicopter station at Imperial Beach.

South of active duty ships, was the largest section of the shipyard, the reserve or mothball fleet consisting of retired World War Two

Photo of San Diego Bay and Harbor

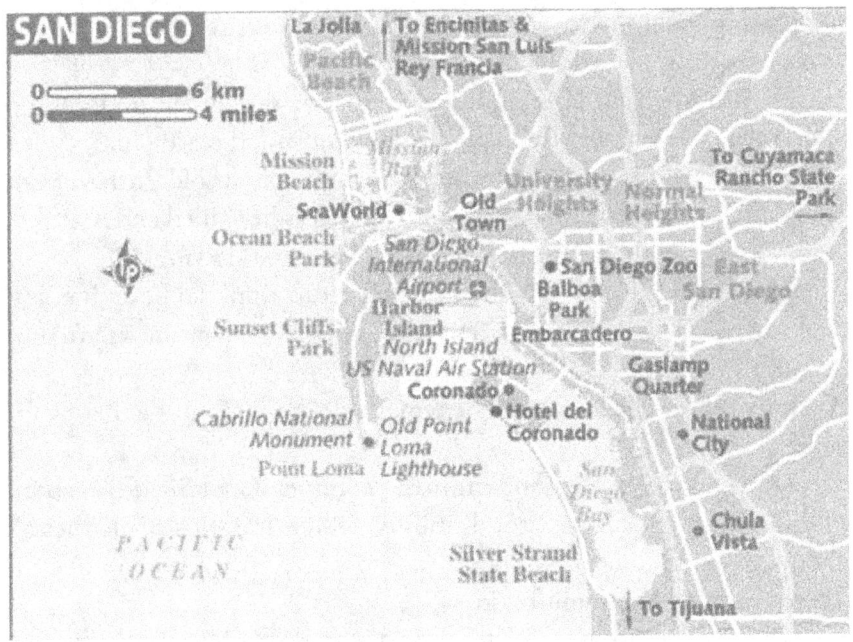

Map of San Diego Bay and Harbor

vessels. On the active ship area, the first few piers were reserved for destroyers, escorts, mine sweepers, tugs and small vessels. Cruisers, large amphibious ships and helicopter carriers occupied the remainder, far from the main gate, guarded by Marines. Jim was elated returning, and the majority of sightseeing was free.

An old 100-foot harbor tug greeted the ship, gently nestling her alongside pier three. Two boatswain's mates threw ropes fore and aft toward a couple of shore sailors who quickly secured them over bollocks and cleats. The 1MC blared, "Now secure from quarters. The Officer of the Deck is shifting his flag from the bridge to the quarterdeck. First Division (deck hands) assume the duty. The smoking lamp is lit, set condition Yankee. Liberty commences at 10:30."

The Navy had three conditions, Yankee, X-ray and Zebra. Each hatch (door) was marked by one or two bold letters x, y or z. Hatches marked Y remained open, signifying a lax condition normally for ships in port—those with X denoted some hatches were secured and others opened at sea—Z meant a serious condition where all openings were dogged, ensuring watertight integrity before a storm or combat condition.

About 150 people stood on the pier gazing up hollering, smiling and waving to ecstatic sailors. Despite the daily Union Tribune newspaper postings of ship arrivals and departures, he wasn't expecting family as most were employed.

As men lined up holding liberty cards, he saw Alden jumping up and down, waving near the bow. Jim ran and stood beside him. Alden looked down at his exuberant wife Janet and two year old, little auburn haired Shannon. Tears rolled down his cheeks as he smiled and hollered, "Honey, I'm here, I'm here. I love you. I'll be right down."

Tom looked at Jim. "Aw shit buddy, I didn't think I'd be crying, but couldn't help it when I saw those two angels. Look at em, aren't they beautiful?"

Jim's eyes swelled a bit and he remarked, "Yeah, Tom, I'm happy for ya pal."

Alden put an arm around him, and continued looking down about fifty feet away where they stood smiling. "Man, Jim, this is what it's all about. Love of God, love of family and country. That's it in a nutshell. There's nothing else, right buddy?"

He smiled. "Listen, enjoy your family ashore and have a great time, alright? I'll see ya after your leave."

Alden ran down, and hollered, "Until that time Jimmy, until that time." He leaned, waved and thought, "What a class guy."

As sailors enthusiastically bounded down brows to liberty, Jim walked aft relaxing in the warm summer breeze while viewing the harbor and shipyard.

Janet, holding Shannon's tiny hand, ran and leaped into Alden's joyful arms, lovingly embracing, and then their lips joined as tears meshed together. He reached, picked up Shannon and hugged and kissed her. "Ya know something honey; it doesn't get any better than this. God, I missed you and the baby. Baby! What am I saying? Wow! She's really grown." Janet laughed as men brushed around, running down the pier, boarding taxis and buses.

She was just above five-three, dressed in a yellow mini skirt. Janet had blue eyes, rosy cheeks, and shoulder-length brown hair. "You didn't think she'd shrink, did you silly? I prayed for you. Each day I put an X on the calendar and was happy because I knew it was another day closer to you. The apartment's nice and the car runs good."

He fought back back more tears. "You know, honey, I tried to visualize our reunion, of what you and I would do or say, but this is so much more. This is real, and you're here now with our little angel." She smiled and kissed him tenderly.

As they walked down the long pier toward the parking lot, she turned and asked, "Honey, who was that man standing next to you? You know the guy you put your arm around when you looked at us?"

He grinned, "That's my good buddy, Jim Hickey, a nice Irishman from Michigan. I'm like the older brother he never had. We get along pretty good. You'll meet him sometime, but today he's got duty. Now, let's go celebrate at a restaurant."

# 5

# "ENVIRONMENT, CULTURE, LIBERTIES, TRAINING"

Dawn broke over the cliffs of the high Cuyamaca and Laguna mountains the following morning, spreading throughout the county and harbor as June waned. After liberty call was announced at 0:900, his buddies and most of the crew scampered down the brow to the pier. He rose, showered, ate, grabbed coffee and walked out on the weather deck.

Alone, he had time to reflect on the past, his family and the reasons for arriving at this time and place. His uncle, Peter Anderson was a merchant seaman and U.S. Marine who fell in love with the area in the early 1950's. In 1958, he moved his family from Michigan to San Diego. Four years later, Hickey's grandfather John Flaherty lost his job in Detroit, consequently, he and his wife Lauretta packed and moved to the golden state settling in an apartment five units from Pete and Jean.

In 1969, eighteen year old Hickey flew west arriving at the Naval Recruit Training Center, joining seventy others that formed company 117. After undergoing twelve weeks of basic training and passing in review of high ranking officers on graduation day was elated embracing his grandparents who were among the hundreds of spectators. He enjoyed liberty visiting his gregarious godmother Aunt Jean, her mellow and tanned husband Pete and his grandparents. After a two week leave in Michigan, he boarded a train and traveled east to Communications School spending two months at the massive Norfolk Naval Base in Virginia.

Upon graduation, he received orders to the Naval Communications Station on Guam. After a brief leave, the sailor flew 7,600 miles west to the largest island in the Marianas. He was assigned duty in circuit control, a top secret area learning to operate equipment, processing classified messages and arranged the daily briefing for the base commander and his staff.

It was an adventurous time on the thirty-mile long volcanic island including boonie stomping, playing golf, going to clubs, hitch hiking aroud, visiting towns and villages; even seeing the Bob Hope Christmas show twice at nearby Anderson Air Force Base.

The climate was hot and humid, but it was an exciting experience for the adventurous young man. Hickey and a few buddies climbed Mt. Finasantos, the second-highest mountain. Upon receiving orders to the destroyer, he was elated; at sea was where the real navy existed.

On this bright sunny day, fresh, salty Pacific air struck his face as he gazed at rows of masts, extending high above gray superstructures near the massive docks on base. Outboard of *Satterfield* , the veteran destroyer *Higbee* sat as her crew aired bedding, placing mattresses over her lifelines. He gazed at rows of masts, extending high above gray superstructures near the massive docks on the base. Hickey was awe-struck, feeling like a small rivet in the powerful American Navy.

Each ship's name in bold, black letters was located just below the sterns. Recently arrived from war, the *Buck, Walke, Rowan, Wiltsie* and *Lloyd Thomas* were among eight "tin cans" docked. Larger, more maneuverable Man o' War 4,500-ton guided missile destroyers and frigates *Buchanan, Lynde McCormick, Henry B. Wilson*, Dale, *Farragut, Halsey*, and *Sterrett* with guns, missile launchers, were imposing with their sharp angled bows, and sleek super-structures as hundreds of sea gulls swarmed between them, seeking fish.

He swallowed java, turned around and looked south at another imposing site. Large 12,000 ton, 460 foot amphibious command vessels *Estes, Mt. McKinley* and *Eldorado* with noticeable double king posts fore and aft, sat idle, as the sun off their sides. Two piers beyond, 35,000 ton 800 foot helicopter carriers *Guadalcanal* and *Inchon* rested.

Since 1901, San Diego has been a Navy town, a prime West Coast liberty port, a haven for merchant seaman and sailors. During the summer of 1971, a first time visitor or tourist would be amazed looking up main street Broadway Avenue at a sea of Navy men in white uniforms

**Destroyers docked at 32nd Street Naval Base, San Diego**

cavorting, while entering and leaving dive bars and establishments during weekend liberty.

Throughout the Vietnam War, sailors normally spent nine to eighteen months overseas on ships before returning to the safe confines of the city. A good number of fleet bars and go-go clubs were located on and off the strip, each having its own character with shuffleboard, dart boards, pool tables, juke boxes and live entertainment.

Places like the Buccaneer Lounge, Golden Nugget, Greens and other pubs served delicious Lucky Lager, Olympia and Coors beers for only a buck. Go-go girls and pretty waitresses in miniskirts hustled drinks and tips from lonely and enebriated military personnel. These establishments monetarily thrived as thousands of sailors converged on weekend liberties, remininiscent of past jaunts during World War Two.

It was common for the Shore Patrol to enter clubs checking I.D's since twenty-one was the legal drinking age. Some young men drove or took buses twenty miles south to Mexico and purchased fake military identifications called "Tijuana Specials" for five bucks.

Conversely, it wasn't uncommon for military police on weekends to swarm into bars, flashing and swinging their night sticks, restoring order after breaking up fights between Marines and sailors. Several brawls with men crashing into or flying over tables, reminded one of John Wayne Westerns. Many were quickly loaded into trucks and detained in the brig.

Back then it was an understatement saying that California was the fastest growing state. Millions flocked from the Midwest and East Coast and jobs were plentiful with companies contracted with the Defense Department, as well as computers, technology and construction. During the 1960's through the 70's the state achieved the highest growth and in 1971 San Diego became it's second most populated city.

According to the U.S. Weather Service, as long as records have been kept, the county had the most pleasant climate in the nation with an average temperature of seventy-two. At times during summer, east blowing and dry Santa Ana winds raise temperatures into the 80's near the coast and city and into the 90's further inland. The cost of living was higher than in most states and consumers paid for it. Construction of new homes and small businesses was rampant in the booming area.

For several years, defense contractors Rohr Aircraft, Convair and McDonald Douglas have had permanence, employing thousands. In 1927, the Spirit of St. Louis which Charles Lindbergh flew across the Atlantic was built by a little firm called Ryan Aviation, which is still there. Eight Naval facilities and a Marine base occupied the county, the majority in or near the city.

The seventy mile coastline and 4,600 square miles made it California's second largest county after San Bernadino. Located 120 miles south of Los Angeles, downtown San Diego is only a half hour drive north of the Mexican border.

The russet topography of the area is unique with several hills in and around the city dominating the immediate vicinity. Further inland, the earth levels for miles and then ascends, reaching the Cuyamaca and Laguna mountains which form a majestic backdrop. Beyond those landmark peaks is wilderness and desert.

The San Diego Coronado Bridge completed in 1969 spanned the city with the Coronado Peninsula and North Island Naval Air Station—moving south on the Silver Strand parallel with the ocean, you'd pass the Naval Amphibious Base where Seal teams trained. The route ends near the naval helicopter base at Imperial Be.ach, not far from Tijuana, Mexico.

On the mainland, lie miles of sand below steep cliffs overlooking the Pacific. Ten minutes north of downtown, rests Mission Bay Park, an immense inland water wonderland surrounding two islands. North, off Pacific Coast Highway is beautiful and affluent La Jolla---forty miles north by Oceanside, lies the world's largest military reservation, Marine Corps Camp Pendleton.

Richard Nixon was president in 1971 and unemployment stood at five percent nationally. Hickey's father was intermittenly laid off from an auto manufacturer in the Motor City, consequently the family suffered, but Hickey took action. He applied for and received a loan through Navy Relief and money was deducted from his bi-monthly paycheck and sent home. His income was less than comparable Third Class Petty Officers, but he was fortunate having about eighty bucks spending money each month. There were significant events that year.

Apollo astronauts made the first ride in a lunar rover two years after Neil Armstrong first stepped on the moon. Communist China was admitted to the United Nations and the 26th Amendment was passed lowerindg the voting age to eighteen. The Federal government banned cigarette advertising on television and the last Ed Sullivan Show aired. The first soft contact lenses were now available. Audie Murphy, the most decorated hero of World War Two died in a plane crash. Hank Aaron of the Atlanta Braves hit his 636th home run breaking Babe Ruth's long standing record, and the Pittsburgh Pirates with Roberto Clemente won the World Series beating the Baltimore Orioles in the fall classic.

The average household income was $10,600 a year and $28,000 bought you a new house. A new Dodge Charger cost $3,500 and gas was 40 cents a gallon. A dozen eggs were 53 cents, milk 1,18 a gallon and you could mail a letter for only eight cents.

Jim Morrison, lead singer of the Doors who's hit Light My Fire in 1968 hit the Top Ten, died in a bath tub of a heart attack from drugs in Paris. Hippie and drug addict Charles Manson and three followers were convicted for the brutal deaths of actress Sharon Tate and six others. The first microprocessor was introduced and the computer disc was created.

On television, people were watching *All in the Family, Hawaii Five-O, The Odd Couple* and *McCloud.* For a buck fifty, you could see favorite movies like *Ryan's Daughter, The Summer of 42,* the scary *The Andromeda Strain,* the violent *Dirty Harry,* and the exciting *The French*

*Connection*; while children loved the musical comedy *Willie Wonka and the Chocolate Factory*. Walt Disney World opened in Orlando, Florida.

For six months in 1971, this was the environment young James Hickey lived. In less than a year he would meet his destiny.

The United States was winning the war and the troop level was reduced to 196,000 from a high of 550,000 in 1968 because of Nixon's Vietnamization Program. South Vietnamese forces were now assuming a larger role in defending their country against bellicose Communist North Vietnam.

In his well researched exposition Vietnam, Looking Back at the Facts, K.G. Sears, Ph.D. Stated that a year before Hickey went aboard his ship, "South Vietnam's government even conducted a long bicycle race over its public highways from the Demilitarized Zone (DMZ) to Cau Mau near the southern tip of the Mekong Delta. Participants were unmolested and the event took place with no, interference from the Communists." Allied forces controlled the majority of free South Vietnam. The U.S. Navy patrolled its waterways and guarded the 1,200 mile coastline, steaming in the South China Sea.

Eight bells rang, and duty called. Hickey went into the radio shack where a skeleton crew read newspapers and retrieved light message traffic. Bearden was ashore. It was calm and tomorrow would be liberty.

That evening after dusk, he leaned against port lifelines and lit a cigarette. In the distance, several bright lights adorned palm tree lined Harbor Drive, and downtown. Small fishing boats with night running lights, snailed, heading out toward the sea. Along docks, vessels slept while crews enjoyed time ashore.

On Wednesday morning, Jim rose at seven bells, showered, ate, packed an overnight satchel with skivvies and civilian clothes, and happily strode down the after brow below a clear sky as others quickly walked down the pier to board a local bus.

Fifteen minutes later, he arrived above a steep hill in Pt. Loma, and walked a quarter mile down until reaching apartments above several carports. He passed a swimming pool below a five-story apartment building, atop an imposing 200-foot, brown hill. Near the pavement's end, the ocean wind swayed tropical plants and scattered palmettos. He thought, this is peaceful and quaint. Suddenly, the feeling vanished as the loud roar of a jet, taking off from nearby Lindbergh, soared over the hill.

Near an end apartment, a cute little Siamese cat scampered inches away, almost causing him to trip. Two rows of flowers flanked the small lawn in front.

Shortly after knocking, a diminuitive brown-haired sixty-five year old lady with fair complexion answered, looked up and smiled. His grandmother, "Mimi", giggled as they embraced after two years.

The grandkids called her Mim, a derivative of the Quebec French Mimi or grandma. Her maiden name was LeDuc, on the French-Canadian side of the family. She was petite and feisty, with a great sense of humor, but tough as nails, having survived the Great Depression.

The large apartment had a spacious living and dining room with a large sliding window door overlooking the parking lot and palm tree lined winding street. Plants adorned the ledge, with with a little foot long red, ceramic Mexican burro sitting nearby.

"Hey Mim, where's Pop?" he asked.

"He's at Center City Ford, downtown selling cars and will be back after five. Why don't you sit?"

After a short lunch, they retired into the living room. She turned on KFMB FM, and listened to *Music, Only for a Woman,* an afternoon soothing music program. "Hey, Jimmy, make me a gin and tonic and let's talk." It was her daily repast.

While consuming three Gilbey's, she rambled about one subject after another, including having an illegal speak easy at their home on Detroit's east side during Prohibition.

Later, his step grandfather entered, wearing an impressive light blue suit. At six four, he was a large figure of a man and gentle as a lamb. He wore glasses on a Roman nose and had neatly combed gray hair. The noticeable half thumb on his left hand was the result of losing part of it several years before when Mim accidentally ran over it while vacuuming a carpet. Hickey gave him a hug and shook his hand.

John Ford Flaherty had been his step-grandfather since he was a baby. A kind and caring man, he'd spent a few years in the Canadian Army between the World Wars; then he moved back to Michigan and worked in the insurance industry several years.

He was an intelligent and voracious reader. People enjoyed being around "Papa" because of his easygoing, dry humor and witty character. He had a pleasant and smooth tone when speaking. His large belly would shake, emitting a low pitched laugh, after she'd tease him or upon hearing a joke. "You know something Jimmy? Papa's an L seven, just a lovable old square."

They were a compatible, cute couple with John towering high above her. At times he was troubled by the availability of money for basic necessities, yet never complained and kept domestic problems to himself. He was an astute tracker of the Stock Market.

As John sat with a drink, he grinned and looked over at Jim. "Hey, Jimmy, why don't you ask one of those big shot admirals when another carrier's coming in, because I'd be selling more cars?" He was a like a squirrel, storing bucks during the lean months. His daughter in-law Jean would jokingly remark, "One month chicken, and next month feathers."

Despite being tired Sunday evening, Pop drove him back to the base, a fifteen minute trip which Jim appreciated. While strolling back to the ship he thought, "I'm lucky and blessed having family here." His grandfathers' kind action was repeated several times before he left for overseas.

On Monday morning, *Satterfield* made her way through the harbor into the sea, joining two destroyers for maneuvers. The three vessels underwent high speed formations and turns for hours. Harrison ordered the ship north within five miles of little San Clemente Island, a government-owned, uninhabited gunfire area, utilized by the Navy.

Aware a dentist was temporarily assigned aboard, Hickey, needing a couple fillings, headed to sick bay to have a couple fillings resolved.

Shortly after a lieutenant gave him a Novocain injection, the vessel shook as the forward dual five-inch mount fired toward the island. The loud cr..a...ack sound frightened him. He'd never been this close to gunfire.

The dentist leaned over, raising his voice, "Listen, sailor, after you're numbed, I'll be careful when filling those teeth. Don't worry." He wondered,"Damn, great timing. How am I going to get through this, with these guns going off and all that shaking."

Every six seconds, loud blasts ensued as both guns fired two 55-pound projectiles into the sky, which then descended, exploding into the island. The power and recoil of each salvo shook compartments throughout the old destroyer. After twenty minutes he questioned, "Damn, will this ever end?"

The dentist carefully finished. "I think you better go back and lie down until the anesthetic wears off before going back on duty."

"Thanks, Doc." He went below as the stern guns fired simultaneously, with the forward mount. Relaxation came later.

Normally during a week, a vessel spent four or five days at sea, conducting drills and gunfire practices, while steaming in various formations with a small task force. Increasingly, the captain became obsessed with obtaining above average results from the crew after implementing an austere program of repeated drills. Crew dissension and better morale didn't exist in his repertoire, and Bearden was a key piece on the captain's chessboard, intermittently berating Jim and others. Harrison ordered general quarter drills several times each day, including abandon ship, fire and collision.

Each ship had a daily one or two page P.O.D. or Plan of the Day, distributed to each department, denoting significant information, including status, ship duties, names of the O.O.D., Junior Officer of the Deck, chow times, and a list of the enlisted, officer evening movies.

Veteran's ruses on new men were common. Jim enjoyed hearing some but felt sorry for the few gullible rookies who entered their webs. A few conspired spreading scuttlebutt about a change in a ship's port call or evening movie.

One late afternoon, the morale of some of the enlisted sank after hearing that an oft repeated old Western *Six Guns West* was being shown. At 2000, about 100 crammed into the mess deck, anticipating another dull film, but were elated seeing bikini clad girls running on a beach on the little portable screen.

Sometimes it was reversed. New men, recently out of basic training or "boots", were excited anticipating a film with pretty women but groaned after viewing opening credits of an old black and white gangster film with Humphrey Bogart and James Cagney. The usual suspects were Thomas and Gates as they at each other, whispered, scanned, and then grinned at the rookies' disappointing reactions.

After four months, Jim had an inkling that Gates was spreading rumors; also, his increasingly closer relationship with Bearden resulted in consternation among some of the men. Jim reflected, "I don't trust him."

Veteran seamen anticipated and planned, initiating gags on new guys such as nineteen-year old Fred Galetti fresh from radioman school who came aboard shortly after the ship's arrival from Seattle. He was tall and slender with black hair above a pug nose. Almost docile, he rarely smiled, seemingly lost in his own little world. Naïve and gullible, he trusted everyone. Raised in Kenosha, Wisconsin by a domineering single mother, he lacked self-confidence, was insecure and quickly became the scapegoat. His Achilles heels were sleep talking and motion sickness.

While steaming ten miles off the Southern California coast, the men in radio were busy sending and receiving messages to and from other vessels as well as the shore base. Loggins supervised. Hickey rose from a teletype machine, walked and grabbed a cup of coffee.

Log approached Hickey, winked, smiled and whispered, "Hey, Jim, watch me get the new fish." Galetti stood fifteen feet away arranging newly received messages and making copies on a mimeograph machine. Log loudly cleared his throat, "Galetti, I want ya to go down to the engine room, see Chief Charley Noble and tell 'em we need a bucket of steam." Charley Noble didn't exist. Galetti looked puzzled. Reemer turned, emitting a low chuckle.

Seconds after he left, Log called engineering and spoke with a chief who laughed, saying, "Yeah, we got another fish, eh? Ha, ha. I'll take care of him."

He got a tour of practically the entire ship as the ruse was repeated. He returned twenty minutes later, embarrassed, and exhausted as the others broke into uproarious laughter. Jim exclaimed, "Don't worry pal, it's all in fun." Troubled by motions, he ran out of the space several times and vomited in the head.

Shortly after, Reemer looked at Hickey. "I wonder what his drift factor is." The term was common among radiomen, denoting a man's mental state after an evening of heavy drinking, during certain situations or after hearing a joke. If the individual didn't quickly grasp something, or was slow responding, his drift factor would be in the high eighties or nineties depending on the severity, with a hundred being the maximum.

"I think his factor's high. He's not the sharpest pencil in the box", replied Hickey.

During chow, after hearing of Log's ruse, Mac exclaimed, "Man, that new guy's so far out there, he must in the *Twilight Zone*.

"Yeah, I agree," replied Reemer.

On another occasion at sea, Loggins again supervised. Tim walked and put an arm around the new man's shoulder. "Ah, hi, Galetti. Do you like *Satterfield* and working with the guys?"

"Sure, but I'm worried about my girlfriend because I haven't gotten any letters from her lately. When do we get mail?"

Sitting a few feet away, Jim turned around, grinned and thought, "Oh wow, Log's got him set up again. The fish's mouth is open."

Log stared at Fred. "Ya want my help, don't ya? Well, I'll tell ya what I'm gonna do for ya. Ya gotta stand the mail buoy watch so ya can get letters from your girl. Understand?"

Galetti's eyes bulged. "What's that?" Log moved within a foot of him.

"Before returning, we go by these buoys, ya see? It's pretty easy. We drop ya off, and all ya gotta do is hang onto the bobbing buoy and wait for a little mail boat to swing by and drop off a bag of mail; then we pick ya up, and ya get your girlfriend's letters. Sounds good, doesn't it?"

Galetti stared and scratched his head. "Loggins, why do I have to do it? What about one of the other guys?"

Log gave a serious look. "Hell, all new guys are required to stand mail buoy duty, and every one of the guys did it. It's your turn."

Gates turned around, looked and chirped, "Yeah, Galetti, he's right. Shit, no sweat. It's a piece a cake."

Loggins ordered. "Go out on the weather deck and see the Chief Boatswain's Mate. You can't miss 'em 'cause he's a stocky guy with a big gut, like me. Its smooth sailin' out there and ya won't need a life preserver. You just tell the chief you're standing the mail buoy watch, and he'll show ya how, all right?"

"Yeah, I think I've got it."

After Galetti departed, they laughed as "Log" lit a cigar and exclaimed, "Well, here's another fish victory cigar. I've lit a few. Shit, I hope the kid doesn't fall overboard even though the water's smooth today."

Galetti walked onto starboard, stood on the forecastle and looked around. The Chief was supervising three deck hands, painting below the bridges' port side. He turned, looked in disbelief at the lone man standing near the forward mount, quickly marched toward him shouting "Now, what in the hell are ya doin' out here on my weather deck, kid? Tryin' ta catch a few rays or somethin'?" Galetti shook his head.

The boatswain glared. "What division are you in, numbnuts?"

"Ah, my supervisor in radio told me to see ya so ya could show me how to stand the mail buoy watch."

Wearing a plain khaki uniform, brown hat with black visor and a large gold USN superimposed over an anchor, the old salt quickly jumped within inches of the startled man, "Ha, ha, ya gotta be kiddin' me, aren't ya, kid?"

Galetti's head quickly shook. "No, chief. You see, I'm new here and was told to come out here."

The veteran backed away, frowned and sternly remarked, "Look, kid, there's no mail buoy out here and never was. Ya probably don't know your ass from a hole in the ground, do ya? Shit, I've been in the Navy twenty years and never seen anyone more stupid than you." He glared and in a booming voice shouted, "Now shove off and get your ass back inside."

Clearly shaken, Galetti walked through a small passageway behind the bridge back into the space. Log approached and smiled, "Hey, kid, you ok?" He told him of being chewed out. The new man's head lowered with an almost tearful expression and Log put an arm around him. "Listen kid, it was just a joke. I didn't mean to get your ass jumped on. Go over and grab some coffee. Some guys go through it and shit, it's like an initiation. By the way, I got a message saying mail call commences before we get back." Log smiled. "Hope ya get one from your girl." He patted his back and sat behind the desk. These types of gags occurred a few times until new men realized they were being had, but it improved morale.

Shortly after the ship returned, mail call was announced. Galetti sat on a bunk smiling and reading a letter from his girlfriend while Hickey eagerly opened one from dad.

Well, son I'm hoping to get back to work soon because it's been rough being off what with all the bills and making ends meet, but I've been doing some art work on the side. Your mom and I really appreciate the money you've been kind sending each month now. It certainly has helped buying food and other necessities. I'm proud of you. Two of your brothers, Kevin and Denny, caddy for a few bucks, Patrick and Mike have paper routes. Kim and Patty babysit neighbor kids some-times. I hope the Navy's treating you well and you're enjoying visits with family out there. Keep the faith son. Love, Dad.

His message renewed hope and confidence in the young sailor. He closed his eyes and thought, "God, I'm happy having a good family. I miss them."

On another afternoon after the ship docked, Larson, Reemer, Thomas, Galetti and Jim walked down a pier toward the parking lot and waiting buses. Fred saw a five-dollar bill flapping in the breeze lying under a small rock. He walked, picked up the note, approached Larson and asked, "Hey, Chief, did you lose this?"

"Yeah, thanks." He quickly winked at Thomas, grabbed and put it in his pocket.

Reemer moved close and whispered to Jim. "Wow, man, I thought I'd seen and heard all stupid things, but this just took the cake today. Man, this guy's not right."

On one occasion while in port, Bearden ordered Jim and Seaman Smith to paint bulkheads outside the radio shack near the hatch. Normally, seamen were assigned that duty instead of petty officers, but he purposely neglected a couple lower-ranked men, singling out Hickey. He thought, "There he goes again, giving me another shit detail."

A few feet from the hatch, they grabbed two four-inch wide brushes and a can and started brushing typical battleship gray paint close to a ladder. While chatting about favorite jazz artists, Smith accidentally splotched a few drops of paint on his dungarees and hands. A minute later, Galetti walked down the nearby ladder and stared. "Ah, what are you guys doin'?"

Smitty's eyes quickly widened in disbelief at the stupid question, gazed at him and shouted, "I got paint on the bulkhead, paint on my hands, paint on my dungarees and you ask what we're doin'?" Jim laughed.

Smith took a few steps and quickly swiped the brush across the surprised kid's face. "That's what we're doin' idiot. How do ya like that?" Stunned, Galetti ran down the passageway into the head.

Jim remarked, "You crack me up, buddy. Man, that guy sure asks stupid questions. He's been harassed and teased by practically everyone. Ya know, in a way, I feel sorry for him, don't you?"

"Yeah, I guess you're right, but how dumb can you be, asking that kind of a question while we're sweatin' our asses out here painting. Damn, that dude's missing a card in his deck. The Navy's gotta get 'em off cause if we get in a bad situation, he could panic or do somethin' stupid and could cost us, ya know?"

" I know. I'll go and check on him." After they finished, Hickey ran, finding Galetti standing in front of a mirror sobbing. "Hey, are you ok?"

Galetti wiped his brow and looked at him. "Yeah, I think so. I guess I say and do stupid things and Bearden's been on me, being the new guy. I wish they wouldn't have sent me here. I don't know what I'm gonna do 'cause it seems nobody's helping me. Everyone goes on liberty, and when I try and tag along, they tell me to get lost or somethin'."

Sympathetic, he put an arm around him. "Listen, Smitty didn't mean any harm. That's him, and he's frustrated sometimes like some of us 'cause of the lifer. If I'm around and ya wanna talk or get somethin' off your chest, let me know. I'll listen. You see, Badass has been harassing me also. There's somethin' wrong with that guy. If I were you, I'd put in for a transfer cause in a few months were sailin' into war buddy, understand?"

"Thanks, Hickey. Would it be ok if I sort of hung around you and maybe have a couple beers with ya sometime?"

"You sure can, any time. Listen, why not get your mind off the bull-shit and read a book in the ship's library? You can relax and concentrate on what you're reading."

"Yeah, maybe I'll give it a try."

Late that afternoon, over 150 men stood in a passageway anticipating a delicious pork chop dinner. Hickey, Galetti and Smitty fell in behind Gates. Gates turned, and then sneered at Galetti and Smith. "Man, our division really got shafted. First, it's Badass, now you, new boy. Ya gotta be the dumbest thing I've ever seen." He grinned and looked at Jim. "Hickey, I see ya hangin' around with the spear chucker, eh?"

Disturbed, Galetti lowered his head in sadness as Smitty glared and shouted, "Watch your mouth, Gates, or I'll deck ya." Several men standing in front turned around and looked.

Immediately alarmed, Jim quickly moved within two feet of the perpetrator and shouted in their defense. "Look, you ignorant ridge-running, blob, I like these guys, and I'm tired of your wise ass remarks. They're in our division, and we all gotta pull together." Jim bellowed. "Shut up. It won't take much for me to hang one on ya. Understand, jerk?"

Smith looked at Hickey. "Hey, keep yer shirt on, Jim."

Gates eye's widened, stunned at the bold response. He expanded his large chest like an intimidating bear. "Ha, ha, that will be the day. Shit, I outweigh ya by fifty pounds. I'll wrap ya around a pole, boy."

Jim retorted, "The only boy around here is you, 'cause of the way ya act. Everyone knows your Bearden's pet." Jim raised and doubled both fists and shouted, "Come on, jackass, ya wanna pick on somebody? I'm not afraid of ya. Go ahead, try me."

Smitty reached, grabbed and pulled him away, "Pal, he's not worth it, and you'd only get both of you in trouble. You're right, he's ignorant." Gates turned around avoiding eye contact and emitted a low chuckle.

A minute later, as the chow line moved closer to the galley area, Smitty hollered, "Ya call me that again, I won't hesitate like Jim here. I'll let loose, and you'll wish ya were dead after I get done with ya. You get my message, boy?"

Galetti leaned and whispered to Jim, "Hey, thanks for helping me. I think I've got a couple friends now."

The following day, Smitty, Galetti and Hickey were on watch, manning equipment and processing messages as Bearden, sitting behind a desk, carefully eyed their progress. Gates slept after a mid-watch and it was routine until midafternoon.

Seated, Badass quickly swung both legs on top of a desk, lit a Winston, smirked and looked at Jim who was working with Smitty ten feet away. "Hey, Hickey, come over here. I gotta question."

He stopped logging in messages and stood before the lifer. Bearden looked up and grinned. "Do ya think I'm prejudiced?" The question surprised him. Puzzled, he scratched his head, pondering why it was posed. "Well, come on, boy, am I or am I not?" Badass raised his voice. "Answer me."

"I don't understand. What's that got to do with our duties?"

He glared, again baiting him, "Hey, ya got a brain, don't ya?" Bearden shouted, "I asked ya question, sailor, now, answer me."

A chill shot up his spine as fear entered. He thought a few seconds. "No, I don't think so, but don't really know."

Bearden reached down, took a long sip of coffee, another drag, stared at him and smirked. "Shit, I'm not prejudiced. Ya see, I think everyone ought to own a few, ha, ha."

Smitty shot up from his seat glaring with hate-filled eyes. Jim's fists clenched. He thought, "No one's ever confronted him. I've had it and gotta do something." Summoning courage, he took a deep breath, placed his hands on the desk, and glared at Bearden. He then turned quickly and snarled at Smitty, "Stay out of this. I'll handle it."

"I know your angle, Bearden. Ya want a reaction, don't ya? Ya want me to fire on ya so ya can write me up, put me in the brig and break me, eh? Well, I'm not a sucker. I know about the two guys ya screwed over and damn it, it's not gonna happen to me." He turned around, looked at his mate and lightly tapped Smith's shoulder, calming him.

With stamina, Jim looked at Badass, raised his voice and asked, "By the way, what in the hell was the Navy thinking when they put you in charge of men? They must have been crazy. You know Communications, but ya sure as hell don't know how to treat men and damn it, we don't have to put up with your racial slur."

Incensed, the lifer sprang out of the chair and walked around within inches of him, steaming. His eyes expanded in rage as his jaw protruded. Bearden glared. "I could write your ass up right now for insubordination, boy."

Tense, Jim's toes suddenly curled as they did when his dad berated him as a boy. He took another breath and stared at him. "Look, I'm only telling the truth, that's all. You're gonna write me up for telling the truth?" His voice lowered as he stared. "Ya know somethin', Bearden? I don't think you're gonna do it, cause it'll never hold up and I got two witnesses sitting right here." Jim at Smitty who nodded.

Bearden's head whipped around and glared at the two. Frightened, Galetti's eyes bulged while his body shook, like a hooked bass. Hickey wasn't finished venting. "Now, if it's just you and me, heck, the chief or Lieutenant would probably believe you." He shook his head and stared. "No, I don't believe you'll do anything, will ya? By the way, I'm not a boy."

With his ego damaged, Bearden walked around a bulkhead, desperately looking for anyone hearing the exchange. Duff was in a rear area spraying solutions and cleaning teletype components, oblivious to the altercation. Innately, Bearden figured Galetti wouldn't back Hickey, fearing retribution, but Smith would.

Frustrated, Bearden sat, never taking his eyes off Jim. He chuckled cynically. "I could write your ass up so fast just for insubordination, but I'm just bidin' my time boy when I'm gonna nail your ass. Ya see, I have two more stripes and got Larson and Stewart in my pocket. What do you got? Shit, nothin'. You think they'll believe you? Hell, no, they won't. What are ya gonna do bout' it, huh?" There was silence for a minute; then Badass chuckled, "Nothin'. I didn't think so."

His comments elicited anxiety from Jim, while attempting to perform duties, distributing messages and quickly sending out classified data on the teletype. Bearden eyed Jim, like a circling hawk preparing a descent, in case he erred. Jim couldn't wait to get off and grab chow.

Walter Bearden's pride had been undermined by a lower ranked man, a person he detested, consequently, he retreated, lying on his bunk, formulating a deceptive plan against the sailor. Planning revenge, he thought, "I'm gonna break him before we get ta Nam, but I'll need Gates."

Smitty and Galetti sat across from Jim on the mess decks. They ate in silence and looked at him. He at the overhead, took a breath and addressed the two. "Think about it, fellas. I'll bet Gates met him in the radio shack this morning before the midwatch ended, and told him about what happened in the chow line yesterday. Hey, otherwise why would he even ask such a question in front of you, Smitty? He knows we're buddies, and he's trying to force you or me into doing something rash so he can write us up. I'm telling ya, there's no other reason. By the way, watch what ya say in front of Gates because he can't be trusted."

They both nodded. Smitty finished, got up and patted Jim's back. "Thanks, Jim. I think ya handled yourself well. We gotta be real careful from now on, right?" They walked outside to relieve tension and inhaled fresh salty air.

Gates was strangely quiet for two weeks, wisely avoiding the three. Jim suspected he was ferreting for Bearden. It added up, since the lifer seemed aware of behind the scenes chatter among disgruntled sailors. Gates behaved like a fly, buzzing in and out of conversations in the radio shack and other areas. Bearden called him "my boy."

One afternoon at sea, Gates encountered Bearden out on the weather deck. Bearden's eyes widened as he raised his voice asking, "What's the latest on the men?"

"Well, I got the feelin' Log's sided with Hickey, Smitty and a few others. It's obvious they don't like ya. Hey, by the way, why ya havin' me do all this sneakin' around? I don't like it."

Bearden grinned, "Now listen, Don. You're my eyes and ears, and you'll do it if ya know what's good for ya. I know ya like favors, and besides, ya really don't want me on your ass like I'm on Hickey's, right?" Gates nervously shook and looked away, but Bearden smiled, placed a hand on his shoulder, calming him. "Donny, I can get early and extra liberty for ya. You'd like that, wouldn't ya?"

"Well, yeah, who wouldn't?"

"See, I'm asking for information, that's all. Listen, we'll meet once a week all right?" Badass smiled. "We'll make a great team. Don't worry about nothing, ok?" Reassured, Gates smiled.

Thomas Alden enjoyed the refreshing two-week leave with his family in a spacious apartment in National City, not far from the base. After returning, he conducted fire-fighting classes for various crew members.

Bearden selected Smith, Carter, Warden, Galetti and Hickey for two-hour sessions each day during five scheduled days at sea. They assembled forward in Repair Two while *Satterfield* steamed ten miles off California. The small compartment had an array of equipment including mechanical foam dispensers, $CO_2$ canisters, a small discharge water pump, large axes, gloves, a few oxygen breathing apparatus or O.B.A.'s, and four and six-inch wide hoses.

The five entered and greeted Tom. "Hey Jimmy, how ya been? I missed ya, buddy. I had a lot of fun with the family. We got around, seeing lots of sights and had a ball at the zoo and probably saw a few of your brothers in the monkey cage, ha, ha."

They shook hands and Jim smiled. "I'm happy for ya, Tom. You have a nice family. Hey, I have a question. I thought you were already in charge of a damage control squad. How come we gotta learn this?"

The group circled around Alden, who turned and looked at each of them. "Hey, fellas, I was told to train you guys firefighting techniques even though you've had a short class in basic. Listen, if one or two of my guys go down, I'm gonna need help in case of fire. All divisions, including you guys in radio, have gotta know this stuff. Hell, I know each space has a $CO_2$ bottle, but ya gotta know basics about the O.B.A. and fire-fighting things. I'll also train you in NBC (nuclear, biological, chemical) warfare defense. Listen, we all gotta contribute in case we're hit and save the ship, right?"

Carter quickly chirped, "Shit, 'Flames', anyone with a brain can grab a hose and put out a fire."

Alden moved closer and stared at him. "There's a lot more to fire-fighting than just picking up a hose. You gotta know which hoses, the proper spraying techniques, back up measures, connections, and other things. Now, suppose the canister on your O.B.A. breaks or ya need to jury rig a hose 'cause the fire main's out. What are ya gonna do?" There was silence. Embarrassed, Carter lowered his head and looked at the deck.

Jim blurted, "Listen, fellas. Tom knows what he's talkin' bout. He's been in longer than any of us and has experience. We gotta learn this."

Alden smiled. "Thanks Jim. Ya see, we gotta react quickly and know what we're doing ta save the ship. She's our home and damn it, we gotta take care of her, understand?" They nodded.

He instructed well in a detail and patient manner. On the fifth day, he assembled the group and grabbed an O.B.A. It was a three-foot long canvas device with a small oxygen breathing canister in the middle, and see-through mask at the top, relatively simple to put on. He explained how to wear it, tighten the canister and other things. "Before we fight any fires ya gotta put this on quick because it will save your lives."

By Friday, he was satisfied they knew considerably more about fire-fighting methods and equipment. At conclusion, he leaned against a bulkhead and smiled, "I'm proud of you guys. You did well. After we tie up, whoever has liberty, meet me downtown at Green's, because I'm buying the first round." They smiled.

Before returning into the tradio room, Jim took Alden aside. "Ya know something, buddy? The lifer hasn't been bugging a couple of us lately. I wonder what he's up to. Maybe he's waiting for the right time for someone to screw up or something. I just don't know."

"Hey listen, you're worried too much. Don't sweat it, pal. You're lucky having family here. Enjoy em', and maybe you'll find another decent babe here." The reassuring words comforted him. They walked outside scanning the pristine ocean, yet Alden looked worried.

"What's bugging you, Tom?"

"Ya know, I just hope if something happens, and I need some guys, they'll remember the training I gave em' and be ready. That's what I'm concerned about."

"Yeah, buddy, don't worry, I'll remember. Ya can count on me because I'm your friend and would never let ya down."

He slapped his back. "Thanks, Jimmy. I gotta run and see how my guys are doing maintaining equipment. Catch ya later."

Twenty years from now you will be more disappointed by the things you didn't do than by the ones you did. So throw off the bowlines. Sail away from the safe harbor. Catch the trade winds in your sail. Explore. Dream, Discover.

Attributed to Mark Twain

# 6

# "YOU'RE ONLY YOUNG ONCE"

Late Friday morning, the ship eased into pier three, but Harrison surprised them by announcing that personnel inspection would commence at 1600 on the weather decks. They expected it each month and normally with a day notice, but this time had only had two hours preparation, knowing liberty would be denied whomever didn't pass.

In berthing, men quickly retrieved inspection uniforms from lockers, grabbed black shoe polish, and old skivvy shirts, and then furiously spit shined shoes. The atmosphere was somber.

Incensed with the captain's last-minute decision, Reemer hollered, "That damn bastard doesn't care about us. This is bullshit. Heck, everyone knows he's biding time waiting to get off this tub and doesn't know how we feel. Hell, all he cares about is getting that full bird captain's rank."

Veins on his neck bulged as he rubbed polish into leather, hatefully looking at the shoe as if it were the captain. "Man, the skipper we had over at San Miguel in the P.I. was ok. Ya see, he cared about his men. A few times he'd walk around and chat with us. This guy's something else. Guys, I can't wait till we get a new C.O."

"You can say that again, Sid," Duff said.

After preparing, men lined the decks at parade rest in dress whites with CR division assembling behind the stern mount. Accompanied by a Yeoman, Harrison carefully halted, eyed each man at attention. If an Irish pennant or thread was visible or a white hat dirty, fingernails unclean and shoes not glassy, the man's name was recorded.

While he inspected near the quarterdeck, whispers were exchanged along two ranks about playing a ruse on the scapegoat. Everyone knew Galetti had motion sickness. Just a week prior, he ran into the head and threw up as the vessel sailed on a calm sea.

While the division stood behind Stewart, Larson and Bearden at parade rest, ten men in two ranks continuously swayed sideways in unison. Jim stood men away from Galetti, who was standing next to the stern lifelines ten feet above the harbor water. Log smiled. Galetti had a perplexed look watching them. A couple guys murmured, "How's it going, Galetti? Are ya getting dizzy yet?"

Jim noticed Galetti's eyes beginning to roll as he stared at the group's motions. Suddenly, he quickly turned and lowered his head over lifelines and then heaved into the water. They stopped, as a few broke out laughing. Bearden quickly turned around and gave a menacing stare.

"What's going on here?"

"Galetti got sick and up chucked over the side," Loggins observed. Badass walked around and grabbed Galetti's neckerchief pulling the stunned man toward him.

"You, idiot, we're not underway and ya get sick at a time like this? I don't wanna see ya. Get your ass below, right now." He tearfully walked away.

Jim felt sorry for him and thought, "This guy needs desk duty real bad at a shore base, not a ship."

Everyone passed inspection, and shortly thereafter, most of the division happily ran down the pier and boarded downtown buses. A few walked into Green's, located two blocks south of Broadway and each produced I. D. before entering.

A shuffle board was located on the right, near the entrance and a long bar opposite. There were a few tables in the middle. Two pool tables and a dart board occupied the rear near a hallway. Hollywood star photos and a large shamrock hung above two rows of liquor bottles, behind the bar. A quarter played three selections on a corner juke box in the smoke-filled lounge.

Jim entered early evening, seeing Alden and six others sitting at a large table. Alden's limit was three beers and he departed after Jane arrived to pick him up. Gates razzed Carter. "Hey Caaaaada, how's it goin with ya beer? Gettin' drunk Baaaston boy?"

Carter was chugging his fourth suds, and made a suggestion, "Hey, how's bout all of us goin' steamin', eh?" Four rose to leave, but Jim declined. Surprised, Thomas looked at him.

"Hey, how come ya don't wanna go? Man, we'll have a blast goin' from bar to bar, maybe even pick up some babes."

He demurred. "I'll walk around a while and maybe catch up with ya guys later."

Yearning to relieve tension, he strolled into Dorothy's Dive, a small, dimly lit piano bar a few blocks west, occupied by a dozen patrons. Fifty-year old brunette Dorothy Conrad sat playing old standards in front of a dozen patrons and allowed him to sing a couple songs from the 1940's.

Afterward, she complimented his baritone voice as he sat drinking a beer. It was comforting listening and being away from the lifer. He returned to the apartment.

His grandparent's Siamese pet Pretty Girl, had grown quite large, frequently roaming in and out of the dwelling. They were renowned, being the most intelligent breed of house cats.

Like his mother, he wasn't crazy about felines. They were sneaky. Beagles were the Hickey's favorite with Bridgett, their current pet, but one evening Pretty Girl surprised him.

On a weekend in August he went steaming with his chums down-town. He returned late after his grandparents had retired. The living room was pitch black as he pulled a blanket over himself and slept. In the middle of the night he felt weight on his upper chest.

Jim's eyes slowly opened, seeing the cat's two golden eyes staring at him, inches from his face. Surprised and frightened, he lunged and grabbed the cat's neck, opened the door and then threw the screaming animal into a row of flowers. Normally, cats land on their feet. This one didn't. He shut the door, turned and murmured to himself, "That damn thing scared the crap out of me."

At nine the next morning, Mim and Pop were eating breakfast in the kitchen. "Have you seen Pretty Girl?" John asked her.

"No, that's strange, " Mim remarked. "She hasn't been around. Hey Jimmy, have you seen Pretty Girl?" He was groggy and rubbed his eyes.

"Nah, Mim, don't know where she is." On succeeding weekends, the feline quickly scampered away each time he neared the apartment.

Jim enjoyed various sojourns alone, losing himself walking through tranquil Balboa Park, or spending a few hours at the zoo. A favorite haunt was Sunset Cliffs Boulevard in Pt. Loma overlooking the ocean. Just north of the harbor entrance, Point Loma was a high peninsula extending into the Pacific. Beautiful and huge million dollar-plus homes rested atop a massive hill, overlooking the road. There were a few small parking inlets near a guard rail along the street, eighty feet above the shore.

Shortly before or after sundown, he'd walk from nearby Ocean Beach and then descend to a small plateau. He sat and dangled his legs over a cliff while viewing waves crashing into rocks on a cove thirty-feet below, watching awesome majestic sunsets as his eyes scanned the horizon. He wondered what lay thousands of miles west. Hearing the sea roar against land brought temporary peace to this soul. Alone, he had time for reflection, away from the boisterous downtown music and idle conversations of sailors on liberty in bars. Their conversing lacked depth. It was therapeutic nesting above the sea. Bearden and *Satterfield* were miles distant and yet the thought of war preyed on him.

On occasion, he frequented a fancy lounge south of Broadway primarily occupied with Black customers. It was another sojourn for enjoying cool jazz and comaraderie.

Normally Monday morning during chow, sailors rehashed weekend exploits. Jim sat with Thomas and Reemer across from Gates, Duff and Carter. "Hey, Jim, how's that family of yours doin'? Have a good liberty?" asked Sid. He related about pastimes and relatives, but seconds after mentioning the club everyone ceased eating, looked and stared in disbelief.

Gates shouted, "You gotta be shitting me. You actually walked in there? Shit, they're all spear chuckers there. Man, you got some balls. Ya wanna get yer throat slit or somethin'."

"Nah, I didn't think about it, because all I wanted was listening to good jazz. I'm tired of hearing rock n roll and country and western music all the time. I had no problems and no one bugged me. They were nice people, and I had a good time."

Reemer shook his head back and forth a few times. Carter exclaimed, "I gotta hand it to ya, Jim, you're pretty brave. Ya probably didn't know it, but that place is practically off limits for us white sailor's because you know all those race riots and protests going around the country not too long ago."

Jim retorted, "Look, I spoke with a couple sailors wearing civvies that night. Heck, they're regular guys. I don't see others as white, black or brown, just people with the same joys and fears like everyone else. Don't be alarmed, I'm not. Guys, they're people and besides, we got Smitty and he's ok in my book."

Thomas blurted, "Fellas, he's absolutely right. Shit, there's so much ignorance and we're all made by the same God, right? What's the big deal? We should understand them better and get along, damn it. You guys know I'm right. Hey, Jim, more power to you, buddy." He thanked Mike who nodded in agreement, but Gates stared at the table and fumed.

August waned as warm Santa Ana winds from the Pacific blew into the county. After four days at sea, *Satterfield* tied up at 1500 on a Friday. Weekend liberty excited Hickey.

In dress whites, he scampered, seeking Alden in Repair Two. Tom looked haggard after hours of drills at sea. Jim smiled, "Hi buddy, how's it going? Wanna go with me to a party with my family on this new tuna boat tonight?"

"Oh, no thanks, Jimmy. I can't. I'm wiped out after training guys and drilling all week. Think I'll call Janet, have her pick me up, grab something to eat and crash at our pad. Listen, have a good time and be cool."

"Thanks, pal." Alden always made him feel good about himself.

Hickey rushed into berthing and caught Log alone sitting on a bunk spit shining his shoes. Sections two and three had liberty and no one was around. "Hey, Log, ya got duty tonight?"

"Nah, just gonna jump into my Chevy, maybe grab some Mexican chow and take in a flick or something since I can't reach my wife."

"Where do ya think she is?"

Tim looked dejected as stress lines appeared on his forehead. "I don't know, but between you and me, I'm not feeling too well because she's been cheating on me and denies doing anything wrong, but every time I suggest we go out she's always got an excuse. I don't think she loves me anymore."

Hickey leaned against a pole, looked down with empathy at the despondent man. "That's too bad. Man, I feel for ya. Is there anything you can do about it?"

"Not much, I guess. Ya see, I've put some pounds on in the last couple years, and she's been in good shape, but ya know it's been hard on both of us, being gone for about a year. I think she desires a younger guy who's in better shape. Hell, I'm the same guy she married seventeen years ago. She didn't want kids, but maybe that's part of it. I don't know."

Loggins turned and looked at him. "You see, between her infidelities and that asshole Bearden causing trouble among some guys, it's tearing me up inside. I'm worried about Badass discombobulating some of the men on watch."

"What the hell's that mean."

"It means to frustrate or confuse others. I came across that screwy word a few years back, but it sure fits his behavior. As you know, when he supervises sometimes, it's not what he says, but how he communicates. Right now I can't do anything because he's got Stewart and Larson's back, but when the time comes I'll have a serious talk with them. I saw the chief corpsman a few days ago 'cause I started having these here chest pains. Heck, I'm only thirty-eight, but feel alot older."

"What did he say?"

"He checked the blood pressure and it's high. Now I'm on medication. Can ya believe it? Shit, I'm not near fifty and here I am talkin' bout those things. I'll exercise more, 'cause I gotta lose weight. I'm not quitting cigars 'cause I only puff 'em. Ya see what I'm talkin' bout, Jim?" Loggins stared at the deck in sadness as his jaw dropped.

"Wow! Log, I never knew that. Maybe exercise will help ya. Word is that ya don't drink a lot, and that's good. Hey, I've got an idea. My family's been invited to this big christening party on some tuna boat tonight, and I don't believe they'd mind if you came along and I think you'll have a good time. How bout it? Wanna go?"

Log at a bulkhead, thought, and then put his shoes in the locker. Tim looked and smiled. "Jim, that's the best offer I've had in a long time. We'll take my car."

Hickey slapped his back. "That's what I'm talkin' bout. Man, we'll have a blast."

An hour later, they jumped into a '65 Blue Chevy Impala convertible parked near the end of the dock, drove through downtown, and headed north on Harbor Drive. The warm breeze was refreshing as they entered Nimitz Highway, exited on to Voltaire and then headed down Famosa toward the apartments.

Log parked on the street and followed him up to his aunt's place. Hickey announced. "Hi gang. How's it going?" Pete, Jean and three kids sat in the living room talking with the grand- parents. After introductions, they chatted briefly before Jean interrupted the conversation. "Hey, Jimmy, I've got something to show you upstairs." They clambered into a cousins' bed-bedroom. He walked in with his back to a closet. Suddenly, a low deep voice asked.

"Well, how are ya doin' there, swabbie?" He turned around, shocked at seeing his smiling grandfather Harold Hickey stepping out of the closet toward him. His eyes quickly expanded in disbelief.

Jean chuckled as they embraced for the first time in four years. He had flewn in from Washington, D.C. the day before for Rhonda's wedding.

When he was a boy, Pop would pull surprises, coming over to the house unexpectedly. His mother, Mary Eleanore, would gaze down while scrubbing the kitchen floor only to suddenly glance a few inches, and see a pair of black, wing tipped shoes. She looked up, stunned, seeing his smiling grandfather wearing a suit. "Well, hi there, El," he'd remark smiling. He was seventy-three with thin receding, gray hair and wore glasses above chubby cheeks on a stocky five-foot eight frame.

Jim's eyes swelled as he smiled, hugged him exclaiming, "My God, I don't believe it. You're here, Pop. Man, what a surprise! This is great. Let's go down below and have one."

It was the second time Harold saw his ex-wife since their divorce during World War Two. For a couple hours they reminisced about family and old times. "Log" enjoyed hearing about Jim's grandfather's exploits during World War One and related some of his own. During a few clean jokes, his large belly shook like a bowl of Jello. Hickey's family was comfortable with Loggins.

That evening, they arrived at a huge well lit marina, just west of downtown. The new tuna boat *Capricorn* was the fifth owned by family friend Jerry Badruga, a large Portuguese fisherman and entrepreneur who enjoyed cigars.

Hickey was surprised at its size. It was almost half the length of Satterfield, having impressive quarters for a dozen men, state-of-the-art radar, and an elaborate captain's cabin.

A seven-piece band on the stern played jazz and current tunes while three young ladies wearing black and white short tuxedos strolled, offering drinks and hors d'oeuvres. Badruga, wearing a fancy white tuxedo, roamed, greeting a hundred guests. His eyes caught Pete, Jean and the others. He walked and gave Jean and Mim a kiss, shook John and Pete's hands, and then was introduced to Pop, Jim and Log.

He was an imposing middle-aged figure, a tanned giant of a man. The lines on his face bore evidence of an individual who'd spent several years fishing. Badrugas dark mustache, Roman nose and eye-brows below jet-black hair was a trademark. He had the largest hands Jim ever seen, and Hickey was relieved when Joe's initial crushing grip lightened up. Jerry was gregarious and loved to chuckle while telling jokes. He was the perfect host. This occasion broadened Hickey's and Loggin's relationship.

Later, in the midst of frivolity, Loggins motioned Hickey over near the stern. After excusing himself, he swayed through several guests and walked aft.

"Log, what's on your mind?" Loggins downed a Jim Beam and water as a serious expression enveloped him.

"Ya know, Jim, when we're on liberty, ya can call me Tim, but aboard, I like the nick-name the guys gave me." Hickey nodded. Tim's eyes took on a serious expression signaling inner turmoil. "I got something real important ta get off my chest. I'm doing it because I like ya. You're a decent guy and a good sailor. Jim you're blessed havin' a nice family here and I trust ya, which is the reason I'm talkin' to ya, see?"

"Come on, what's eatin' ya, Tim?"

"I've been observing what's been goin' on with Bearden and some of the men. I'm tellin' ya, don't trust Gates. He's a snake and has his nose up Bearden's can. Ever notice he gets early liberty a lot, and Badass never jumps on him when he screws up in the radio shack?"

"Yeah, come to think of it, I have." He told Loggins about the altercation with Gates and subsequent confrontation with Bearden.

Tim's eyes bulged as he stared at him, "Wow! Someone finally challenged him. You know, he was baitin' ya, and now you're really in his dog house. Be careful. His question had nothing to do with the navy and your duties. Yeah, I know his angle."

"Tim, there's at least three of us and maybe more who think Gates is a ferret." In the navy, few things are worse than a spy aboard ship. Log moved closer.

"Look, watch yer back, Jimmy, because I think it's gonna get worse when we get ta WestPac.

When the time's right, I'm gonna speak to Bearden if I can. I came aboard bout a year ago, and know what happened to those two guys."

"Were your close to Badass before?"

"No. Well, ya see, we only went on liberty a few times, but I know the man and see right through him. He knows the men are comfortable with me cause I'm fair with them; that's why he despises me. Badass knows he's lost a considerable amount of loyalty. Before I leave, let me say something else, than ya can return to your family."

He stuck out his large chest and breathed heavily, releasing built up tension. "Damn it, Jim, I'm not gonna let him destroy anyone else cause we gotta restore morale, with everyone pulling together, see? Well, I needed to get this outta my system, and besides, I've been quiet about this too damn long. Keep it between us shipmates, ok."

"Tim, ya got my word. Let's watch ourselves and be cool. Can I trust Thomas, Reemer, or a few other guys I hang around with?"

Log's eyes shifted toward downtown building lights reflecting on the harbor then he paused and thought. "The first two are ok, and maybe Smitty, but Kennel has loose lips and ya know the old sayin' bout that, don't ya? Keep Galetti out of it. That kid's got some real psychological problems, and he's kinda messed up. I feel sorry for 'em. He's sheepish around Bearden."

"Yeah, I know."

Loggins concluded, "The more guys know about the ferret and our strategy, the worse it'll get, 'cause someone will spill the beans and he'll know everything. As you said, we gotta be cool. I'm gonna start writing a little secret journal later about what's goin' on, 'cause we may need it in the future. I know it's against Navy regs, but I gotta do it. If something happens again, let me know, but make sure no one's following ya. Let's go and eat some of that good swordfish, buddy."

Hickey patted Logs back. For the first time he felt relieved a senior petty officer was getting involved. Loggins was a class act and Hickey admired his courageous spirit.

After a couple hours, Log thanked the Anderson's and his shipmate for the invitation and enjoyable time. "Have to run, Jim. I've reached my three-drink limit. Have a great time at the wedding, and I'll see ya Monday."

As Loggins walked down the pier, Mim stared at him then turned to her grandson. "Ya know Jimmy, he's a good man. Stick close to him and you'll learn some things." Hickey's family departed at eleven after thanking Badruga for his hospitality.

The following day, the wedding reception was held on a spacious lawn behind a large home owned by one of the Anderson's friends. Servants moved about, catering to a hundred guests. Hickey was proud of his grandfather's poise, carrying himself well in public. Harold didn't over indulge in alcohol, but could still handle a few brandys, while engaging in meaningful conversation. He didn't have an enemy in the world, and enjoyed making people laugh, drawing others like a magnet, not for his own pride, but for who he was.

With a combination Eastern and Southern accent, Harold's complexion brightened while smiling. Hickey had that rare talent of making everyone feel good about themselves aside from a great gift, of singing and harmonizing. On occasion amid people, to their surprise, he'd suddenly bellow out old World War One standards like *Down by the Old Mill Stream* and *Dear Old Gal*.

He took his grandson briefly aside, and advised, "Now son, ya watch out for those pick- pockets overseas and those wild women, 'cause a lot of em' are no good, ya see?"

"Ok, Pop." He delighted seeing Mim and Pop getting along well, again. It would be their last time together.

Sunday after Mass and breakfast, they entertained the usual weekend friends around the pool. Later, Flaherty offered to drive Jim back to the base. Jim embraced Pop Hickey as tears quickly formed. Harold smiled, placed a hand on his grandson's shoulder and advised, "Now, Jimmy, you take care of yourself over there in that damn war, ya hear? Be a good boy. I love ya son." He never saw him again. Within two years, Harold passed out of this life.

September came and the destroyer breached the harbor's entrance early on a Monday, sailing alone a hundred miles west. Harrison ordered test firing of the new ASROC system.

Each rocket had a warhead with a 1-5 mile range. Throughout the ship, men heard successive "*whoosh*" sounds as each armed missile was fired into a blue sky, and then plunged into the ocean, thousands of yards away. Sonar then tracked each to its predetermined depth, monitoring the subsequent explosion. Several tests were run for a few hours while fire control petty officers analyzed the data.

In radio, men went through routine functions, sending and receiving message traffic. Larson, Bearden and Loggins carefully observed subordinate's behavior as they manned equipment and processed messages, and were pleased with their efficiency. Jim's teletype speed increased to over fifty-five words a minute, beyond the required fifty. Hours of education and training were paying off for the communicators. Galetti and Smith ran the mimeograph machine and distributed messages. Duty went smooth, yet at times Jim and others were uncomfortable as Bearden's eyes homed in, like a heat-seeking missile.

During the next four days, the captain relentlessly pushed men through a variety of drills until he was pleased with the results. Sailors grumbled as they often do, but were relieved Friday afternoon after the public address sytem blared. "Now hear this. Make all preparations for entering port. The smoking lamp is out."

After docking, radiomen showered, donned dress whites and civvies for liberty. Thomas approached Hickey, sitting and polishing his shoes. "Hey, buddy, ya wanna go down to Tee Town with us?"

Puzzled, he rubbed a hand over his cheek. "Where's that?"

Thomas grinned, "Well, hell, that's what we call Tijuana. Man, we're gonna have some tequila and maybe get a few senoritas in the sack."

"Nah, I've heard about G.I.'s getting locked up in that filthy jail there for jay walking or getting drunk and I'm not looking for hookers. Ya better be careful, Mike, ok?"

"Oh, that's all right. You have a good liberty anyway, pal."

At 1700, Hickey approached the O.O.D. standing on the quarterdeck and flashed the required yellow card. "Request permission to leave the ship", he said.

"Granted." He saluted the officer, turned, looked at the small American flag hanging ove the stern, repeated the action, ran, then boarded a bus and went downtown.

He sat alone, thinking at a quaint little park off Broadway. "I've gotta focus on meeting and socializing with some new girl. Perhaps this will temporarily wash away the fears of Bearden."

Hickey walked and saw a little drug store on a corner and entered to purchase gum. A short, cute brunette wearing a white blouse and green slacks smiled behind the counter as an old pharmacist while filling prescriptions behind a glass barrier in the background.

The sailor stood and smiled. "Hi, what's your name?" A surprised expression came over her.

"Why do you wanna know?"

"I like your smile and ya look nice, that's all." She had green eyes on a lightly tanned oval face. Her forehead seemed to jut further out than normal and the neatly brushed brown hair fell below middle neck.

No customers were around. She leaned over and whispered. "Hey, that's the owner back there. I just got this job a month ago. He told me never to speak with sailors because they're all alike and only want one thing."

He at the proprietor busy filling a prescription, moved near her and whispered. "Hey, I got news for ya. He's wrong. We're not all wild, but some do stupid things, get outta control and give us a bad reputation, understand? Sorry to bother ya. Here's a quarter for the gum." He softly remarked, "Listen, I'm gonna keep comin' back here until ya tell me your name, got it?"

Her eyes sized his countenance. She grinned. "That's up to you, I guess." He turned and started walking out. She quickly looked back toward her employer, then hurried around the counter stopping him as he grabbed the door knob. "My name's Diane. I'm twenty-one, from Sacramento and a junior, attending San Diego State. My folks have lots of money, but I work here part time because I want some responsibility and a little extra cash each month, see?"

He grinned. "I'm Jim, stationed on a ship, have family here, and I try spending a lot of time with them. Listen, I don't wanna get you into trouble. I'll see ya later." He left, turned, and watched her gait as she returned behind the counter. She smiled, raised a hand and waved. He was happy and would see her again.

Night fell as thousands of lights from high rises reflected on the harbor. Jim desired another musical environment to relax. In the distance high above, he looked at the lighted bold letters EL CORTEZ near the top of a building, sitting on a hill, north of downtown. After a fifteen-minute climb up steep Ash Street, he entered the historic site.

Several affluent, well attired guests mingled. Decorated and imposing chandeliers overhead brightened an array of tropical plants on each side of the main hallway. The conspicuous fifteen- story hotel was built in 1927 on the site where General Ulysses S. Grant's son's home once stood. It had thirty-two suites, eighty-five apartments and an attractive glass elevator that quickly brought the visitor up to an impressive top floor lounge. Two seven-story connecting buildings flanked each side of the high rise. It was an imposing site, viewed from the harbor.

After stepping off the elevator, his eyes brightened as he walked into the Sky Room. The large, quaint room had stools surrounding a half bar on the left. Along both sides next to viewing windows were round tables, and comfortable lounge chairs. In a corner, a quintet with a vibes musician in front played a variety of smooth jazz and old standards.

Behind a piano along a corner wall were immense windows. As others socialized over cocktails, he walked near the edge, gazing in awe a few minutes at a panoramic view from 175 feet above the city. Countless lights flickered from buildings, yachts, ships and homes. Below downtown, a loaded jet sped down a runway and lifted off from Lindbergh Field, soaring over the Marine Recruit Depot and Pt. Loma. Light from a full moon over the peninsula reflected on the harbor along marinas and naval bases, giving it a breathtaking romantic flavor. Toy-like fishing boats with tiny, white running lights shuttled in and out of the harbor.

He sat a front table near the entertainers, thinking about inviting the girl there, but a quick glance at the menu confirmed his suspicions; too expensive for his blood. Uncle Sam didn't pay much. His eyes again shifted toward the windows. He thought, "I'll never forget this beautiful scene."

After ordering a bourbon and water, he closed his eyes, listening to various Latin tunes, at peace and away in his own little realm. Before departing, he downed another drink, again venturing near a window gazing at the resting city.

Hickey had duty Saturday. A new man, nineteen year-old tall and slender Al Franklin joined Gates and Log supervised. It was a slow traffic day with mainly routine messages and battlefield reports from COMSEVENTHFLT about the war increasingly being assumed by South Vietnamese forces.

Gates was strangely pensive, out of character, negating exchanges in idle talk among the skeleton crew in the radio room. Log would speak with Jim on the mess deck during noon chow. Fewer than a hundred sat enjoying burgers and fries. They faced each other while a few men from the supply department sat nearby.

Shortly afterward, Hickey related about the wedding, meeting a new girl and a journey to the El Cortez. Loggins suggested. "Hey, if ya wanna impress that girl, take her there, and if ya need a few bucks, let me know."

"Thanks Log, you gotta big heart, but I don't wanna burden you."

"Nah, no problem. Ol' dad here will help ya and if I'm not around there's a couple veterans aboard operating slush funds. Ya know what they are?" He shook his head.

Loggin's leaned forward, pointing his right forefinger and related. "Hell, it's illegal, but been goin' on as long as I've been in. It's a little business normally done by married guys who need extra money to help support their families and other reasons. Let's say the ship's in port and some guy needs money for whatever reason; he borrows five ten, or twenty bucks, then on pay day the guy has ta fork over seven, fourteen or twenty-eight bucks to the loaner. Yeah, it's high interest and some single men take advantage of it, but if an officer discovers it, the guy's normally busted."

Hickey's eyes widened. "Ya mean this always goes on in the fleet and shore?"

"Yeah, listen, my advice is only taking advantage of it if you really need it or you're desperate."

"I understand." Loggins took a long sip of coffee, but suddenly his composure changed as his jaw dropped.

"What's wrong, Log?"

He whispered, "Lately, I been doing a lot a soul searching 'cause of my wife's indiscretions, and the problems with Larson and Bearden. Confidentially Jim, this is real personal and I trust it's between me and you. Hickey leaned forward, intently listening. "Well, if I can't patch up the problem with my wife before we sail overseas, I'm gonna take her off as my insurance beneficiary, and put my folks on who are retired, living on Social Security back on the farm in Iowa. Now, she won't even know I did this until after I croak, see?"

"You're pretty serious, aren't you?"

"Damn right." His forehead wrinkled indicating stress. It pained him discussing it. "See, Jim, like you, I don't trust too many people, 'cause I've been back stabbed before and the reason I'm even telling you about it is because ya got values. Like I told ya before, you're a decent young man with a good family. In a way, I envy ya."

"Thanks Log, I appreciate it", he smiled.

"Have ya ever heard of WESTPAC widows?"

"No."

"Listen. They're married mostly to veterans, ya know, career men and some have kids. What happens is when their husbands are overseas, they go bar hopping and wanna hit the sack with another sailor or civilian, especially if the guy's got money."

Hickey's eyes quickly expanded, his mouth opened, and he remarked, "Ah, that's not cool."

"Yeah, it's been goin' on for years all over the Navy. I'm not saying they all do it, because some are still loyal, but the Navy has the highest rate of divorce now. They probably do it cause they're lonely, bored or don't love their husbands anymore. Logs eyes moistened as his jaw dropped and the voice quivered, "Jim, it's pretty hard saying this, but my wife's a WESTPAC widow."

"Are ya sure? How do ya know?"

"I've gotta buddy stationed here, married, with a couple kids. Last year when we were over-seas, he took his family to a restaurant, saw my wife sitting close with some younger guy and both were real friendly." A large tear slowly descended down his left plump cheek. "Yeah, they were holding hands and hugging. Man, I send a lot of dough to her each month and sure, I've had my chances, but damn, I don't need this crap. Heck, we hardly talk to each other and she's busy working part time at a clothing store. I suggested we see the base chaplain and a marriage counselor, but she won't because she's stubborn and full of pride. Jim, I know she doesn't love me anymore. If ya wanna know why I been kind of quiet sometimes that's the reason. I hope ya understand and will keep it private." Hickey reached across and placed a hand on his shoulder and reassured him.

That night, wearing a short-sleeved shirt decorated with palms he hopped on a bus and arrived at the Red Sails Inn on Shelter Island near Point Loma to ponder Tim's predicament. The palm-lined narrow strip of land across the channel from the air base was popular among the Hollywood elite and tourists with its exotic hotels and clubs, including the Bali Hai where Hawaiian dancers entertained.

Opened in 1957, Red Sails greeted visitors with an imposing stuffed sailfish over a long bar on the left, a large black white photo of actor Robert Wagner who occasionally stopped in, hung on the right, and beyond was a dimly-lit romantic dining area. Outside was a large wooden deck, Tikki bar, and a dozen round tables with umbrellas, overlooking a huge marina. Several scenes from the popular 1960's T.V. program *The Fugitive* had been filmed there. It was therapeutic and peaceful sitting by the rail, listening as water lapped against idle bobbing yachts.

A couple hours during the next few weekends, he rented a board and surfed at Ocean Beach. He wasn't too adept, as opposed to local youth who frequently rode higher waves, but the escape required concentration, easing his mind from the stress of Bearden.

Strolling through the beach town, he was unnerved, seeing pot-smoking Hippies getting high and loitering. He reflected, "These fruitcakes and punks probably are the same kind I've read about who burnt draft cards and the flag we represent." Hickey loathed and disrespected the low lifes, rebelling against order and values he and most others cherished.

On two occasions, he dropped by the pharmacy and briefly spoke with Diane, but most of the time he socialized with men and desired female companionship. In the Fall, his persistence was finally rewarded when she consented to seeing a movie and dining.

He tried impressing Diane, spending the majority of funds at one plush restaurant, yet was unnerved seeing her unmoved by the gesture; as if she expected nothing less. Later, she dropped him off at Mim's apartment in her new brown Cougar.

Before departing, he moved close to her. "Listen, Diane, thanks for taking me back. I enjoyed being with you." She smiled, quickly leaned over, planting a long soft kiss on his lips to his surprise.

"See you again, Jim. Give me a call."

He waved goodbye, watched her speed away on Famosa Boulevard and thought, "Man, a kiss on my first date with this babe." He was elated.

During the ensuing two months, she accompanied him to a couple family gatherings and parties at the plush Bahia Hotel near Mission Bay, yet her behavior smacked of someone coddled most of her life. In a large crowded room, she motioned him toward a corner, grinned and whispered in his ear, as a few others looked.. "Jim, I'm kind of jealous of your family."

"Why?"

"Well, most of the time my family is reserved as we quietly go about our business and lives.

You see, I've never been exposed to such gregarious behavior."

"Ah, what's that mean?"

Her eyes closed a few seconds as she bit her lip, studied him and frowned telegraphing disgust at his lack of vocabulary. She whispered "It's simple. It means an outgoing person and not introverted, understand?' He nodded, but felt insulted by her nonverbal gesture.

Diane was spoiled, raised as an only child on a ranch near Sacramento. After receiving a sizable inheritance, her parents sheltered and catered to her every whim. The lady's behavior smacked of Scarlet O'Hara fame relishing sycophantic males who heaped praises on her.

He reflected, "She's not a diamond in the rough, yet I'm infatuated with her beauty. You've gotta be a patient gentleman." When speaking, her tone was soft and pleasant. She had an engaging personality, yet was cognizant of her intellectual superiority over him. Despite these factors, she was merely a temporary antidote to Bearden.

The next week on a calm sea, he grabbed some coffee after watch, went topside and gazed at the far horizon, thinking, knowing Satterfield would be sailing west in eight weeks. After a few minutes, a hand touched his shoulder.

"Hey, Jimmy, how's it going, buddy?"

"Tom, you're a site for sore eyes." He related about his enjoyable liberties and family, but his buddy sensed a troubled soul.

"There's something bugging ya, isn't there?" He nodded, informing about the confrontations with Gates and Bearden, the trust developed with Loggins and a few others. Hickey finished the drink, leaned against the lifelines and looked at the sea. "I met this rich girl recently and really like her. I'm kind of sad 'cause we're leaving soon, and she'll probably find someone else.

"Jim, ya gotta understand something, pal. You have no control over the situation, and besides you'll probably get to see that Filipino girl. Don't worry about nothing, because everything's gonna be fine. God's in the heavens and knows what's going on. Don't sweat it."

"Yeah, you're right, and I guess ya make sense, so why get too choked up about it? Besides, we have enough problems here, right? It's just that she makes me feel good when I'm around her, away from that asshole, if ya know what I mean."

"I understand, Jimmy. Just hang in there, pal, and maybe think about that Filipino girl. Don't even think about getting serious with this one. I got a feeling she's not right for ya."

"Tom, you have a gift of making a guy feel better about things. Thanks for being my friend."

Alden put an arm around him, "I think you're taking the right approach with the lifer. Watch you're back, do your duty, and be cool." Jim smiled and breathed a sigh of relief.

Two weeks flew without significant incidents aboard. After numerous drills, the crew's efficiency pleased Harrison. After a four-day exercise with other vessels, the ship headed south toward the Baja Peninsula for an hour, then turned and steamed back, north parallel to the coastline.

Hickey and a few others in dungarees temporarily rested in bunks, waiting for two bells, which signalled chow. Suddenly, a boatswain shouted over the loudspeaker. "Now hear this, whales off port side."

Excited men scrambled up decks or leaned against lifelines seeing about two dozen large mammals rise and plunge in the saltwater. One behemoth swam within 100 hundred yards of the ship.

Sid nudged Jim, "Hey, look at em'. Wow! Aren't they something? I think they're heading down to Baja to mate." Again, Hickey felt exhilarated, as if he were back in time aboard an old sailing vessel, looking at their majestic black tails rising above the surface. Shortly after, she returned to port.

That night, he stood the midwatch with Sid, Mike and Loggins, but was yearning to see Diane on Saturday. Early that morning, Log sat, lit a cigar and addressed the three."Now, what I'm telling you guys will stay here, understand?" They stopped, nodded and swore to secrecy.

They had never seen him this serious.

Loggins thought deeply, stared and stated, "Listen, I'll make this short. Keep your eyes on Gates because I don't trust him. He's running interference for Bearden. Watch what ya say around 'im. After we leave for WESTPAC, I'm gonna try and ta talk sense with him about how he's been treatin' a few of you guys.Yeah, I know some fear him, and Jim here had the guts to face him which I believe was justified. I think he's gonna do everythin' he can to break him 'cause his pride's been hurt."

He paused, took a long puff on the tobacco stick and continued, "Men, we're goin' back ta war and we gotta have some harmony around here. This guy ya call Badass, I think he hates himself. He's sick inside and takes his frustrations out on others and that's wrong. Yeah, he's very smart, been in a long time and I'm sure he's earned his rank, but damn it, I won't sit still and have another repeat of what happened last year. Let's pull together and don't give him an excuse to jump on ya. Let me handle this for now, all right?" They nodded in agreement.

Thomas blurted, "Ya make perfect sense, Log. It's good advice. Listen; speaking for us three, I wanna thank ya."

Log smiled, "We'll get through this, I promise."

Saturday was only sixty-two, a little chilly and partly cloudy. Jim grabbed lunch aboard and scampered in dress blues down to the pier, then ran, barely making the downtown bus and walked into the store. While a few customers milled, he thumbed through a magazine which was sitting on a rack in the corner.

The owner was inattentive as Jim approached her. She wore a tight yellow sweater, brown slacks and silver turtle like designed earrings. Diane grinned, "You look nice in those blues, Jim."

He leaned over and whispered, "My grandparents are goin' out tonight and aren't returning till late. Why don't ya come over and we'll have a couple drinks and watch a flick."

"That sounds good. After I'm off, I've got some studying, but I'll swing by around eight, okay?"

"Good, see, ya later."

After departing off a bus, he bought ingredients for her favorite drink, the screwdriver, then walked down to Mim's. She arrived at eight as he chased the cat out. He wasn't used to liquor, but made two double screwdrivers and turned on NBC's *Saturday Night At The Movies*.

They sat on the couch, idly chatting, and consumed two more drinks during the next hour. He kissed her lips while embracing her, as she closed her eyes in willing response. She stopped, sipped the drink and looked at him. "I need my hard contact lenses out, and have to put them somewhere." He went into the kitchen and grabbed two small glasses of water, placing them side by side. She walked in, looked and said, "That's a good idea, honey."

"Yeah, see? Port and starboard, like aboard ship."

She dropped one in each glass. An hour later, after passionate caressing and kissing, the alcohol was affecting him. As they sat close, she gazed into his eyes. "I really like you, Jim. You're a gentleman. I had these preconceived ideas about sailors which I know now aren't true. Listen, I wanna invite you to meet my parents up at our ranch next weekend. Can you fly or take a bus? We have a large place, a spare bedroom, and we'll have an enjoyable time together. Is your ship in port then?" Her invitation surprised and delighted him.

"Thanks, honey, that sounds great. Yeah, I can take a bus up there next Friday." She smiled and quickly kissed his lips.

Shortly afterward, she requested another drink. He hurried into the kitchen and mixed another. Numerous times out of habit, he'd quickly clean Mim's counter. The hard liquor was having an effect. For a few seconds, he forgot about the lenses and without thinking, grabbed the left glass and quickly poured the water into the sink.

Suddenly he thought, "Oh shit, what have I done? That was stupid." He mumbled a few words to himself as she walked in.

"Oh, thanks for making me one. By the way, where's the other glass?" Clearly embarrassed, a he lowered his head as she glared.

Nervous, he swallowed and stared at her. "You're gonna think I'm an idiot, but I wasn't thinking and accidentally threw the water into the sink. Gee, I'm sorry."

Diane was incredulous as her mouth opened and her jaw dropped. She looked like she'd seen a ghost as her eyes bulged. She shouted, "How could you do such a stupid thing? Damn it.

That's for my left eye and these things are expensive."

He thought, "If I had her money, I'd burn mine."

He grabbed a flashlight out of the drawer while she impatiently stood nearby folding her arms and gritting her teeth. He placed it over the garbage disposal drain as fingers from his other hand explored the bottom, desperately searching. He stopped and looked at her. "Listen, I've got an idea. Let me run down and borrow an Allen wrench from my uncle so I can lower the disposal then I might be able to get it out."

Her lips pressed together. With her patience exhausted, she stammered, "Yeah, you'd better do that right now."

He ran past five apartments until reaching the Anderson's at the end, and knocked. Pete opened the door wearing a bathrobe as his nephew excitedly blurted out what had occurred. Pete's face brightened into laughter, "Ha, ha, boy oh boy, Jimmy, I thought you were kidding at first, but looks like your gonna blow this one. Wow, I don't believe this. You gave me the laugh of the day. Hold on, and I'll get ya one." Jim thanked him. Pete blurted, "Good luck, ha, ha, you're gonna need it."

After returning, he knelt and started undoing the bottom bolt. She couldn't contain her anger and started berating him, much to his surprise. "You're an idiot. Do you know that? I've seen all kinds of mistakes, but this one takes the cake. Don't you realize if you can't find it, I'll be driving back with only one eye?" He chuckled softly. "That's not funny," she shouted. "Come on, hurry up and get it. I haven't got all night, damn it."

He turned around and grinned as she stood with her hands on her hips. "Everything's gonna be all right, baby doll," he reassured.

She fumed, "Don't baby doll me." The rage and hollering near his ears surprised him.

He thought, "Now, I'm seeing her other side."

After ten minutes, he was unsuccessful. Again, he grabbed the flashlight and fingered around, frantically trying to locate the tiny object. Her ranting never ceased as stress increased within him. Instead of encouraging him, she continued raving. He thought, "I'm not gonna put up with her crap." Raising his voice, he exclaimed, "I can't take this anymore." He turned and flipped the power switch on.

The machine quickly ground the lens and tiny bits of food. She ceased bantering as her eyes widened without blinking, like someone hypnotized. "I don't believe what I just saw."

He took a deep breath, looked at her and softly remarked, "I'm sorry this happened, but I couldn't stomach any more of your shouting." She took the other lens, placing it in an eye, paused and stared at him.

With open arms, he stepped near to console her, but she quickly backed away and announced, "I'm going back now." He handed her purse to her. She swiftly grabbed it, shrugged her shoulders and started marching out like a little queen who'd just been insulted.

He blocked the door and said, "Listen, Diane, look on the bright side. You have one eye and it's better than no eyes, right?"

"That's not funny", she snapped. "Now let me out."

He followed her down the steps where the vehicle was located in a car port. She hurriedly jumped in and rolled down a window. He was concerned about her safe return. "Hey, I'll guide ya out, okay? Call me when ya get back. I'm worried about you."

With an angry expression, she squinted, saying nothing as he guided her down the driveway.

She turned, peeled rubber, and sped off. He watched as the car disappeared into the night and wondered why someone with one eye would drive like a maniac.

He thought, "Women, I'll never understand them."

During breakfast Sunday, he related to his grandparents what had happened. They broke into uproarious laughter. Mim remarked, "Well, Jimmy, I think it could only happen to you. Ya know this could have been a blessing in disguise cause even though all of us liked her, she behaved like a little princess. We thought she had the attitude she was better than us, and I picked up on that during the party. She's probably a spoiled brat. Don't worry, you'll find someone better."

He thought, "Yeah, God willing."

On Monday, Jim received a verbal "Dear John" from Diane over the phone as Loggins, Thomas, and Smitty sat in the radio room. Minutes before, they had chuckled after hearing of the escapade. After she refused his plea at making amends and compensation, he slowly placed the receiver down as his expression turned maudlin. He lowered his head into his hands.

Mike put a hand on his shoulder, "Hey, pal, I feel for ya, buddy. Man, this is the first time I've ever witnessed a phone D.J. Jim, I think you ought to get tanked tonight."

Log inserted, "Hey, Jimmy, from what ya told me, she was probably a gold digger and self-centered. Listen, look at the positive side. There's more fish in the sea and you're gonna see that Filipino babe, anyway."

He looked up, wiped his moist eyes and nodded, "Yeah, guess you're right, but this isn't easy, Log."

Loggins smiled, "Hey, ol' dad here will take care of all you guys. Just come and lay it on me anytime."

He walked a few paces, grabbed a cup of coffee, lowered his head and thought, "Damn it, here's another thing I've failed at." He decided to focus and work hard at his profession.

In November, weekday maneuvers and gunnery practices went well. The captain was satisfied with the previous month end reports, submitted by department head officers. His mission was getting both ship and crew prepared again for war.

The lifer's behavior was strange. He ceased looking over guys' shoulders, being jittery and impatient, but the difference was an increasing animosity toward Hickey, clearly noticed by others through nonverbal behavior and his eyes.

Later that month, Jim had an enjoyable Thanksgiving dinner with his family. When short on funds, he meekly approached Mim asking her if Pop had a few bucks, and was elated when given an extra five or ten greenbacks. His grandfather continued driving him back to the base before ten on Sunday evenings. He never forgot the generosity. In three weeks, he would fly East and home.

# 7

# "LEAVE"

That fall, daily temperatures fluctuated from sixty two to seventy degrees. Notice of mandatory inoculations was posted as the vessel idled near the pier. At 1400 the loudspeaker blared, "Now all hands muster with your division topside for shots." Sailors wearing dungaree trousers and skivvy shirts congregated on weather decks as the sun's rays off the superstructure.

Eight hospital corpsmen were positioned with air guns to innoculate the crew with anti-disease protective serum. Officers assembled on the forecastle as 285 enlisted joined their respective departments on the main deck, port, starboard and fantail areas.

CR Division fell in single file between the stern mount, and the DASH flight pad, and rolled up their white shirt sleeves. Gates stood in front of Jim, six behind Larson. Two flanking corpsmen held gun-shaped pneumatic tools, attached to inch-wide, long gas air hoses which instantly shot anti-cholera, Asian Flu, Yellow Fever and Typhoid agents into into arm muscles.

Standing behind Jim, Reemer murmured, "I hate the gun and would rather have the needle any day. Hey buddy, remember, don't flinch when they hit ya with them." Most of the men were silent. The only sounds were low pitched, firecracker like "bangs" after each corpsman simultaneously pulled a trigger, releasing fluids into muscle and flesh.

A corpsman announced, "Next."

Gates stepped forward, however, as each trigger was pulled, he panicked, and quickly jerked his right arm. Tiny bits of flesh and blood shot into the air. "Oh, damn, that hurts," he screamed. The frustrated corpsman dropped the gun on the deck, quickly raised Gates arm up and placed a small patch over the wound. Frightened, Gates moved a few feet away.

"Ok, next," the corpsman shouted. Hickey stepped forward and took a deep breath. Initially, it felt like he'd been quickly stung by a few bees, but slowly the pain subsided as he stepped forward, joining the others.

A few returned into radio with aching arms, manning equipment. While lying half asleep in berthing, Jim listened as Thomas exclaimed, "Man, I'm glad we're through with those damn shots. They're sure a pain."

Carter chirped, "Look on the bright side, at least they're not a pain in the ass."

"You can say that again," Thomas replied.

Shortly before Christmas, several men took leaves. His chit (request) was approved for a 30 day leave and after paying the stand by fare, he boarded a TWA flight for wintry Michigan.

His dad greeted him at the airport and happily embraced him as a twenty degree wind blew above the three inches of snow. The area south of town was commonly referred to by north siders as "fertile valley" because five to twelve children comprised the average family. Boredom didn't exist.

Located in an attractive lower, middle-class subdivision, it was a sixteen-year old two story brick house with a large, square picture window in front. There were five bedrooms. A small kitchen and dining area adjoined a spacious living room. His father's study and art room encompassed a third of a tiled floor basement. In the corner of a large, garage-less back yard was an apple tree.

Two sisters had a small bedroom on the main floor near his folks bedroom. Upstairs, five brothers occupied three beds in a large dormer while two girls slept across a short hallway in another room.

He couldn't wait to savor mom's great cooking. After entering, the kids yelled, "Jimmy's home, Jimmy's home," as they ran and hugged him. His mother slowly walked around the kitchen corner with her sweet Irish smile and they embraced. Tears quickly swelled in his eyes.

"It's so nice having you home, Jimmy," she smiled.

"Oh mom, it's so good being here."

The smell of fried chicken, gravy and mashed potatoes permeated the area that joyous Sunday evening. Throughout dinner, he patiently answered questions from siblings and parents. Later, they congregated in the living room, conversing for a couple hours.

His five foot six good humored mother Mary Elenore had beautiful auburn hair and rosy cheeks on her five-six Irish frame. Ten siblings were present. The eldest girl, Christine, her career Army husband, and infant son were in Germany. Second oldest son Mark, an Air Force tele-type repairman, was stationed in Japan.

They were a good Irish litter and each was unique with God-given talents. Father had lead singing roles at a nearby community theater group and taught art once a month in the basement. The boys partici-pated in sports at a nearby park and created outside activities, building tree forts, playing street football, earned money shoveling snow, paper routes, and collecting old magazines and newspapers. A few caddied at a local golf course. The girls helped with mountains of laundry and a couple babysat neighbor children for a buck an hour.

Their father's talents had filtered into a few. Kevin and Dennis played folk and pop music on string guitars and Kim excelled in art. Both Kim and Patricia had impressive melodic voices, while seven year old and youngest Lauretta, practiced cheerleading on the front lawn.

Second youngest Paul was taciturn, with red hair and freckles. In the evening after homework and dinner, the boys enjoyed ping pong, and paperwad fights in the basement until someone shouted in pain after getting hurt; then the game or fight ceased after hearing dad exclaim, "Oh ok, that's it, come on up boys."

The seemingly never-ending activities attracted the neighborhood Jettie, Murphy and Youngs kids as they filtered in and out of the house. The atmosphere was a carbon copy of an old Henry Fonda and Lucille Ball movie," *Yours, Mine and Ours.*"

Patrick eight and Michael seven were two inseparable little scala-wags. Every time you turned around, something was happening, and they got in trouble.

Jim asked, "Mom, anything important happen last summer?"

She recollected and grinned, "Well, I told those two never to go down to the creek." She related that one early dark evening, the boys hadn't returned for supper. Worried, she thought about calling the police, but instead, said a prayer. Shortly after, there was a knock at the back door.

Two dirty-faced ragamuffins stood on the porch with sullen faces, looking up at her. "Where have you two been?" she asked.

Patrick, in dramatic fashion, immediately took charge, concocting a story. He looked up and said, "Well, ya see, mom, we ran into a bad man whosaid, 'Boys you gotta go down to the creek and catch some pollywogs and frogs.'" Stifling laughter, she listened further to the outlandish tale.

"What happened then?" she inquired. It was obvious he had rehearsed his little speech after telling his brother to keep mum.

"So we did what he told us to do. We went down to the creek and got some pollywogs." Keeping her composure, Elenore gazed down at them and asked, "What happened next?"

Patrick lowered his head, paused and thought, then looked up into her brown eyes.

"Mom, the cops came and they got (emphasizing "got") that bad man and told us 'Boys, ya gotta go home now with those pollywogs and eat some supper.'"

Seconds after opening the door and letting them in, she ran down the hall into the bathroom, closed the door and laughed uproariously.

On another occasion during chore time on a Saturday, Mr. Hickey vainly searched for lanky, seventeen year old Dennis. Exasperated, he approached Kim while a few teen siblings stood nearby. "Ah, where's Denny?"

"He went to see Gordon Lightfoot."

He paused, thought, and turned, looked at her and ordered, "Well, call Gordon's house and tell him to come home right now because I need him here for chores." They broke out laughing.

Puzzled, he inquired, "Why are you all laughing? Now, stop that. I'm serious and I need him to help out."

Mary stopped, took a breath and smiled,"Ah, dad, Gordon Lightfoot's a popular entertainer, and Denny's at his concert."

He chuckled with the others as Patricia reached and patted his back chirping, "That's ok dad, you didn't know."

Mr. Hickey was off and on diets and at one point in 1971 was fifty pounds over his normal 180 pound weight. As usual, he never took himself seriously while poking fun at his expanding stomach.

On his birthday, Patricia bought him a pair of trousers. The family watched as he placed them against his waist, and then carefully looked at the label inside, which read "extra-large." He grinned, and said, "Oh, thanks, Patty, but I can't figure out why the label says American Tent and Awning." Everyone broke up.

Though an alcoholic, he was a good provider, loyal to his wife and children. At times he had a quick temper and would put the fear of God into the kids, but did his best teaching values and the Catholic Faith. Though prayerful, he was a troubled man which originated with his parent's divorce as a teen, resulting in insecurity. Nevertheless, he loved his family, and each Sunday everyone attended nine thirty Mass, attired in their best.

Jim slept on a short couch in the living room. Sometimes, one of his brother's buddies spent the night upstairs. Hickey visited a few pals and a former girlfriend, returning late on a few occasions. After entering the rear door and taking off shoes, he tried creeping near the couch in darkness. A voice from a rear bedroom inquired, "Is that you, Jimmy?" It was mother. He thought, "Well, nothing's changed. She could still hear a pin drop."

It was impossible sleeping in as each morning kids and teens moved about talking and giggling while eating breakfast. With the exception of weekends, he resigned to getting more sleep by retiring earlier. He enjoyed socializing with siblings, discussing navy life, playing sports and helping with chores, but refrained from manifesting the Bearden problem. Jim had no intention of unloading on his parents about Bearden since they had considerably more worries.

The day he bid adieu to his family, then took his dad aside pouring his heart out to him. "Dad, I remember when I was twelve during a Little League game striking out three times and letting the winning run in as a fly ball sailed over my head in center field. I sat in your car and cried my eyes out for letting the team down. You reached, hugged me and were so understanding. You've been a good father."

Mr. Hickey nodded, put a hand on his son's shoulder and responded, "Yes, I remember son, but you did well pitching as a teen in Babe Ruth ball." Mr. Hickey lowered his head, wiped a small tear from his eye, and looked at him. "Son, I've made some bad mistakes in my life as a father and should have treated you better, but I want you to know how sorry I am. Please forgive me. You see, I'd like us to be close again like when you were a boy."

He put an arm around his father's shoulder, turned, and looked at him. "I do forgive ya. It has to be tough being a father and I can't even imagine doing that. Ya know, I think back of failing my teammates, failing geometry and failing in other things. I'm sorry. I couldn't live up to your expectations, but damn it, I will not fail my shipmates." Mr.

Hickey took a deep breath, exhaled and looked at him. He pulled him close and they embraced as their eyes moistened.

"We'll be praying for you son. Be careful."

# PART II

## ODYSSEY

I wish to have no connection with any ship that does not sail fast; for I intend to go in harms way.

John Paul Jones

# 8

# "THE PACIFIC AND PEARL"

On 14 January, Hickey returned and had a last dinner with his grandparents. Pete and Jean came over and bid goodbye. "Now Jimmy, be careful and don't volunteer for anything," warned his aunt.

"I'll try, but sometimes the Navy does it for ya, if ya know what I mean."

"How long are ya gonna be gone?" Mim asked.

"Probably nine months to a year."

After hugging each, Mim wiped a tear from her cheek. Pete looked at them and exclaimed, "Hey, listen, he won't be on the ground getting shot at. Don't worry, he'll be safe aboard that ship."

That evening, Pop drove eight miles, dropping him off in front of the main gate. He hugged and thanked him for everything. Chilly air struck his face as he buttoned his pea coat. The temperature plunged to fifty while he walked through the gate. There it was again, fog! It enveloped the harbor. The same eerie feeling rushed into his soul as in Seattle eight months before. He thought, "There's something about fog. Was it a portend of impending evil?"

Around eleven, small groups of sailors staggered and walked along the dock, boarding vessels. He wondered and asked hinself, " Where's my ship?" Bow and mainmast lights poked through the thick camouflage of fog as he strolled by each ship trying to read hull numbers. Suddenly, the unmistakable white painted 816 bow number came into view. He was back, and Bearden waited.

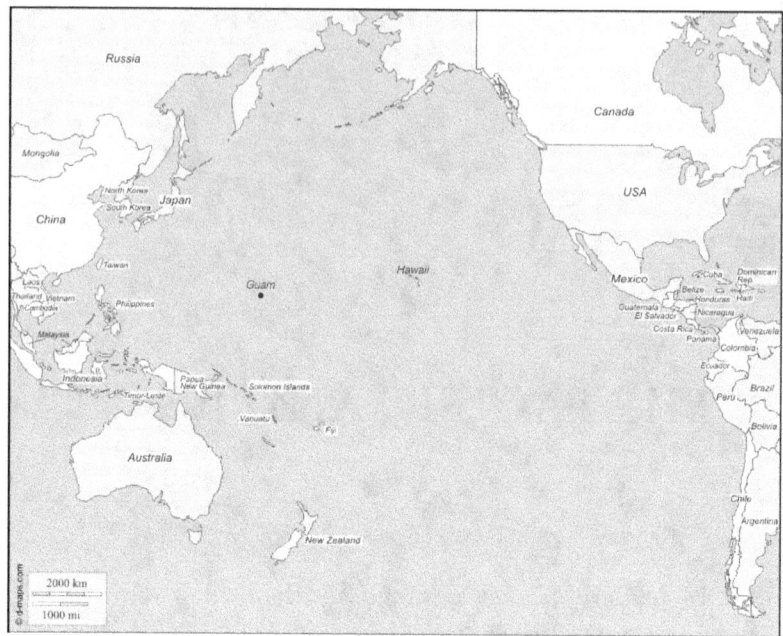

**Map of the Pacific**

At 0:800 on a cloudy Monday, a hundred people gathered on pier three. Sailors mingled among civilians, kissing, embracing loved ones as girlfriends, wives and children shed tears. Tom huddled near Janet and Shannon. He wondered. How six months could fly this quickly.

She choked back tears. "You just take care of yourself honey and return safely."

His eyes moistened as sadness crept in while lookinfg at her. "Listen, honey. The best decision I ever made wasn't joining the Navy. It was marrying you, and I thank God every day for you and our little girl."

She wiped tears and embraced, replying "Oh, Tommy, you always have a way with words. I'll pray for your safe return every day. Remember, I love you." He pick up Shannon, kissed her little pink cheeks and hugged her. He lowered her to the pier and gently planted a long kiss on his wife's receptive lips.

Suddenly, the ship's loudspeaker interrupted their embrace. "Now, make all preparations for getting underway. Set the special sea and anchor detail. The smoking lamp is out. Deck section two, man the lines." Men were going to war. Alden clamored up the after brow with others in dress blues, assembling at parade rest along lifelines. Hickey and mates lined the starboard.

"Cast off all lines," the O.O.D. ordered.

The boatswain announced over the 1MC, "The officer of the deck is shifting his colors from the quarterdeck to the bridge."

While onlookers waved, she slowly backed away, and then turned, leading three destroyers at eight knots, snailing past downtown. In naval tradition, it was an honor bestowed by the high command being the point ship for other vessels. Satterfield exceeded training expectations earning the coveted E for excellence, and the large noticeable white letter was painted on both sides of her bridge.

The 160-foot patrol, motor gunboat (PGM) USS *Travis* with twenty men aboard, brought up the rear. Named after a California city, she had an enclosed three-inch gun mount forward, single forty-millimeter gun aft and fifty-caliber machine guns. *Satterfield's* duty was escorting and providing necessary refueling for her during the voyage.

After rounding the marinas and North Island, she moved past the sub base into the channel.

Jim gazed at high Cabrillo Peninsula as men stood at parade rest with legs spread and hands clasped behind their backs. Nearby, hungry white gulls dove toward water like World War Two dive bombers, snapping fish.

The announcement came. "Secure from sea, anchor detail and quarters. Set condition X-ray. The smoking lamp is lit."

Standing on the bridge in khakis, Harrison barked to the helmsman, "Increase speed to twenty knots, course zero nine zero."

Quickly, the reply came. "Aye, aye, sir, twenty knots, and course zero nine zero." Three other "tin cans" followed her wake, each spacing 600 yards on a calm sea.

The TBS (talk between ships) systems were tested, and then *Satterfield* sent *Travis* a message ordering the little vessel to assume position three hundred yards ahead. Capable of forty knots, she revved up jet engines, swiftly moving and maintaining position. Eight thousand miles west men were dying in war.

Radio division dispersed. Jim went into berthing, quickly changed into dungarees, then went topside and leaned on stern lifelines watching the California coastline slowly diminish as the destroyer's wake increased. Feeling somewhat homesick, he was preoccupied by the unknown and precarious adventure, far beyond the horizon.

For thousands of years men have put to sea for a variety of reasons: adventure, travel to distant lands, love of country, escaping homeland drudgery or strife, physical or mental challenges, fulfilling youthful dreams, and an incessant quest for life's meaning for water calms and stimulates the soul.

After noon chow, he walked on the main deck, viewing expanse of ocean. Bright sun now dissipated morning clouds. He moved near the forecastle (focs'le) pulling the white hat snug above his ears and looked fifteen feet down at the gray bow plowing through blue salt water as a chilly a breeze struck his face.

Swift dolphins looped up and down alongside, and then quickly scurried away. At peace, he smiled, comforted, far from the noise and confusion of cities. He thought, "Wate's unique. It floods a sailor with tranquility and like baptism, cleanses the soul."

On the ocean, a man thinks clearly and delves into his being, reflecting on many things including family, but also his destiny. In awe of God's creative power, Jim felt like an excited child wandering into an unknown realm or dark forest, apprehensive of his future, but yearning for the adventure, beckoning him.

At sea, five men stood one of three eight hour watches in the radio room, and transmitter spaces, yet most desired midwatch duty because of low traffic volume with better transmission and reception. After a nap, he changed into working dungarees shortly after six bells before going on watch at 1600.

Many U.S. Naval traditions were inherited from the British. Sailor's tell time when a ship's bell rings. Eight bells (0800) begin's the day watch to 1600 or 4pm. Even bells ring on the hour, odd, half hour. For example, 0:830 one ring, nine, two rings, noon eight, and the cycle is repeated.

Thomas, Gates and Hickey relieved the day watch. Bearden supervised. Message traffic was light as Jim sat near a teletype machine quickly sending out classified messages to Hawaii and Guam.

Sitting at a desk in view of them, Bearden was unusually quiet. Between checking messages, he had a weird habit of staring intermittently at a clock on the bulkhead or at subordinates sometimes for an hour while repeatedly sliding a fore-finger and thumb up and down on a pen. It was as impossible determining his thoughts or motives as it was to unravel an enigma.

Since Thomas was second in rank, Bearden let him rectify any arising problems, thus harmony ensued,. Few trusted Bearden, remembering past volcanic eruptions for infractions and his attitude toward Jim.

Harrison conducted various drills a couple hours each day for those not on watch. Men in communications were concerned about Galetti's daily bout with sea sickness despite calm seas. While others slept, he inadvertently babbled classified information. A few men without top secret clearances resting just twenty feet beyond awakened, listening to his broken words. The last thing *Satterfield* needed was for a sailor (without a clearance) to disclose secure data to other unauthorized individuals.

During that period, a Navy chief warrant officer on the East Coast was passing top secret fleet broadcasting information to the Soviet KGB (intelligence) officials.* Two days before arriving, Larson met with Galetti after conferring with the lieutenant. The captain cut orders for his transfer to Hawaii for temporary duty. Word spread. Thomas ran down into berthing and spoke with Jim sitting on a bunk spit-shining his shoes.

> Since 1968, cryptologist John Walker Jr. spied for Communist Russia passing classified information to the Soviets. It became the biggest spy scandal in U.S. history. In 1985 he was arrested and convicted. His reason: "I needed money." He died in prison in 2014.

"Hey Mike. Man, you're out of breath. What's up?"

Mike's eyes widened and looked down at Jim. "Shit, that kid's one lucky son of a gun. We're dropping him off at Pearl, and he's probably getting two or three months temporary duty in an office or something until new orders come."

"Are you serious?"

"Hell yes, I am."

"Well, it's probably for the best because he's the type who may crack when we get into combat or go on port and starboard watches. Galetti's been singing in his sleep during the middle of the night so I think he's better off ashore and may even lose his top secret clearance."

After Thomas left, Galetti walked down and spotted Jim. Galetti's jaw dropped as his eyes swelled with tears.

"Hey Galetti, what's wrong pal?" Jim asked.

"They're transferring and giving me clerk duty at the base in Hawaii. I wanted to be with you guys over there and see some places." He took a deep breath, sighing relief. "You and a few other guys have been good to me and I'm sure gonna miss ya. Is there any way I could stop them from doing this?"

Jim ceased polishing, got up and thought, "That was a stupid question." "Unfortunately no, because they don't want unauthorized guys receiving classified information. We can't have secure data compromised. I'm sorry for ya. Stewart spoke with the old man and approved it. Hey, look on the bright side. They'll probably give ya a day job in a comm center, and ya won't have to put up with crap aboard here anymore. There are a lot of guys who would gladly swap with ya cause of all those pretty dishes running around Waikiki Beach.

Shit, it could be a blessing in disguise."

"I think yer right cause I get sick, and guys razz me. Bearden makes me nervous, and I can't help talking in my sleep."

Jim put an around him and smiled. "You'll be ok and learn some things. Don't worry. Listen, don't trust too many over there. There's back stabbers everywhere. We'll miss ya. Now, let's get some chow."

In four days they reached the Hawaiian Islands. At 0:800 on the last morning, the loudspeaker blared. "Now make all preparations for entering port. Set the special sea and anchor detail. The smoking lamp is out. All sections not on watch assemble on the weather decks for entering port." Imposing Diamond Head loomed east of Honolulu as the task force sailed between the channel buoys. Seawater changed from dark to light blue as they moved near the harbor.

*Satterfield* led the ships as *Travis* assumed rear guard in slow procession into what sailor's called "the bottleneck" channel. They passed Barber's Point Naval Air Station off the port beam while most of the crew wearing tropical dress whites assembled at parade rest along both of her sides. Hickey and others stood near port lifelines, below the DASH flight deck, proudly facing outward. More than two years prior, Jim landed at Honolulu Airport for a one hour layover, but never left the terminal, before flying west to Guam. Now he would have two days liberty in paradise.

As colored signal flags on halyards flapped in a tropical breeze, the destroyer slowly moved into Pearl Harbor on a cloudless, bright morning. A two-deck white excursion boat filled with numerous tourists, motored twenty yards away alongside, while onlookers filmed, snapping photos of the man-o-war.

Off starboard, giant mobile cranes towered above the massive ship-yard past Hospital Point. An intense feeling of pride engulfed him as trade winds smacked his face while steaming past Ford Island in the harbor's middle. The morning was serene, as on that dreadful Sunday in December 1941 shortly before the U.S. was attacked.

She moved near the *Arizona* Memorial where over 900 sailors were still entombed in the sunken vessel. An ivory memorial rested across her mid-ships. Small circular spots of oil rose from her bowels, expanding on the surface. After thirty-one years, the *Arizona* still bled. Unmistakable, a couple rusted gun mounts sat just above forty-feet of water Briefly, his mind shifted, imagining what those poor men endured on that fateful morning when Japanese planes descended from three directions against the surprised fleet.

The vessels turned into a loch with three tying up near a large admin-istration building, while *Satterfield* and *Travis* tied up across at southeast loch near the submarine base. Several destroyers, escorts and frigates hav-ing returned from the Far East, were docked for weekend liberty.

Half the radio gang had liberty along with most crew. Galetti said his goodbyes, lifted his seabag, and walked over toward a large, two story administration building nearby. Jim would miss him.

It was strange seeing Gates, Bearden and Larson together, walking down the pier and jumping into a cab. Everyone knew Bearden and Gates came from the same town in Alabama, but high ranking NCO's typically never associated with seamen. Why were they going on liberty together? A puzzle began forming.

In berthing, Jim changed into dungarees for evening watch while an excited McGovern shouted, "I can't wait to get back to Hotel Street with all those bars and pretty babes."

"Well, have one for me buddy, but don't get too drunk and rowdy cause there's shore patrol around, and ya don't wanna get busted," Jim warned.

"Yeah, I know. Besides, I'll be with Dog and Smitty, and we'll watch out for each other." Reemer, Hickey, and Loggins had duty from 1600 to 2400. Traffic was light. During idle moments, the three conversed. Reemer at Log, "Hey why don't we play a little trivia and the winner gets a few bucks?"

"Nah, got some thinking ta do topside. I won't be gone long. You guys go ahead. Not much going on around here."

He left the space in a pensive mood, walked down the ladder out near the stern lifeline and looked east. While gazing at the Pali Pass and mountains in the distance he thought, "I will not tolerate my wife's indiscretions."

Before leaving the mainland, Loggins received another check up with the doctor, who increased his blood pressure medication to 500 milligrams a day. He filed for divorce and changed the beneficiary on his life insurance policy at the base legal department. In the event of his death, Logs retired parents would receive 100,000 dollars, tax free. He reflected, I'm glad I did it since they're on social security and still running the farm.

Another dilemma confronted him. He wondered, "How can I maintain the status quo with Stewart, Larson and Bearden whose respect has declined, and keep a relationship with men who can barely tolerate them?" Two opposing forces inexorably were colliding in the distant future. It was a dichotomy.

His stress level increased as he became a buffer between the triumvirate and the men. He thought, "Damn it. I've gotta have a meeting with Bearden and Larson. His conscience bothered him as he thought. I'm ashamed of being apathetic during last year's crisis involving those two young men."

Loggins mind flashed back to the inquiry on the quarterdeck in front of Harrison. Tim had listened, innately disgusted, as the three testified, outright lying about what had occurred, including the sailor's performance, covering their own sterns. His impression had been that Stewart was apprehensive but had decided to placate Larson and Bearden opposerisk to risking confrontation with the senior petty officers.

Loggins had stood at attention facing the captain, feeling the stares of the triumvirate behind.

Fear of being ostracized and of possible retribution by the three had consumed him. Harrison's words rang in his brain, "You've listened to their statements. Have you anything to add, Loggins?" As Loggins heart had palpitated, he closed his eyes, almost a minute, thinking in silence.

"Well, come on sailor, speak up", Harrison had barked.

He had taken a deep breath and murmured, "No, sir."

"This hearing's closed. You're dismissed."

As the four walked aft, Larson and Bearden had put they're arms around Tim, guiding him near an outside hatch, while Stewart had left for the officer's mess. As Larson reached out his hand to shake Tim's

Bearden had cynically grinned and remarked, "Hey Tim, thanks for supporting us. Ya did good. Ya know, we had to do this cause in a couple years we're retiring, and don't need any trouble, right?"

Dejected, he at the two and responded, "Yeah, we sure covered our asses all right, didn't we at the expense of the two kids, one of whom will never testify."

Bearden smiled, "Well, I'm glad that's over. Let's get coffee."

Loggins had moved closer and gazed into his eyes. "I hope ya won't have trouble sleeping Walt, because I sure will. Thanks anyway, but I'm going below." While he laid on his bunk, he reflected. By complying, he felt mentally sick, like the title character in *Mr. Roberts* upon disappointing the sailors after the captain's tirade aboard the fictitious *USS Reluctant.*

Men were amazed at Loggins conciliatory attitude toward the conspirators and began distancing themselves from him. Shortly thereafter, during liberty in Hong Kong, Thomas, Reemer, Duff and Carter found him in a drunken stupor, sitting at a bar. He broke down, pouring his heart out and crying, "Please forgive me, fellas. I was wrong and tried covering my own ass."

He'd promised to make amends and re-earn their respect. Hesitant, they'd been reluctant to understand, but later helped him aboard a little shuttle boat, which transported Log back to the anchored ship. Wounds sometimes heal longer. It would be months before he regained their trust.

Log lit a cigar and thought, "Since those incidents, my conscious has been bothering me for over a year, and I'm ashamed for not speaking the truth. I took the cowardly route to avoid confronting Larson and Bearden. I like my men and I'm responsible for their well-being. I've gotta take a stand and atone for my inaction. I'm tired of repressing thoughts and will address a few of the men. I've got less than three years before retiring and won't tolerate another tragedy. He murmured a short prayer, "God, give me the strength to do the right thing."

Thomas ordered Carter to temporarily stay in radio while Reemer and Jim met Loggins on the mess deck for coffee. Thomas joined as the three sat, facing Log. Tim stared at his cup while thinking. "Listen men, I believe you're the only ones I can trust in the division." He paused, and then explained his thoughts while on deck. "I'm gonna do everything I can to back you guys so we don't have any trouble overseas."

"Well, just what are you gonna do against those three?" Mike asked.

"I'm gonna talk with Larson and Brarden, and try and to get Badass to ease up on some of the guys, especially you, Jim. I don't know if it'll do any good, but I've gotta at least try. Jim, you showed him up in front of Smitty and Galetti, and he's lost some of his pride. I think he's gunning for ya and will even trying busting ya down a stripe."

They quickly at each other. Jim took a swig of coffee and nodded, "Yeah, your right, Log. I'm gonna avoid eye contact with him, but try and do the best I can. He's gonna be on my ass, trying to get me riled and baiting me to lash at him. I've just gotta be cool."

Mike chimed, "Your right, Jim. Heck, that's all ya can do."

"Log, what about that ferret, Gates?" Reemer asked.

Loggins finished his coffee, and reflected. "I trust em' as far as I can throw em'. Keep your eyes on him fellas. Look guys, I need all of you to swear now, before God and me what we say and plan here, stays here. Do ya understand and agree?" They nodded.

Thomas gave Log a serious look. "We're with ya, Log and gotta trust each other.

There are a few guys that can't be trusted. Let's guard our words." Reemer and Jim both turned, slowly scanning, seeing if anyone was within earshot. They were alone.

Log told them to keep their eyes and ears sharp regarding the relationship between Badass and Gates. "They can't suspect anything. The key is information about any devious plan they may have. When the time's right, I'll speak with Larson and Bearden and let ya know.

Mike, since you're Second Class, one stripe under Badass, he respects you. Ya can't let on that you're close with Jim here and a couple others."

Thomas finished his drink and looked at him. "Yeah, that makes sense. I gotta be cool."

Loggins gazed at them. "There's one more thing. Ya have ta really watch your body language with each other around Bearden. Ya know, he's got this weird habit of just staring at ya, as the wheels turn in his sick head. Man, in all my years, I've never seen his kind. Well, good talkin' with ya, and let's stick together. I'm with you." They extended their arms, reached and shook his hand. Tim smiled.

Jim woke at eight bells, showered, ate breakfast, and then joined Tom for liberty. In mid- after-noon they went ashore wearing colored, tropical shirts and white slacks while carrying small overnight bags. As they left the main base gate, the warm tropical winds relaxed them.

The bus eased onto Nimitz Highway, motoring past nearby Dole Pineapple Company and stopped at Hotel Street in the city's oldest section. Before Hawaii became a state, Old Honolulu was the business and tourist district, which included shops, stores, clubs and restaurants. During World War Two, thousands of G.I.'s enjoyed liberties on Hotel Street, infamous for places of ill repute and dive bars where brawls were common. There was cheap liquor; several tattoo shops and plenty of women.

They stopped briefly at a fleet bar and had a beer while listening to rock n roll. Tom said, "Jim, these places get old, but I know Waikiki Beach. Let's buzz over there." The bus whizzed by the huge Ala Mauna Shopping mall, and then entered Kalakaua Avenue, the main drag through Waikiki Beach. High palm trees flanked the street, and in the distance Diamond Head stood, like a Pacific Rock of Gibraltar, beckoning travelers below to its sandy beaches.

The men walked inside the International Marketplace, a busy palm covered area of unique shops, restaurants and clubs along a labyrinthine, winding sidewalk. Duke Kahanamoku's Club was the main attraction where the "Hawaiian Sinatra" Don Ho performed, evenings.

He was amazed at seeing several foreign tourists including Japanese, congregating and purchasing souvenirs.

"Hey, let's go for a swim", Tom suggested.

On famous Waikiki Beach, thousands of civilians and foreign tourists sunbathed, jogged, walked and swam as two-foot waves crashed against the shore. High-rise hotels like The Outrigger Reef, Princess Kapiolani, the old Royal Hawaiian and others formed a majestic back ground behind palms.

As they ran into the ocean, Tom shouted, "If this isn't paradise, I don't know what is." The warm seawater refreshed them as they swam toward two outrigger canoes filled with onlookers. Trade winds swayed palm trees guarding the long beach.

Shortly thereafter, while lying on white sand, gazing at blue sky, Tom remarked, "You know, buddy, this reminds me of a scene from an old flick, *Mutiny on the Bounty*. Fletcher Christian and his friend Bynum were lying on a beach, below palm trees, marveling at the beauty of exotic Tahiti."

Jim smiled, "Yeah, I remember seeing it some years ago. Man, it doesn't get better than this."

After two hours swimming and sunning, Tom suggested, "Let' have beer at Shipwreck Kelly's. You'll like it. They entered nearby Lewers, a side street off Kalakaua, the main drag.

A few feet from the door, a South American green, yellow macaw sat in a small, wooden cage suspended six feet below the roof, squawking and repeating jokes. Tom moved within inches of the cage, looked up and smiled. "Hi, Gus, it's been a long time, birdie birdie. Jim, this is Gus the screwiest bird around. Tourists stand here and tell him jokes, and then later, all he does is repeat one after another." The bird stopped chirping and stared at them.

"Come on, Gus, tell us a joke," said Jim.

Tom grinned, "Heck, just our luck. Man, great timing. Now, he clams up when we show up. Let's go."

Seconds after entering, he was surprised seeing sea life in a dark environment. Numerous tropical fish, including small sharks, swam above twenty patrons sitting at the bar and nearby tables along walls. Below the overhead, were a dozen large aquariums built into wooden walls surrounding the entire lounge and bar. An old, wooden ship's wheel, sextant, green sea urchins, small mast, and a five-foot wooden bow and spyglass adorned bulkheads. His eyes quickly adjusted. To the right, was a two-foot-high stage and nearby a long bar with several circular tables. In the rear, was a lighted, fine dining area. Sitting in a corner a few feet from the stage, was a four-foot windlass with anchor and chain.

He smiled, "Wow, Tom. This looks a lot like the inside of an old nineteenth-century ship.

"Yeah, buddy, I knew you'd like this place. Let's go have one."

Happy hour would end in an hour. They sat at the bar, looking at a large mirror and middle-aged Hawaiian bartender, who figured the two were sailors by their short Princeton haircuts.

"I'll buy the first round,"Jim said. He put a buck on the bar. "Hey, give us two Michelobs."

The man gave him a strange look and exclaimed, "Ah sailor, that's two bucks. You're in Hawaii."

After they gulped a few swigs, he asked, "You guys want any poo poos?"
Jim grinned and quipped, "Not particularly."

Tom laughed, looking at the man's puzzled face, "You'll have to excuse my buddy because he's never been here. Hey Jim, it's Hawaiian for snacks."

"Well, I'll be damned, I never heard of that. What are they?"

Impatient, the man repeatedly tapped a forefinger on the bar and leaned forward.

"Look, they're little hot dogs stuck between small hard biscuits, or you can eat the little smoked turds, but please use a tooth pick. Do ya wanna know anything else?" They shook their heads and giggled.

"Yeah, Jim, they're good so let's have at it."

After a shrimp dinner, four Hawaiian musicians and a singer in tropical shirts walked on the stage. The Aloha Seasons were the featured group and played every weekend. The lead singer had a smooth, melodic voice belting out popular and Hawaiian songs. A short, stubby blind man wearing sun glasses was on piano while a drummer, sax man and guitar player backed him up. The club was filled primarily with tourists, some of whom snapped away with small flash cameras during their performance. In between songs, the singer told jokes, delighting patrons.

Later, after enjoying the show and a few brews, Tom remarked, "Hey buddy, it's getting late. Let's get a cab and head back to the ship."

"Yeah, good idea. I liked Shipwreck Kelly's. You have good taste."

The last day of liberty Jim, Log and Tom took a launch and motored to the *Arizona* Memorial. She's still a commissioned ship. Each morning at 0:800, a few sailors and a Marine raised the American flag above her, lowering it at dusk.

The original large, dark brown ship's bell sat twenty feet from the names of over 1,000 crew in black letters on a bright white wall. The men are entombed in forty-feet of water above fifteen- feet of mud. A four-foot model of the ship sat inside a rectangular glass case in the middle of the area. A dozen tourists maundered, listening, as a middle-aged mustached guide announced. "Folks, if you must talk, please whisper. Where you stand is sacred." He took a deep breath. "I was a young sailor sleeping aboard the battleship *Maryland* thirty-one years ago. We were inboard from the *Oklahoma*, here at Battleship Row when the first bombs hit. They called general quarters and said it wasn't a drill." His voiced quivered as he lowered his head in obvious pain recalling that horrendous morning.

"I thought I was having a nightmare, hearing screams and bombs going off. I jumped into dungarees and went up, helping man an anti-aircraft gun. We hand passed three-inch wide shells into the gun. The Jap planes were diving all around us. The *Oklahoma* got hit with a few torpedoes and capsized. The explosions shook our ship. We shot down a few planes and cheered, and raised our fists in anger at the enemy planes."

His tanned face saddened, as his eyes swelled with tears. "I saw the ship you're standing over blow up after a bomb went down through the decks, exploding the magazines where a lot of shells were stored. These men's names you see on the wall here didn't have a chance. Many drowned. As you can see outside, she still suffers, bleeding oil. I still have nightmares. Remember these brave men for they'll always be my shipmates. You may now continue viewing the memorial. Thank you."

The three walked out, gazing down at a rusted gun mount, as globs of oil slowly rose, floating to the surface. It was an eerie silence as the sailors eyes met and again looked down at what once was a 30,000-ton fighting ship. During that moment, they intuitively received an inkling of their own mortality. Tim whispered, "We can never let this happen again." Tom and Jim were somber as they nodded at Tim.

After returning to base, they walked through the large complex and waited for a bus. Tim suggested, "Let's see that dormant volcano above Waikiki." Tom looked puzzled.

"Tim, I've been ta Pearl a couple of times and never heard of a dormant volcano. What's the attraction?"

"It's a huge cemetery built on top of a dead volcano."

Jim scratched his head and asked, "You're kidding, right? Who in their right mind would wanna go there?"

"Just stick with dear ol' dad here, and ya won't be disappointed. I promise you."

Tom remarked, "Hey, I thought we were going sightseeing. Well, no guts, no glory I guess."

"Fellas, this is sightseeing you'll never forget."

The bus motored east, through Waikiki Beach toward Diamond Head. After leaving, Tim gazed up at a sloping hill, which flattened at the middle, then turned around, pointed and said, "Look up. What do you see?"

They began ascending; then Tom exclaimed, "Wow, there must be thousands buried here."

Tim announced, "Guys, this is the National Cemetery of the Pacific. It's called Punchbowl. Wait till we reach the top."

After a ten minute climb, the earth leveled as they walked on a tree-lined avenue past rows of white tombstones where 34,000 fallen personnel of World Wars One and Two, Korea and Vietnam rested. Upon climbing several steps, they stopped and gazed in awe, looking at a thirty- foot sculptured Lady of Columbia statue, attired in ancient Greek garb, her right hand extending toward the fallen as if saying 'these are my sons I watch over.' Above and just behind on a long white edifice, were the bold names of major Pacific battles: Wake, Bataan, Coral Sea, Midway, Attu, Tarawa,Saipan, Peleliu, Leyte, Iwo Jima and Okinawa.

Tim ordered, "Follow me." Under the roof on a long wall, were map murals of major battles on blue background, showing casualty figures. Because of the structure's overhang, it was shady. "Now, look at this."

They gazed upward, focusing on each unique, watercolor design. Outside, other mural maps flanked the statue. It was somber and inspiring. "Wow! It's really something. God, this is remarkably beautiful," said Tom. A few tourists milled around snapping photos.

The sailors beheld a panoramic view below of the University of Hawaii: on the left was formidable Diamond Head, to the right was Honolulu and in the distance was the airport and outline of Pearl Harbor. Jim thought, "This imposing scene is breathtaking. I'll never forget it."

"Well, what do ya think?" Loggins asked.

"Man, Tim, I'm blown away, being here on sacred ground," remarked Tom.

"Yeah, me too," chirped Jim.

After an hour they boarded a cab and enjoyed a few beers at Shipwreck Kelly's. Sitting at a rear table, enjoying music Jim narrowed his eyes, focusing on both of them.

" Hey, what's on your mind?" inquired Tom.

Jim put a bottle slowly down, and took a deep breath before speaking. "There's a reason I asked both of you to come with me today. You're my best friends, the only men I trust other than Sid, Mike and Smitty."

He at Tim. "Do ya think I should mention our plans about Bearden and Gates?"

"Heck yes, he's your buddy and a good shipmate. Tom and I met over a year ago. I respect what he's done training guys." He looked at Tom. "Ya got class, 'Flames.' Go ahead, Jim."

Jim explained their strategy regarding Bearden and Gates as Tom intently listened. "What do ya think, Tom?" Jim asked.

Tom thought a few seconds, lit a cigarette as both leaned forward to lisen. "All I can say is this. Ya have to be careful. Watch your backs, do your duties and don't let on you're wise. Log, if I were you I'd have a serious talk with Larson and Badass. That's your last resort cause if it doesn't work, the shit may hit the fan. Ya know that asshole has it in for Jimmy here, and he's liable to do anything."

Tim nodded in agreement and smiled, "In case you haven't heard, scuttlebutt has it we're getting a new skipper by the end of the month, and I hope he's better than what we've had for almost two years. Listen, when the time comes, I'll do what I can and speak with Larson and Bearden.

Jim grinned, "That's good news. Thanks for your input, buddy." Night drew near as they returned and walked through the main gate of the base. Jim assumed Log would solve the problem with Bearden, or so he thought.

# 9

# "THE ABYSS"

Two days later, the ship was refueled and followed *Travis* out of the harbor, sailing into the ocean as morning sun off the decks. The Pacific is a precarious and strange creation.

It can be peaceful and calm as a vacant cathedral, or violent, like an out-of-control roller coaster.

Monstrous winds originating in China blow eastward, causing rapid weather changes.

Throughout history, numerous ships and men have traversed various sea lanes, marveling at its beauty and precarious character, yet not all have realized one, poignant characteristic until too late when fate intervened—it's vastness!

The smooth ocean accelerated as rolling waves from the northwest struck the little ships off their starboard beams. It was 3,300 nautical miles from Hawaii to the Marianas Islands, and sailors saw nothing but water for six days.

Below 300 fathoms (1,800 feet) is an immeasurable deep chasm where the graves of wooden and rusted steel ships once holding men were strewn about, like broken toys. Over many years tropical storms, hurricanes and typhoons were prevalent throughout the expanse of ocean.

Sea birds were nowhere in sight as they steamed at twenty knots and passed over the 180th Meridian (the International Date Line) into tomorrow. A basketball-shaped balloon with spike antennas was sent skyward from *Satterfield's* stern, rising above the clouds, transmitting atmospheric and weather data.

All divisions secured chairs and loose items with quarter inch ropes. Bearden supervised every other watch Jim manned. Radiomen received messages from CINCPACFLT, Guam and the Philippines while Travis steamed fifty yards off *Satterfield's* starboard.

Concentration on accurate typing and sending classified data on teletype machines was difficult as the vessel rose and then plunged into four foot swells. Badass sat behind the desk reviewing frequency reports and messages. Intermittently, he turned, gazing at Jim's back, like an eagle eyeing prey. Cognizant of his gaze, Jim felt like an insect being examined under a microscope. He thought, "Don't think about him, stay focused."

The lifer rose, strolled over and leaned behind Carter who rapidly typed. Stressed, due to his presence, Carter made a few mistakes. Bearden shouted, startling Jim and Sid, "Hey, don't ya know how to type, jackass? Shit, my little niece could do better than you. Now, pick up the pace, damn it."

After being relieved, they ate pork chops on the mess decks. Carter dove into mash potatoes and gravy while his other hand held the tray from sliding because of the ship's swaying motion. He blurted, "I can't wait until Log speaks with that jerk. I can't stand him anymore belittling and harassing us like some sort a slave driver." They nodded in agreement.

At sea weather changes transform both men and ships. Stress elevates short tempered men on duty, during poker games or after the psychological effects of reading "Dear John" letters from girlfriends back home.

The balloon relayed a strong inclement storm, brewing hours west as the ship steamed directly toward it. Before sunset on an overcast late afternoon, Jim went topside, meeting Tom near the stern gun mount. They looked starboard, seeing the gun boat riding high and then crashing into wave after wave, sending a torrent of salt water over bow and gun mount. Gathering his thoughts, Jim was in awe of this deep and immense body of water.

Tom suggested, "Hey, Jim, let's spread our legs, balance ourselves and see who's the first ta slide." The vessel now plunged when a six-foot wave hit from starboard, causing her to sway to port. In the distance, a huge rolling wave incessantly approached their watery home. Suddenly, Jim lost his balance as water poured over the portside. He slid ten feet, hitting the stationary four-foot lifelines, and then fell onto the deck. His body shook with fear while his heart pounded. Tom quickly walked over and squatted.

"Are you all right, pal?"

Jim took a deep breath as Tom grabbed and pulled him away as another wave struck. Hickey regained composure as his buddy led him back inside the hatch.

Tom put an arm around him and grinned, "Ya gotta a little wet, didn't ya?"

He at the ocean,"Yeah, scared the shit outta me."

They grabbed coffee on the mess deck as the boatswain announced over the 1MC. "Now hear this. Rig for foul weather. All hands are pro-hibited on weather decks. Secure all hatches for watertight integrity, and set condition Zebra."

Shortly thereafter, he returned into the radio room. Sid approached him. "Man, I feel sorry for that radioman on Travis. I just sent him a short message asking how he felt. He said he's got a shit can between his legs in case he throws up."

"Yeah, I don't envy him."

Within three hours, what started as a gale became a violent storm with seventy knot northwest winds that howled like Banshees in Irish folklore. He was thankful for being off watch as half the crew manned duty stations.

Now the storm's full fury struck as torrential rain lashed down from the heavens. Twenty-foot walls of seawater smashed over the forward gun mount, striking the bridge as the ship dove into valleys between waves. Men cursed, falling out of their racks, some heaving their guts out. Inside, a man attempting to climb a ladder toward the head, fell breaking an arm when the vessel plunged through a large swell.

Jim was glad he'd taken dramamine early and grabbed both sides of the bunk, holding on for dear life. He was stressed remembering a scene from the film *The Caine Mutiny* when a violent typhoon tossed the destroyer minesweeper about like a plastic toy in a bath tub.

Communications were non-existent. It was unpredictable if the ves-sel swayed port or star-board. Harrison and the junior officer of the deck stood on the bridge, a few feet from the helmsman, peering out between large windshield wipers swishing torrential rain over the glass windows.

"Steady as she goes. Rudder amidships, speed ten knots", Harrison ordered.

"Aye, aye, sir, rudder amidships, speed ten knots", replied the helmsman.

A few minutes later as the young sailor perspired, the wheel shook despite grasping it with both his hands. He desperately turned and addressed the skipper.

"Ah, sir, I'm having a hard time keeping her steady."

"Damn it, sailor, hold that course."

"Yes, sir."

Harrison grabbed an internal communications black phone, "Engineering, how's it going down there?" The duty chief's voice quivered with apprehension.

"Sir, one of the boilers are out, but we're working on it."

"Very well, keep me informed. Good luck."

Men heard creaks in stanchions throughout the old sea dog. In the radio shack, Log sat on a chair singing an old sea shanty *Blow The Man Down,* attempting at comforting and cheering their spirits as sitting men tightly grasped chairs.

Harrison's anxiety increased as stress lines were evident on his forehead. The helmsman shouted, "Captain, she's taking twenty-degree rolls, sir." He brought the ship back on course after making an adjustment while quickly spinning g the wheel.

She groaned like a woman going into labor while both of her sides shook. Fear showed on the four in the radio space. Reemer, sitting ten feet away, hollered at Loggins. "Hey, why is this old tub moaning? It's getting on my nerves." Tim tried being an example of calm leadership.

Innately scared, he responded, "Those groans gotta be coming from the rivets in her sides, Sid. Don't worry, men, we'll get through this. Old dad here's been through a few of these fellas. If anyone has a quick prayer, I'm all ears." He thought, "I've been through these before. Be cool and don't show alarm. I don't want the men to panic." There was silence, but Smitty closed his eyes and spoke with the Almighty. In other areas, a few World War Two veterans looked worried, but tried calming younger subordinates. The men were trapped in a steel tomb.

It seemed the violent storm would never cease as encased souls heard fierce winds continuously hitting *Satterfield*. Some men were busy fighting against the sea after someone failed to properly secure a hatch below the bridge's port side. While a torrent of seawater poured through, four men lunged against the hatch and finally closed it as others formed a bucket brigade, tossing water into toilets and sinks in a nearby head; others pitched in, quickly swabbing the deck.

The ship too has a soul, for she's a home and a feeder despite her pains in the maelstrom. It was as if Neptune with immense hands tried reaching from the bottom attempting to pull her down into the abyss. The storm lasted almost twenty-four hours. No one slept through the horrific night.

The next morning, Jim went topside, checking on possible damage to *Travis*. She was unscathed. He turned, looking above *Satterfield's* superstructure. Four halyards had snapped. It was a miracle there were no major damages, and she survived.

Three days later after a mid-watch, Jim strolled out near the bow, gazing at the horizon on a calm sea. On the main deck, the maximum range for the human eye to see is about four miles toward the horizon before the earth's curvature begins. After ten minutes straining, he saw a tiny speck in the far distance. As the destroyer steamed at twenty knots, the object expanded until his eyes beheld a mountain. He thought, "My God, it's Guam!"

"Make all preparations for entering port", the announcement came. He was returning after almost a year. She tied up at a pier in Apra Harbor, about ten minutes from downtown. It was a typical hot and humid day on the thirty-mile long U. S. Trust Territory island. Things changed. A new McDonald's had opened in the capitol city, Agana.

With a mere eight hours liberty granted, Jim didn't have time for traveling north or visiting friends at the communications station in Finegayan. Sid, Mike, Tim and Jim jumped into a cab and went into Agana for lunch and beer.

Marine Drive was the main thoroughfare, appropriately named after Marine leathernecks retook the island in tough battles against the tenacious Japanese in 1944. Several small shops, stores and restaurants flanked the two lane road as palm trees provided a tropical backdrop.

Hickey suggested, "Let's eat at Bob's Whispering Palms, one of my favorite joints." It was a cozy little place, right in front of a beach with a shuffle board table on the right and a long bar opposite. A large stuffed swordfish, barracuda and hammerhead shark adorned three beige walls. An eight by ten colored photo of a smiling Bob Hope and other celebrities on a stage hung above the entrance door. A twelve-foot long rectangular window behind the bar overlooked six palm trees and the nearby shore in the rear. Six circular tables were scattered about, four near the front windows for patrons viewing passersby off Marine Drive.

"This is a cute little place, Jimmy," remarked Log. They were surprised at seeing only four Guamanian civilians eating shrimp fried rice near the front. Sitting at the bar, they perused unimpressive five by seven menus as a silver-haired, middle-aged slender man with a protruding gut leaned over the bar and smiled.

"Hi, sailors. It's good seeing another ship pull in. Heck, at the sub base we only have the old tender *Proteus*, but those guys come in on weekends." He reached and shook their hands. "My name's Gene Harper from Pittsburgh, and I retired a few years ago as Chief Radioman on this rock. I sort of manage this place because it gives me somethin' ta do. What will it be?"

Loggins stared at the menu, and looked up, "You sure don't have much on here, do ya?"

"Aside from burgers, hot dogs, fries and chili that's about it, but we got some great shrimp fried rice one of the locals makes and its only four bucks."

Reemer suggested, "Yeah sounds good. How about it guys?" All agreed.

Log blurted, "I haven't had a Falstaff in a long time. I'm buying the first round. Ya got any?

Gene's face brightened, "Yup, sure do and only a buck."

Thomas walked, put a quarter in a juke box and played a half dozen country tunes as they wolfed down the delicious food and beer. Shortly thereafter, the old salt paused and looked at them. "Look at those palms swaying and waves hitting the beach in back. Isn't that somethin'? I fell in love with this place first time I came in here and got to know Bob. He's a good guy, but getting' up in years ya know. It's good seeing fellow radiomen for a change. How are they treatin' ya?"

Log took a long swig, pressed his lips together and replied, "Pal, ya don't even wanna know. It's why we four stick together."

Jim took a sip of beer, looked at Gene and remarked, "I was stationed here eighteen months at the communications station and miss some of those guys."

"They come once in a while," Gene said.

Suddenly, Harper quickly turned from washing glasses and addressed them, "Hey, fellas, ya know what just happened here? "Just yesterday I was reading in the paper about two fishermen who ran and tackled this old Japanese soldier on a beach here the other day. Can ya believe it? The guy was still wearing his torn up uniform and carrying a rifle like World War Two was still goin' on. Man, unbelievable."

Jim shouted, "Oh my God! I remember when I was here being woken up a couple times in the middle of the night by our Marines running out of the barracks with packs and rifles, looking for a sniper who took pot shots at our gate guards. The grunts went searching the boonies, but never found the guy. The next day I walked out, waiting for a liberty bus in front and saw a half dozen bullet holes in the glass shack, where two Marines stood duty. Here's this war goin' on in Nam, and these guys on U. S. territory are getting' shot at. Man, it surprised me."

"Yeah, I heard about that," Gene said. "Ya see, according to the local paper The Guam Eagle, I guess the guy somehow knew the war had been over for over 25 years, but those guys were trained never to surren-der and were a tough bunch. From what I gather, I think he was just too damn scared to give himself up. He saw a jet take off and thought it was some sort of secret weapon or something. The two guys turned him over to the local police, and the naval authorities got involved. Through an interpreter, they asked how he survived all these years. He hid in jungles, fished, lived in a cave and survived off the land. The guy was a modern day Oriental Robinson Crusoe, absolutely amazing."

"What happened after that?" Tim asked.

"They somehow got ahold of a couple relatives." All four leaned forward, listening. "Well, they flew em' down here and man, all three cried, hugging each other. Wow! I saw their photo in the local paper. That was really something, and I'm glad it ended that way. Yup, it was big headlines here and in Japan."

Thomas stood up and lifted his beer high, proposing a toast, "Here's to the survivor." Harper joined as each bottle clicked.

Shortly afterward, Jim suggested, "Hey, why don't we catch a flick up the street?"

Mike said, "Nah, we're gonna hit a couple other joints on the strip. Are ya coming?"

"I'll just meet you guys back aboard."

They took a cab, dropping him off in front of an old warehouse, rebuilt into a movie theater years before. A few hundred locals sat on portable, wooden chairs viewing a Clint Eastwood western.

As he ate popcorn in the dark, something quickly brushed over his shoes. He thought, "My God, it's a rat." He turned, looking at a stray cat chasing another along the aisle, swiftly moving through another row. The Guamanians acted like nothing happened while glued to the screen. He thought, "That's weird." Later, when speaking with a manager, he learned that a few pet dogs and cats would follow their masters inside, occasionally cavorting about. He returned, took a nap and joined his mates in radio for midwatch.

# 10

# "THE SIBUYAN, CONSPIRACY, SUBIC AND MANILA"

For two days, *Satterfield* and *Travis* sliced through the 1,500 mile wide Philippine Sea toward the scattered, massive island archipelago. Saltwater mixed with fresh as they entered the five to nine mile wide San Bernadino Strait then into the Sibuyan Sea, separating the southern border of Luzon from Samar Island.

He rose shortly after daybreak and stood on a weather deck, gazing at the 5,100 foot dormant volcano, Mt. Busulan, two miles off starboard. In this area in October 1944, a major portion of the most famous naval engagement in history took place. In the Battle of Leyte, the American Navy defeated Japanese forces in three different areas of the Philippines, and their navy ceased being a significant threat thereafter.

The gun boat steamed at fifteen knots a quarter mile ahead into the Sibuyan, and the course frequently changed because of islands dotting the majestic body of water. The sea is practically surrounded to the north by Luzon and to the south by the immense islands Masbate and Mindoro.

Mike and Sid joined Jim on deck. Bright sunlight danced off the water as they looked down at hundreds of flying fish skimming over the glass surface. Thirty yards away, a lone slender, middle- aged Filipino fisherman, miles from home standing in a little banca boat smiled and waved as the passing Americans returned the gesture.

For many years, modern-day pirates traversed the area seeking to rob families in boats, who were attempting to attend fiestas and fandangos on other islands. The large speed boats, loaded with armed thugs were, and are an ever-present threat to the good Filipinos. Mike and Sid knew about these occurrences. "I'll tell ya, guys, if we see any of those idiots trying to harass these good people, our ship will blow the bandits right out of the water and not ask questions," Mike said.

Sid confirmed,"Ya can say that can that again."

They steamed passed Masbate off port, entering the widest expanse of sea. Before reaching Mindoro, cloud patterns rapidly changed. Cyclonic storms were endemic, producing consternation among the crew.

In the distance, a black sky formed as one water spout (small tornado) after another hit the surface, dissipating shortly after. As humid tropical breeze struck his face, Jim thought, "Wow! What a sight." Because of stifling heat, you could fry an egg on the deck as the sun's rays baked the gray vessel.

Dark clouds merged as *Satterfield* steamed directly toward an inky horizon, a bad omen. In several spots, intermittent light from the heavens pierced the oncoming dark sky and struck water. He thought,"This is the weirdest thing I've ever seen." Suddenly, the afternoon sun flashed and dissipated the once-gloomy area looming beyond. They were relieved. Sailors never relish any storm.

Later that day, Bearden woke Gates and shouted, "Hey, get up. I've gotta talk with you. Gates rubbed his eye's and put on dungarees.

"Let me get a cup of coffee first."

"All right, but make it fast." Bearden motioned to follow him down into the engine room.

"Why are we going down there?"

"You'll see."

They descended into the ship's bowels while boiler tenders and machinist mates manned equipment and checked gauges. Two large shafts revolved at half speed, turning twin screws below the surface. Sweat poured through each working dungaree of the "Black Gang", a name given to men who worked on the lowest deck of coal burning ships many years ago. The 150-degree environment was almost unbearable despite two fans and a one-foot diameter tube continuously blowing circulating air.

"Hey chief, how's it going?" asked Bearden. The chief engineer was a portly forty-year old with a handlebar mustache.

"Well, Walt. We can't wait to get ta Subic and out of this heat box. What's up?"

"I wanna have a little chat with one of my men here."

"All right, have at it, but I wonder why you'd want to come down here in this hell hole. I'm sure you'll wanna go topside after five or ten minutes."

They walked over near the side, above the ship's hull. "What's on your mind?" Gates inquired.

Badass leaned and stared. "This is where it starts and I need your help nailing Hickey. Now, I know ya don't like him 'cause he tried pickin' a fight with ya, right?" Gates nodded. "Let me tell ya somethin', Donny. He challenged me, standing me up in front of Galetti and Smith. Nobody does that ta me and gets away with it. I guess ya heard about it. I'm gonna break 'em, and it all starts here, see?"

Gates scratched his head. "What do ya mean it starts here?"

"Listen, ya know I've given ya extra liberty before because ya have been good feeding me stuff about some of the guys. I know ya got a girl in Subic. We're gonna be in for at least four days, and men will be standing port and starboard (day on, day off) watches. How would ya like three days liberty and only one duty day? I can arrange it."

Gates face brightened into a smile. "Shit, that would be great."

Bearden grinned, "Sounds good, doesn't it?" All ya got to do is be a lookout. Ya see, I heard he's gonna pay someone ten bucks for standing his watch and put in a chit for an extra liberty day cause he wants to see some Flip girl in Manila."

Gates puzzled, scratched his head again. "What's that got to do with me?"

"It's simple; here's the plan. He's gonna go looking for me to sign the chit, and I'll be hiding down here for a little while. He won't think ta look for me here. What you're gonna do, just in case, is keep an eye on him. If he decides on coming down, you're gonna stand near the hatch and tell him you were just down here seeing a buddy and didn't see me."

"Oh, I get it. Ya want me covering for ya, right?"

"Yeah, something like that."

Bearden smirked with a devilish grin and put a hand on Gates shoulder, "Listen, what he'll do is get Stewart and Larson's signatures and they'll tell him that I've gotta sign the authorization. He'll look around and be frustrated at not finding me. I'm hoping he'll leave and get to Manila. When he returns, I'll write him up for jumping the chain of command and going A. W. O. L.

Harrison will bust him down a rank, and I'll have my revenge. Payback's a bitch, ya know. That's my plan. Are ya in or out?"

Gates stepped back and looked down as his eyes wandered. "Yeah, I can't stand the guy. He's buddy buddy with Smith, Log and a couple others. Remember when he wanted to take me on in the chow line? I miss that babe in Subic and wanna be with her as long as I can."

Bearden put an arm around him and smiled. "That's my boy. Don't worry about the chief, cause he likes ya, and Stewart's in my pocket. Ya know somethin'? I think that dumb lieutenant's afraid of me, the way he agrees with everything I say or do. Shit, Donny, I've got it made here. I'm gonna nail Hickey. By the way, do you think anyone suspects you been feeding the chief and me info about a few of the guys?"

He shook his head. "Nah, no way, but I don't trust Thomas, Reemer, Smith and Loggins because they're close ta Hickey. What are ya gonna do about Larson?"

"Look, don't worry, he doesn't have to know. Besides, he's being transferred soon and I'll be in charge."

Bearden grabbed his hand, held it and gave a serious look, "Now, listen, I gotta swear ya ta secrecy. If ya sing or word leaks out, I'll deny everything, saying it was your idea, because you've gotta a motive." He glared, applying pressure on his hand. "After that, you'll wish you'd never come aboard when I get done with ya. Shit, you'll be in my doghouse a long time, and ya wouldn't want that, would ya? Understand?"

Gates face reddened with fear. Bearden released the grip and put an arm around him. "Hey, don't sweat anything. It's foolproof. I'm with ya on this." Walt smirked. "Everything will be cool and go according to plan. Listen, don't worry Donny, all right?"

Gates thought, "I wonder if I'm doing the right thing. I don't like Hickey, and Bearden's got my back, so why not?" They climbed back up to the main deck.

The two ships approached the eastern edge of Mindoro Island as sailors viewed a mountain chain running the length of the interior. Shortly thereafter, they passed exotic palm-lined beaches of Batangas, located southeast of Manila, and then turned northwest toward Subic Bay. Liberty would commence in two hours.

Chief Larson joined Bearden on the mess deck for coffee, leaving Thomas in charge in radio. Loggins approached, sat across from both and folded his hands together. "Hi Walt, Chief. It'll be nice being in port a few days after surviving that damn storm."

Larson responded, "Yeah, Tim, what's up?" Log's motive wasn't intimidation while leaning his bulky shoulders over the steel table, but rather communicating relevant information. Anticipating his intention, Badass lowered his head, avoiding eye contact. He was haughty, pride being the root of all sin.

Larson stared at Loggins, "Well, come on, what's on yer mind?"

Tim took a deep breath and said, "Some of the new men are stressed, including Hickey and Smith. Now, I know what's been goin' on between you and Hickey, Walt. Heck, the guy does his duty and gets along with most of the men. Why are you hard on 'em? You've been on the kid ever since he's come aboard." Larson frowned. Log continued. "Look, I'm trying to improve morale and am getting frustrated hearing several complaints from the men."

Larson and Bearden turned and then looked at each other. Bearden tipped the cup slowly while taking a sip as his eyes squinted, gazing at Tim. "Well, look what we got here, Chief, a real defense attorney aboard. I didn't know the Navy had lawyers at sea, did you?" Larson was silent. "Listen, I know how friendly you are with some of the men, especially Hickey. They look up to and respect ya, and that's ok, but you're taking this too far. I'll tell ya this much, the training I've given em' will come in handy when we get into combat. I know a few fear me, and I don't give a damn because I'm doing my job. If some of the men don't like my methods, they can put in for transfers."

Tim retorted. "Well, no shit, Sherlock. A few have already done that cause of you." Walt gave another devilish smirk. Tim thought, "Man, I'd like to blast that grin off his face."

Larson inserted, "I'm supporting Walt because he knows all the systems and is one of the best I've ever seen. As for supervision, as you know, there's always going to be those that don't agree with your methods, but you can't please everyone. We want men sharp because we're going into combat soon. Shit, this isn't a democracy. It's the Navy! Men have gotta obey orders, and if not, they're in trouble."

"I couldn't agree more, Chief, but Walt, I don't like your methods on a few men. Heck, even some veterans are upset about your tactics. You've got em' so keyed up and stressed, they're having trouble doing their duties. There's another thing. I know your still pissed at Hickey challenging you, cause he's the first having the courage to do it. I know he should have kept his mouth shut, but he had a good reason."

Bearden's menacing glare surprised even him. In all his years of naval service, Tim had never seen such anger and evil eyes. Blood quickly surged into Walt's face. He lunged within inches of Tim and shouted, "Damn it, Loggins, ya mind your business and quit kissing his ass. I don't have to take this crap from you or anyone else, so you'd better steer clear of my bow because I'll pull a few strings; have the lieutenant recommend a transfer, and you'll be off this ship in no time. Do ya hear me?" His stressed and shriveled prune-like face reflected pure hatred.

Exasperated, Tim gazed at Larson. "Chief, I'm at a loss. All I did was try communicating with ya. Yeah, I understand why the men call him Badass. He doesn't out rank me and been in only a year longer. Regardless, that doesn't give him the right treating me this way." Larson turned and patted Bearden's back.

"He's right, Walt. Cool it, will ya?" Bearden glared at Log.

Tim slowly rose, leaned and stared at them. "All I can say is this. I know about the cover up on those two other sailors you were both in on, and I'm ashamed I didn't say or do anything. It's been eating me ever since. Damn it, I'm not gonna let it happen again."

Cynical, Walt laughed. "Oh really, now, how are ya gonna do that, Log?"

"Bearden, I see right through you and know you're a vindictive person. You're a sick man, but unfortunately, you don't know it. What saddens me, chief, is that you go along with him, who's a poor excuse for a leading petty officer. Well, I'm going to do everything in my power and see ya don't break anyone else. Put that in your pipe and smoke it. Damn it, I sure wasted my time with both of you."

The altercation elevated Tim's blood pressure. He went below to think and rest. Bearden wondered, "What were Log's methods? Would he speak to the lieutenant? There's no way he'd believe him since they had Stewart right where they wanted him." Time would tell.

In late morning, the ship, with gunboat following, reduced speed to eight knots, and entered Subic Bay. Huge Bataan Peninsula jutted down from the mainland, splitting Subic from the wide and massive Manila Bay to the east. It was on Bataan that the largest surrender of American troops in U. S. history occurred after Japanese forces conquered the peninsula and nearby Corregidor Island in May1942. Thereafter, starving Filipino and American troops walked fifty miles north in extreme heat to prison camps in what became known as the Bataan Death March. Thousands were killed during the trek.

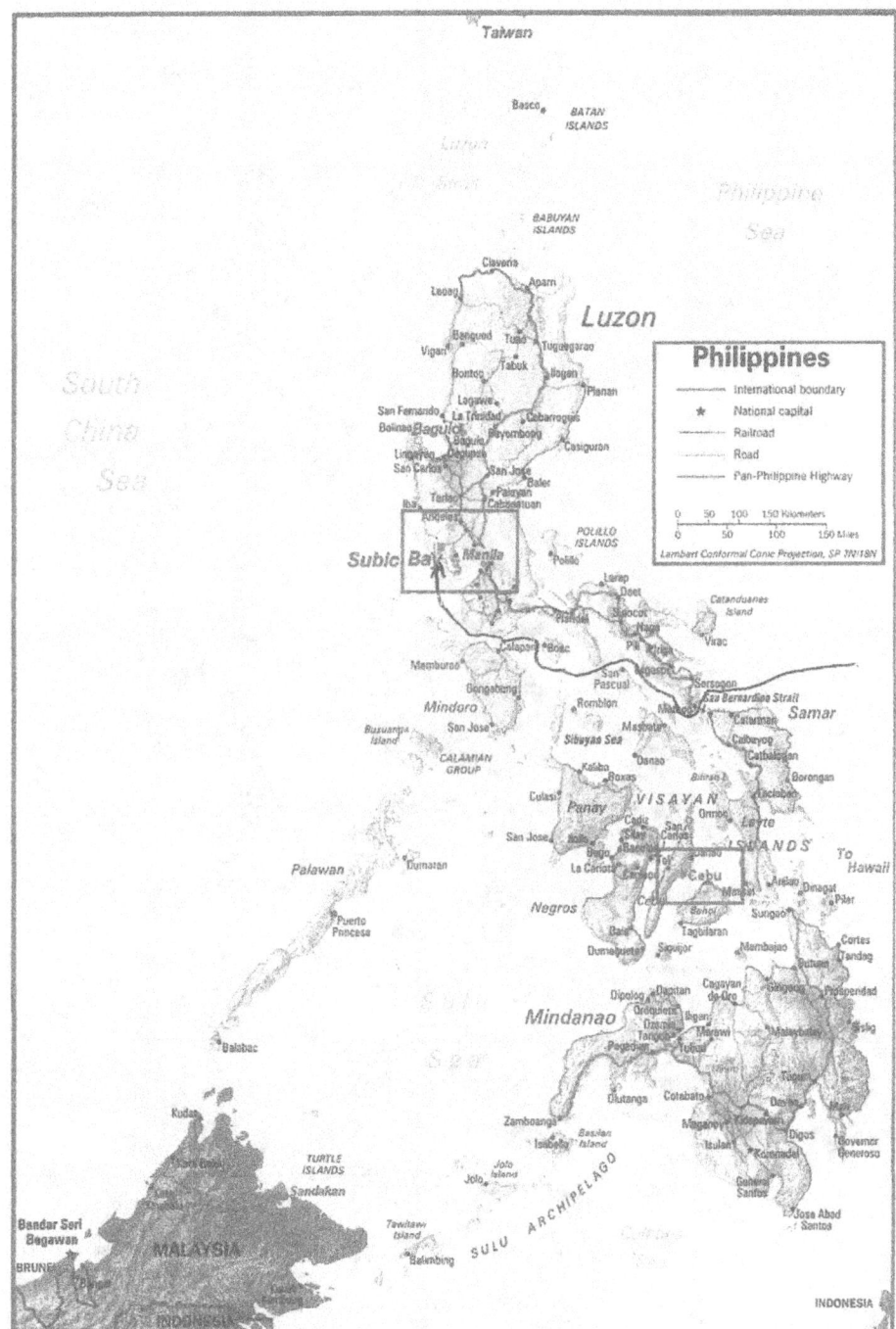

**Satterfield's course through the Philippines**

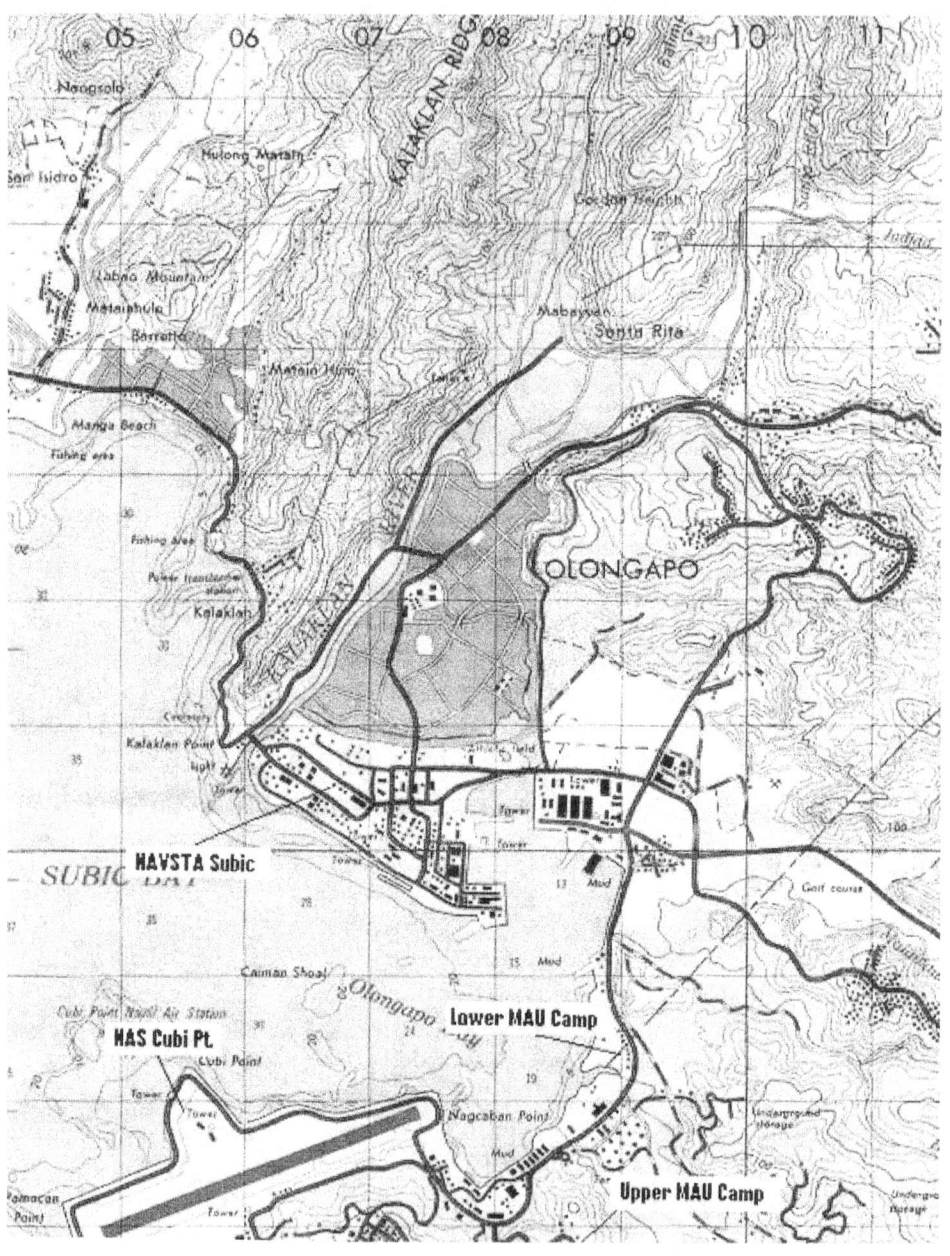

**Map of Subic Bay**

**White Rock Beach
in Subic Bay**

**U.S. Naval Station Subic Bay, Philippines**

Since the Spanish American War, the U. S. Navy maintained a presence in the Philippines from the old Asiatic Fleet before World War Two to the Seventh Fleet during the Vietnam conflict. Subic Bay with nearby Olongapo City was a favorite respite for sailors and merchantmen.

Satterfield passed the peninsula, little Grande Island, (navy recreational location) near the middle of the bay, then proceeded past Cubi Point Naval Air Station off starboard before turning to port and tying up at Alava Pier. Most of the men were excited, chatting about plans ashore while donning short sleeve tropical uniforms and civilian clothes.

Jim paid Thomas ten bucks for standing his duty for an extra liberty day. The lieutenant and chief signed his chit, but Larson stopped Jim before he left the radio shack. "Hickey, you know you gotta have Bearden sign it."

"I know, chief." He was excited about meeting the girl. He wandered, asking shipmates if they'd seen the lifer.

Duff remarked, "Ya know, I just saw 'em bout ten minutes ago walking midships. Maybe ya can catch him around there."

Tim supervised the first watch as Jim walked in. With only routine message traffic coming over teletypes, Reemer and Smith relaxed playing cards. "Have ya seen Badass, Log?" Jim asked.

"No, not since we almost came to blows a couple hours ago on the mess decks."

"No kidding, really?"

"Yeah, I caught Larson and Badass having coffee and tried making sense with them about his treatment of you and the other guys, but I couldn't get through to either one. Matter of fact, he got ticked for me defending ya, so I told him what I thought of 'em. He got pissed. Hell, I would have decked him on the spot if Larson wasn't there."

Jim asked, "Listen, if I can't find him, could you sign my chit for an extra liberty day?"

"Sure, let me know." Tim shook his head in disgust. "Jim, I'm frustrated with Larson and Bearden and feel like puttin' in for a transfer, but damn it, I made a promise to myself that I'd support you guys. I don't wanna see that asshole break ya." Sid and Ron turned and listened.

Jim smiled, "I understand. Thanks Log, I appreciate that. You're a class guy."

Meanwhile, Bearden clambered down to engineering and sat hiding behind a large black panel with several gauges, as Gates guarded a hatch near a ladder leading down as planned. As excited men departed,

Jim walked into the mess decks and a few departments, including CIC, supply, damage control, and machine shop searching for Bearden. Disappointed, he ventured amidships and saw Gates leaning against a bulkhead, smoking.

"Hey, Gates, have ya seen Badass around?"

Gates grinned, "Nah, haven't seen 'em."

"What are you doing here?"

Clearly nervous, his eyes shifted, side to side and he responded, "Ah, I just came up from visiting one of my snipe buddies down there, and ah, waiting for 'em to go on liberty."

Jim stared at the suspicious looking man. "I'm going down because I gotta find him." Gates quickly moved sideways, blocking the entrance.

"What in the heck are you doing?"

"I'll save ya the time because he wasn't around when I was there," he snapped.

"Listen, let me see myself, all right?"

Gates glared. "Look, damn it, Bearden wasn't down there, and besides why would he be?" He raised his voice. "Now, back off." Jim stared and slowly retreated, frustrated.

"Yeah, guess you're right, see ya later." He thought, "It looks like he's trying to protect somebody, but whom? Gates is either lying, hiding something, or both."

He returned to radio, catching Log with his feet up on the desk reading a military newspaper *The Pacific Stars and Stripes*. "How did it go with Badass", Log inquired.

"I've practically looked everywhere and can't find him." He told him about Gates' strange behavior, preventing him from seeking Bearden down in engineering.

Log put the paper down, and rose. "Yeah, I agree with ya. It's obvious he didn't want ya down there, but why?"

"Log, I've been looking forward to meeting that babe, but now it looks like I'll only have one day."

"Listen, I'll sign it for ya, but ya know Bearden's supposed to. I can't promise it will fly, but will give it a go, all right?"

"Thanks, Log, I appreciate it."

He quickly scribbled his name and handed it back. Jim turned and started leaving. Loggins shouted, "Have a blast in Manila, Jim, and be careful. I'll try and cover for ya while you're gone."

Jim back, smiled and walked to the quarter deck. The officer of the deck reviewed the chit. "Looks, good."

"Request permission to go ashore, sir."

"Granted," came the reply. He saluted the lieutenant and the stern ensign and walked down to the pier.

A few minutes later, Bearden slowly emerged from engineering after Gates hollered, "All clear. He left the ship." Badass put an arm around the ferret and shook his hand.

He whispered, "Nice going, Donny, Now, he's in the trap. I got 'em where I want 'em and can't wait to see his face after I write 'em up. Now get going, see that Flip girl and have a good time." Gates smiled, left and went ashore.

Five minutes after Jim departed, Tim took a break since message traffic was light. He grabbed a cigar, left the room, went down on the main deck catching fresh air and enjoying the tropical scenery.

After descending a short ladder near the main passageway, he turned, looked and saw Bearden and Gates standing sixty feet away, talking near the engineering hatch. Immediately, he backed out of sight, and then peeked around a bulkhead seeing Bearden put an arm around Gates shoulder. He thought, "They didn't see me. That's strange. I just saw Hickey ten minutes ago and signed his chit after he said Bearden wasn't aboard. I'll track down Walt and see what's going on."

Shortly thereafter, Tim went into berthing and saw Bearden getting ready for liberty. "Hey, where ya been? Hickey was looking for ya all over cause he needed ya ta sign a chit for extra liberty."

Wearing skivvies, Bearden quickly turned and stared at his opened locker, avoiding eye contact.

"Ah, see, I had to run down to the pier and speak with somebody bout something, and after I came back, Gates said he was lookin' for me."

"Is that all he said?"

"Yup, that's about it."

He thought, "Something's not right. This guy's lying like a corrupt politician." He moved within two feet and confronted him. "Man, that's crap and you know it. Heck, he came in frustrated and related that Gates said you weren't in engineering. He asked me to sign his chit, then left. The kid's only been gone less than fifteen minutes."

Enraged, Bearden's face turned red as he turned, and shouted, "Are ya callin' me a liar? You had no business signing his chit. That's my responsibility, see? Why did ya do it?"

He backed away. "Look, I thought it would be ok since you weren't around, and besides, I felt sorry for him because you've been on his can for months. He's worked hard and does his duties." Loggins was unaware of any conspiracy.

After dressing, Bearden sat on his rack, tied his shoes and looked up, "Well, ya shouldn't have done it, Tim. Listen, if he's not back by 0800 tomorrow, I'm writing his ass up and there's nothin' ya can do about it, see?"

Log clenched his right fist, gritted his teeth and thought, "I wanna fire on this jerk real bad."

Bearden up and smirked, "Yeah, I know you'd like to try and deck me, wouldn't ya?"

Irate, Tim walked near a ladder, turned and shouted, "Ya know something Baaaaaadaaaasss? I wouldn't waste my time because you're not worth it. I'm looking at the reason why some of the men aren't shipping over. Oh, by the way, I wonder why Gates wouldn't let Hickey look for ya in engineering. Think about that one, asshole."

Bearden's eyes quickly shifted as he murmured, "Ah, I wouldn't know about that."

Log went topside, leaned over lifelines and gazed at the Bataan Peninsula thinking. "There's a snake in the grass and someone's lying. It's not Jim. I suspect Seaman Gates and will find the truth, but the ferret will be gone a few days." He wondered. "How did Gates warrant more liberty than anyone else? Just about everyone knows he's a brown nose. I think Bearden's behind something. My soul feels it. It couldn't be anyone else."

Meanwhile, carrying a small overnight bag with civvies, Jim, attired in dress white uniform, walked through the base as tropical air struck his face. The intense heat was like standing next to an open hot pizza oven. Palm and banana trees swayed on a green lawn nearby as he hurried. A surge of freedom enveloped him as he walked a quarter mile past the enlisted men's club and arrived at the main gate.

He produced a liberty card for a Marine guard and started walking toward a bridge leading to downtown. Hot air streaming over a mountain blew stench nearby. He wondered, "What's that smell?"

Sailors called it "shit river." A two-lane, hundred yard, concrete bridge spanned a narrow putrid river where human waste floated. Several tin roofed shacks on a small hill above lined the dark water.

**Bridge connecting Subic Naval Base to Olongapo City**

He walked, looking down at two little Filipino kids standing in a small wooden canoe.

"Hey, Joe, hey, Joe, you throw coin, you throw coin." As other sailors teased and chuckled at the destitute children, he tossed a quarter, but it missed the boat dropping into the stinky water. A ten-year old quickly jumped in retrieving the coin. He thought, "I feel sorry for them and never seen such poverty."

The sailor walked down the main street of Olongapo. Throughout the city were several dive bars, air-conditioned clubs, and a few restaurants. Canvas-covered, decorated jeep taxis or jeepneys motored up and down picking up passengers as hundreds of military personnel roamed entering and exiting establishments.

Local young, attractive women in mini-skirts were employed as dancers, hostesses and waitresses in places like D'Cave, Pauline's and the Top Three Club. Skinny male Filipino bands mimicked American rock n roll music in large smoked-filled lounges. The exchange rate was seven pesos to the U.S. dollar and you could retire and live well on eight-hundred bucks a month. Prostitution was legal, and numerous women profited instead of laboring in rice paddies, farms and sweat shops.

Word quickly spread when several ships or an aircraft carrier docked in Subic, consequently, more women flocked into the city from rural areas. Tom warned him about succumbing to the ploys and charms of girls preying on G.I.'s using tactics as, "Hey, Joe, I love you, no shit, buy me dink." Venereal disease was common, and several ladies of the evening carried required up-to-date shot cards. Essentially, it was The Tijuana Mexico of the Far East.

After exchanging dollars for pesos, he stopped in a small, dimly-lit tavern, had a popular cold San Miguel beer, then briskly walked up the street and hopped aboard an old former school bus called Victory Liner. Inside the gray-painted twenty-year old vehicle above windows, were color advertisements of local movies and consumer products.

The lone American sat on a rear wooden seat and put a window down. Dust flew as motorcycles sped by. Night approached as several locals with children boarded for the seventy-five mile, two-hour trip southeast for Manila.

The uncomfortable creaky vehicle motored into a few small towns aspassengers babbling in Tagolog arrived and departed. At each location, a boy clambered aboard, running down the aisle shouting "baluts, baluts." The delicacy was a fertilized duck embryo in a baseball- sized shell rich in protein after boiling. The nauseating smell permeating the hot air was overbearing.

Arriving on a moonless night, the unfamiliar surroundings were confusing. He thought, "I feel like a Pilgrim in a strange land." The massive city of three million plus buzzed with activity as buses, taxis and jeepneys motored along palm-lined Rojas Boulevard, the main avenue parallel to the large bay.

He checked into the tropically decorated, plush Filipinas Hotel and was glad employees spoke English. To the right of the lobby was an attractive restaurant and bar. Twenty yards behind the front desk was a kidney-shaped pool flanked by a variety of tropical plants and banana trees.

After leaving the fifth-story room, he hailed a taxi outside on Rojas. He leaned inside and asked, "Do ya know where the Malate area is?"

The young diminutive cabbie smiled, and with a rapid, squeeky voice replied, "Sure, Joe, not too far. I take you." A wide grin came over his face, knowing the passenger was an American. His eyes darted to and fro as he sped into heavy traffic. The car zig zagged around several autos unnerving the sailor.

The cab pulled into an area a notch above destitute poverty. He was lost. After tipping the driver, he walked, stepping on boards placed after a recent downpour among small aluminum-roofed wooden houses. Two little boys played nearby. "Hi, boys, do you know where the Hernandezes live?" They merely stared, pointing toward a small dimly- lit wooden house tucked near a corner between two others.

He knocked. A wrinkle faced middle-aged man wearing a tee shirt answered, "Ah, you must be Jim, the American my daughter been writing. Come in." Despite an accent, Mr. Hernandez spoke good English.

By American standards, the living room was small with only two little lamps on end tables providing dim light. Three small children sat with their short, petite mother staring at the visitor. Her husband gave a firm handshake and smiled, "Here, sit on couch. Linda be out soon." He felt comfortable.

Small talk involving domestic issues ensued for twenty minutes. Her dad was employed by the Philippine Constabulary, comparable to the American State Police. He rambled about being a guerilla fighter against Japanese forces before General MacArthur returned in 1944 liberating his nation.

Mrs. Hernandez was sedate as the kids giggled, looking at the Yank. While impatiently eyeing a bedroom door, his heart beat faster, anticipating her arrival.

Suddenly, she emerged. His eyes widened as if seeing an angel. Jim looked and grinned. She smiled, but her eyes quickly shifted as if embarrassed. His heart was joyful as she sat inches from him. Instantly, there was reciprocal attraction.

Linda had a cut white flower above her left ear and jet black hair falling just inches below the top of the neck. She wore a bright yellow, green sleeveless mini dress over a five-three, 110 pound frame. Wearing little makeup, her deep brown eyes conveyed sincerity above a slightly turned up nose and immaculate white teeth. She had smooth medium-brown skin and her smiling face brightened, sending a chill up his spine. She was more than he expected and enchantingly beautiful.

Her father pressed, desiring knowing more about the stranger. He relaxed, discussing his family background and spoke proudly of naval service. After a half hour, he quickly wrote the hotel phone number, folded the note and discreetly slid it into her hand.

Jim was tired. Her father insisted on accompanying him back to the hotel, but he objected. "Oh, sir, that's all right, I can make it on my own."

He gave him a stern look. "Listen, Jeem, der lot of gangs out der, and I don't want someting happen, so I go wit you, see?"

"How do you say thanks in Tagalog?" he asked her.

Linda turned and smiled. "It easy. You say *salamat*." Her soothing, pleasant voice sounded almost angelic.

He rose, smiled and shook Mr. Hernandez' hand, "Ok, salamit." The kids giggled.

After waving goodbye, they hailed a taxi, but the man insisted on paying. He thanked him again and entered the hotel, returning to the spacious room in stark contrast to the environment he'd left.

Before sleeping, his eyes closed, focusing on her beauty and he reflected. She's wonderful.

Here's this borderline poor family, barely surviving. They don't have much, yet they're happy. The queen-size bed provided comfort a few feet from a large window overlooking the avenue.

She met him in the lobby late next morning. They strolled on Rojas Boulevard, with Linda assuming the role of tour guide, showing sites of beautiful downtown Manila. They walked into Luneta Park, a large area near the bay. Various lifelike historical statues were scattered about including Manuel Roxas, the first president when the nation became independent, and patriotic leader Emilio Aguinaldo, their George Washington, who fought against the U. S. during the Philippine Insurrection early in the Twentieth-Century.

They jumped aboard a jeepney and entered Intrameros, an old Seventeenth-Century Spanish fort and walled city near the Pasig River, which separated Quezon City from Manila, the Philippine capitol. MacArthur Bridge spanned the waterway to the old city.

The massive rectangular structure had eight-foot thick stone walls rising twenty-two feet high. The fort was infamous as thousands of civilians, including American nurses, were incarcerated and tortured there during the Japanese occupation. Several square cells stood facing a grassy courtyard; giving evidence of their plight long ago. It was a sobering for him.

Both walked slowly among palm trees facing a dozen merchant vessels anchored in the huge bay. He turned and looked at her. "Why is your middle name Chu?"

She grinned. "I'm half Chinese and have relative in Hong Kong. Maybe you go sometime, and I meet you der."

"Ya know, we might be going there for a few days." He stopped and gazed at her. "This is a tropical paradise, Linda. I never would've imagined it in my wildest dreams." He slowly moved an arm around her and stared into her eyes. She felt uncomfortable until he grinned. "Wow! Here I am halfway around the world in this beautiful place with a pretty girl I hardly know. I'll never forget this." She looked up at him and smiled.

Linda had a relatively quiet demeanor and listened intently, enjoying his extroverted personality and gregarious character. She had a soft voice, like an eighteen-year-old teenager. After speaking one or two brief sentences, she would abruptly stop and stare at him. Despite social status, her classy behavior was reminiscent of Ann and Laura. She was a lady, the antithesis of the bar girls hustling G. I.s.

She was a junior at the University of the Far East, studying nursing, and occasionally worked weekends as a cashier at her aunt's club in Olongapo. He was surprised and asked, "Why don't ya work here in Manila?"

"Jeem, I have auntie who let me stay nice house for two day when I work. I will take you der some time." He smiled and quickly thought, "Things are going smooth."

He took her into an elegant restaurant for dinner, ordering fish, rice, soup and salad. She put the menu down, looking concerned. "Jeem, if you don't mind me saying dis, but dis costs hundred pesos. It too expensive for you."

He thought, "She's considerate and probably has never eaten in such a nice place."

"Listen. I can afford it and besides, this is a special occasion."Afterward, they danced to a few melodic songs from a juke box. Initially still leery, she moved closer, attracted by his pleasant voice softly singing near her ear.

The day faded as they sat on a bench at a shore near the bay watching the sun sink beneath a red sky over the horizon. He moved closer. "Linda, there's an old nautical saying, 'Red sky at night, sailor's delight. Red sky in morning, sailor, take warning.'"

She grinned placing her head on his shoulder. He turned, planting a brief kiss on her willing lips. It was dark as traffic increased along the bay. He hailed a cab, returned to the hotel, paid the return fare and kissed her goodbye.They would meet the next day.

The following morning, Linda brought her sister Ellen to meet him in a park near the bay.

They climbed aboard a jeepney traveling throughout downtown, the girls pointed out various landmarks and the majestic Catholic cathedral near the heart of the city. He reciprocated treating them to a delicious shrimp and pancit lunch.

Her sister was twenty and a few inches shorter, with long black hair and wore a light blue dress. Ellen had a cute, girlish smile but was shy and quiet. They walked a mile along the palm-line shore near the water. He stopped, looking east at a peninsula jutting into the bay. "What wrong, Jeem?" Linda asked.

He pointed and grinned, "That's Sangley Point, our naval air station. I sure wish I was stationed there to be near you." She moved her head, placing it against his shoulder and smiled.

Throughout the afternoon, he learned some of the language. He asked. "What do I say if I need a taxi or jeepney or just wanna say hi to someone?"

Linda replied, "You say *hoy*. That mean hey or sometime hi."

"Thanks, that's easy. How about I love you?" He grasped her soft hand, looking at the lovely face.

She smiled, looked down, somewhat embarrassed and then replied, "You say *ini ibi kita*."

He gleamed. "Wow! That has a nice ring to it. I'll remember it." Both sisters were impressed how quickly he grasped the language.

Night drew near as the sun descended. He stood near her. "Listen, I've gotta get on a bus and head back. Here are a few pesos to get back home." She smiled and moved closer under a palm tree as Helen stood a few feet away. He slowly moved his head, planting a short kiss on her lips.

She smiled, "I will miss you, Jeem, and write you. When you come back?"

He put an arm around her soft shoulder. "I don't know, maybe a month or longer. Listen, I've really enjoyed getting to know and be with you. God, I like you so much."

She grinned, "I like you to, Jeem. I have good time. You good man, and I pray for you." He turned, smiled and departed. A slight tear formed in his eye.

He jumped on a bus returning over rough roads into Olongapo, arriving around nine, entered a lounge and sat at a bar, thinking of her. Sailors filtered out, staggering along the street toward the base and ships. He thought, "This is the best weekend I've had since joining the Navy, and I can't get her out of my mind."

Before Jim finished his beer, Sid ran in out of breath, surprising him. Standing nearby, his eyes widened. "Man, you know how many joints I've been in looking for ya? Word's around Badass wrote ya up for being over the hill. If I were you, I'd take off and stay with that babe, 'cause the crap's gonna hit the fan after ya get back. Heck, I wouldn't wanna face that lifer."

Upon hearing the words, his heart jumped sending a chill up his spine. He took a last swig, thought, then looked at his buddy. "What do ya think I should do?"

Sid cupped his hand thinking and replied, "I can loan ya bout fifty bucks ta live on, which should tie ya over till I can send more."

Jim was despondent as he lowered his head toward the bar. "Listen, Sid. Thanks, that's decent of ya, but ya know I can't take it."

Reemer put a hand on his shoulder. "Look, think about it. This tropical paradise and girl, why they're just fantasies. The ship and Badass, now, they're real."

"What are you trying to say?"

"Only that right now you're focused and thinking about her instead of what's ahead."

Jim looked into his eyes, and agreed. "Yeah, you're right. Besides, if I'm A.W.O.L. thirty days, I'd be a deserter and have the military and local police looking hard for me. Heck, I shudder just thinking about what would happen after they'd catch me." He lowered his head, closed his eyes and thought. "I'm not going to abandon my shipmates."

"That's right. Come on, I'll walk ya back. Just lay low until tomorrow."

They returned. Before Jim went below, Loggins encountered him walking through a passageway. "Hey listen Jim, I heard about Bearden writing ya up and tried covering for ya today on watch, but he said ya violated Navy regs. He knew I signed your chit but wouldn't listen when I said ya couldn't find 'em a couple days ago."

"Yeah, I figured that might happen. I'll just have to take the medicine."

"I hope ya had a good liberty. By the way, how was that girl?"

He smiled, "Log, she's everything a sailor could want, a real lady and gorgeous."

Log placed his hand on Jim's shoulder. "That's good, I'm happy for ya. You'll probably have captain's mast, but I'll try being there as a witness and back ya." Tim put an arm around him trying to console him. "Listen, I can't promise they'll let me, but damn, it's the least I can do, ok?"

"Thanks, Log."

Tim took a few steps, turned and addressed him. "I'm bound and determined to stop 'em from breaking ya. Ya better get some z's, cause you're gonna need it."

Jim laid down, said a prayer and slept.

# PART III

## WAR

He is the best man who when making his plans, fears and reflects on everything that can happen to him, but in the moment of action is bold.

Herodotus

# 11

# "THE GUN LINE IS WEST"

In the course of the war, the majority of U.S. ships spent 30-45 days off Vietnam's "gun line" coast before being relieved for a week. In 1968, during the height of the conflict there were 70,000 sailors aboard 150 ships and patrol boats along the 1,200 mile coastline from the Tonkin Gulf to the southern tip of the Cau Mau Peninsula. By 1972, that number had dimished as the now trained South Vietnamese navy assumed a greater role aboard smaller vessels in preventing enemy incursions along its shores.

During bombardment and gunfire support missions, some U. S. destroyers were damaged by North Vietnamese shore batteries, killing and wounding sailors. The "tin cans" were particularly vulnerable to enemy shore fire because enemy forces positioned, and then fired the Russian built 120-and 175-millimeter heavy artillery, outranging the five-inch guns on destroyers.

In several missions, the ships steamed one to two miles off hostile areas accommodating their five-inch rounds to reach a maximum effective seven to eight mile range inland. Consequently, numerous casualties were sustained aboard these vessels during furious gunfire exchanges. Twenty-nine ships were damaged by enemy shore fire during the war.

Off the coast, the 18,000 ton heavy cruiser USS *St. Paul* bristling with powerful eight inch-wide bore guns, sustained a hit from a North Vietnamese shore battery, resulting in minor casualties. A few months before a peace treaty was signed in 1973 "twenty-one sailors perished after a defective eight inch projectile exploded inside a gun barrel, igniting fires in a turret aboard the 20,000 ton heavy cruiser USS *Newport News* during bombardment near Quang Tri. It was the U.S. Navy's largest one day loss during the war."(USS *Newport News Reunion Association/Territi*)

The daily general quarter calls aboard ship, coupled with routine work details exacerbated stress among sailors in the U.S. Seventh Fleet. After duty on the "the gun line," they sailed east into the major American naval base at Subic Bay, Philippines for replenishment, repair, and R&R for ship and crew.

COMSEVENFLT also granted ships liberty in Hong Kong, Tokyo, Bangkok, Sydney and Manila, yet Subic was a favorite haven for sailors because of the friendly and hospitable Filipinos in nearby Olongapo with its bars and clubs.

Men were educated and cautioned about widespread venereal disease, with many infected undergoing painful shots. Numerous sailors were enamored with young women with jet black hair, attired in miniskirts covering alluring brown bodies. While G. I.'s sat in attractive air conditioned lounges listening to live rock and roll, working women circled like sharks seeking prey, charming inebriated sailors.

During the war, a several men put in requests to marry foreign nationals. The native women's goal was often marriage, thus securing free passage to the U.S. and opportunity, far from the poverty-stricken Philippines. They used every trick in the book to lure American fighting men.

Business thrived in Olongapo, particularly after a carrier arrived for a week. Sailor pursuits while in ports varied from sightseeing, purchasing inexpensive clothing, stereo equipment and souvenirs to consuming liquor, dancing and socializing with women. Yet, all pleasures swiftly ended to the chagrin of many, and it was back west to "the line" and war.

The United States Ship's *Satterfield* and *Travis* got underway early Monday afternoon, clearing the bay, entering the calm South China Sea. They steamed twenty knots, 720 miles toward Da Nang, Vietnam.

After evening chow, Smith, Thomas, and Hickey relieved the second watch in radio. The evil eyes and cynical grin of Bearden sitting behind the desk greeted and unnerved Jim as he turned and sat down in front of a teletype machine. Others manned equipment and processed message traffic. Jim thought, the lifer's quiet demeanor, strange.

Jim rose to get coffee. Badass approached, holding a five-by-seven written form and shoved it in front of him.

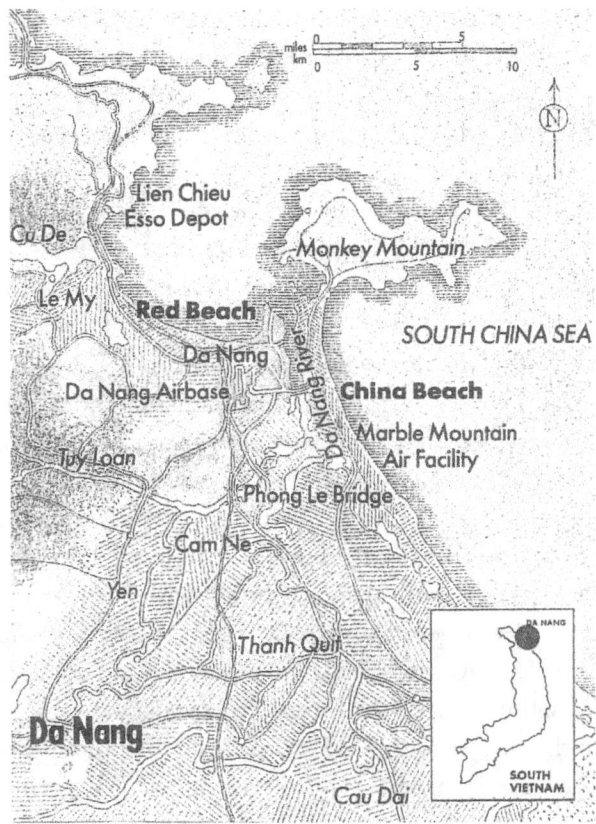

**Da Nang Harbor**

"Here, Hickey, sign this."

"What is it?"

"Well look, boy." The notice stated the specific violation of naval regulations including the time and date of infraction along with Bearden's name. There were two counts, absence without leave and breaking the chain of command.

He grabbed it out of Bearden's hand, quickly scribbled and handed it back without making eye contact. Bearden walked a few feet and leaned against a bulkhead, fixing his eyes on the form.

While pouring coffee, Jim heard an evil chuckle. "Ha, ha boy, I've got ya right where I want ya."

Standing a few feet away, Smitty gave a menacing stare while clenching his fist.

Badass sneered, "What are you looking at, squirrel? Get back to work and don't eyeball me again, ya hear?"

During evening chow, five shipmates listened to his excursion into Manila and about the new girlfriend. Loggins, Thomas, Reemer, Smith and Duff were sympathetic regarding Jim's predicament. "If he gets ya busted, we're gonna plan something and get rid of him because we can't take 'em anymore," Thomas snapped.

Loggins finished his pork chops, looked at Mike and countered, "You can't do anything illegal or physically harm 'em. Are you guys crazy? You wanna spend the rest of your lives in prison with dishonorable discharges?"

"So what in the hell do we do, Log?" Sid asked.

He lowered his head, thinking, and then responded, "Right now, nothing. We gotta be patient because things are gonna get rough shortly. Let me think about it. I already told Jim I'd try and back him up if I can at Captain's Mast." The men were sullen because in a day and a half they would be thrust into an unavoidable situation and environment.

The following day, Satterfield was only hours from war. Before sunset, Harrison ordered general quarters, including testing all guns and the drone. The destroyer followed *Travis'* wake, but dark clouds formed north toward China, giving the impression of a bad omen.

At 0700 the next morning, a mountain chain loomed ahead. South Vietnam! The captain ordered Condition Three or war time cruising, where a third of the crew manned stations.

The ship entered Da Nang on an overcast day as a dozen naval and merchant vessels anchored in the horseshoe-shaped harbor. Off starboard was a large mountain chain, and facing the sea on a peninsula was imposing 400-foot Monkey Mountain. Atop the mountain were clearly noticeable large, sophisticated communications equipment and radar. Below, lay the Naval Support Activity base near shore, Tien Sha landing, and nearby Highway One was a long aircraft runway – just South, China Beach invited tired G. I.'s to its shore for rest and recreation. Two-lane Highway One zig zagged, down the banana shaped coastline.

South Vietnam's second-largest city was 115 miles south of the Demilitarized Zone and 400 miles northeast of the capitol Saigon. This was a major hub for allied forces in the northern zone the U. S. military referred to as I Corps. At the large, busy base and port, ships, aircraft and personnel were routinely shuttled engaging North Vietnamese forces. Huey gunship choppers swept along beaches and the harbor like hawks; keeping a sharp eye for any hostile activity.

The republic's topography varied, from numerous beautiful white sandy beaches along its shoreline down to the Mekong Delta, a vast marine labyrinth where sixty percent of the population lived. West of its shores, was russet land, rice paddies, several high hills and small mountains which spread throughout, overlooking and flanking villages and towns. Between elevated areas was double and triple canopy jungle infested with poisonous reptiles, wild boar, malaria carrying mosquitos and even tigers.

Throughout the war, the majority of fighting was located north of the Central Highlands in the five major provinces below the DMZ. This landmass spreads west through mountainous terrain flanked by the Laotian border, a key sanctuary for the NVA.

Shortly before arriving, gunboat *Travis* departed, motoring at high speed toward Vietnam's "rice bowl", providing support for ARVN troops in the Mekong Delta region, south of Saigon. CINCPACFLT ordered both ships to serve a year in the Far East, but fate intervened on one.

*Satterfield* dropped anchor in the harbor's middle and lowered a motor whale boat with four armed men into the water. Their orders were to scout, slowly motoring around the ship while keenly eyeing the surface for bubbles indicating enemy swimmers. Two men carried hand grenades and Thompson sub-machine guns, the others M-16 automatic rifles.

It was standard operating procedure for the Navy to post at least two armed deck sentries aboard ships in port due to their vulnerability to explosive mines and frogmen. A few years before, the LST USS *Westchester County* sustained major damage in the Mekong Delta after enemy swimmers placed explosive near her hull in the middle of the night, killing 25 men, including 17 sailors, making it the Navy's worst one-day fatal attack of the war.

Both mounts swiveled, training four guns toward shore, as extra shells were hoisted from the upper handling spaces below. Two roving deck sentries armed with rifles were posted fore and aft.

Larson dispatched McDonald and Kennel to board a launch and retrieve classified messages ashore at the Naval Support Activity. Wearing pistols, they walked down a short ladder into a whale boat and motored to a nearby pier.

Because of the monsoon season, the temperature dropped to the low sixties. Hickey and two others from divisions were ordered to wear dress blues and assemble on the quarterdeck for Captain's Mast.

Captain's Mast was a hearing under Article 15 of the Uniform Code of Military Justice or UCMJ, utilized for minor offenses. According to the Naval History and Heritage Command, the article specifically refers to "non-judicial punishments certain limited offenses a commanding officer can impose on an individual." The accused had a right to represent himself and make his case, or refuse and request a military court martial on a later date. A man's statements during a hearing could be used against him at a court martial, consequently, most men charged, preferred mast. In the majority of court martial proceedings, the deck was stacked against an enlisted facing senior officers in judgment sitting behind a long table.

Tim rushed into radio, confronting the lieutenant and chief. "Sir, with all due respect, I'd like permission to assemble with Hickey at Captain's Mast as a witness."

Stewart demurred and replied, "There's no need for that, because Bearden will be there. Listen, I'm upset one of my men went over the hill and I need you here." He at Larson. "What do ya think, chief?"

Larson avoided eye contact with Tim, focused on the officer and answered, "Ah, I think you're right, sir. I concur and don't think it's necessary."

Tim's blood pressure rose as his lips pressed together and then exclaimed, "Sir, I think Bearden set him up, intending to break him. In Subic, Hickey couldn't find him, so I signed his chit. He had no intention of going A.W.O.L." The palms of his hands opened as he pleaded.

"You gotta believe me, sir. Don't you see? I just wanna back him that's all."

Like Pontius Pilate, Stewart washed his hands of the affair, glared and raised his voice. "Request denied." Loggins stared at both, shook his head in disgust, and departed.

Harrison, wearing a khaki uniform, sat near a hatch on the starboard quarterdeck a few feet from a Yeoman, who held a pad and pen. Two other men were charged with disorderly conduct and drunkenness; Hickey with fourteen hours of unauthorized absence and violating the chain of command.

In berthing, Sid and Mike slapped Jim's back, wishing him luck before climbing the ladder and facing "the old man" and Bearden. Jim thought, "The evil presence I felt when I first came aboard is now upon me.' Fear rushed through his soul. He whispered a prayer, "God help me."

Two other senior petty officers and Bearden stood at attention, facing the captain as the Master at Arms, wearing a .45-caliber pistol, escorted the three up to the quarterdeck. In the distance there was combat, but Jim felt like a criminal. He thought, "Damn it, why am I feeling this way? I did nothing wrong." He stood, gazed upward, hearing the *whosh, whosh, whosh* blades of helicopters descending and flying over the ship's mast, returning from battle several miles inland.

The first two men were reduced one rank and restricted aboard ninety days. Standing at attention, Jim struggled to maintain his composure, his eyes quickly blinking like those of a nervous child on his first day at a new school.

Commander Harrison called his name and read the prepared statement. The Master at Arms looked at him and ordered, "Hickey, front and center." He moved forward and stood before him at attention.

"Radioman Third Class James Hickey is accused of violating Navy Regulations, to wit, unauthorized leave of absence for period of fourteen hours and breaking the chain of command."

He stared into his eyes and asked, "How do you plead?"

"I'm not guilty, sir." Harrison frowned and leaned forward with a stern expression. "Explain yourself, sailor."

His voice quivered while relating what occurred in detail as Bearden stood two paces behind. "Sir, I was frustrated at not finding Bearden, so I asked duty petty officer Loggins to sign because they both have equal rank and then"—Harrison quickly cut him off.

"How long have you been in the Navy, Hickey?"

"Three years, sir."

The skipper stared, gritting his teeth, refusing to hear anymore and snapped, "I find it hard to believe you didn't know you had to have Bearden's signature since he's under Larson in the chain of command. I think you were trying to play a fast one on the Navy, sailor. Well, it doesn't work."

He over Jim's shoulder and asked, "Petty officer Bearden, what's your analysis of Hickey's duty performance?"

"Sir, he had a habit of getting things mixed up and didn't perform well like a few others." Jim quickly turned his head, glaring at the lifer.

"Eyes front, sailor, you're at attention" barked the captain. He took a deep breath as his heart palpitated and then looked at the captain.

"Sir, that' absolutely not true. There are two petty officers including Loggins that'll back me up. My intention wasn't to break the chain of command. I felt it would be ok if Loggins signed my chit, because they're both equal in rank."

Bearden requested to speak and retorted, "Ah, sir, Hickey's been a problem since he's been aboard. He challenged me and was insubordinate in front of other enlisted men. I tried giving him slack, but he's never respected me. He convinced Loggins and a few others to oppose me. They started calling me Badass behind my back. That's uncalled for, sir."

As the yeoman quickly noted the proceedings, Harrison lowered his jaw, cupping it with a fist, shook his head, emitting a low chuckle, and then looked at Bearden. "Badass, eh? Ha, ha. Well, Bearden, aboard my ship you sometimes have to be a bad ass, keeping men sharp."

"Request permission to speak, sir", Jim inquired.

"Denied, I've heard enough", he snapped. Impartiality was nonexistent. He gave Jim a stern look and said, "This is my decision. I'm reducing you one rank and giving you forty-five days' extra duty. That is all. These proceedings are closed." Hickey about faced, lowered his head in disgust and walked toward the bow, thinking, as others dispersed.

A light rain descended from the heavens as more ominous clouds formed beyond Da Nang. He would lose sixty bucks a month ($342.00 in 2015 dollars), but more importantly, his pride and self-respect. Jim walked forward, stood under the bridge for shelter, and reflected, "This is wrong! It's an injustice. That jackass is wallowing in victory now. Damn it! He's not gonna break me. I'm staying the course and not cracking." He was a nervous wreck returning into berthing.

As with the previous sailor, Bearden had lied and convinced the skipper.

After changing into dungarees, he laid on his bed attempting to relax. Reemer and Thomas approached and looked down. Mike said, "I heard what happened. What they did ta ya is bullshit." In a fit of rage, Sid quickly took off one of his shoes and threw it against his locker denting the aluminum door. He shouted, "That's what I think of Badass. I hate that bastard."

Jim remarked, "Yeah, he put on a good act and lied like a devil. I can't wait until we get a decent captain. I wonder where my extra duty will be."

Thomas said, "I heard him talking with Larson when I went into the shack to grab my mail.

They said you'll be in the chief's mess helping some other guy cook meals. That's ridiculous; can you believe it?"

"Ya know, by now nothing surprises me aboard this ship, but I didn't join the Navy to be a cook. It's demeaning and shit, they know it; that's why they're doing it."

He dropped off his dress blue and white jumpers at the laundry for new Seaman First Class stripes to replace the petty officer crow patch. Afterward, three black angled stripes were sown on the upper left arm, while identical white stripes went on the blue jumper.

It took two years to make Third Class Petty Officer (E-4 pay grade), but after the injustice, in ten minutes Seaman stripes were stitched on his uniforms replacing the respected non-commissioned officer (NCO) crow rank insignia. He was now equal in rank with the ferret.

Aside from watches, work entailed an extra four hours per day, including rushing into radio whenever G.Q. was called. He felt like an outcast thrown into a deep well, gazing up into darkness. Was there a glimmer of light or hope?

Bearden's undercover conspiracy resulting in Hickey's demotion, coupled with Harrison's intransigent behavior, increased the already volitle atmosphere among the communicators. Men in radio smelled a rat. A ship is like a small town where rumors or scuttlebutt abound. Jim went topside, leaning over lifelines, thinking. Shortly after Tom heard the news, he went looking for his buddy, finding a sullen mate staring toward the sea.

"Jim, how are you?"

"Well, not too well, but I'm not jumping into the harbor here to end it." Tom put an arm around Hickey's shoulder, consoling the depressed sailor. For a minute, Jim was quiet, but then he told Alden about his new girlfriend and Sam Mallos premonition, "five hurt, two overboard."

Jim turned and whispered, "You're the only one aboard who knows about that guy, Tom. I don't know how things are gonna turn out, but I promised I'd tell one man cause it's hard trusting most guys, and besides, they might think I'm losing it. After what happened, I just hope I don't crack cause then the lifer would have another victory notch in his sick head."

Tom listened, lowered his head thinking and remarked, "Man, I hope the old salt's wrong about our ship. It's got me thinking now. Listen, if ya wanna get away, just sit and relax, ya can swing by my space in repair two because it's quiet in there sometimes. Hey, think about that cute girl back in Manila 'cause you'll see her again. She'll perk up your spirits, and ya gotta good family back home, so try focusing on positive things."

He smiled and looked at Alden. "Thanks, Tom. I'm glad I've got a few good shipmates aboard this can. I don't know what I'd do without you and the others because we're all in this mess. I've gotta get some sleep before watch. See ya later." Tom stood, watched him leave, looked down at the harbor and shook his head.

Shortly after McDonald and Kennel returned, Satterfield weighed anchor and turned, heading south along the coast. Hickey and another young man quickly learned to cook meals in a small mess, accommodating a dozen chiefs. Each day or night on watch, he left, after working two hours of extra duty and grabbed a quick bite after serving senior petty officers.

One night at 2200, COMSEVENTHFLT ordered the ship to proceed two miles off Nha Trang to assist another ship in gunfire support, while South Vietnamese troops were attacked by superior enemy forces. "All hands man your battle stations. This is not a drill," barked a seaman over a loud-speaker. While others leaped out of their racks, and ran to their stations, Hickey and mates quickly donned working uniforms, tucked dungaree trousers into their socks in case of flash fire, and hurried into the radio spaces.

Ground target coordinates, including range and bearings were received, processed into the ship's fire control system, and sent via internal communications into each gun mount. Normally, 15-27 Seamen and Gunner's Mates worked in three uncomfortable hot gun spaces forward and aft. The magazine room was located two decks below each mount where shells and 15-pound black powder bags were stored while two fans circulated air.

In chain gang fashion, they placed shells into an electric hydraulic hoist, sending each into an upper handling room, one deck below the mount. There, each round was primed and assembled into a 26-inch long casing and hoisted up the mount where two shell handlers placed metal casings into twin firing breeches. Precise teamwork made it possible to assemble and fire a maximum total of 35-44 rounds per minute in four barrels.

The twin Mark 5"38 caliber gun mount could fire two 21-inch long 55 pound projectiles simultaneously from 13-foot barrels every four seconds to a maximum nine mile range. After each shell was fired, the unit quickly ejected the hot casings out through a hole in the mount

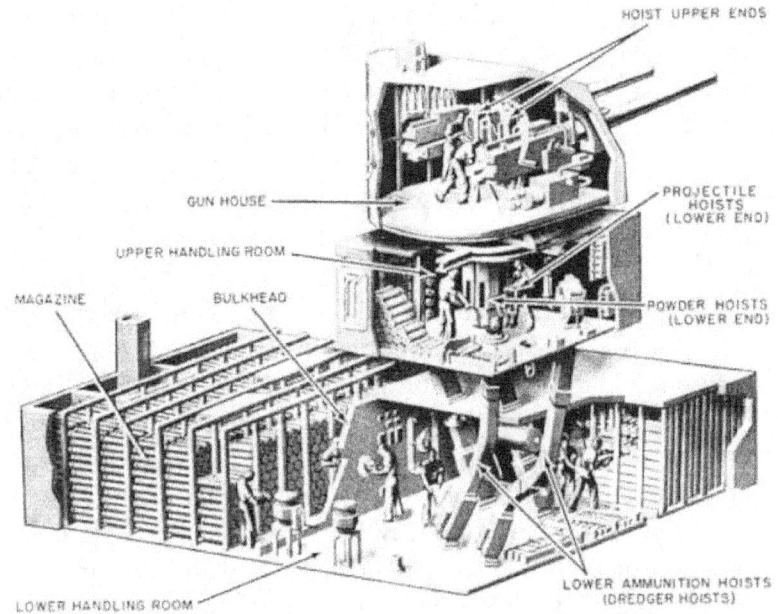

**Diagram of gun mount showing upper handling room and magazine**

**Destroyer Firing on Enemy Targets off Vietnam**
*Used by Permission, T.C.S.A.*

onto the deck. In sweltering heat, each sailor had specific duties some of which were black powder and shell handlers, who placed projectiles into breeches, and a phone talker. Key duties were a trainer, who gazed into a technical device to lock on targets after receiving coordinates from fire control, the pointer raised and lowered or depressed a barrel. A gun captain, normally a petty officer, was responsible for maintenance, safety and supervision to ensure the team performed in a timely and efficient manner while conforming to operational standards. Other than carrier flight deck operations, these duties were the most dangerous and arduous performed aboard naval surface ships by men in combat.

Harrison, standing on the bridge ordered, "Mounts 51 and 52, commence firing." For two hours the old vessel shook like a rag doll as salvo after salvo flashed into a black night. Hundreds of 54-pound five inch diameter shells rained down upon advancing NVA troops five miles away. After punishing naval gunfire obliterated hundreds of enemy, scattering body parts over a wide area, South Vietnamese troops counter attacked, resulting in victory as the remnants fled.

The next morning on the mess deck, Loggins spied Hickey finishing breakfast. Jim looked dejected.

"I've never experienced what you're going through, Jim, but I'm gonna find out what happened if it takes me the whole tour."

"Thanks, Log. I appreciate it. Ya know I suspect Gates had a hand in this but can't prove it. All I can do now is take my medicine and grind it out."

Log took a sip of coffee and stated, "Badass has a new guy with only six months' experience doing your job, while you hustle, mimeographing hundreds of messages. That's hogwash. Heck, ya got over two years' experience, and he's got some rookie doing your duty. Hell, that doesn't make sense."

"Yeah, you're right. Looks like he's looking for new meat, but wait until the kid screws up; the crap's gonna hit the fan again." Loggins smiled.

"What's so funny about that?"

"Nothing, but here's some good news; we just got a message from COMSEVENTHFLT and BUPERS saying we're getting a new captain in a few days."

"That's good. I just hope he's better than Harrison. We sure need someone who'll support the crew better."

Log slapped Hickey's back and remarked, "Absolutely, I couldn't agree more."

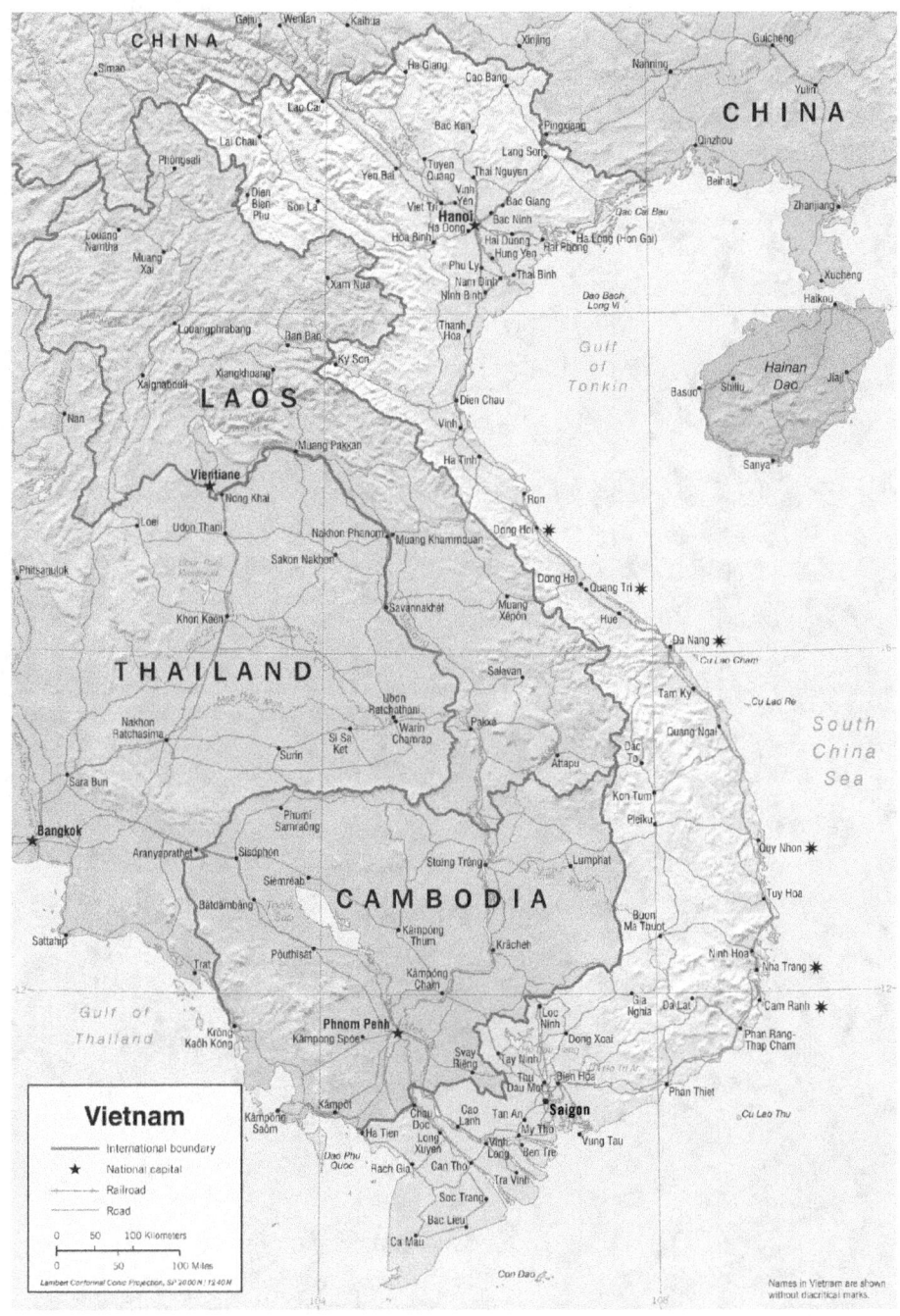

**\* Indicates: Satterfield areas of operations**

# 12

# "A NEW CAPTAIN AND BANGKOK"

On 30 January, the destroyer steamed south, dropping anchor in Cam Ranh Bay on Vietnams' central coast in early morning. The massive base was one of the most secure facilities throughout the war. A bright, sheet-like beach overlooked the half- moon bay. In the background nearby was a large airstrip with hundreds of small buildings, steel built support and supply structures.

At 0:730, wearing a brown uniform, Chief Larson, waved goodbye and walked down an aluminum ladder into a bobbing whale boat, which transported him to the base, a brief stopover before his next duty station. Standing near the bow, Log at Sid, Mike and Jim and remarked, "Good riddance. I'm glad he's gone, and I think you guys know why."

Although no replacement was forthcoming, it was good news, however, Bearden now reigned supreme. Thomas now assumed the vacant watch supervisor's duty.

The entire crew attired in tropical whites, assembled topside at attention to view the change of command. Harrison got what he desired, promotion to Captain and skipper of a light cruiser in the Atlantic. Most of the crew, including several petty officers, were relieved seeing the insolent officer depart.

Leland Kowalski, with five conspicuous rows of colored ribbons on his white uniformed chest and wearing three rectangular gold bars above each black shoulder pad, stood near a microphone behind the forward gun mount and read his orders.

From Bureau of Naval Personnel: To Commander Leland J. Kowalski, U.S.N.

You are hereby to assume command of destroyer USS *Satterfield*, DD816 at 0800, 30 January 1972 at Cam Ranh Bay, Republic of South Vietnam.

The former executive officer of a destroyer and recently promoted Commander was an enlisted man for ten years or a "black shoe" in naval terminology. The forty-year old's twenty-two year career was noteworthy.

After achieving the rank of First Class Gunner's Mate and completing courses part time, he earned a college degree and was commissioned an Ensign. He spent the majority of time as a department head in various capacities aboard frigates and destroyers while happily married with four children. Satterfield was his first command.

At five ten, the tanned and medium-built Kowalski had sandy gray hair combed to the side. His handsome face mirrored that of renowned Hollywood actor Cary Grant, yet the blue eyes conveyed sincerity and honest character. Though taciturn at times, the new captain was all navy. Throughout naval history, some of the best commanding officers were former enlisted men.

After a formal meeting with his twelve-officer staff, he dismissed them, and motioned Pursell over. "Sit near me."

"What's on your mind, captain?"

"Chad, you're aware that one of your duties is the morale of the men, right?" Lee stared into his eyes, unnerving the executive officer.

"Ah, of course, I am."

"Mister, I'll get acquainted with the crew because a ship's only as efficient as those manning her. If you have some bad apples disrupting morale, dissension spreads like cancer throughout a body. We can't have that aboard this ship. understand?" Pursell nodded, repressing thoughts of the previous year.

"Tell me, how you would rate the crew morale now?"

Pursell's eyes shifted while thinking. "Well captain, I'd say pretty good now. There were a few minor incidents last year, and recently a few enlisted were busted at mast, but aside from that, I believe things are running pretty smooth."

Kowalski listened, took a sip of coffee and stared at him. "I read the previous year's log regarding the two sailors no longer here, including one who committed suicide. What do you make of it?"

Pursell folded his arms, looked up at the overhead, and replied, "Ah, well, a board of inquiry convened, and no further investigation was warranted."

Kowalski gazed up at a ten-by-fourteen black and white photo of the ship's namesake hanging next to a large picture of the destroyer on the bulkhead.

"Have you ever read about Heliena Satterfield, Chad?"

"No, not really. All I know is that she was a Navy nurse."

"Well I have. I'll enlighten you because her behavior has something to do with morale."

He related that Satterfield headed the U.S. Navy's Nursing Corps during World War One, treating numerous wounded including several patients stricken with the deadly disease influenza. Despite losing some of her associates who had succumbed and contracting the illness, she steadfastly continued treating sick veterans and survived. Morale among medical personnel in the Washington hospital improved due to her unselfish leadership qualities and example. The Navy awarded her the nation's second highest medal, the Navy Cross. It was unique because she was the first woman to earn it.

Kowalski's eyes lowered, then turned to Pursell.

"Chad, I really admire that wonderful woman who was willing to sacrifice herself for those men, so you see, morale's very important aboard this ship named in her honor. Don't forget it."

The skipper closed his eyes, thought, and remarked, "You'd better be right about the crew because morale's significant and you know we're going to be facing more heavy combat soon. I don't relish problems, understand?"

Pursell clasped his fingers together and swallowed. "Ah, yes, sir."

The new skipper roamed about speaking with each division head, including senior and junior petty officers, desiring as much knowledge about the men as possible, unlike his predecessor. Shortly after a brief gunfire support mission, he knocked on the radio hatch, surprising the few men inside.

"Men, this is the captain, open up."

Loggins sat checking messages. Lee entered. "Attention on deck," Tim shouted. All four quickly rose.

Lee smiled and spoke in a low tone, "At ease sailors." He walked over and shook Log's hand, then turned asking each man his name. Jim put a stack of messages down on the counter, smiled and greeted him. Kowalski grinned, looked him in the eyes while giving a firm hand shake. "Where are you from, sailor?"

"Michigan, sir."

The skipper smiled. "Well, that's good. I've got a few relatives living there and remember visiting with them some years ago. I enjoyed the kielbasa they made."

"Captain, where ya from?" Log inquired.

"Allentown, Pennsylvania, Loggins, but I haven't been back there for some time." He smiled, "Listen, sparksmen. I've been pleased with your duties maintaining and operating the ships' vital communications. Keep up the good work."

As he turned to exit, Log ordered, "Attention on deck."

The captain turned around near the hatch and looked at them. "Not necessary, Loggins. I'll let you men get back to duty."

A minute later, Tim lit a cigar and breathed a loud sigh of relief. "Men, I think there were a few guys praying we'd get a better skipper. Now, I'm a pretty good judge a character, and am tellin' ya, this officer's a sailor's captain, because he's been enlisted and knows how we think and endure. Man, am I happy." Carter and Reemer turned around from the equipment, and nodded in agreement. One problem remained, Bearden.

Two weeks of intermittent day and night gunfire support, watches and extra duty took a toll on Hickey's psyche. He lacked proper sleep.

Bearden's outbursts at two inexperienced new men and impatient behavior compounded and exacerbated the already stressful watches in radio. Behaving like a rudderless ship, Badass was inconsistent and weird, a Jekyll and Hyde. At some times he'd joke, laugh, acting like their buddy, fellow shipmate, then he'd suddenly shift gears, angrily berating a man for having the temerity of asking what he considered a stupid question.

Off duty, he became the topic of whispered conversation among small groups of men.

Stressed, chagrined faces were evident after seeing their names under his on the next day's watch schedule. "Well, I'm shafted again, got the Badass watch," said Reemer. They hated being around him.

One morning, Log stood on a ladder and shouted down into berthing, "Hey, fellas, I've got great news."

"We could sure use some,"replied Mac.

"The skipper's giving us a four-day liberty in Bangkok, Thailand the day after tomorrow."

"Yeah, bout time cause we've been on the line a month now," exclaimed Mike.

Two days later, *Satterfield* rounded the southern tip of Vietnam's Cau Mau peninsula, steaming at twenty knots, 635 miles north of the equator. After a mid-watch, Jim went topside as the ship sailed into the Gulf of Siam, two miles off the Cambodian coast.

Alden approached as Jim gazed at the mountainous landscape, "Well, how ya been, buddy?"

"Not, too good, Tom, because ya know I'm lucky getting five or six hours sleep with those damn guns going off and the extra duty. I've only got four weeks left of this crap."

Tom quickly patted his back. "Yup, don't worry. You'll do it, mate."

After passing Sattahip, he nudged Jim and exclaimed, "Hey, look, a school of sea snakes." Jim turned, looked starboard, and saw a dozen seven-foot brown serpents with yellow bands swimming thirty yards away just under the surface. Alden looked at him. "Man, don't fall in, because they're real poisonous." Intense heat from the afternoon sun incessantly beat down on the destroyer. The Philippines were hot and humid, yet Jim had never experienced this much unrelenting heat.

Speed was reduced to ten knots as the ship moved north into a narrow two-hundred yard wide, brown river leading to Bangkok. He marveled at the topography of the jungle as palm and banana trees swayed among numerous little wooden dwellings. In the background, gold and silver-roofed Buddhist temples gleamed in the sun, rising high above tropical under-brush and banyan trees, indigenous to the Far East.

She tied up astern of a large freighter at the commercial pier as enthusiastic sailors donned whites and assembled before going ashore. He gazed down from the stern, seeing three teenaged girls attired in shorts in a little hollowed out bamboo canoe, looking up, smiling. "Hey, Joe, you want Coca Cola?" one asked. Without local currency, he shook his head.

Hickey, Reemer, and Loggins stood duty that night as the rest enjoyed liberty. Message traffic was light. Log took Jim aside and whispered, "Hey, listen. I know Badass has ya doing crap detail around here and regular duties, but when the time's right, I'm gonna investigate. Ya see, I think there was some sort of conspiracy goin' on and I aim to prove it. I wouldn't be surprised if Gates was involved. I'll go down to engineering and find out if anyone saw Bearden on the day we entered Subic cause that's the only place you didn't check, right?" Jim nodded.

Tim puffed the cigar and blew smoke. "Ya see, I believe they had some kind of a deal, and he possibly covered for Badass. I think Gates lied when ya saw him and would've stopped ya going through that hatch cause of his size. See what I'm talkin' 'bout?"

"Yeah, that adds up because we almost got in a fight. He doesn't like me and besides, everyone knows he's Bearden's boy."

Tim put a hand on his shoulder. "Now listen, I've gotta be quiet about this cause I can only trust Thomas, Smitty, you and Sid. I don't want anyone knowing what I'm doin', especially Bearden." Men were relieved Badass was ashore.

Before a naval ship docked at a foreign port, sailors were given little guide books, showing a map of the city, points of interest, local culture and monetary exchange rates. Clearly emphasized were prohibitions of entering certain out of bound areas, but at times some ignored the warnings, to their detriment.

On departure, a lone sailor or Marine would fail making muster and be declared missing or absent without leave. Later, his body would be found with stab wounds after a robbery. In the Bangkok handout, they were warned against venturing at night through small fields between buildings near the downtown area because of deadly cobra and krait snakes.

In late morning, Sid, Mike and Jim went ashore, taking in the sites of the cosmopolitan city of three million. After an enjoyable visit to the zoo, they entered a snake farm with mingling tourists and locals gazing down over a large four-and-a-half foot high circular, concrete structure at small cobras, kraits and other venomous reptiles slithering among small plants and brush.

Highlighting the display were two young, slender Thai herpetologists, clad in long white medical garb, wearing gloves. They approached twin ten- foot rectangular boxes on a table in the center of the pit. As patrons snapped photos, one snake handler carefully unsecured a latch, opening a door as the other quickly grabbed a tail, slowly pulling out a ten-foot brown monster, the King Cobra. Immediately, a doctor swiftly reached, grabbed the head, placing it above a small glass jar as the tail furiously lashed.

Two large fangs protruded as extracted venom dripped into the container, and the process was repeated with the other snake. The crowd of about a hundred applauded after each demonstration as the sailors looked on in awe.

Shortly thereafter, the heat was overbearing. Mike exclaimed, "Damn, it's so hot I'll bet you could cook on a sidewalk. Man, we need air conditioning." They jumped into a taxi and journeyed to the posh Golden Lion Hotel, a popular tourist lodging for affluent foreigners. Two sculptured, six-foot high, gold painted lions with opened mouths flanked the entrance of the five-story building. Several circular tables, each with an open umbrella, surrounded a large pool. Just a few yards beyond, banana and palm trees provided a little shade.

After checking in, they donned bathing suits, purchased quart bottles of beer in ice and sauntered near the pool. The water refreshed their sweaty bodies, and the cold suds were tasty. A dozen tourists from France and England sat under umbrellas, conversing.

He noticed a distinguished, middle-aged gentleman with a handle-bar mustache wearing checkered Bermuda shorts, sitting alone in the corner. Jim walked over and introduced himself. The English man smiled, "Have a seat, Yank."

The portly gentleman had softball-like cheeks flanking a Roman nose, sandy hair and a large, tanned forehead above a monocle. He was cordial, yet inquisitive, questioning the young sailor.

He guarded his tongue when asked about the ship's next destination. Spies circulated through- out known American liberty cities.

"Mister, all I know is we're going back, but where, I don't know."

"I see. Would you like a cognac, Yank?" Jim shook his head. "I say, Yank, you've never had cognac? Why, it's great. I'll pour you two shots in this glass." That was Jim's first mistake.

The stranger proposed a toast, "To all the Yanks and Brits who've ever sailed the seas, here, here, ol' chap." The sailor took a few swigs.

"Wow! That's strong, but good." Across the pool, Sid and Mike exchanged pleasantries with two bikini-clad local women.

The foreigner rambled for an hour about merry ol' England, his family and Shakespeare, as Jim listened. Within an hour, the Englishman was getting on Jim's nerves because of his repetitive habit of mouthing, "I say Yank."

After another cognac, the worm turned. He thought, "I'm getting tanked. Ah, thanks Mister, but I gotta go."

"Well, ta ta, Yank. It's been fun talking with you."

He staggered near his buddies and sat. They laughed. With alcohol clearly having an effect, the sailors were jovial and cavorted, throwing a couple of willing foreigners and each other into the pool after sunset.

The following morning Sid woke him, looking down and grinning while holding a hot cup of black coffee. "Here, this will sober ya up."

He rubbed his eyes, looked up and murmured, "Ah, thanks, I needed this. By the way, do ya know what I did last night?"

Sid shook his head back and forth a few times, and chuckled, "Wow, you put on a show for everyone. Ya ran inside, put your jumper on, stood on the end of the diving board, sang an old song, but lost your balance and fell into the pool. You were plastered and funny. We all busted up. Man, you were totaled and could hardly swim, but Mike helped ya out. I'll tell ya, those high-class, prissy foreigners were shocked."

"Ya gotta be kiddin' me. I did that? Damn, must have been the cognac and the beer. I've never been that drunk before, but we had fun, didn't we?"

"Yup, sure did. Ya even threw a few surprised Brits into the pool, including the old guy. Hey, jump in the shower, and let's get going.

After grabbing lunch, they hailed a cab and motored throughout downtown, marveling at Buddhist temples and foreign architecture. Later, they strolled into a little air-conditioned lounge.

It was a rectangular, dimly-lit pub with six black leather booths opposite a long bar.

Four circular tables occupied by locals were scattered in the rear near a juke box. Upon entering, they saw a well-inebriated Electronic Technician, George Hanley, with his head resting on the bar.

Two hookers in dark, silk miniskirts were busy pilfering money from the Tennesseans' pockets. Mike quickly grabbed baht (currency) out of one girl's hands while Sid shoved the other aside. Irate at being denied, both shouted unintelligible Thai at his rescuers. Jim knelt, and picked the remaining money off the floor as the thieves ran laughing toward the rear.

Hickey shouted at the bartender, "Hey, call a taxi."

The skinny, middle-aged owner leaned over the bar and hollered, "Hey Joe, it ok, we take care heem."

Sid lifted George's face as Mike pulled the 180-pound Southerner off the stool, sliding him over into a nearby booth. Aboard, everyone liked George's good nature and demeanor.

Sid leaned over the bar, angrily glaring at the man, "Damn it, you knew he was drunk, being hustled by these sluts, and did nothing. You were expecting a piece of the action, eh? Well, listen, asshole, we take of our own. Ya got any coffee?"

Frightened, the Thai entrepreneur grabbed a phone, looked and snapped, "I ca shoe patol now."

Sid grimaced as veins expanded on his neck. He leaped on the bar and shouted, "You dial that damn phone, we'll destroy this place. You hear me, jackass?" With eyes bulging in fear, the Thai's hands shook while placing the receiver down.

"Ok, ok Joe, all good." The owner poured a hot cup of tea.

Mike hollered, "Hey, bring us three beers, too."

Hanley wanted sleep, but the last thing the men desired was the shore patrol entering and transporting the sailor to the brig. Sitting near, Jim moved his head back and forth, shouting in one ear, "George, George, wake up." Hanley's eyelids slowly opened as Jim held his head.

The groggy face brightened as he looked across, seeing Reemer and Thomas. "Ah, hi sparks men. What in the heck ya doin' here?"

"Here, take a sip of tea, they don't have coffee," Jim said.

He slowly brought the cup, touching his lips and drank. Mike gazed at him. "You know, it's a good thing we bopped in here before those broads finished hustling ya."

Thomas turned, staring again at the bartender, "Yeah, I gotta believe they were all in on it. Hey, you're valuable Georgie, because ya do a good job testing and repairing our equipment. We're not gonna let anything happen to ya, buddy." He began to sober as a dozen others stared while consuming beverages nearby.

Shortly thereafter, a short elderly woman with black hair and Indian headdress, holding a crystal ball entered and approached three people sitting at a rear table. "Boy, a fortune teller, man just what we need," remarked Thomas.

After reading a young couple's fortune, her eyes shifted side to side. She slowly moved like a serpent seeking another victim near their booth. Covering her slender, frail body was a long red and yellow, one-piece silk outfit. The sailors saw her crooked little nose protruding between almost black eyes. She gazed, staring deeply into each of their eyes studying and analyzing, like a mechanic staring at an engine. They were nervous.

Her tone was low, almost hypnotic. "You, young American say las. I am Krisnaveni. I fom India, tell fotune for only twelve baht, real cheap today."

Mike downed a beer and snapped, "Ah, no thanks, lady, we're not interested."

"This old lady's strange, but I'm fascinated by what she says," Jim thought.

Her eyes darted from one to another, then focused on Jim's eyes immediately reading his inquisitive mind. She leaned inches away, her unblinking deep eyes piercing his.

"How bout you?"

He shook his head, "Nah, I don't believe in all that crystal ball stuff." She pulled a chair near them and put the ball on a nearby table.

"I read you palm say la man, ok?" He quickly turned and looked at Sid and Mike who nodded. He handed her the equivalent of three American dollars.

"You give me left hand, relax, and don't move." His buddies curiosly stared as Jim extended his left arm and open palm. She placed her left hand under his gently holding it, and closed her eyes a few seconds. For a few minutes, her right forefinger slowly moved over the palm lines tracing each tributary while deep in thought.

The strange lady stared into his eyes. Her tone was soft, almost hypnotic. "You come fom big family. Good people." She told him a few domestic facts regarding his family that no one, but God could have known. His heart beat faster. He was stunned. With the palm still up, he asked, "Will I live a long life?" She stopped moving the finger and looked at him.

"Yes, good long life and you be happy with two daughta and wife in cold land."

He pulled away as she rose and asked, "What's that all about?" She was mum, smiled, backed away, turned and left. He was puzzled and looked at his friends, "Wow, that was somethin'."

Sid replied, "Ah, don't worry about it. A lot of times these types are just blowing smoke and hustling bucks."

George finished the tea. The three toasted. "Here's ta a long life for all of us, shipmates," exclaimed Mike.

Jim remarked, "I've never had my fortune told because I figured they're all crack pots, but damn, she knew things about me and my family nobody else did. I don't know how she knew, but I hope I live a long life, buddies."

"Yup, ya can say that again," replied Sid.

Mike was unusually quiet and pensive as he looked down at the table thinking. He finished his beer, then looked at Jim. "That was the most bizarre thing I've ever seen."

They helped George outside and hailed a cab. Sid put an arm around him and remarked. "Man, you look like Grant took Richmond, buddy."

He fluttered his eyes and slured, "Ah, ah, that's not, not funny. I'm a Reb, ya know." They chuckled.

Jim leaned over and looked at the driver. "Take him back to the commercial pier." George waved as they departed.

Night approached as they entered the Thai Heaven, a popular dance club. A large round, gleaming, silver ball rotated above a stage as a rock n roll band played. "Man, there must be four hundred people in here", remarked Sid. Sailors off the ship danced with attractive mini-skirted women.

They spotted Carter, Mac and Warden at a table and sat down. All three were drunk. A short, slender, long-haired girl in shorts ventured near Jim. "Hi, Joe, I like you. You want buy me dink and go hotel?" He shook his head and thought, why am I surprised? This is getting old.

"No, why don't you try somebody else" They turned, fixing eyes on her beauty. Linda was decent. He would be true.

Reemer smiled, putting an arm around her waist and said, "Listen, baby doll. I'll buy ya a drink, but ya can't sit down. I know your angle, and you're tryin' ta hustle us, and besides, we gotta get back." She got the drink, moved away and repeated the sales pitch for others nearby.

Mac muttered, "Ah, ah Hickey, ah man, ya know she's so fine and just tryin' ta make a livin.' Why did ya screw that one up?"

He took a long swig of Tiger beer and replied, "Listen, it's the same old bull-shit thing with these babes, just like Subic and Seattle. All they do is hustle and hit the sack with ya. There's really no love. Man, there's many fish here getting hooked. They reel a guy in and get married, and then it's a free pass to the good old USA."

Thomas nodded, "You know, he's right. We were here before and things haven't changed."

Jim inserted, "Listen, I got a nice girl in Manila, and her letters cheer me up. She likes me for who I am and isn't interested in a slam dunk marriage." It was getting late as the six left in taxis and returned aboard. Two days later, the destroyer departed as trouble brewed in the war zone.

# 13

# "THE VIETNAMESE
# AND LIBERTY"

By March 1972, 98,000 Americans remained in South Vietnam, down from 550,000 in 1969. The majority served in advisory and support capacities as ARVN assumed the majority of the fighting. At least two-thirds of all provinces were secure from Communist forces. After being decimated in the 1968 Tet Offensive, the remaining southern born Viet Cong units operated on squad (10-15men) or platoon (20-40 men) levels, with the NVA comprising the bulk of opposition forces.

Because of U. S. Navy Operations Market Time, Game Warden, and Giant Slingshot successes, commercial waterborne traffic flowed with few incidents in the Mekong Delta, south of Saigon, where sixty percent of the population resided. To be sure, there were sporadic, isolated small battles near villages and cities from NVA insurgents entering Delta tributaries from Cambodian sanctuaries. ARVN units backed by American air and naval gunfire repeatedly thwarted attacks by enemy forces. Without the U. S. Navy, America wouldn't have been able to sustain the war.

After the Chieu Hoi (open arms/surrender) program was initiated a few years prior, thousands of enemy troops converted to South Vietnam's side, coupled with a successful urban pacification plan, and increased waterborne commercial traffic, resulted in significant economic growth. Trade increased as rice production reached an all-time high. Most people were free of Communist domination, though enemy activity was volatile in the five northern provinces below the DMZ.

The brief incursion into Cambodia in 1970 by U. S., and ARVN forces eradicated large concentrations of NVA as thousands of tons of supplies, ammunition and weapons were seized, thwarting a major invasion by two years. By 1972, North Vietnam was resupplied by Russia and China, consequently, the Communist high command in Hanoi planned another massive offensive into South Vietnam.

*Satterfield* steamed two miles from land between Nha Trang and Qui Nhon. During the next two weeks, she provided gunfire support along the coast, then was ordered south, to support ARVN units under fire in Delta areas. Kowalski ordered port and starboard watches for the entire crew. Stress increased as men awakened in the middle of the night hearing general quarters. A man was fortunate to get a few hours of rest each day.

Between G.Q., normal and extra duties, Jim's anxiety exacerbated. In the war zone, hundreds of messages were sent, received daily in the ship's communications spaces where radiomen had to quickly think and react, creating a stressful environment. Shortly after three one morning, Jim's heart palpitated and raced, awakening him. He struggled and rolled out of bed, then staggered near the ladder like a drunken man, slowly climbed up and collapsed on the top step. He wondered, "My God, what's happening to me? I've gotta make sick bay."

Jim crawled sluggishly on an empty passageway, but his eyes couldn't focus clearly. Fire hoses, CO2 canisters and large axes on bulkheads quickly swayed back and forth. He asked, himself, "Am I hallucinating or something?" For the first time in his life, he thought he was dying as his heart beat faster.

The five-minute journey seemed like an hour as he crawled over another open hatch and banged on the sick bay door, waking the duty corpsman.

A twenty year-old broad shouldered blond duty petty officer opened the hatch as Hickey collapsed inside.

"Hey, sailor, you all right?" he asked.

After picking Jim up and placing him on a nearby gurney, he grabbed a syringe and plunged a needle into a vein in his left arm. "Now, rest here buddy, and I'll wake you in a few hours. I think you'll be ok."

Shortly after reveille, Jim was still groggy, staring at the overhead. The corpsman sat nearby at a desk, writing an incident report. Jim gazed at him. "Ah, thanks buddy, for helping me last night."

"Yeah, you almost didn't make it with your rapid heart rate. You had a severe anxiety attack. I'm recommending two days light duty for you."

"Thanks, doc. I think I need it." Surprisingly, Bearden approved the request, ordering him to stand two day watches making copies of received messages with no extra duty.

As Jim sat near a mimeograph machine on a table, Log was sympathetic. "Wow, Jim, that was a close call you had last night."

"Yeah, as my grandfather use to say, 'I almost bought the farm.'"

He asked, "How much extra duty ya got left?"

"Only two weeks, and it can't come too soon."

Log grinned, "Well, that's good, because in a week we're goin' back ta Subic for a few days, and you're gonna see your girl again." Jim smiled, immediately feeling better.

Bearden slowly descended into berthing, catching Gates sitting, polishing his shoes. He leaned against a top bunk, looked down and grinned, "Well Donny, guess ya heard what happened ta Hickey, eh?" He stopped the chore and gazed up.

"Yeah, word got around."

"Well, I'm breaking the bastard. He almost didn't make it the other night, but I'll get him before he finds out anything else. Listen; keep your eyes and ears sharp around Loggins, Hickey and the other two. Let me know what's goin' on. Remember, you're getting extra liberty in Subic."

"Ok, will do."

Attempting to improve morale, Kowalski ordered the ship to drop anchor at Vung Tau, an old French resort city near the mouth of the Mekong River, 45 miles south of Saigon. Located on a peninsula jutting into the South China Sea, it was among the many secure areas in Vietnam, a favorite respite for weary G. I.'s. To the sailor's delight, the captain secured several cases of beer from naval supply on shore.

Log, Sid, Mike, Jim and others wearing dungarees came ashore and boarded buses. Each vehicle had checkerboard like steel mesh protecting windows to suppress flying shrapnel in the event of an ambush or detonating mines. The old green vehicle lumbered over a dirt road a couple miles, dropping the men off near a patch of trees overlooking the beach.

Other G. I.'s wearing bathing suits basked in bright sunlight as tiny waves from the sea lapped the shore. A few small children with their mother mingled with the Americans as fishermen banked a wooden craft nearby.

The men were allocated five hours socializing and swimming as cold beer was distributed. Sailors ran, diving into the warm sea; others milled around telling jokes. The four sat at a picnic table, exchanging toasts.

A skinny nine year old boy wearing shorts, and younger sister carrying bags of hats, meandered a few feet away. G.I.'s nicknamed all Vietnamese "*gooks*", a common, but demeaning word used during the conflict.

The little boy approached, smiling, "Hey, G. I., G. I. you want buy hat? Numba one, reo good, reo good." Piasters were local currency, but most sailors brought no money. Jim thought, "Damn, I wish I could give em' something. They look so poor." Their daily goal was surviving another day and living free.

The lad wearing a brown hat smiled, gazing up at him. Jim shook his head slapping his dungaree pockets. Disappointed, the boy lowered his head and walked among others, attempting solicitation.

Tim, sitting atop a wooden picnic table, chugged a beer, jumped into sand, ran and spoke with the kids. He knelt, reached into a pocket, smiled and gave each a five-dollar bill. Excited, the two giggled, jumping up and down as if on pogo sticks.

He motioned them to follow while their mother stared nearby. During the next hour, he built a two-foot high, ten-foot long sand castle, including a moat, to the joy of the excited children who assisted.

Thirty feet away, Jim and Mike leaned against a tree watching as they relished the suds. Mike remarked, "Ya know? Log really loves kids. I heard he did some volunteer charity work for orphans back in Diego."

"I admire that," replied Jim.

Tim rose, wiped sand off, walked near the two and asked, "Hey, fellas, enjoying your selves?"

"Yeah, this is great. Shit, ya don't even know there's a war going on here", Mike said. Log gazed in the distance beyond palm trees, reflected and then looked at them.

"Believe me, there is. That's why we're here fellas."

Jim complemented, "You're good with kids, Log. Ya got any back home?" Tim sat a few feet away, thought and looked at both.

"She never wanted kids." His head bowed. "It gets to me some times. I've been married 15 years, and yeah I've had my chances with other babes, but stayed the course despite what she's done."

After two beers, the veteran's tone changed to melancholy. "I never told anyone bout this guys, but several years ago, I was stationed at San

Miguel in the P.I. at the Communications station. After making petty officer, the navy flew my wife over, and we lived in base housing, and later adopted Billy, a five year-old Filipino boy. Man, it was great!"

They moved closer, listening. "Well, after a couple years I was sent to Long Beach, and he went to school like most kids while my wife worked in a department store, and later we got transferred to San Diego, which was nice."

"What happened after that?" Mike asked.

His expression quickly changed, becoming maudlin, "its tough saying this, but here he was, a ten year old kid having fun playing Little League and then she tells me she didn't wanna bother to continue raising him. He was getting on her nerves and an extra cost to us."

Tim looked down at the sand, pressed his lips together, and swayed his head back and forth. "Can ya believe it? Shit, the kid had his moments like they all do, but overall, was a good boy, respectful, and got along with other kids. I taught him all his prayers and stuff."

Sid exclaimed, "Sounds like she has a big ego and selfish Log."

"Guys, it was a sad time when we drove back east ta my folks' place and they agreed to take care of him."

Jim got irate. "What the hell was wrong with her Log? That's bullshit, ya know.

"Yeah, see, for years she's been consumed with herself, wanting material things, and that bothers me. I'd fly back at least once a month for a couple days, spending time with him when I was on another tin can stationed in Diego."

He brightened with a smile. "Ya know somethin'? My boy and I are real tight and I get nice letters from him. Billy's seventeen now, plays baseball, is on the golf team and even has a girlfriend."

"That's great, Log" said Mike.

"Yeah, I'm blessed. He works his can off helping the folks on the farm, and I bring 'em souvenirs every time I return from overseas. Man, I love that kid." He smiled and waved at the children sitting near the castle. "Hey, excuse me guys, but I've gotta run and play tag with em'."
He jumped up, ran, kicking sand as his stomach jiggled while chasing the laughing kids as others looked and grinned.

Mike at Jim. "Look at 'em, laughing and running around with that huge belly shakin' like he's a kid again. Ya know something, pal? I've known 'em well over a year and never regretted it. He's got a magnetic personality, and a good spirit. Log's a special guy and a great role model. After what happened to the two others, we were sort a pissed at'em for siding with Larson and Badass. He apologized and it was tough, but we got over it."

Jim took a swig, looked toward the sea, and reflected. "Guys, I'm sure he's not gonna let us down. He'll get to the bottom of what happened in Subic."

Alden broke away from a couple buddies and moved near the radiomen, "Hello, Jim. Man, this beer tastes good. I heard the cases were in cargo holds of old World War Two Liberty ships for weeks, but heck, its cold and that's all I care about. How ya been?"

"Ok, I guess. I'm just hanging in there." A few other men from another division cavorted, flexing muscles while others laughed at the tomfoolery.

Later, Tom looked at the two siblings, who continued wandering around the beach, peddling. He lowered his head in sadness and mumbled, "Ya know something, Jim. Take a good look at those kids and their mother. She probably works hard in a rice paddy. Ya see, these people are what we're fighting for so they can live free, not controlled by the Commies."

"You're absolutely right. Let's toast ta these people" he told them. They chugged and walked on immaculate sand toward water to speak with a middle aged fisherman who had just beached his craft. He was short and skinny like most Vietnamese. "Ah, what's the rifle for buddy?" inquired Tom.

The man looked down inside his little boat and responded, "It for shark, Joe. Day get in net some time."

Jim lightly patted his back, "Well, good luck, pal."

Later, as sailors returned and boarded, Kowalski stood on the quarterdeck smiling as the men saluted, thanking him. The ship steamed north near Nha Trang, and anchored nearby. A chopper swooped low, hovered ten feet above the stern and dropped a large brown sack of overdue mail.

Jim and Log went topside and sat reading letters. Log said. "Well, here's another letter from my wife complaining about this and that. The divorce should be final soon, and that chapter will be closed." He briefly at Jim. "I'm impressed with the new 'old man.'"

According to Windas in Traditions of the Navy "A vessel's captain as applied to the merchant service is a courtesy title only. His official rank is that of Master Mariner and he's generally called the 'old man.'"

"Yeah, he's been pretty supportive of us so far."

Jim's eyes quickly scanned a letter as he chuckled. Log asked. "Ah, what's so funny?"

"My mother always writes nice letters, cheering me up. Ya see, we've had this beagle now for some years. In my last letter, I asked what's new. Here she says 'well, Bridgett's pregnant again, so what else is new.'" He laughed then turned and looked at Tim. "For years there's been this forty pound black and white dog down the street called Prince. He's the stud of the block, and when he wanders around, everyone runs and gets their females inside." Tim grinned. "What cracks me up is that he's got this bell dangling below his neck and he just hunts around, looking for another mate, and you always hear that bell ring. He's like a canine Good Humor ice cream man. A couple of my brothers throw rocks trying to keep him away from our yard."

Tim uproariously chuckled, getting everyone's attention, "Ha, ha, man, I sure needed a good laugh."

Jim was elated receiving a warm letter from Linda. "My Jim, I think about you each day and miss you. Come back soon."

After six weeks, the ship pulled into Subic Bay and tied up at Alava Pier for liberty and replenishment for four days. He was granted two days liberty after Loggins spoke with Stewart. Bearden signed his chit.

She took a bus from Manila to visit an aunt in Olongapo. They met at a little club and embraced, and slow danced to an old Andy Williams selection as she enjoyed listening to Jim again singing near her ear. She melted in his arms. That afternoon, sailors filtered in.

"Jeem, you want go White Rock Beach with me? I meet cousins."

"Sounds good, let's go."

It was a narrow, almost quarter-mile long beach located on the northwest corner of the bay. An old rusted LST was beached two hundred yards away. Just beneath swaying palm trees were a half dozen bamboo and open wooden shelters for picnickers. Her two cousins were short, young ladies clad in tropical skirts. Linda wore attractive brown shorts above a two-piece bathing suit.

Trade winds refreshed them as they waded into the mixed salt and fresh warm water. In the near distance, a destroyer slowly passed an imposing mountain chain on the Bataan Peninsula. She couldn't swim, but he boldly stroked out into deeper water, and stopped to treaded water. He thought, "There may be sharks here. Better not go far." After swimming back he waded and grinned at the three Filipinos standing on the beach below palms. He reflected,"Here I am with a pretty girl in a tropical paradise. It doesn't get any better than this. I wish the day would last forever." War seemed far away.

Shortly thereafter, she sat on a bench inside a shelter posing for him in shorts as he snapped a picture. Three hundred yards away, locals and sailors swam and frolicked around a large enclosed pool.

The following evening, he got a visitor's pass and escorted her into the Sampagita Club, a popular on-base enlisted man's lounge. He was surprised seeing Log and Tom sitting together.

After introductions, Jim and Linda slow danced near a live band playing soothing music. Both mates enjoyed her personality and lady-like demeanor during the few hours.

Later, the couple walked along the shore under a bright full moon, overlooking the beach. Romance filled the air as he planted a long kiss on her receptive lips. He withdrew a few inches away from her beautiful face and stared. "Listen, we're gonna be gone for a while, and I don't know when I'll be back cause I think things may get rough over there." She lowered her head in sadness, then looked into his eyes.

"Jeem, I pray for you ebery day. Dat is what I do."

"Thanks, honey, I'll need it. Linda, your letters lifted my soul. Thank you." She pulled him close to her.

**White Rock Beach**

They sat on a bench looking at the moon and water. Before leaving, he drew near and hugged her. Tears formed in her brown eyes. He moved a forefinger slowly over each and wiped them, and then planted a long kiss as she pressed against him. The sailor moved his head back a few inches gazing into her sad countenance. "Honey, I will miss you until I see you again."

He thought, "God, I hate going back, but duty calls." Shortly before 2400, Jim returned aboard. Soon, his life would significantly change.

*Satterfield* sped west toward Da Nang, back to war. During the thirty-six hour trip, Kowalski ordered general quarter drills and evasive zigzagging maneuvers in the event of air or artillery attack. The ship performed sporadic gunfire support for ten days. Suddenly, the captain and crew were surprised at a lull in enemy activity as a strange tranquility settled over the northern provinces.

Steaming east of Hue City, the C. O. stood on the bridge scanning a mountain range then turned and looked at the J.O.O.D. (junior officer of the deck). "I don't get it. There've been no gun fire requests for five days. I've seen recent intelligence reports, and there's no evidence of heavy enemy activity up here. I feel somethings gonna happen soon."

He'd developed a sixth sense, having served two previous combat tours as an executive officer aboard another destroyer. "Yeah, captain, I think our minds are in sync because I've been wondering about it too. I do know this: the crew's sharp, and we'll be ready for any eventuality."

"I concur, they're well trained."

# 14

## "THERE ARE SOME DAYS YOU DON'T FORGET"

After completing extra duty, Jim returned to regular watches in radio. Bearden's behavior puzzled subordinates. Mike took Sid and Jim aside out on a weather deck. "What's bugging ya Mike?" Sid asked.

"Man, I'll tell ya Badass is sure weird. I've known him almost two years and have never seen him so quiet like this. Are you guys surprised at his patience? Heck, I don't get it. It's like there's somebody else inside the guy, a Dr. Jekyll cause of his mellow tone. He's not impulsive, but nothing's changed and he's still eyeballing a few of us, especially you Jim."

"Yeah, I've noticed that."

However, the internal conflict and Bearden's behavior would now be greatly overshadowed by surprising events unfolding in the war torn nation.

Throughout the war, hundreds of American naval ships alternated off South Vietnam's shore line providing supplies, as well as logistical, air and gunfire support to Army, Marine and ARVN forces. Thousands of sorties were flown against belligerent targets from carriers steaming north east of the DMZ in an area of the Tonkin Gulf called "Yankee Station."

Flight deck crews worked fourteen to sixteen hour days on dangerous navy flattops where mistakes and accidents meant almost certain death. Over two hundred were killed by tragic explosions and fires aboard carriers *Oriskany* and *Forrestal*.

In March, COMSEVENTHFLT dispatched Satterfield, joining the destroyer Merton, 14,000 ton light guided missile cruiser *Rapid City*, and guided missile frigate *Sterling* in commencing an intensive shelling of Communist targets north of the DMZ.

The majority of bombardments occurred shortly before or after sundown. The destroyer got so close to the flour like sandy beaches there was fear of running aground, yet daily work routines and general quarters again increased stress among sailors aboard Seventh Fleet ships.

One evening, Jim attempted to catch a few hours' sleep before a mid-watch. His mind flashed back ten years to a simpler world, lying on his backyard grass, gazing at slow floating cumulo-nimbus clouds on a bright spring morning, wondering about his destiny.

Suddenly, general quarters were sounded. Jim ran into radio central. While standing on the bridge, Kowalski peered through binnoculars at the shoreline and calmly ordered, "Commence firing." The destroyer's guns opened up blasting strategic enemy targets. Lookouts spotted several huge explosions from ammunition dumps which illuminated the sky.

The Communists were incensed, consequently, several large guns commenced return fire, sending large ten and twelve-inch diameter shells at her. There ensued a furious exchange of fire between the shore batteries and *Satterfield*. Shells from North Vietnamese guns exploded just feet above the mast as hot shrapnel quickly rained down, striking the bridge and superstructure.

Men in radio sat, quietly listening to the constant recoil of both mounts as the vessel shook with each salvo firing shells into an ebony night. One incoming round exploded, sending a torrent of hot lead above their space just aft of the bridge. Sitting behind a desk, Log exclaimed, "That was close, guys. I've been on two other war cruises, but this is the worst."

Bearden returned from transmitters and leaned against a bulkhead while his eyes quickly shifted to each man. Jim thought, "This is the first time I've seen him this nervous." Everyone was aware of his consternation. Fear spread. Sailors quickly realized their own mortality while each looked at the overhead, hearing prang, prang, prang like sounds as marble and walnut sized hot shrapnel struck above them. A shell exploded 20 feet above the mainmast, raining a torrent of hot shrapnel into the superstructure.

As she sailed past shore based guns, it was a scene reminiscent of huddled German sailors hearing depth charges exploding above their

U-boats under the Atlantic during World War Two. This was Hickey's world now, far removed from joys of peaceful youth. While gazing up at the overhead, Jim shook with fear. He closed his eyes and thought of Linda, wishing he were cuddling, lying next to her on a quiet beach. The reflection relaxed him momentarily.

After two hours, the vessel ceased firing. Numerous holes permeated the superstructure, but there were no casualties. He thought, "My God, that was scary. I hope it doesn't happen again. Maybe now I can get a couple hours' sleep."

For four days, he man o war poured hundreds of shells into North Vietnam, hitting specific military targets including an airport. Between Haiphong and the DMZ she conducted harassing gunfire raids, striking the Dong Hoi airfield and incensing Communist officers on the mainland.

Suddenly, shore-based enemy artillery fired large rounds, a few exploding, creating 40-foot geyser like splashes within twenty yards of *Satterfield* as she steamed at flank speed. She heeled 25 degrees, zig zagging, avoiding rounds as shrapnel pierced holes into the helo deck.

Standing on the bridge observing large shells exploding, Kowalski quickly turned and at the J. O. O. D. standing nearby, "Damn it, we can't match the heavy stuff they're firing at us." Within minutes, the intense hail of large incoming shells started bracketing her while Lee intermittently shouted commands to the helmsman, "Right full rudder, left full rudder." *Satterfield* quickly turned, desperately attempting escape. He ordered, "Let's get out of here." The ship exited the area, steaming further east out of harm's way. It was a miracle she survived.

Midnight on the last evening, Kowalski stood on the bridge, leaned near the window, peered through binoculars, then looked at a lieutenant. "Mister, we've sure been taking it to em'and we're almost out of ammunition. Cease fire." The guns were silent as seaman and gunner's mates removed several empty shell casings from the deck and mounts.

The skipper turned, ordering the lieutenant, "Call radio and send this flash message to COMSEVENTHFLT. 'Ammunition practically expended. The majority of selected targets destroyed. Heading east out of artillery range and hostile area for next day replenishment, will advise with status report, accordingly. Kowalski, C.O.'" Reemer quickly sent the dispatch as the ship steamed away into the night.

The following day on an overcast morning, Jim caught Tom leaning against a lifeline, gazing east toward the horizon. "How's it going, buddy?" he asked.

Alden looked sad, turned and looked at him, "Ya know something, Jimmy? God, I miss both of them more than the last WESTPAC cruise. I guess it's because of all the incoming fire we've been receiving. I just hope I see 'em again. If ya aren't scared, there's something wrong with ya." His eyes widened. "It's never been this bad, but the old man knows what he's doing and I think we'll be all right."

He put an arm around Tom's shoulder in consolation, "God, all those shells going off above scared me half ta death. Man, I never thought it would be like this. I'm sure they're praying for ya . You're a blessed man having those two. Don't worry; we'll get out of this damn mess. I'm glad we've got a good skipper."

"I needed a shot in the arm. Thanks pal. Hey, I almost forgot, today's Good Friday and Easter's right around the corner. Maybe we'll get a turkey or a ham dinner on Sunday."

Three hours later, after a massive artillery land barrage, the North Vietnamese Army initiated the largest coordinated offensive of the war against South Vietnam in what became known as the Easter Offensive. At least 200,000 crack troops, supported by tanks and artillery, attacked from four directions, surprising thinly positioned ARVN and their American advisers along the DMZ, Laotian, Cambodian border regions and Central Highlands. Initial confusion ensued, largely due to the ubiquitous nature of the planned assaults.

The spearhead attacks originating across the DMZ (I Corps) in the northern provinces overwhelmed retreating allied forces as thousands of terrified civilians fled in panic down Highway One and other areas. Cognizant of U.S. troop withdrawals, and the 98,000 Americans remaining, the Communist timing was perfect.

Allied intelligence was caught off guard largely because of communication difficulties and the failure to understand and act upon factual information. Two years before, the successful incursion into eastern Cambodia by U.S. and ARVN forces resulted in the seizure of thousands of tons of military hardware and ammunition. Because of this, officials mistakenly believed that North Vietnam was incapable of mounting another major offensive for quite some time after absorbing significant setbacks during 1970 in their timetable for conquest.

Like the intelligence mindset toward the end of the European Campaign in World War Two, their pride and arrogance was surprising in underestimating the enemy's true capabilities. History repeated itself like in December 1944, as the British and American high command

**The Easter Offensive, 1972**

were convinced Hitler's forces wouldn't launch a major offensive. The result was widespread disaster as German soldiers poured through the Ardennes Forest into Belgium; consequently, thousands of G.I.'s. perished during the Battle of the Bulge.

In his book, The Easter Offensive of 1972, W.R. Baker expertly stated and referenced Colonel Robert S. Allen, succinctly pinpointing the major problems of "command and control problems within allied intelligence." After thorough analysis based on facts, Baker reasoned that "like commanders prior to The Bulge in December 44' who had ample information and were cognizant of German movements. In 1972, Allied officials were overconfident, but failed to act upon the relevant intelligence they possessed on the large NVA troop deployments. They wrongly assumed the Communists couldn't stage such a large operation until all American troops had departed the following year."

The four pronged offensive spread into the Mekong Delta, north of Saigon, the Central highlands (III Corps.), and down Highway One. During tenacious engagements, Quang Tri was captured and later retaken by ARVN.

There were two U. S. carrier battle groups steaming in the Tonkin Gulf, but all land and sea based aircraft were grounded by overcast weather. The only supporting and preventative measures were destroyers sailing off the coast. The NVA's goal was to thrust down Highway One, retake the old imperial capitol Hue City, continue south, and seize South Vietnam's second largest city, Da Nang.

After available coordinates were sent by American advisers assisting ARVN west of the highway, commanders aboard ships ordered massive round-the-clock bombardment against rapidly moving enemy armored units. During the first forty-eight hours, thousands of shells rained inland, striking targets and troops attempting to halt the Communist juggernaut. Thousands of NVA were killed, wounded or incinerated while numerous tanks and armored personnel carriers were destroyed by a constant barrage of exploding five-inch shells.

By the third day, carriers Coral Sea and Hancock, comprising 140 aircraft in the gulf, launched practically round-the-clock sorties against the bellicose Communists. Within a week, they were joined by carriers Midway, Saratoga, Kitty Hawk and Constellation providing massive air assaults in a desperate measure at halting the belligerents. Because of intensive naval response, thousands of civilian and military lives were saved, including people in Da Nang and Hue City. Retired American Navy Captain Mark Tempest admired the role destroyers played during the first two days of the offensive:

> Because of inclement weather conditions, no tactical air support was brought to bear on the North Vietnamese ground forces. Naval gunfire became the only reliable source of supporting arms during the first forty eight hours of the offensive. History will record that destroyers were of immeasurable value in holding back the North Vietnamese attack down Highway One to Da Nang and Quang Tri City.

Additionally, there was the heroic, suicidal, but successful action of a courageous U.S. Marine who single-handedly thwarted the enemy's assault. On that Sunday, two NVA divisions comprising roughly 30,000 men supported by 200 Russian tanks advanced down the highway approaching the town of Dong Ha. Their goal was to advance across a key bridge spanning the Cua Viet River which snaked through the area. If successful, the Communists would have a free ride, swiftly traveling south, to assault and respectively take the major cities of Hue and Da Nang.

Opposing them was the vastly outnumbered crack 700 man 3rd Battalion of South Vietnamese Marines and their American advisers Marine Captain John Ripley and Army Major James Smock. A dozen supporting tanks and ARVN opened fire against the advancing enemy, vainly attempting a tenacious defense as civilians fled.

Despite airstrikes and intense fire from destroyers, the massive column moved slowly toward the bridge. Ignoring warnings from the Vietnamese commander and without regard for his own safety, for five hours under hostile small arms fire, the tall, lanky Ripley intermittently carried 500 pounds of dynamite, placing explosives in various areas beneath the long concrete, Navy Seabee built steel expanse, three stories above the river.

As South Vietnamese Marines provided covering fire, hundreds of incoming rounds flashed, hitting cement and steel inches away while he secured dynamite one section after another. Shortly before his death in 2008, he recalled dangling under the bridge, loaded with explosives, "moving his arms, hand walking, grasping each beam, praying repeatedly 'Jesus, Mary, get me there. Jesus, Mary get me there.'" (John Grider Miller, The Bridge at Dong Ha, U.S. Naval Institute Press)

The prayer worked. He completed the mission, returning opposite of the structure after cutting his body while running through sharp barbed wire before joining the Marines. Shortly thereafter, as enemy tanks columned ready to advance, the dynamite erupted, exploding tons of concrete and steel high into the air, collapsing the span. Later, six miles south, while the NVA were taking Quang Tri, friendly forces and residents quickly retreated. Ripley helped a dazed mother carrying a child, then ran and hopped aboard an evacuating truck shortly as a mortar round exploded just yards away.

Destroyers poured hundreds of rounds into stalled armor, obliterating several tanks. For bravery and unselfish devotion to duty, Ripley was awarded the Navy Cross, the nation's second- highest medal.

On 4 April, President Nixon ordered the Seventh Fleet to mine approaches to North Vietnam's main port of Haiphong Harbor, which had been receiving thousands of tons of military hardware, ammunition and supplies for years from the Soviet Union and China. Aircraft from the USS *Coral Sea* dropped hundreds of mines in an effort at stopping foreign shipping from entering the location.

Eleven days later, Nixon ordered the heaviest bombing campaign of the war against North Vietnam's capitol Hanoi, and Haiphong which previously were off limits. This was in response to the flagrant enemy's Easter Offensive and the U.S. attempt at resuming peace negotiations in Paris, which were on hold at that time.

During the majority of the conflict, the U. S. committed 40 percent of it's military and fought a limited war with the goal of maintaining South Vietnamese independence, but had no desire to conquer North Vietnam. American pilots were handicapped by controversial R.O.E.'s or Rules of Engagement ordered by Defense Secretary Robert McNamara. This policy frustrated a majority of officers and enlisted. In addition to "no fire zones" in the South, the aviators were prohibited from bombing canals, dikes and targets eleven and a half miles from the nearest town or city in North Vietnam.

Seven months after the defeat of the Viet Cong and NVA in the 1968 Tet Offensive, President Lyndon Johnson ordered a permanent bombing halt against North Vietnam because of the upcoming U. S. elections, and to gain a bargaining chip during peace negotiations. Tactically and effectively, his decision prolonged the war for over four years.

Now in 1972, the gloves were off as elated Air Force, Marine and Navy pilots struck at the heart of the Communist industrial capacities for the first time. The intensity and success of the two-day bombings enraged North Vietnamese leaders.

During the afternoon watch on the 17th, a flash message was received in radio. Before sending it via the pneumatic "bunny" to the captain on the bridge, Loggins quickly perused the classified priority coded dispatch.

```
ZNR SSSSS
P0934Z 17 APR 72
FM COMSEVENTHFLT
TO USS SATTERFIELD
INFO/USS RAPID CITY, USS MERTON, USS STERLING
CINCPACFLT, NAVSUPPACT/DA DANG, COMNAV-
FORPHIL
CTF 77.1.1, COMNAVFORV/MACV
BT
SECRET//NO08739//
YOU ARE TO PROCEED DONG HOI VICINITY
AT 1500 4/19 JOINING TF 77.1.1 TO COMMENCE
INTENSIVE BOMBARDMENT OF ENEMY TARGETS
UNTIL MISSION ACCOMPLISHED. INTELLIGENCE
REPORTS HEAVY CONCENTRATION LARGE SOVIET
PRODUCED ARTILLERY POSITIONED IN AREA.
AVOID POSSIBLE EXTREME HOSTILE GUNFIRE AND
TAKE NECESSARY EVASIVE ACTION
BT
```

On the morning of 19 April, the ship was replenished by a large navy supply vessel miles out in the Tonkin Gulf. The action required excellent seamanship. Two ships would steam parallel between thirty to fifty yards at equal speeds port to starboard. It was a delicate, risky task, since both helmsmen had to maintain the same course and speed despite at times high waves. A line would be shot over onto the supply vessel where a six inch diameter fuel hose was attached, and then sent to the warship for fueling. Pallets loaded with shells were high lined and brought by helo where deck personnel offloaded and stored ammunition in magazines below mounts. Shortly thereafter, she joined Task Unit 77.1.1, again comprising *Merton*, *Rapid City* and *Sterling*.

They sailed west toward Dong Hoi for a gun run, shelling enemy surface to air missile sites and other significant enemy war infrastructures.

The 8,000-ton *Sterling* maintained position two miles northeast, responsible for monitoring and protecting the small force against enemy aircraft since she carried highly accurate Terrier missiles in twin launchers, and a single rapid firing gun aft that shot five inch diameter shells.

The city of Dong Hoi (Lat. 17.30N, 106.38E) lies a few miles west of the sea off Highway One, fifty miles north of the Ben Hai River and 17th Parallel (DMZ) separating North and South Vietnam. Near the city were key military supplies, fuel storage facilities and major radar control center near an airport, a vital area supporting NVA units fighting ARVN, and Americans south of the DMZ.

A week prior, a heavy and furious exchange of gunfire ensued for hours between the NVA shore batteries and 7th Fleet ships with four vessels struck. Despite casualties, none sank. North Vietnamese high command's objective was to sink at least one American ship, the result being not only a military triumph, but a psychological one as well for propaganda purposes over the powerful United States.

At 1600 on a bright, cloudless, but hazy afternoon, *Satterfield* following lead ship *Rapid City* initiated a high-speed gun run shelling enemy SAM sites. The task force in column formation with *Merton* following in *Satterfield's* wake, proceeded south, just a few miles off shore. Meanwhile, Sterling sailed northeast as her alert radar men scanned for any bogie's (hostile aircraft) in the area.

After almost an hour of shelling, the ships ceased firing, turned and steamed north before turning again on a southerly course to prepare another bombardment. General quarters were temporarily cancelled to assess target damage.

Shortly before 1700 during the brief hiatus, Tom in work dungarees walked toward the stern and leaned against starboard lifelines gazing toward land. Off G.Q., Jim grabbed a Coke, walked outside and stood next to his friend. "Hey, Tom, how ya been?" His expression showed a tired sailor.

"Jimmy, I've never seen it this bad with all the return fire and ships getting hit. I hope we get out of here with our skins."

"Yeah, I know what ya mean. I don't think there's a guy aboard who isn't scared." Jim gazed down toward the water, looking despondent.

"What's the matter, buddy?"

"Ya know something? I'm just wondering why in the hell were here anyway. The generals and Pentagon made stupid decisions."

Tom's eyes expanded in surprise. "What are ya trying to say?"

"Well shit, five years ago, I read where CINCPACFLT Admiral U. S. Grant Sharp at Pearl three times asked Defense Secretary McNamara to have the Navy blockade North Vietnam. The reason was to halt supplies coming from Russia and China and shorten the war, but he was turned down."

"Gee, I didn't know."

Frustrated, Jim continued, "Ya remember those poor guys in the 101st Airborne Division?

They suffered heavy casualties assaulting and taking Hamburger Hill back in '69, then after the top brass ordered it evacuated, the 'Gooks' occupied it again. Back in '68 when I was a senior in high school, those 6,000 brave guys of the 26th Marines held Khe Sanh for over six weeks against overwhelming odds. Ya know what happened? A few months later, they were ordered to destroy the base and vacate. Can you believe it? What in hell were they thinking? That's bullshit. Those decisions made no sense; that's why a lot of guys were pissed off, and damn it, I don't blame 'em."

Tom threw an arm around his shoulder, and looked at him, "Hey what's gotten into you lately? Remember those poor little kids we saw on the beach down at Vung Tau?"

He took a long breath and exhaled. "Yeah, I remember. Who could forget. They were good."

"Well, I agree. There's still hope as long as the Navy's around. We've still gotta try and help these people while some stupid politicians and generals call the shots. Yeah, it's frustrating, but there's still hope, and that's a good thing."

"Yeah, I suppose you're right."

In silence, they looked toward shore at a mountain range beyond, when suddenly, two camera-like flashes discharged from shore. Tom asked. "What the hell's that?" Seconds later, two huge splashes erupted twenty yards away, stunning both. He quickly at Jim. "What's going on? Shit, they're firing at us, and I don't think we're ready for this. We better get going, Jimmy, because these guys are serious."

Frightened, Jim's eyes widened. "Yeah, let's get out of here."

On the bridge, Kowalski swiftly turned his head, looked at the boatswain and ordered, "Sound general quarters." Seconds later, everyone heard the loud order. "General quarters, general quarters, all hands man your battle stations. This is not a drill." *Gong, gong, gong, gong* came the warning as three hundred men sprinted toward stations while she steamed out of gunfire range.

Shortly after 1700, lookouts aboard spotted three rapidly-moving silver objects miles away, rising over a mountain chain and diving over the beach toward the sea. Enemy planes! An excited seaman rushed on to the bridge and stood a few feet from Kowalski. "Sir, hostile aircraft are fast approaching."

He calmly responded, "Very well, sailor, return to your station." Lee at a lieutenant. "Ya know something, mister? They must have figured out exactly what we were doing, because they've scrambled three Mig jets. Heaven help us." A veteran Gunner's Mate quickly manned a single .50 caliber machine gun a few feet outside the bridge while Thomas ran and assumed duty as emergency phone talker on the quarterdeck.

The Communists reacted to the on-going evening shelling, ordering jets to attack the U.S. task force with a vengeance. The Russian produced Migs were originally designed for aerial combat, but a few were modified to carry bombs because of the intense American naval bombardment on their military facilities. The Mig-17 jets capable of Mach 1 speeds (760 m.p.h.)swept over a beach below radar, zooming only 50 feet above the calm water toward the ships.

Kowalski ordered, "Commence firing." The vessel opened up with all guns, desperately firing at the planes with her old World War Two weapons since she was practically defenseless without rapid-firing anti-aircraft guns or missiles. The enemy attempted dropping a bomb amidships, targeting the ASROC mount. Kowalski peered through binoculars at the oncoming jets; then he looked at the young tanned crewcut officer. "Damn it, their bomb bays are open. If a bomb hits the ASROC mount, it will incinerate the ship, and they'll never find a piece of us." The vessel was authorized to carry nuclear rockets, yet many were unaware they were aboard.

While shooting and perspiring, the gunner thought, "Damn it, we're firing like crazy, and all we've got are these old weapons and a machine gun.

The first jet made an initial pass, dropping bombs, exploding less than 50 yards off her star- board quarter. The next plane swung around and banked, dropping a 250-pound bomb near portside. It tumbled between the aft stack and ASROC launcher exploding into the sea in such close proximity that the shock from the blast resulted in extensive damage to her internal stability, including separating the vital fire main.

Initial confusion ensued, and quickly vanished because of men trained in a variety of hazardous conditions. Small fires broke out near Tom's G.Q. station in Repair Two, located near the bow but were quickly extinguished by men using CO2 canisters. Sailors quickly sprang and ran, attempting to repair damages. Tom shouted to his men nearby, "Let's get going!"

Shortly thereafter, a second Mig, with an unmistakable large red star on its tail came roaring in so low the gunner's mate saw the pilot grin. The deck machine gun blasted hundreds of rounds resulting in the melting of the barrel.

Standing on the bridge, Kowalski shouted to sailors standing nearby, "We're gonna get hit, men. Brace yourselves!" The jet dropped a 250-pound bomb on the aft deck, which skidded across, penetrated the main deck, went into the upper handling room and exploded. The blast shattered the sprinkler system, the after steering, ruptured fuel tanks and detonated ammunition. It was a volatile situation, since the ship had just been rearmed and fueled.

The explosion blew the top of the gun mount skyward like a fire-cracker, descending some- where in the gulf, and the sides of the mount peeled off like a banana skin.

Shortly before, men escaped instant death when a hot round (shell lodged) was declared in one of the aft gun barrels, and twelve men immediately evacuated the mount. Men in Repair Team Three were in the process of attempting to cool down the round by sticking a ten-foot applicator into the problem area.

The explosion and shrapnel opened her hull to the sea. It was a disaster in the mount and surrounding spaces because the blast ignited punctured fuel lines and ammunition, creating a large hole on the left side near the ship's store. Hot shrapnel and flames shot into the handling room as men screamed in agony crying, "Help, help, get us out of here!" Black smoke from burning oil engulfed the entire area.

Kowalski charged out of the bridge on to the weather deck and gasped, "Oh my God, we're hit." He re-entered, grabbed a phone and called a seaman phone talker standing aft. "Sailor, what's the situation back there?"

The kid's voice reverberated with fear. "Sa, sa, sir, it's pretty bad back here. There's wounded guys being removed out of the upper handling room and a huge hole in the ship. Waters pouring in like crazy down

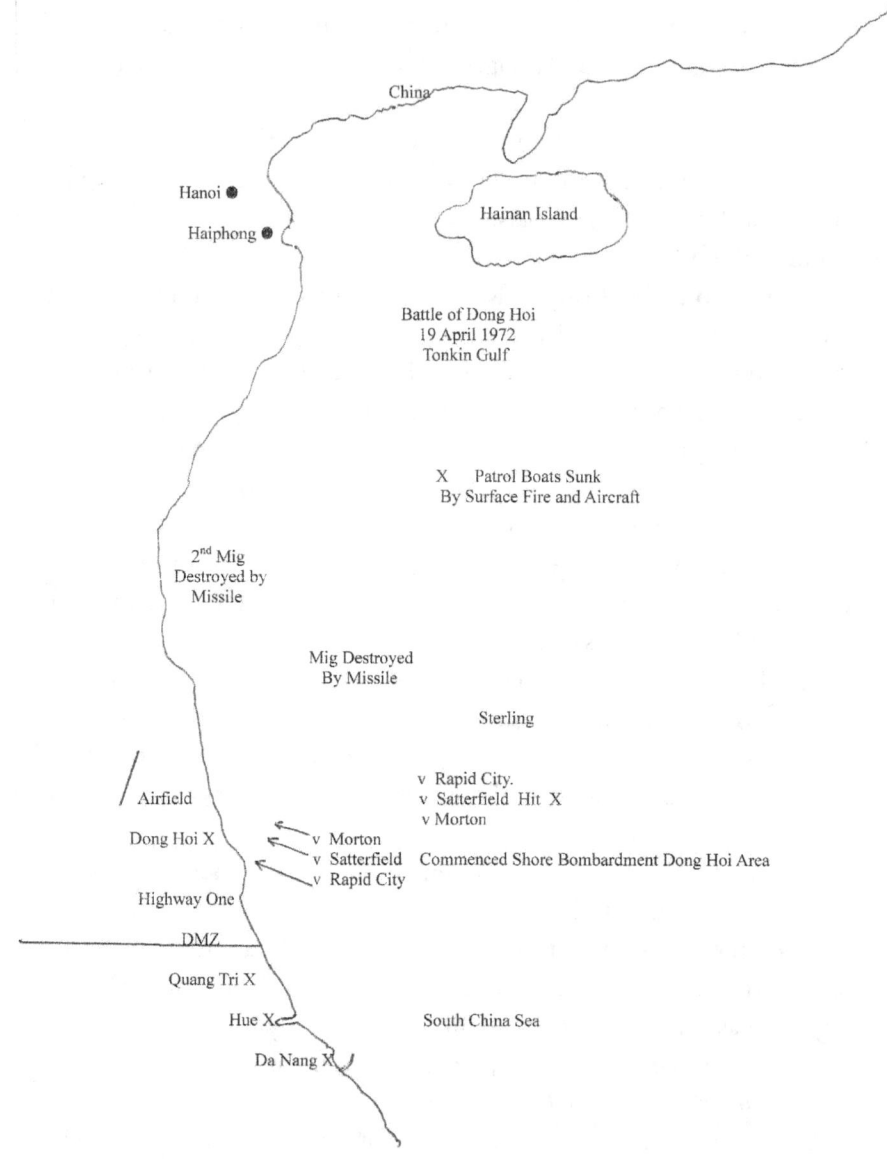

China

Hanoi ●

Haiphong ●

Hainan Island

Battle of Dong Hoi
19 April 1972
Tonkin Gulf

X      Patrol Boats Sunk
By Surface Fire and Aircraft

2$^{nd}$ Mig
Destroyed by
Missile

Mig Destroyed
By Missile

Sterling

v  Rapid City.
v  Satterfield  Hit  X
v  Morton

Airfield

v  Morton

Dong Hoi X

v  Satterfield      Commenced Shore Bombardment Dong Hoi Area
v  Rapid City

Highway One

DMZ

Quang Tri X

Hue X

South China Sea

Da Nang X

**Battle of Dong Hoi**

there, and the gun mount's blown up. There are several holes in the hull. We need help, captain."

The captain took a deep breath and replied, "Ok, sailor, don't panic, we're sending men."

The skipper looked at Thomas. "Call a few divisions and tell em' we need men back aft, right away."

"Yes, sir." Mike called radio, informing Bearden, and other departments.

Meanwhile, *Rapid City* sustained shrapnel damage to her sides after another Mig dropped bombs close by. After unleashing ordnance on the destroyer, one jet attempted escaping back north when *Sterling* launched two surface-to-air terrier missiles at the bandit, but missed with the first.

The plane climbed to full throttle, vainly attemping escape, fleeing west toward a group of mountains when a second missile struck, disintegrating the target. Numerous sailors on four ships clapped and raised their clenched fists, shouting victory cheers.

The second intruder took off, heading for land when the frigate fired another missile. As the jet began climbing over a mountain, the warhead struck. Lookouts viewed jet black smoke and an explosion was heard by several men. Flying overhead, two Air Force F-4 Phantom jets observed the Mig plunging and crashing into the earth while the remaining jet roared over a mountain chain, escaped and landed at an airbase near Dong Hoi.

Later, eyewitnesses standing on cruiser's bridge near a seated Rear Admiral viewing the battle, reported his flippant remark, "This looks like a John Wayne movie." His comment infuriated many sailors aboard the ships.

Kowalski grabbed a phone and called engineering, down in the hold, "Lieutenant, what's the situation there?" The tanned, lanky twenty-five year old hollered, "Sir, we're taking in some water down here. I suggest we stop all engines."

"Very well, mister. I want a situation report every five minutes."

"Yes, sir." Damage controlmen sprang to action.

The skipper ordered, "All stop." She crawled, stopped; then he grabbed a phone on the bridge and called radio. "Loggins, get a flash message to COMSEVENTHFLT, COMCRUDESPAC, Da Nang and Subic. 'Sustained bomb hits, hostile aircraft, extensive damage aft mount, upper handling room and near spaces, *Merton* assisting. Attempting to control hazardous situation, casualties. Will advise accordingly developing situation. Kowalski, C.O.

Loggins scribbled, then ordered, "Get this out now, Mac." Mark quickly sent the flash dispatch on the wireless circuit.

The *Merton* slid alongside. Sailors passed pumps to men standing near the stern. In Da Nang, two auxiliary fleet tugs (ATF's) were dispatched, then they proceeded at flank speed to assist the stricken vessel. A chopper from *Rapid City* hovered above Satterfield's helo deck lowering gallons of fuel necessary to feed the extra pumps.

Bearden walked over, gazing at Jim and Smitty, "I want you two ta stand by outside the hatch in case they need help fighting those fires." They left and leaned against a nearby bulk- head outside the space.

Incensed, Loggins shouted, "What the hell you sending these guys out of here for? Send the new kid. Hickey's our fastest man on teletype and you'll have a neophyte doing his job." He pleaded, "Listen, they've got plenty of guys aft." Badass, standing near a corner, fingered his mustache, stared and grinned.

Loggins thought, "He's trying to get rid of Jimmy. There's no other reason." Badass walked within a few feet of Log as others observed. Log continued. "Listen, they're gonna need more guys back there. I know our guys are at G.Q., but they'll need all the help we can give 'em. That's it."

Seawater rushed into Satterfield as screaming men scurried about escaping. Tom led six others in rescuing the men. Four wounded sailors, including one on a stretcher with third degree burns, were safely carried out of the upper handling space. The severely burned nineteen year old, fresh out of basic training and the others were rushed into sick bay and treated.

Because of the tremendous pressure from the sea, men in repair teams grabbed four-by-four and four-by-six boards to shore up bulkheads in adjoining compartments and pounded wooden pegs into hull openings to prevent increased flooding.

Just after the explosion, Tom ran aft from, but upon reaching midships, was shocked at finding no fire main from there to the aft section. The fire main operating system was significant because it ran through practically the entire ship, providing seawater to flush toilets and was necessary to fight fires. The forward main was operational, but he was unaware of the pressure level and after inquiring, was informed it had about 125 pounds. He shouted to his men, "Let's get to work." It was a two-stage operation since there was stifling heat in the damaged compartment. Fear spread among men that remaining ammunition would explode, destroying the entire ship and killing practically everyone aboard.

Tom took a deep breath and poundered, I've gotta do something and do it quick." He looked at his eight-man team standing nearby and gazed into their fearful eyes, yet his calm demeanor momentarily comforted the sailors. "You guys rig a two-and-a-half jumper hose from mid ship ta aft, port and starboard, while I go and help Kennedy fight fires."

He ran, grabbed a hose, joining the man, and frantically sprayed gallons of water into the hot compartment, attempting to cool it down and flood the spaces. Seawater continued pouring into her. The result was increased weight in *Satterfield* with only one foot of free board from waterline to main deck because of severe damage to the ship's watertight integrity (the ship's ability to resist sinking after sustaining damage), in the stern area. She was sinking and began dying.

The damage control chief quickly called the bridge. "Captain, she's sinking badly. We've only got a foot of free board."

"How are the pumps doing?"

"They're pumping as much as possible, but we need more. The guys are fighting the fires as best they can, sir."

"Ok, thanks, Chief, keep me posted."

"Yes, sir"

Stunned, Kowalski leaned against a bulkhead as the words 'abandon ship, abandon ship' suddenly flashed into his mind. He closed his eyes and thought, "One of my heroes was Medal of Honor winner Commander Earnest Evans, a full blooded Cherokee Indian." Though mortally wounded after Japanese battleship shells demolished his destroyer during the Battle of Leyte in '44, he went down with his ship, the destroyer USS *Johnston* while the last gun was still firing. He murmured, "Damn it, I'm not abandoning her."

He turned, looked into the eyes of a frightened lieutenant and remarked, "She can't take any- more, but we're not giving up. If that ammo goes, we've had it. Those men have gotta save her."

As the compartment blazed, hundreds of gallons of fuel oil gushed. Tom knew he had to get permission from the C.O. to flood the magazine space. The gun was so hot, that he knew if the space wasn't flooded, the ship would blow from there to kingdom come.

His task was getting the fires extinguished, but the only solution was leading a team down into the fiery space. He thought, "God, that's suicide." The possibility that no one would survive flashed into each sailor's minds.

Fire shot up from the mount as he lined up the team on the main deck, each holding a section of a long rigged hose. While holding the nozzle, he jumped on top of the mount's side, pouring water into the upper handling space, trying to flood the room because of the intense blaze.

Tom grabbed ahold of the hydraulic system connected to the magazines and turned the handle, opening the valve to flood the space, but was surprised it was easy. H thought, "Damn it! There's no pressure and no hydraulic system." It had been blown away; consequently, there was no fire-fighting capability. The only alternative for extinguishing the flames was descending into the infernal compartment.

Alden turned and gave an order to a phone talker, "Tell the captain I need permission to flood magazines because the hydraulic system's not operational." Within seconds, Kowalski gave the order to flood that compartment.

Bearden quickly opened the hatch, stuck his head out, and snapped, "Hickey, get your ass back aft and help those guys fighting fires." Jim gazed at Badass. There it was again, the evil smirk he despised.

Suddenly, Loggins ran out, grabbed Bearden's shirt and shoved him against a bulkhead and hollered, "What in the hell are ya doing? Ya know the chances of anyone coming out of there alive are slim to none with all that ammo. I know what you're up ta, jackass." Tim released his grip and backed away.

Temporarily stunned at the aggressive intrusion, Bearden turned, glared and shouted at Jim. "Shove off."

As he departed, Log hollered, "Good luck, Jimmy."

Jim grabbed an O.B.A. hanging nearby and ran aft, scampering down a ladder toward men who were feeding a long hose down into the burning space. Despite Naval regulations prohibiting personnel from keeping a diary, at that moment, Tim decided on recording a secret little journal about Bearden's behavior, and a possible conspiracy.

Tom, wearing an O.B.A. with a young seaman standing a few feet behind him, descended while four others stood on a ladder holding and feeding the hose to them. As they carefully swooped, the seaman panicked crying, "I can't go down there, I'm too scared, I, I, I, don't wanna die."

Tom quickly turned, looked at him and shouted, "Damn it, you're not gonna die. Now get your shit together and your head back on cause we've gotta fight this fire."

The frightened kid pleaded, "I'm sorry, I can't do it."

The focused veteran turned around again, shouting, "Get outta here, heck, I need help."

Tom thought, "I kind of know how he feels because I'd feel the same way and could lose my life down there. Shit, I'm no damn hero and scared too, but we gotta save the ship."

Jim ran aft as the frightened seaman walked and stared at him. Jim stopped, and looked at a man consumed with terror. The kid asked, "Hey, are ya going down there?"

"Yeah."

The sailor continued walking, then stopped, turned and hollered, "You're crazy if ya do."

After arriving, a burly Chief approached. "Ya see that kid? I guess he was just too damn scared. Are you the guy Bearden sent?"

"Yeah"

"From what I gather, you've had some training in fire-fighting, right?"

"Yup, just a little."

"Well, Bearden says you're his best guy. Now, listen. There's another man who volunteered standing right over here. It's dangerous down there and ya don't have to go, understand?"

Jim lowered his head, cupped a fist under his chin and reflected, "Fear's plagued me for years, fear of my father, fear of Bearden and fear of failure. It's taken hold and wrapped its tentacles around me far too long. Damn, I've had it. I'll face it or die trying."

He took a deep breath. "Chief, that guy down there needs help. I'm your man."

"Ok, put the O.B.A. on and get down there behind the lead guy. If he goes down, you're it."

Jim thought, "Badass must have called after I left and lied about me being his best. He wants me dead, but I'm goin' down fighting, if it's the last thing I do."

The oxygen-breathing apparatus was a three-foot long, harness canvas unit with a small oxygen canister in the middle, a mask, and two attached air tubes to facilitate breathing, common in firefighting. It was mandatory the seal canisters be tightly secured.

Upon securing the unit, he walked down the ladder, grabbed the hose, taking position six feet behind Tom. They slowly descended, reaching the deck, unaware of the others identities.

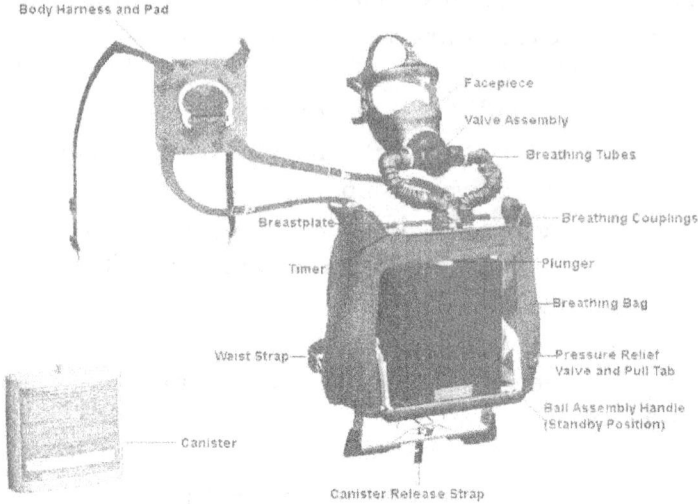

**Oxygen Breathing Apparatus (OBA) Type A-4**

The space was black as a deep cave. Fire shot toward them from burning surface oil. Tom turned on the nozzle, began spraying and thought, "Man, it's so damn dark I can't see my hand in front of my face." Twisted steel and sharp jagged metal gave evidence of horrific destruction as flames scorched the destroyed space.

Like a swift stream, the sea continued rushing into a four-foot wide hole, pushing his 180-pound frame back and forth like a bobbing channel buoy. The only visible objects were numerous red flames burning above oil, skipping and hopping like locusts, from one area to another.

After the ATF's arrived, lines were thrown on their sterns and secured. The little vessels began towing her, when shortly after 1900, *Sterling's* radar tracked three fast-moving surface objects nine miles away, racing toward the stricken ship. P. T. Boats! The Soviet-built eighty-four foot Komar class craft had forty-knot plus speeds, carried rapid firing guns, missiles and torpedoes.

The TBS system rang and the captain quickly grabbed the receiver and listened. "*Satterfield*, this is *Sterling*. Three hostile craft approaching northwest. Speed forty knots. We are attacking, out."

Kowalski peered through binoculars at the craft, shook his head, and looked at the O.O.D. "Those damn bastards know they got us, and now they're trying to finish us off. I hope those guys on Sterling are good shots."

Now the frigate, steaming two thousand yards from the stricken ship's starboard, locked the targets into her fire control system, and fired several rounds in rapid succession from the 5"54 stern gun destroying two of the boats. As their companions sank, the remaining boat quickly turned 180 degrees, retreating toward land, when an F-4 Phantom jet, cruising at 5,000 feet, swept down like a vengeful eagle and fired several bursts of 20 millimeter rounds, detonating on board ammunition. The boat exploded into fireballs, shooting thousands of pieces of flesh and metal skyward. Two groups of sailors standing on Satterfield's main deck clapped and cheered.

A few feet from Kowalski, a lieutenant exclaimed, "Take that, you Commie bastards. Yeah, that's what I'm talking about. Great shooting."

Lee wiped sweat from his forehead. "Thank God they got em', but the men have gotta save her."

Back aft, Lt. Frank Chapell, a tall damage control officer wearing glasses, was satisfied after inspecting hastily shored up adjoining frames near a passageway. He phoned a chief who was standing under the drone flight deck observing the fire-fighting team. "Chief, what's the situation down there?"

The excited veteran shouted, "Sir, fire's still out of control. Two men are fighting, but theres' a lot of live ammo and I believe they're stepping all over it. Shit, they could detonate any minute."

"Thanks, I'll inform the skipper."

Chapell wiped sweat off his forehead and quickly dialed the bridge. Lee grabbed a phone. "This is the captain. What's the status back there?"

The officer, breathing heavily, shouted, "Skipper, it's Frank. We've completed temporary repairs, stabilizing three frames, but there's live ammunition moving around in the damaged upper handling space. The chief says the blazes are still out of control and two men are down there fighting it."

The skipper's jaw dropped. He paused, and thought, trying to contain himself. "I understand, Frank. Keep me informed if anything changes."

"Will do, sir"

Pursell, standing nearby, at his worried expression and inquired, "Do you think we've got a chance of making it, Lee?"

He looked at the X.O. "There's live ammo back there, but we have a good crew, and I'm sure those men are doing everything they can. The pumps are working. There's hope."

As four enlisted stood nearby listening, he moved within a foot of Pursell. "Chad, if you're not a praying man, I suggest you start now, because we're sinking, and this old girl could blow any minute." The X. O.'s eyes widened. He quickly blinked, backing away as fear enveloped those around him. Both hands of a 19 year old Seaman nervously shook as Pursell at nearby men. Kowalski turned, walked a few paces, lowered his head and murmured a prayer.

Meanwhile, as they fought blazes, Tom stepped on large, cylindrical foreign objects, almost losing his balance. He thought, "What's that?" Unstable live shells sluggishly rolled on the deck beneath the surface, but the men were unaware the fuses were broken off. A chill ran up Jim's spine.

He thought, "It's an inferno down here. God, if these things go off, we'll be dead men, and they'd never find a piece of either of us."

They felt the rapid beating of their hearts. Alden swayed the nozzle side to side while waves of bright flames flashed all around. Tom reflected, "This is the closest to hell I've ever been." He prayed, "God, please help me do my job and save our ship."

Four P250 pumps pushed water out of the vessel at 250 gallons per minute as hatches were opened, ventilating the damaged compartment, yet she continued sinking. As tugs sluggishly pulled the stricken vessel toward Da Nang, the bow rose as saltwater rushed in, creating an irreversible condition in the stern.

As Jim stood, grasping the hose behind him, a dreadful thought entered Tom's mind while spraying on burning oil. He thought, "If oil is introduced into the O.B.A. canister on my chest, I'll blow into a thousand pieces and I'll never see Janet and Shannon again." Within an hour, seawater rose against their chests, yet both spread legs, maintaining balance while tenaciously extinguishing fires.

Numerous drops of sweat poured down their faces as they grimaced, fighting blazes. There is something within the spirit of warriors in combat that cries from the heart and soul. Never surrender.

Tom pondered, and remembered reading poignant words given by a dying U.S. officer long ago. "Don't give up the ship" were Lieutenant James Lawrence's last command to his men in 1813 aboard the USS

Chesepeake during a battle with British ships in the War of 1812. For over 200 years American Navy men have indelibly marked this motto into their souls Jim stepped on a large shell just as seawater struck his chest, thrusting him sideways, causing the nozzle to spray upward, off target. Tom quickly turned around, eyeing him as he regained his balance.

Dreadful thoughts quickly entered Tom's mind. "If we sink, it would be a horrible feeling for us to drown. Our last actions on earth would be futile in preventing seawater from rushing into our lungs after coughing up burning ship oil. It would be traumic watching our ship plunge into the sea and die, and then having our unfortunate souls descend into the abyss."

Jim uttered, "*Holy Mary, mother of God, pray for us sinners now, and at the hour of our death. Amen.*"

After two hours, their muscles ached from grasping the high pressure hose as hundreds of gallons gushed. Oil mixed with saltwater repeatedly struck their bodies as they struggled maintaining composure and balance.

They fought the blazes five hours, and then Alden noticed they started containing fires in a quarter of the space. He reflected, "I won't let my shipmates down. I have to save the ship." The water started receding as the remaining fires were extinguished. Tom thought, "Man, I feel like a cowboy now. We got this thing beat."

The men had to exit safely, but the only avenue was the hose, which functioned as a lifeline.

As numerous five-inch rounds covered in oil rolled, they turned, clutched the hose, and began moving slowly away in darkness toward the ladder as four men standing on the steps, pulled them up on to the deck to safety.

Tom looked into the opened magazine space seeing the space hatch had sprung with the bulkhead and frame gone. The frame was flooded with oil and unstable ammunition. A Chief, standing on deck, gazed down, ran into a secure space and called the bridge.

"Captain, the fire's out."

"Thank God."

"Sir, we got a lot of unstable ammo back there and need an ordnance guy to assess the situation. Skipper, these shells could go off any minute."

"Very well, chief, I'll send someone right away. Keep me informed."

"Aye, aye, sir."

A short muscular E.O.D. (explosive ordnance disposal) specialist ran back, looked, cupped his jaw in his hand, thought, and then turned addressing the chief. "Tell the men to grab mattresses and put 'em on the deck here. Set up a chain gang and carry up the shells. They're gonna have to handle each one like a newborn baby, chief. They've gotta be jettisoned over the side including boxes of thirty and fifty caliber ammo and grenades."

After the two emerged topside and took off the masks, they were stunned looking in disbelief at each other. Jim exclaimed, "Oh, my God! I had no idea it was you, Tom.

Alden wiped sweat off his brow, smiled and threw an arm around him as a dozen men back slapped and shook their hands. "Jimmy, I'm just as surprised as you, pal. Man, ya hung in there with me good. Thanks for volunteering."

"Well, Badass volunteered me, figuring he'd get rid of me, but I would've helped ya any time."

Tom smiled, "I know ya would, because we're close buddies, right?" He nodded, and grinned.

The chief walked up, placed blankets over both, and smiled, "You guys did a hell of a job down there and saved the ship. I think you need showers now."

Tom grinned, "Yup, good idea. See ya later, Jim." Alden turned and asked the E.O.D. man. "Do ya have any idea why the ammo didn't ignite down there?"

"I think all the oil in that space had a negative effect on the fuses and mechanisms."

"Well, thank God."

Walking back toward radio, Jim thought, "Before showering, I wanna see Bearden's expression."

He entered radio, glancing behind the desk as water and oil seeped from his dungarees. A few feet away, Bearden's eyes bulged, staring in disbelief, the expression reminiscent of the eyes of a deer seconds before being struck by a Mac Truck. McDonald, Reemer and Smith's jaws dropped in astonishment.

Sid quickly rose and shook his hand as others patted his back. Smitty chirped, "Jim, we got scattered reports of what was happening and thought for sure you'd be a dead man."

Jim glared at Bearden. "Surprised eh? Sorry to disappoint ya Badass, but I'm back." He turned, and smiled looking at the others and exclaimed, "Too bad ya gotta put up with me again, guys."

The three struck up singing *For He's A Jolly Good Fellow,* bringing a wide smile across his face. He left, took a shower and tried sleeping, but intermittent explosions prevented rest.

In the evening, sailors carefully removed ordnance, placing them on mattresses near lifelines. The shells were heaved over the side, but every fourth or fifth round detonated beneath the surface like depth charges, shaking the destroyer's already-damaged hull.

The ordnance man observing, remarked to the chief, "This old girl's frightened, but she's tough and still seaworthy. I hope we make Da Nang in one piece."

"Ya can say that again."

At 2300, *Satterfield* entered Da Nang Harbor, tying up at Tien Sha Landing next to a repair ship at the Naval Support Activity Base. Kowalski walked outside approaching the Chief Master at Arms. "Chief, I know everyone's tired, but the enemy knows they've badly damaged her and wanna make damn sure they sink us. I want six men posted outside in case of enemy swimmers."

"Yes, sir." Deck sentries armed with machine guns and grenades were sent out on the weather decks.

The U.S. Navy was cognizant of the situation and there was concern that enemy frog men might desire to blow her up, consequently, a safety net was initiated. Daytime sentries were posted on deck, scanning the surface for bubbles, indicating suspicious underwater activity.

The following late afternoon before dusk, she was towed from the harbor into the sea toward the horizon, out of harm's way. Throughout the evening, as a precaution against the eventuality of enemy swimmers, a few crew members threw percussion grenades (designed to detonate-beneath the surface) over the side. Fortunately, there were no incidents.

A few days later, after temporary repairs, the still-leaking vessel slowly steamed east into Subic Bay for total repair and overhaul. As she neared the shipyard, Kowalski, standing on the bridge, noticed a floating dry dock wasn't ready. A large ship had blocked her approach.

Infuriated, he grabbed a bull horn, ran out on the quarterdeck, shouting at officers and supervisors standing on a dock, "Damn it, get that ship out of our way, we're sinking and need your help." Shipyard officers quickly made arrangements for the floating dock. The vessel was moved and the stricken warrior slid safely inside.

During this period there were few reports of the Battle of Dong Hoi because of heavy coverage of the Apollo 16 Lunar Landing. The Navy provided scant publicity.

The successful bombing airstrike by an enemy jet plane on a U. S. ship was unprecedented in Naval history. Like four years prior, when North Korea seized the spy ship USS *Pueblo*, top naval brass were embarrassed. The *Satterfield* Incident was recorded among the hundreds of engagements against enemy forces, yet the Navy attempted stifling information.

Shortly thereafter, Kowalski, cognizant of the high brass decision, stood on the pier, observing repairs. He lit a Kool, turned around and slowly walked away, joined by engineering officer Chapell. Lee stopped, took a drag, and stared at his wounded ship. "Ya know something? We fought our guts out there a couple weeks ago. I received a Well Done message from the Admiral, but saw only A. P., UPI and *Stars And Stripes* carried reports. Hell, this should have been front-page news." He gazed toward the bay. "My men deserve better."

"I concur, skipper."

The following day, Kowalski sent COMSEVENTHFLT a message requesting Alden and Hickey be awarded Silver and Bronze Stars respectively.

For three months the old girl underwent repairs performed by several Filipino civilian contractors and ship's crew. A crane removed what remained of the two stern gun barrels and mount. A large square steel slab was welded on top of the opened and destroyed mount while extensive repairs were completed on the hull and damaged areas. Because the vessel was immobile in dry dock, the crew slept in barracks on the base.

The long hours of tedious work in extreme heat took a toll on Tom. In July he flew home for two weeks leave, seeing his father in Pennsylvania. Jim traveled by bus to Manila.

As Jim walked in Luneta Park on a bright day, his eyes swelled with joy as Linda ran toward him with arms extended, her black hair flapping in the summer breeze. They embraced and kissed as tears streamed down her cheeks, "Oh, my Jeem, it been so long. I thought something happen you. I missed you so much." He wiped her brown cheeks, planting a long tender kiss on her lips.

"God, I looked forward to this day, sweetheart." They sat on a wooden bench beneath palm trees overlooking the bay as commercial ships rested in the near distance. He spoke about the battle and his role in helping Tom fight the fires. Her eyes gleamed as she nuzzled aside him.

"I pray for you ebery day, my Jeem."

"Yeah, I'm glad, because it sure helped out there, honey. Listen, we're gonna have liberty in Hong Kong soon. It'd be great if ya could make it. I know ya got relatives there. I'll pay for a one-way flight if ya can afford return fare."

She smiled, "Let me tink and see. I let you know, my dear." After walking a couple miles in Manila and dining, they hugged tightly. He looked into her sentimental, kind eyes.

"Are ya going back up ta Subic soon?"

"I tink sometime July. I write and let you know. Goodbye, Jeem. I love you." She rose, smiled, turned and departed. He watched her gait as her body swayed beneath a bright yellow short skirt; then she was lost amid the throng of Filipinos.

Throughout summer, several battles raged as Allied forces inevitably pushed the NVA back into the northern provinces, Laos and Cambodia. It was another three months of fighting before the military situation was stabilized. The Communists suffered 100,000 casualties, including 40,000 killed largely due to Naval, artillery and airpower while tenacious, crack ARVN forces, and American advisors successfully counterattacked.

# 15

## "HONG KONG"

Aware and pleased with the crews' hard work and determination readying the ship for sea, Kowalski rewarded his sailors with liberty in Hong Kong. After completing repairs, the ship weighed anchor and steamed out of Subic Bay, destination northeast. Shortly before departing, Jim called Linda, informing her that he would phone her after the ship arrived.

The first day at sea on a bright cloudless August afternoon, Leland addressed the crew over the 1MC.

> This is the captain speaking. I'm aware of all the hard work you have endured during these last few months. Our ship is now fully repaired thanks to your efforts. I wanted to tell you from the bottom of my heart how proud I am of your devotion to duty before, during and after the devastating attack on our ship. Because of your dedication, they couldn't sink us. I will never forget your attitude and unselfish actions as sailors of the U. S. Navy. I am honored and proud to be your captain and lead you. We're going up to Hong Kong for a few days. Be good and enjoy your visit. You've certainly earned it. That is all.

His speech sent a positive shot throughout the crew as morale soared. A day and a half later, she entered Victoria Harbor and Hong Kong. Like Gibraltar and Singapore, Hong Kong Island, Kowloon and the surrounding territories were a British Crown Colony inhabited by four and a half million people, mostly Chinese. The sixteen-square mile harbor is flanked by numerous skyscrapers and high-rises on the island across from Kowloon on the mainland. Large three- decked 300-foot boats shuttled thousands of passengers and cars daily between the two land masses. Twenty miles inland lay the New Territories and the Communist Chinese border. British soldiers were quartered, performing border guard duties facing the Reds.

A tongue of land jutted into the harbor from Kowloon. Near the tip was the renowned Peninsula Hotel, a favorite respite for affluent tourists, nobility and politicians from various countries. Rising behind tall buildings on the island was imposing Victoria Peak where cable cars hauled visitors 1,800 feet to the summit.

She dropped anchor in the harbor 300 yards from a large merchant vessel on a sunny morning. Numerous immobile ships from around the world scattered about, while little wooden canvas covered boats chugged between, selling everything from souvenirs to produce and clothing.

Jim showered, put on tropical whites, and ran up joining Smitty, Mike and Sid gazing down at a tiny craft motoring nearby. Jim scanned in awe the majestic topography and massive cities a mile away. One little boat filled with six kids and their parents moved alongside, bobbing up and down, while the Yanks leaned on lifelines and waved at the family below. When word spread that an American ship had entered or anchored, floating stores rushed from shore, surrounding vessels like bees around a honeycomb hoping for quick cash.

The kid's father stood on the bow, holding a white, short-sleeve shirt sprinkled with little palm trees wrapped in see-through plastic. He looked up, smiled and hollered, "Hey Joe, hey Joe, you like shirt? Only tirty Hong Kong dolla. Here, you ty."

Despite a ten-knot breeze, he reared back, tossing it toward the ship. Mike leaned, extended an arm, and grabbed it. After unwrapping, he placed it against his chest. "Looks good on ya," Smitty said.

Thomas smiled, "Yeah, I like it, but we haven't been ashore yet exchanging bucks for their currency. Heck, he's only asking five bucks. It's a hell of a deal." He started reaching for a five spot when a stocky Chief petty officer walked over.

"Hey, sailor, you can't do that here." Sailors were prohibited from using American greenbacks until they went ashore. "The old man will probably get pissed off. Why don't ya just throw the shirt back?"

As the little craft bobbed, Mike looked down at the destitute family in ragged clothes, sitting and eating rice out of bowls. He stared at the chief, "Listen, no officer's around, and I feel for 'em. Hell, they're just trying to make a living, chief. It's not like I'm committing a crime, is it?"

The Chief gazed at the poor family, looked back at the bridge and addressed Mike, "Well, I guess not. Go ahead." Thomas reached into a jumper pocket, grabbed a five-dollar bill, rolled and then tossed, but the wind caught it, carrying the money ten yards from the craft. The father turned, shouting a command. A skinny eight-year old boy wearing shorts quickly jumped into the oil-spotted green water, swam and retrieved the currency. After climbing back aboard, the sailors smiled and applauded the kid's brave efforts.

The Chief stared at Mike and the others. "Listen, don't say a damn thing to anyone about this, all right?" They nodded.

Mike looked at his buddies, "Ya know something, guys, I'll bet there's some big shot rich guy ashore who owns lots of these floating markets and probably keeps the lion's share of profits, but these people gotta eat too. I'm glad I did it and just had a thought. I'm the first one who got a souvenir." Everyone smiled, and Thomas went below, storing his new shirt.

The four walked down an aluminum ladder into a bobbing water taxi. The fifty-foot wooden craft motored to downtown Hong Kong, where they exchanged money at the China Seaman's Club. After a hearty lunch, they ventured across from the Hilton, stood on a curb gazing at lorries (double decked busses) speeding past.

Leery of oncoming traffic, Jim left, but unthinking, began stepping across the two lane highway when suddenly Mike grabbed his shoulders, pulling him back, second before cars flashed from the opposite direction a few feet from the sailors.

Hickey shouted, "Wow, thanks, buddy, that was close. Ya probably saved my life."

Mike said, "Hey, Jimmy, you were looking the wrong way. Ya didn't know it, but they drive on the left side, like in England."

Momentarily stunned, he replied,"You're right. I'm use ta looking the other way. Heck, in Manila they drive on the right side like stateside."

They enjoyed a few beers at the Chicago Club, The Dragon Lounge and Suzie Wong Bar. Each establishment had a little Chinese man standing in front, hawking in broken English. "Ah, hi, sayla mon. You likee petty gil? You likee coo beer?"

After a couple hours, Sid suggested, "Let's take in a flick and fire down a few more." Smitty looked chagrined.

"What's up?" Jim asked him.

"I hate disappointing ya guys, but I think I'll take a ferry over ta Kowloon and walk around sight-seeing. Jim, ya wanna come along?"

"Sure. Hey you two, remember ta stay away from out-of-bounds areas. I don't wanna hear about ya getting rolled or knifed. See ya back aboard."

Jim and Ron jumped into a cab which sped to the Star passenger car ferry. Crowded with locals, and a few British, the boat slowly motored across the harbor, and finally discharged autos and passengers.

They strolled about on a bright afternoon, weaving through narrow two lane streets until Ron saw a men's clothing shop. "Hey, Jim let's see what they've got."

Nahraja's was a small rectangular gentleman's clothier flanked by numerous shops. Two middle-aged skinny Indian men wearing tropical shirts stood in the rear chatting. Alone, the sailors scanned various business suits that were displayed high on a wall above racks of trousers, shirts and ties.

As Smitty browsed, a little ten-year old Chinese boy excitedly ran near Jim. "Hey, Joe you sit, you sit." He chuckled at his enthusiasm and sat. Assuming an immediate sale from the American, one proprietor smiled and approached with a measuring tape, stretching it across the sailor's back. Jim grinned and thought, "They must think I'm loaded."

The boy retrieved a cold bottle of beer, handed it to the sailor, grabbed a towel and quickly fanned him as if he were royalty. He took a swig, and smiled. "You like, you like, saila mon?

Now, you stand, you stand." He rose, and then the owner measured a pant length, looked and smiled.

"Suit reo cheap, G. I., custom made. You get po ony 360 Hong Kong dolla, (60 bucks) ok?"

Smitty walked over chuckling, "What in the hell would ya do with a suit anyway? Besides, ya can't afford it buddy."

Jim sat down, looked and pointed, "Hey, all I want is that short sleeve, blue, silk shirt hanging over there." The man's friendly expression quickly changed to disappointment. He lowered his head while biting his lip.

"How much is it?" Jim asked.

"Sixty Hong Kong dolla, G.I.," he sternly announced.

"Good, I'll take it." The boy grabbed and placed it in a plastic bag as Jim paid.

Smitty leaned and whispered, "I get the impression they're tryin' ta hustle us. Let's go."

"That sounds good to me. Let's check out that big hotel over there." The taxi dropped them in front of the renowned Peninsula Hotel.

Opened in 1928, it was the oldest hotel in Hong Kong and faced the harbor, a few blocks away. The gray brick structure had two-seven story attached wings flanking a wide court-yard entrance with a small continuously gushing fountain in front.

The G. I.'s entered the lobby and marveled at an array of exotic plants, flowers in large vases hanging on huge pillars on each side of a long stairway leading to rooms. Forty feet from a long check-in counter, a row of beige square twin stanchions with brown circular designs flanked a lengthy dining area. White-vested waiters scurried about serving delicacies. Guests in immaculate suits and dresses impatiently waited near two elevators. They gazed in awe at the epitome of luxury.

Jim suggested, "It's their tea time. Let's sit and try some." Dining tourists and locals socializing at the Americans. A slender young Chinese lady smiled and approached as both viewed large menus. Jim looked up and raised two fingers. "Tea, please."

Shortly after returning with three-inch high oval cups of dark English tea, she stared at Smitty stirring his drink. Her English was good. "Are you with American Navy?" She'd never seen a Black U. S. sailor.

Smitty, sitting three feet from Jim, , winked at him and gazed up. "Oh no, I'm in the African navy." Jim lightly chuckled. Her eyebrows quickly rose, as a puzzled expression came over her. She shook her head and retreated.

He placed an arm around Smitty's shoulders and smiled. "Smart ass, that was great. Ya crack me up." Initially, the English drink was strong, surprising them. Both added extra cream and decided to observe tourists.

Numerous guests entered, walking about clad in expensive attire. Jim looked and exclaimed, "Hey, check this out." Their eyes focused on a middle-aged Indian. The dark skinned man wore a gold headdress as he led his attractive slender wife toward the check-in counter.

Several clients focused on a large diamond on her middle forehead as her eyes from side to side. She was immaculately dressed in a gold silk gown, trailing on the floor as three servants lugging suitcases followed her. The couple's arrogant, snobbish demeanor and upturned long noses conveyed royalty.

Later, two elderly Russians entered. The gentleman was clad in a dark blue suit below a large cossack hat resting on his head, but his wife drew everyone's attention. She wore heavy makeup, six-inch long, snake-shaped, silver earrings flanking blond hair, extending just above the waist. Her low cut, long, flowing white dress sparkled like the dresses of movie stars in old Hollywood films, yet her face was out of the ordinary with a pointed nose below light blue eyes. Both sailors turned, looking at each other.

Jim remarked, "I've never seen someone this white before, Smitty."

"Yeah, me neither. I wonder if she's an albino."

After an hour Jim suggested, "Listen, let's shove off. I wanna see how the other half lives. It's probably out of bounds, but there are two of us. We should be ok. How about it?"

"Yeah, sounds good, I like adventure."

Shortly after debarking off the ferry, they took a cab and motored through downtown, past thousands of wooden boats occupied by families adjacent to several piers. Near the outskirts, they entered a narrow street barely accommodating two small vehicles side by side. It was flanked by six-and eight-storied brown tenement apartments where thousands of laundry hanging from windows, flapped in the hot breeze.

Numerous Chinese leaned out of cramped high rises, gazing down at a throng of shoppers as the men snaked past mom-and-pop produce stands. Locals gibber jabbered, staring at the young foreigners.

Jim stopped and remarked, "Smitty, I think we're the only G. I.'s within miles." Ron quickly pinched his nose.

"Pee you."

"Hey, what's wrong?"

"What in the world's that smell?"

"Yeah, was wondering that, myself."

They walked a hundred yards, seeing a row of a dozen small, open-air wooden stores. Several locals pointed at fish and reptiles hanging from roofs above the counters as proprietors quickly received money, and wrapped the products in newspapers.

The steamy air blew the putrid smell, enveloping the area. Swarms of flies buzzed on a variety of seafood including squid, octopus and shark. The men stopped and gazed at several six-foot long skinned snakes, slimy eels and large frogs. Little skinned dogs and cats with exposed genitals dangled and swayed in the breeze.

The Orientals didn't mind. It was another routine market trip. Almost on cue, both held their noses while people quickly and laughed. "Man, I wouldn't eat that stuff if ya gave me a thousand bucks," remarked Jim.

He chuckled, "Yeah, even if ya did, you probably wouldn't be alive to collect because your stomach would be destroyed. Their systems are a lot different from ours, pal."

Passers-by, clad in ragged trousers and shorts, waved, gawked and smiled at the visitors. Jim thought, "The Asians are a friendly and strange race, but human nature's the same all over.

Their only goal is daily survival."

They continued walking, gazing up at little children peeking out of windows at rickshaws scurrying about carrying passengers. Several adults with tots merely sat against buildings, their arms extended, begging for food as warm air circulated the stench of human waste. The sailors reached into their pockets, retrieving a few H. K. dollars, handing it to a little old woman who smiled and bowed, giving thanks.

Others, hiding under cardboard boxes, peeked at the G.I.'s strolling by. The sailors had never been exposed to such destitution. The brief sojourn was a poignant contrast to the affluence they'd viewed earlier.

After a half mile, they turned a corner. Night would arrive in two hours. Smitty stopped, leaned against a building, lit a cigarette and looked at his buddy. "Man, I thought I saw poverty in St. Louis, but shit, this takes the cake. I've never seen anything like this."

Jim took a deep breath, "Wow, you can say that again. Some of these people don't live; they only exist. Ya know, seeing this really makes ya appreciate what we've got back home."

He took a long drag and exhaled smoke through his nose, "Right on, man, right on. I couldn't have said it any better. It's getting late, let's head back."

A skeleton crew were on duty the next day, including Jim, Smitty and Log. Amazingly, Tim was quiescent, the antithesis of the man they'd known over a year. "Something's wrong with him," Jim thought. Tim sat reading a letter from his parents and a back home farm report. His pensive behavior was out of character, alarming them.

After logging incoming messages, Jim took a break and approached him. "Excuse me, Log, but are you all right? You look worn out." He stopped, slowly put the paper down and looked upward. His slow enunciation of words in a mellow tone were indicative of a troubled man, attempting to relax and gather his thoughts.

"I'm fine, Jimmy. I stayed aboard yesterday doing a little detective work. Ya probably didn't know it, but I filed for divorce with legal in Subic. My folks are now beneficiaries of my life insurance." Smitty listened.

"That's good. What do ya mean detective work?"

"I went into engineering and spoke with a senior petty officer, a guy I've known for a while and asked who had duty there after we first tied up at Subic in January. I mentioned my suspicions about Gates, Bearden and their possible role in setting you up."

"I see. What did he say?"

"Well, while we were in the P. I., he overheard two young seamen boasting about the quickest twenty bucks they ever made from a First Class Radioman for agreeing with some kind of a ruse on a guy from radio. It was you Jim."

He took a step back, and frowned "I don't understand, nobody played a joke on me. What's he talking about anyway?"

Tim lit a cigar, put both legs on top of the desk, and stared, "I don't understand, but I got a sneaking suspicion there was a conspiracy with Badass behind it. I've got an idea about what happened and am putting the pieces together because I'm going to uncover it. He gave me a couple names and after we put to sea, I'm gonna confront both and find out what transpired."

Jim nodded, "Yeah, I'd sure like to know. I'll tell ya, Log, the way you were quiet, ya had us worried."

Loggins smiled. "Did ya guys enjoy liberty yesterday?"

Smitty grinned, "Yeah, sure did."

Loggins closed his eyes thinking and quickly blurted, "Don't worry about me. Ol' dad's like a rock here, and I'll take care of you guys. I've got a lot on my plate with all the bullshit we've been through with that asshole ordering ya back ta that hell hole, and my soon to be ex-wife and everything." They were relieved, but concerned.

Jim sat, thought, and looked over at Log. "With all due respect, why did ya wait this long checking this out?"

Log closed his eyes, puffed on tobacco, turned and responded, "I'm sorry. I shouldn't have and damn it, I'll make it up to ya, Jimmy. What's been eating me were problems with my wife; then tolerating Bearden's behavior and his relations with you guys, all the combat and my health condition. Ya know, there's no love lost between Badass and me. Shit, I spoke with the lieutenant about my concerns and Bearden's treatment of some of you guy, but get frustrated because he supports that jerk. I hope ya both understand."

They thought in silence for a minute; then Jim responded, "Thanks, Log. Now we know. We'll keep our eyes on the ferret. Let me know if ya find anything else out."

Tim replied, "Right."

A messenger scampered down the ladder at 0900 the next morning, waking him. "We got a message from some girl name Linda asking you to meet her at one o'clock at the Star Ferry pier."

He rubbed his eyes, gazing up, "Ah, thanks pal." He thought, "My God, she made it."

Jim caught Tom shaving in the head, "Hey, that babe I was tellin' ya bout is here. I'm gonna see her this afternoon. Why don't ya meet us at the Star Ferry around seven-thirty, and we'll go up to Victoria Peak. I think it'll be a great adventure."

Alden finished, looked into a mirror and grinned, "Yeah, sounds good. See ya later, Jimmy."

He jumped aboard a bobbing water taxi with others motoring to the island on a cloudless, warm day. He then took a cab exiting at Star Ferry pier, and awaited her arrival. After fifteen minutes, he saw the boat approaching across the harbor and docking downtown. Hundreds of passengers debarked along with several autos, as he stood on the pier. "Where is she?" he thought.

A few stragglers exited. Dejected, he began trekking back toward one of the main streets when a sweet voice pierced the air. "Jeem, Jeem, I'm here, I'm here." He turned around seeing her slowly approaching, wearing a light blue skirt just a few inches above the knees. Her contagious smile was captivating, sending a chill up his spine. He ran, threw his arms around her, picked her up and they kissed. Several onlookers laughed in amusement.

After putting her down, they clasped hands and walked. He gazed at her. "Oh, this is so nice having you with me. Man, I never thought you'd make it. When I got your message, I was stunned. How long ya staying?"

She grinned, "I stay one week at auntie's apartment in Kowloon."

He looked at her. "That's good. Listen, honey, we've only got today being with each other.

Let's make the most of it. I've got duty tomorrow, and we're leaving the next day. A buddy of mine is meeting us tonight and we're taking the cable car up that mountain. Sound good?" She smiled.

They reached the street as she scanned, then she pointed above skyscrapers toward the imposing peak. "You mean we go all way up?"

He grinned, "Yup, all the way, baby doll, and it should be fun. Let's get something to eat."

She was familiar with the area, occasionally visiting relatives. After dining, they arrived in Kowloon. "I take you meet uncle, auntie and cousins."

"Sure, I'll follow you."

The small yellow cab sped past busy Kai Tek Airport, where the main runway greets the harbor; it then turned into a myriad of six-and-eight story apartment buildings in close proximity to each other. She entered a building, scampering six flights of stairs with him behind. She stopped and looked back. "What's your hurry?"

"I excited for dem meet you. We have little time, you know."

A tiny bathroom was located near the entrance and a small lamp on an end table provided dim light in the large one room dwelling. Four mattresses lay on a tiled floor a few feet from a small couch. A twelve-inch wide black and white television sat on a wooden table in a forteen square foot kitchen. Six bowls of uneaten rice and pork lay on a small table.

Hot air blew through two large open windows a few feet above the sleeping area. A long paved street separated the olive block-long building from its twin across. Numerous laundry dangled from clothes lines strung over the street. He thought, "My God! This is all they've got." He was in their world now.

Six pairs of eyes looked, surprised at the uniformed American. Her uncle, Mr. Chu smiled extending his right hand as he reciprocated. The middle-aged slender man was just under five two with salt and pepper hair above baggy eyes and stress lines on his light yellow face. The four children, aged five to ten clad in shorts, and wearing rubber sandals huddled near her aunt, a petite lady. None spoke English.

She quickly assumed the role of interpreter, speaking Mandarin while standing and pointing at Jim. Jim asked, "Where does he work?"

Linda wiped sweat from her forehead. "He cook at Chinese restaurant. Not fa."

Adults asked a few questions about his background and ship. He was comfortable answering inquiries. She listened as the uncle desired to know if he was a hero or warrior.

"Oh no, just a sailor doing my duty."

Linda turned toward him and remarked, "My auntie say she no like Communists. They take feedom, and kill many people in China. Mao, bad man."

He looked at the aunt and responded, "That's why Americans are helping Vietnamese."

Her little eight-year old cousin picked up a bowl of rice, smiled and placed it in his hands. He took a few bites, put a hand on his stomach and shook his head. Linda grinned, addressing the family in Chinese. "We eat not long ago. I think he full."

After an hour, he thanked them for the brief hospitality. She hugged the relatives, and they departed. While promenading down a stree,t he stopped, lit a cigarette and gazed up at the tenements.

"Ya know something, honey? Your relatives don't have much, but they're really nice people and happy cause they've got each other and that's important. Things don't make ya happy. It's the family that matters most because that's how God planned it." She moved closer, gazed into his eyes and squeezed his hand.

As he took a drag, his eyes moistened. Innately, he felt sorry for their condition as opposed to the materialistic, arrogant and rich people he earlier witnessed. She pressed herself near him. He looked into her eyes and wiped a little tear flowing down her brown cheek. "You good man, Jeem. I can tell you have nice family in States." She moved within inches of his face. Her expression changed to intimacy. "*Wo ai ni.*"

Puzzled, he asked, "What's that mean?"

"It mean 'I love you in Mandarin.'"

He smiled, "I like it. It's soothing and nice as you are. I love you too, angel."

After reaching the pier he suggested, "Let's take a harbor cruise on a large junk. I've always wanted to sail on one."

"That sound good my Jeem."

Holding hands, they walked parallel along the harbor until a large sign greeted them. ONE HOUR HARBOR TOUR/60HK DOLLARS. A 150-foot two-masted wooden junk bobbed near a dock as a few British tourists and Chinese quickly scampered aboard. He thought, "Bucks are getting tight, but heck, let's do it."

They went aboard, sitting near the stern of the wooden craft as the Chinese crew babbled and cast off. Warm breeze struck canvas as they sailed into the harbor past several small tarpaulin-covered boats selling produce near merchant vessels. He felt relieved, unencumbered from the constraints of Bearden. They moved past majestic high-rise buildings in Hong Kong, sailing north, viewing thousands of dilapidated little tin and wooden shacks huddled, spreading along the shore below a high mountain chain.

The boat turned and headed south 500 yards from land. She nuzzled near him, looking into his wandering eyes. He reflected, "Here I am, half a world away in one of the most exotic places on earth, sitting near a wonderful Oriental whom I love. God, I'm living a dream." He planted a short kiss on her receptive lips.

"Linda, remember this moment in time. It will never happen again, honey. This time, this place, I mark in my heart forever."

A tear formed again in her brown eyes, "Oh Jeem, you have wise word, but make me cy." He wiped her tears with his forefinger.

The boat scurried between several craft traversing from the island toward the mainland as the summer air blew, hitting the sails. Suddenly, he caught sight of *Satterfield*. He rose and pointed. "There's my ship Linda." The junk sailed a mere thirty yards from her bow as Linda stared. Jim asked, "Isn't she a beauty?"

"It nice looking, but no gun in back." He briefly explained the bombing incident, avoiding mentioning his role. She needn't worry. They returned as night approached.

After a delicious shrimp dinner, they strolled and saw Tom patiently leaning against the cable car ticket counter downtown. He smiled, "Good seeing ya again, Linda. My, you look beautiful." She smiled, but looked toward the pavement, embarrassed.

Despite his objection, Tom paid the fair, turned toward him and remarked, "I get a lot more dough than you, pal. Don't worry, my treat."

They boarded the Peak Tram (first operated in the late 19th Century) with seven Caucasian tourists. The fifteen-foot steel-built enclosed tram had no windows and slowly rose on a narrow track above skyscrapers. Jim was nervous and thought, "Last week I read an A.P. report on the teletype about some cables snapping here, quickly plunging a car and eight victims 1,200 feet to their deaths." Sitting in a rear seat as both flanked her, he turned, gazing down at a steep incline, thinking about the accident and murmured a short prayer.

The car now climbed higher, rising above elegant million-dollar homes resting on small escarpments, overlooking the city. They were in awe of lush tropical foliage and banana trees swaying ten feet away, on each side blocking a descending sun.

As Jim and companions ascended the mountain, Walter Bearden covertly followed four radiomen at a distance as they entered a bar. Standing outside, he lit a cigarette and thought, "Somehow, I've gotta get their loyalty back and convince them to ally with me."

He was a troubled, unhappy man, feeling isolated for months from some of the men, lapsing into periods of depression and anxiety. He soloed in liberty ports, wasting time, attempting to temporarily drown his guilty conscience and insecurity through excessive drinking and foreign women. In China, he had purchased a colorful silk dress for his wife.

He walked into the well-lit lounge, looked and spotted them sitting at a large circular table. Their eyes opened wide in stunned disbelief as he smiled, shimming himself between Duff and Warden sitting opposite McGovern and Kennel.

Bearden grinned, quickly whipped out and flashed a small stack of money, "Hi, fellas, how's it going?" They didn't respond, but nodded and turned, viewing a young male rock quintet, performing on stage, fifty feet away. Gates entered as planned, and sat near Bearden.

Initially, the four merely acknowledged their presence. Shortly thereafter, Walt's tactic deployed after buying a few rounds of drinks, and launching into a litany of dirty jokes attempting to lighten the atmosphere. He proposed several trivial toasts while each time raising a glass of rum and Coke. Holding court, within two hours they were like clay in a sculptors hands as Gates sat, quietly observing and grinning. He knew the game.

Bearden enjoyed their company, feeling like a kid again, but subtly changed character when his victims were nearly inebriated. He chugged a shot of bourbon, looked across at Kennel and smiled. "Hey dog, what do some of the guys say about me huh, buddy?" Bearden quickly circled a hand, ordering another round as a mini-skirted young waitress stood nearby. He lit a cigarette and raised his voice. "Come on, come on, tell me pal."

Doug's blurry-eyes shut then slowly opened as his head weaved side to side like an out of control plastic dummy on a ventriloquist's lap. He looked and slurred, "Ah, ah, ya know they, they have these here secret meetings. Ah, ah Reemer, Smitty, Thomas, Hickey and Log. When a couple of us come round' all a sudden they h h h hush up. Shit, man, they don't like you though and Log's their buddy. Ya see, Badass, I think they're planning somethin' 'cause Hickey got busted." His head bobbed up and down. "Ah, well, that's all I know."

Bearden chugged another drink, lowered his head and was pensive. He rose, gazed out a window, returned to his seat and squinted while scanning each. "Yeah, I figured that. Thanks." The others were more focused on the band and trying to maintain composure.

Gates and Bearden rose as Don bellowed, "See ya guys back aboard." Both exited, desiring the company of ladies of the evening.

Meanwhile, after arriving at the summit, Jim and friends debarked from the tram and sauntered near a huge open-aired oval restaurant. Several outside circular dining tables were arrayed in front, a mere ten feet from a steep cliff. Jim asked, "How about a couple Singapore Slings, Tom?" She never drank alcohol. Tea was her favorite.

Shortly thereafter, they sat marveling at the panoramic view 1,800 feet above the vast metropolis. Jim stood a few feet from the cliff and looked down, scanning the harbor. Excited, he pointed, turned around and shouted, "Look, there's *Satterfield*. She looks like a little toy boat floating with others in a huge bathtub."

Tom rose and chimed, "This is really something. Let's walk over and look west."

The sun touched the horizon as a light red sky enveloped the area. They stood and gazed at Repulse Bay, guarding the harbor. A few minutes later, night swept over, as Tiki lights were ignited among several visitors dining outside. Hong Kong and neighboring Kowloon teamed with life as a myriad of lights glimmered among high rises, hovering over numerous ships resting in the dark water below.

Tom smiled, proposing a toast, "This is ta both of ya, and may you find happiness together." The couple smiled, and lovingly gazed into each other's eyes, then toasted. Jim thought, "What an evening this is, high atop one of the most famous cities on earth."

After an hour, Tom stood, looked out toward sea, turned and grinned, "Well, Jimmy we'd better return to earth. Day after tomorrow, we're heading back to sea and war. Hope it goes quick because I sure miss those two wonderful people back home."

"Yeah, I'm sure ya do, buddy. Let's go."

**Hong Kong and Harbor viewed from Victoria Peak**

The cable car returned. Alden inquired, "Ah, Jim, do ya want me to wait for ya, or ya just wanna spend more time with her?"

"I'll walk her back and catch ya later. Thanks for comin'."

"It was great, and I enjoyed it. See ya."

He placed an arm around her, walking toward the pier. Passengers boarded. They had but few minutes. He gently pulled her close, studying her now sad expression. "Honey, I think we might be gone four or five weeks, but we're coming back ta Subic. Don't worry, we'll see each other again." With his cheek pressing hers, he whispered, "This has been one of the best days of my life, Linda. I'll never forget it." He broke away, reached in his pocket and handed her return flight fare.

"You kind man Jeem, salamit." She took a white handkerchief from the little brown purse and wiped tears streaming down her soft cheeks. He drew close, embracing her. When the final boarding call was announced, their lips pressed together. She drew back within a foot and said, "I pray por you each day my Jeem. I write often. You be safe. I love you."

His eyes teared, and he softly murmured, "Ini, ibi kita, Linda." She smiled, turned and quickly walked up the brow onto the boat. He walked near the end of the dock, watching her leaning against a railing, and never taking their eyes off each other as the ferry slowly moved farther, and then he watched until her countenance faded in the night.

While motoring toward the ship in a water taxi, he sat alone thinking. I love that girl and already miss her. He gazed at several stars, whispering a prayer. God, keep her safe until I return. At 2200 he lay in his rack thinking of the day's events and possible turmoil ahead.

The next day's watch under Thomas was uneventful. In late afternoon, Jim saw Log leaning against a lifeline puffing on a cigar, gazing toward the shore, thinking. "Hi ya, Log. How are ya?"

Loggins turned around, paused and stated, "I got the two snipes' names from the guy I saw in engineering, and I'll confront em' real soon."

Jim smiled, "That's great. We're making progress. Why don't ya give me the names, and I'll go down cause I need to know what happened."

He shook his head, "Nah, this is my baby. I'll take care of it." He thought, "I feel somewhat responsible for what happened to the two other guys and must atone for the lack of action in not opposing Bearden."

Log lowered his head mumbling, "I'm gonna make it up, gonna make it up."

"What did ya say?"

Tim quickly swiped his brow and replied, "Ah, nothing, don't worry about it."

Jim inquired, "Hey, any word on how long we'll be gone? I can't imagine it gettin' any worse than it's been."

"I don't know, but I'll tell ya something, Jimmy. This next war patrol's going to be something. Before leaving Subic, they installed a T.O.W. aboard and trained a few guys on it. I wish we had it when we were attacked. It could have made a difference."

The device was a hand- held tube-launched, optically tracked, wire-guided dual purpose weapon. It was primarily used as an anti-tank killer, but was also effective against close enemy aircraft in battle.

At 0800 the next day, *Satterfield* weighed anchor and steamed at ten knots out of the majestic harbor, southwest and back to war, but a significant incident occurred shortly before the sailors returned home, unexpected by all, save one.

# 16

## "THE FINAL INCIDENT"

As she steamed, Tim went into the engineering space, investigating and approached a stocky second-class petty officer who was sweating profusely. "Are Kirby and Spencer on watch here?"

"They're working near the bulkhead, why?"

"I'd just like ta yack with them a few minutes, if it's okay."

"Sure ya can, but just a few minutes, all right?"

He moved slow eyeing the men, wiping sweat in the 150 degree heat. The two nineteen year old's were checking and recording steam pressure guage's on a panel as he approached. "I'm Loggins up in radio. You two were on watch here after we first pulled into Subic some months ago, weren't you?"

Kirby, a short brown haired-freckled face sailor responded, "Yeah, why?"

"Did ya see a radioman named Bearden down here that day?"

Nervous, they quickly eyed each other as Spencer's hands fidgeted. He was six feet with blond hair and fair complexion on a gangly frame.

Kirby replied, "Ah, I don't think so. Why?" Tim thought, "I see right through him and he's lying." Tim moved within a foot of him while Spencer stared at his imposing large gut and frame.

Tim leaned forward with a stern expression. "Now, you listen to me. I know you're hiding something, and if ya don't tell me what happened, there's gonna be serious consequences for both of you. Do you understand?" He shouted, "Damn it! Tell me now."

Stunned, both repeatedly blinked. Kirby observed him. "Listen, I'll tell ya."

Spencer turned, stared at Kirby and quickly blurted, "Ya better shut up if ya know what's good for ya." Log was incensed. Kirby lowered his head and brooded. Tim jabbed a forefinger against Spencer's chest and gazed into the frightened man's eyes.

"Boy, I'm not playing games. Ya better start talkin' now, damn it."

Spencer at Kirby, who nodded approval. "This guy came down here asking if we'd each like making a quick twenty bucks. We said sure, who wouldn't." Log described Bearden.

"Yeah, that was him. He said he was playing a joke on somebody, and in case the guy came down here looking for him, we were supposed ta say he wasn't around."

"Did he say the guy's name was Hickey?"

Spencer looked at the overhead, reflecting. "Let's see, yeah, come to think of it, it was." He cupped a hand under his chin thinking, and then inquired. "By the way, wasn't he one of the guy's that got busted in Da Nang?"

Tim nodded. "Go ahead, continue."

Kirby contributed. "Ya see, he said that if we told anyone about it, we'd regret it and get transferred because he had connections at BUPERS in D.C."

Tim cut him off and retorted, "You believed him, right?"

"Well yeah, shit, he was pretty convincing, and we thought it was kinda weird then, but we needed money and went along, thinking it was just a joke he was playing. The guy walked around and hid behind one of the steam pressure gauge panels for about fifteen minutes until we heard some other guy holler down from topside."

Tim lowered his head, thought, and asked, "Do ya remember what he said?"

"I think he said something like'all clear, he's ashore.'"

"I see. What happened then?"

Spencer interrupted, "This guy Bearden, walked over, gave us money, shook our hands, but before leaving, he turned around, and stared at us. Man, that guys' got the creepiest eyes I've ever seen. He said we did good. Shit, we really didn't do anything."

Tim shook his head disgusted and looked at them. "Ya swear it's the truth?" They nodded "You fellas know something? He set em' up, got him busted and then lied to Harrison. You see, Gates is his stooge, the other jerk who stopped Hickey coming down here looking for him. It was a conspiracy and an injustice." His eyes narrowed while gazing at them. "Now, that's the truth, and I'm gonna do something about it."

Both looked at the deck with dejected expressions. Kirby's eyes widened. "Wow, what a crock of bullshit. Listen, Loggins, we're willing to back ya up as witnesses if ya need us."

"Thanks, fellas. Now, listen. I think he was just trying to scare ya bout being transferred if ya sang. Don't worry about it. I may speak with you again. Now, I've taken enough time. Ya better get back with your duties."

He climbed the ladder, went through an opened hatch on to the main deck and turned, walking aft. Seconds earlier, before stepping through the hatch, Gates, walking on the quarter deck, saw him emerge and quickly ducked out of sight in front of the bridge. The sneaky ferret peeked back as Log walked near the stern and lit a cigar.

Gates wondered, "Why was he down there? I'll bet he was asking questions about Bearden. There's no other reason. I'd better tell Bearden."

Tim gazed at a calm sea and a clear day, but feeling stressed from the information. He puffed on the cigar, thinking. "Of all the low down tricks to pull, this takes the cake. I've gotta play my cards right and can't let on ta Bearden and others about what I learned. I can't break the chain of command and bypass Badass or Stewart. Stewart probably wouldn't believe me anyway. When the time's right, I'll confront Bearden when he's alone and I'll make notes in my diary. Tim, be cool, just be cool."

At noon, Gates approached Bearden eating chow with Duff, Carter and McDonald. "Hey, ya got a minute? I need to talk with ya." Bearden excused himself, rose and walked a few paces toward him. His nervous expression caught Bearden off guard.

"Why ya so uptight, Gates? You're my eyes and ears. What's goin' on?"

Standing a foot away, he whispered, "I think Log found out something. I saw 'em earlier comin' up from engineering."

"Did he see ya?"

"Nah, I was standin' on the quarterdeck when he came up. Log turned and walked aft."

He lowered his head and thought, "Ya did right tellin' me. If ya notice anything out of the ordinary in the other four, let me know immediately. We have to assume the two kids blabbed, and he's gonna let Hickey know. He won't tell Stewart because he probably wouldn't believe him. Listen, don't worry about nothin'. Let me handle this. I've got a contingency plan in case he sings to 'em."

During the two-day voyage back to "the line" the contemptuous relationship between Bearden and Loggins increased particularly during watch changes, as one relieved the other. It was protocol informing an oncoming supervisor of significant information relative to the vessel's communications status.

Before departing the space, Tim verbally manifested the latest updates, including relevant priority traffic sent and received; contrary to Bearden's quiet but hateful expression which was clearly noticed by subordinates. Tim asked, "Anything new? What's going on?"

Bearden was silent but walked, turned and pointed toward scribbled notes on an eight-by-ten pad sitting on a nearby desk. Tim retorted sarcastically, "Yeah, thanks for letting me know."

Because of his intermittent irascibility, watches practically became intolerable for the unfortunate few assigned under Bearden. Shortly after the weekly watch schedule was posted on a bulkhead behind the supervisor's desk, confident and joyful dispositions quickly changed to moodiness when seeing their names listed under his. The adversarial relationship between the two leading petty officers exacerbated as both avoided eye contact with other.

Sid Reemer sat on his rack, spit shining dress shoes as Smitty, Carter, Mac and Thomas dressed after showering. Sid exclaimed, "Damn, I'm cursed again. Shit, I'm scheduled under that bastard five times this week. It's hard concentrating sometimes with him around. I'm telling ya guys, it's all I can do not to deck 'em. Shit, San Diego can't come soon enough."

Mike stood near his locker with a towel wrapped around his waist, and responded, "Yup, Sid, I know exactly how ya feel. Here we are, going back to war and damn it, we have another war aboard this old tub with him." He grinned. "Look on the bright side. Each day that passes is another step closer to home."

"I guess that's one way of looking at it," replied Carter.

They arrived at Da Nang Harbor in the morning. Before dropping anchor, Kowalski ordered deck sentries posted fore, aft, port and starboard. Four men ran out carrying rifles, machine guns and grenades.

In radio, Jim looked surprised at seeing an A.P. news release printing on an unclassified teletype order wire about *Satterfield*. He quickly tore it off and handed it to Log. "Hey, check this out. I think the captain will find this interesting."

He quickly scanned the report and told him."Yeah, I'll bring a copy to him on the bridge in a few minutes after we're relieved."

After Thomas assumed the watch, Tim strode a few spaces forward, entered the bridge, saluted and handed the dispatch to a young crew cut Ensign recently out of officer candidate school. "Mister, I think the captain should see this."

"Ok, thanks."

He quickly perused as his eyes widened in disbelief and rushed outside near Kowalski, who stood gazing at land through binoculars. Excited, he rapidly spoke, "Sir, look at this. I don't understand why the Navys' letting the world and enemy know we're back in action. I thought ship movements were classified."

The news report stated." Today, the U. S. Navy announced that the destroyer USS *Satterfield* has returned for combat duty off Vietnam, after a brief stay in Hong Kong. The vessel spent three months being repaired at Subic Bay Naval Base after being attacked by enemy aircraft last April during the Easter Offensive."

Kowalski quickly scanned it, stared, and chuckled. Four sailors turned and smiled, enjoying his laughter. He looked at the young officer. "Relax, Ensign. This was deliberate. It's beautiful. I love it."

The officer demurred, puzzled at his reaction. "Mister, don't you get it? There's a hidden message here. Read between the lines." The Ensign lowered his head thinking, but Kowalski raised his voice for everyone within earshot. "They couldn't sink us! We're back in action. The Navy just gave those Commie bastards a punch in the solar plexus. Now they know we're here. Their goal was to sink us because it would've been a propaganda victory they could boast about, but here we are back in Da Nang."

Lee grinned, putting his hand on his shoulder, guiding him near a hatch and asked, "Now, mister, do you understand?"

His head lowered in embarrassment; then he nodded, "Yes, you're right captain, I'm sorry."

As they say in the Orient, the officer "lost face" near the sailors, but Lee was conciliatory, putting an arm around his shoulder. "Nothing to be sorry about, Ensign. Listen, you've only been in a short while, but you'll learn. Observe some of the senior petty officers aboard who've served many years."

An NCO turned and whispered to another, "Ninety-day wonder Ensigns, they're all the same."

In August, ARVN, assisted by American advisers, fought several battles, gradually pushing large NVA forces back into the northern I Corps provinces south of the DMZ. U.S. ships were called upon again to provide gunfire support offshore. COMSEVENTHFLT ordered her and two sister ships north to shell the remaining enemy units still operating in Quang Tri Province. As she sailed on a sweltering afternoon two miles off the coast, Kowalski stood on the bridge, turned on the 1MC (microphone), addressing the crew.

> Good afternoon, men. This is the captain. The last few months have been tough for us. As you know, we survived a devastating attack. This ol' gal is repaired, sailing back into action. They couldn't sink her, thanks to your devotion to duty. Our firepower has been reduced to the level of a World War Two destroyer mine sweeper with one mount operational, but we're taking it to the enemy because I'm sure you all know we have a score to settle. Let's accomplish duties to the best of our abilities and get back home. I'm proud of you. That is all.

Officers and enlisted smiled. His message shot confident adrenaline through everyone. In radio, Loggins lit a cigar, rose, climbed onto a desk, bellowing to his surprised men. "Yeah, that's what I'm talkin' bout. That was great. We got the best skipper in the Navy. Let's take it to em." Smitty, Jim and Sid rose, and clapped.

For five weeks Satterfield roamed the sea like a vengeful shark searching for prey; any Communist prey seeking to impose hegemony on the free people of South Vietnam. On the bow, mount 51 pumped thousands of rounds into enemy forces, destroying tanks, vehicles, and staging areas after the ship's CIC (combat information center) received accurate intelligence from daring unarmed spotter pilots above—in jungles and mountainous regions where brave reconnaissance teams stealthily operated. The P.O.D. informed them of successful gunfire missions primarily in areas north of Quang Tri; consequently, an atmosphere of high moral and espirit de corps pervaded.

Because of reduced weaponry, Satterfield was ordered to perform plane guard duties on several occasions. Numerous sorties were launched from aircraft carriers steaming twenty plus miles out in the Tonkin Gulf, in an area called "Yankee Station."

It was standard operating procedure during launch and recovery for a destroyer steaming 1,000 plus yards astern behind a "bird farm's" wake to retrieve any pilot forced to ditch. Off duty men enjoyed these missions as a respite, catching extra rest as opposed to interrupted sleep during G.Q.

The ship accomplished duties admirably when two airmen ejected after their F-4 Phantom jet engine malfunctioned, catching fire after being launched from the flight deck, a few miles from their carrier. Satterfield's lookouts spotted men wearing life vests, bobbing in two-foot-waves as Lee ordered full speed ahead.

After a davit lowered four men in a whale boat into choppy water, the craft motored a hundred yards toward the men. The unharmed pilots, wearing life vests, were pulled into the boat and shortly thereafter were safely aboard.

After climbing on to the deck, both smiled while shaking their res-cuers' hands as one pilot blurted, "Boy, we're glad seeing you guys." After showering and grabbing a snack, they were high lined back aboard the carrier.

For months, Loggins prepared for the Navy-wide Chief Petty Officer's exam by studying manuals and completed required data in all aspects of communications, including advanced leadership. He lay in his bunk and closed his eyes thinking. "I've flunked twice, but damn it this time I'm reaching my goal and passing."

A week later, confident of success, Log supervised a day watch as Jim, Smitty and Duff busily sent and received several messages over wireless and teletype. With a short cigar dangling from his mouth, he strolled, gazing down at a teletype machine printing a classified message from BUPERS to all commands with test results and promotions.

"Yee, hah, I finally made it!" he shouted. He quickly tore off the completed dispatch and grinned. The men turned and smiled. Buddha (Duff) rose and approached him.

"Let me be the first to pump paws with ya Chief Log."

Jim and Smitty turned around and clapped. "Way to go, Chief!" bellowed Smitty.

Bearden wasn't as fortunate. Though excelling in communications, he failed, specificly in difficult decision making and situational scenarios determining leadership. Psychologically, it was his Waterloo.

Results of tests and news of promotions quickly spread. Despondent, Gates ran and caught Bearden leaving the mess deck. "Hey, Donny, ya look like ya lost yer best friend. What's up?"

Gates cupped his hand, brooded and related, "Hate tellin' ya this, but I heard only Log made Chief. I'm sorry for ya."

Bearden's eyes bulged in disbelief. Furious, he pressed his lips together while doubling both fists and exclaimed, "Damn it, this changes things. I have to employ Plan B, Donny." He lowered his head, slowly walking toward berthing.

Tim lit a cigar, climbed, stood on the desk, looked down, raised a fist above his head, and hollered, "carpe diem", befuddling them.

"What the hell's that mean?" Duff asked.

Tim took a quick puff, and blew smoke as his face brightened with another smile. "It's Latin for seize the day. I figured I just did. Fellas, I'm real happy about this after seventeen years."

Jim rose, extended a hand and smiled, "Congratulations, Log. I'd give anything to see the look on Badass' face when he finds out."

Log grinned. "Well, guys, I'll let ya know, but first I've gotta take care of some unfinished business."

Two days before completing gunfire support, Tim sneaked down to wake Gates in berthing. They were alone. He shook Gates and hollered, "Get up, I wanna talk ta ya."

Groggy, he rose, sat up, blinked and asked, "Why are ya waking me up? Shit, I've got watch in a few hours. What's on your mind, Log?"

Standing nearby, he gave a stern glare. "I don't give a damn what you've got, ferret." Clearly nervous, Gates eyes shifted back and forth. "Ya see, Gates, I know what happened in Subic, how you and Badass set Hickey up. Two snipes told me what happened. You're in deep shit fella."

Gates arms crossed defensively, avoiding eye contact as drops of sweat quickly appeared on his forehead. "You're crazy. I don't know what you're talking about. Besides, I'm not saying anythin', and ya can't make me talk."

Ignoring him, he rolled over, but Tim grabbed his waist, pulled him out, and shoved the stunned man against the middle rack above. Gates vainly tried wiggling away, but strong hands pinned him against the mattress bar. "I'm gonna beat the crap outta ya unless ya talk now, damn it."

His voice quivered as a tiny tear formed in one eye, "He, he told me not to say anything, so I can't. Please let me go, you're hurtin' me." Log moved inches from his face and shouted.

"Who told ya?" Gates pleaded, "No, no. I can't say." Loggins released him and stepped back.

"I know who it is. Gates, don't ya realize you're in hot water?"

Suddenly, Kennel came bounding down. "I heard some hollering and wondered what was going on here." Shaken and scared, Gates jumped back into bed.

Tim, standing a few feet away, at the intruder. "Ah, nothing Kennel. We're just having a come ta Jesus talk, weren't we Donny?"

"Ah, ah, yeah, that's what it was 'Dog', no big deal." Tim quickly turned, reached into a dungaree pocket, retrieving a pill and swallowed. He looked at Kennel.

"Listen, don't ya have duty or somethin'? Get out of here." Kennel quickly ran topside. Tim gazed down. "I'm gonna speak with Stewart. Ya better thank the man upstairs Kennel came down. Better get some sleep."

Walking back topside, he thought, "Kennel probably will let Bearden know about the altercation, but at this point, I don't care." Suddenly, he felt a sharp pain in his upper chest. He thought, "I've gotta take it easy."

That night, Thomas supervised Duff and Gates in radio while Tim changed into his new light brown Chief Petty Officer's uniform. One two-inch long conspicuous gold anchor adorned each lapel on his short sleeve shirt.

Tim caught Stewart walking through a passageway before evening chow. "Sir, do ya have a couple minutes? It's important." The officer stopped, rolled his eyes, irritated at the intrusion.

"All right Loggins. What is it?"

"Sir, here's a chit. I'm requesting a special Captain's Mast."

"Why?"

He mentioned the lifer's attitude and behavior toward Hickey, including racial comments made by Gates and Bearden. Log continued, "Mr. Stewart, I believe Hickey was set up by Gates and Bearden in Subic. They didn't like him. Bearden's been on his can since Bremerton and I know there was a conspiracy getting him busted after I received information from two men in engineering."

Irritated, Stewart snapped, "That's nonsense. Why didn't you speak with me about this before? It happened six months ago. What difference does it make now? "

"Ah, well sir, I've had some serious personal problems with my wife and my health hasn't been well. I wanted to be sure before speaking with you."

Stewart glared, unnerved. "Hickey's had Captain's Mast and was reduced in rank for violating Naval regulations. He had his chance explaining at that time. What do expect me to do? I'm leaving."

He walked away. Frustrated, Tim quickly reached, tapping his shoulder. Irritated, he turned around and snapped, "Now, what is it, Loggins?"

"Sorry, sir, but you gotta believe me. Those two guys in engineering were paid to lie for Bearden, thinking he was playing a ruse while Hickey looked for him to sign his liberty chit. Bearden hid down there and Gates covered for em'. It was an injustice." He handed him the chit in order to manifest the affair at a special Captain's Mast. Stewart frowned, reached and grabbed the form. "Sir, could you sign this and give it to the X.O.?"

He stared at the petty officer. "Hell, you expect me to believe that? This is too far-fetched. It's purely conjecture. I need actual facts Loggins. Listen, the matters over and done. That's it sailor."

Stewart departed, but Tim shouted, "I'm just asking ya ta speak with Pursell and give him the chit, that's all."

The officer halted, gazing ahead. "All right, let me think about it. Oh, by the way, congratulations on making Chief."

"Thank you, sir." He went below, opened a locker, retrieved the diary and wrote.

Stewart joined ten other associates and the X.O. in the officer's mess. While enjoying a steak dinner, he was pensive, focused on Loggins' remarks. He thought, "It wouldn't hurt speaking with Pursell."

As they enjoyed dessert, Pursell observed. "Bob, you haven't said a word. That's unlike you. What's on your mind?" Stewart finished the Neopolitan ice cream, shoved the bowl aside and looked at him ten feet away.

"I'd rather talk with you after everyone's left if you have a few minutes."

"Sure, but it better be important because I'm busy, understand?" Minutes after the others departed, Stewart grabbed coffee, sat across and stared, surprising Pursell.

"Mister, why are you looking at me that way?"

He took a long swig of java, and lowered his head. "You probably wouldn't believe me if I told you, sir."

"Well, try me." He related Loggin's comments after placing the chit in front of him on the table. Pursell lit a Salem, took a drag and toward a large framed photo hanging on a nearby bulkhead of uniformed nurse Heliena Satterfield.

"Stewart, you actually believe this is significant?"

"Ah, yes, I do. I think we should thoroughly investigate. Loggins' is a good petty officer and men are compatible with him. There may have been a surreptitious plan against Hickey. I'm thinking about signing Loggins' chit for special Captain's Mast."

He at the request, shook his head and snapped, "Damn it Bob, we've got more important matters and another couple days on the line before heading back. Now, I appreciate your concern for men you're responsible for, but it's a dead issue. The sailor was busted in January. We've gotta move on. Understand?"

His jaw dropped in disbelief. "Yes, sir, but why would Loggins even bring it up? I think it's valid and we should look into the matter."

Pursell rose, put the cigarette out and stared. "Lieutenant, don't you get it? He's had at least six months to disclose his claim and now he's bringing it up. Listen, speak with Bearden and get his take on it. I really don't wanna hear any more about it. Request denied, understand?"

Looking dejected, he briefly closed his eyes, rose, and started walking toward the hatch when Pursell arrogantly raised his voice. "I said, understand?" Stewart stopped, turned and gazed at him.

"Yes, sir."

The following morning, Stewart told Bearden to meet him in his stateroom. Bearden left Duff and Warden in radio and knocked on the officer's door. "Come in, Bearden. Sit down."

"What's happening lieutenant?"

He informed him of Loggin's comments, paused, and asked, "Were you and Gates involved in this?"

Bearden didn't blink, but looked him right in the eye, and in a smooth tone replied, "No, sir. The only reason I can think why he'd say those things is because we don't get along. He's alienated some of the men against me, lieutenant. This is so far out, I don't know what to think. He's dreamed this up out of envy and revenge against me. Sir, I think he might be losing it cause of his high blood pressure and problems with his wife. Heck, yesterday he woke up Gates and tried picking a fight with him. I'm telling you, the man's losin' it." It was a masterful performance.

Stewart cupped his jaw in his hand thinking, and looked at him. "Oh, I see. Listen, I spoke with Pursell. Loggins requested special Captain's Mast, but I don't think the X.O. will pursue the matter. You could be right. Keep an eye on him. I've known about his animosity against you for some time, and it makes sense." He placed a hand on Bearden's shoulder and grinned. "You've done a fine job keeping the men sharp, and I've received good reports from the captain about our department, including the signal men. I won't pursue this further. Carry on, Bearden."

"Thank you, sir."

Bearden reentered radio, lit a Winston and thought, "The fat man spilled the beans eh? Log just passed the CPO test, and now he'll be in charge." He sat, gazing at the desk, slowly moving a forefinger, and thumb up and down a pen, contemplating suicide. He reflected, "Power has fled. I'm feeling isolated and trapped. Maybe I'll end it by jumping over the side tonight. On the other hand, the only avenue of escape is getting rid of Log before it gets out of control." Bearden formed an insidious plan to alleviate the final obstacle.

The next afternoon after supervising the day watch, Bearden walked into the mess space and sat across from Loggins eating chow. He stared and grinned. "How ya been, Tim?" His calm tone was unusual, uncharacteristic of a man he'd known two years.

Log didn't acknowledge, but looked at the tray and stated, "I spoke with Stewart and put the fear of God into Donny."

Bearden stirred his coffee, and then stared at him with a noticeable smirk. "You're pissed off and I understand. Listen, let's try and get along, all right? Oh, by the way, I guess congratulations are in order, right?"

Tim refused eye contact, lowered his head, chewed mashed potatoes and continued. "I got all the facts from two in engineering and Stewart's aware. Ya must have programmed Gates well cause he didn't chirp. Now, I've gotta break the chain a command and speak with the X.O."

Bearden smoothed his mustache with a forefinger, thought a few seconds and retorted. "Listen, I spoke with Stewart. He said the X.O. denied your request. The matters closed. Ya know ya can't break the chain of command."

Tim glared, and raised his voice. "Yeah, right. I'm sure ya told him everything. If I believed that, then there's gotta be oil on my folks farm. You've forced me to do this, leaving me no other alternative, Bearden."

Suddenly, he switched to other sensitive topics. "By the way, how's your wife and blood pressure been?"

Tim's eyes squinted as he glared at the intrusive man. "What's it to ya? This isn't your style Walt. Why do you care about my personal business?"

He was deceptive in replying. "Oh, I just figured with your other problems, maybe you're losing it or somethin', that's all."

Tim snapped, "Hell no, I'm not."

Bearden leaned across, grinned and whispered, "Hey, calm down."

Bearden closed eyes as his head bowed and reflected for a minute. There was a hush. Suddenly, his expression turned maudlin. A tear formed in his left eye, then he raised his head and looked at him as his lips quivered. "Listen, I was wrong. I'm coming clean and giving you a statement tonight about the whole affair. I'm just askin' ya not to reveal it until after I'm gone, Tim. My life's over."

Log sipped his coffee. "What are ya gonna do, jump over the side? Damn it, face the music like a man, not a coward." Bearden wiped his eyes and looked down.

"No, not gonna do that. I'll lose face in front of the men. Tim, just do me this one favor, meet me near the stern at 0:300 and I'll hand ya my written confession, then ya can leave me alone. It'll make ya happy gettin' yer revenge, watchin' me die. That's how I wanna go out."

Tim at a bulkhead and thought a few seconds. "No, I don't wanna watch ya die. I'm not that kinda guy. If I hadn't made chief, I doubt you'd even consider being this forth-coming, Walt. Now, you're off your little throne."

Bearden's eyes squinted, and he grinned. "Shit, next January, Hickey's rank will be reinstated anyway. Listen, this has been eating at me ever since Subic." Bearden rose, extended his right hand and stared. Convinced of his sincerity, Log wiped his brow with a napkin, paused, looked up and shook his hand.

"Ok, I'll meet ya later, but ya better have all the facts on paper and sign it."

Tim contemplated. "What have I got to lose? Sounds like he desires coming clean, but why? He pondered. "I need his statement to exonerate Jim and will no longer tolerate Bearden's nefarious behavior. If I have to drag him myself in front of the captain, but I'll give him the benefit of the doubt. I still don't trust the snake and not gonna let 'em commit suicide. I need em' alive, but I wonder if there's another motive."

At 23:45, the second watch was relieved by Loggins, McGovern, Gates and Warden as Hickey, Smith, Reemer and Thomas left retiring for the night. Message traffic was unusually light during the next three hours. Gates avoided eye contact with Tim as he logged, and made copies of dispatches while Mac and Warden operated the wireless, sending and receiving code.

Two hours earlier, Bearden grabbed a few hours rest, anticipating meeting his adversary later. Shortly after 0:245 he woke, put on dungarees, white hat, went topside and walked toward the stern.

At 0:300, Loggins tapped McGovern's shoulder as he finished typing a received message. Mark put the ears down. "What's up Log?"

"Listen, traffic's not bad tonight. Take over a little while because I'm going aft and think for a spell and I won't be long. Have "Squeeks" man the wireless, all right?"

"Yeah, sure will, no problem."

Tim started leaving, and turned around. "Hey, if ya get an emergency flash message, run and get me." Mac nodded.

Early that evening after a successful six-hour shelling against enemy positions, the vessel expended all her ammunition. Shortly before 2300, Kowalski ordered cease fire and retired to his stateroom. A third of the crew stood watch as Condition Three (wartime cruising) was set as she steamed at seventeen knots (half speed) southeast, three miles out, parallel along the coast near Chu Lai on a moonless night.

Gleaming stars sprinkled the sky as twenty-knot north easterly winds blew a choppy sea. Due to wartime conditions, the smoking lamp was out on weather decks. As most slept, the only sounds below outside the weather decks were two-foot waves striking her sides, and engines powering twin screws, churning water below the stern, creating a 500-yard wake on a black sea, while gently swaying, like an old baby cradle. Except for small, dim red and green running lights on the mainmast, it was an eerie darkness as she plunged into small swells. You could barely see a hand in front of your face.

Tim walked out, held onto both railings, slowly descending the ladder toward the starboard weather deck. Cautiously moving aft, he timed his gait as the destroyer sluggishly moved up, down and port to starboard. He reached and halted, standing on a large, flat steel slab that once was a gun mount. Just below, were repaired, but empty upper handling and magazine spaces.

Within twenty seconds his eyes adjusted, beholding the ship's wake below the stern. He strolled a few feet toward the stern, and then saw a dark shadow like figure standing near the lifelines facing outboard. Bearden. They were alone.

Looking aft, Bearden heard footsteps as he stared at the wake reflecting on the successful subterfuge employed tactic. "I knew you'd meet me here. Tomorrow, you're headin' back to the P. I., then home. I'll bet you're looking forward to it, aren't ya?"

Tim walked, stopped a few feet behind, and confronted him."Of course I am. Let's cut to the chase. Listen, don't do anything rash Walt. Ya got your statement?"

Bearden slowly lowered his right hand, retrieving a weapon in his dungaree pants. He opened the recently sharpened four-inch blade, and quickly turned around flashing the weapon, three feet from Loggins. Surprised, Tim's eyes bulged while he retreated.

Badass gazed at him, exclaiming, "What do you take me for, a fool or somethin'? Did ya actually believe I'd slice my own throat and make amends?"

Tim quickly backed away and thought, "He convinced me earlier. I shouldn't have trusted him." Holding the knife upright, Bearden slowly advanced, as Log retreated saying, "I thought you were a man of your word, but ya fished me out here. I was hoping we could settle this as gentlemen, but was wrong. You're a snake and will always be one."

Bearden quickly swung the knife inches from his target's chest while Tim jumped back as his eyes suddenly widened. "What in the heck are ya doing? Are you crazy or something?"

Hateful eyes glared as he shouted, "I'm settling this right now, fat man. When I'm done with ya and roll your ass over the side for the sharks to feed, my problem's solved cause they'll figure ya fell overboard. You see, no one knows I'm out here, but you." Log raised both fists, carefully retreating. Badass laughed and crouched, stalking him as his right hand wiggled the knife.

"Ya see, I went back into engineering yesterday and spoke ta the two kids. Ha, ha. They're not gonna sing again, cause I scared the shit outta em'. There goes your great witnesses. Shit, I even convinced ignorant Stewart you were plotting against me. Ya see, all I gotta do is get rid of ya and I'm home free. I've been waiting a long time for this, now it's just you and me."

He rapidly swung the weapon twice, missing Tim's hands by inches, and then chuckled, "You're slow, fat man." He was never obese, but hated being called that as a youth. His blood pressure rose as he backed near the starboard lifelines. Like a fencer, Bearden quickly lunged his

his arm toward Loggins stomach. Tim stepped sideways and swung his left fist, landing a blow against his cheek and lip sending the surprised attacker staggering back.

Tim stopped and shouted, "Listen, Bearden. This is crazy. We've gotta stop this." He thought, "My God, he's trying to kill me. I'll try luring him near the side."

Bearden quickly shook his head, wiped blood off his lips and shouted, "You're not singing anymore ta anyone Log." He relentlessly swung the weapon as Loggins continued jumping away, while the vessel swayed. Tim tried balancing himself, spreading his legs while retreating as the ship shifted to port, when suddenly Badass swung; the blade ripped through his short sleeve shirt, slicing his upper right arm. He winced in pain as blood trickled on to the deck. Bearden sinickly remarked, "Ha, ha. I got ya, man, you're slow. This is easy."

Now the aggressor lunged again as Log jumped back against the lifelines. Cornering him, Badass smirked, menacingly flashing the blade side to side while stalking his prey. Tim had never seen such hatred in a man.

Bearden thought, "I've got 'em and gonna finish him." Brandishing the knife four feet away, he bolted and charged, but Tim quickly dropped, hitting the deck away from the onrush. The attacker's momentum carried him over lifelines as the weapon and white hat flew overboard, but instinctively, his left hand grabbed a bottom line halting a fall into the sea. He screamed, "Log, help me, help me."

Tim turned, looked at the victim and rose as blood dripped to the deck. Bearden wiggled, dangling, like a hooked fish, banging against the vessel's side each time she moved to port. She swayed starboard as whitecaps lashed over him like a squid's tentacles, attempting to pull him into the deep.

Tim had never seen such fear as was in the bulging eyes of a frightened man. It is strange how human behavior quickly transforms in seconds, from extreme hatred into absolute terror.

Tim reflected a moment. "He just tried killing me and now wants help. Damn it, I want 'em alive." Bearden desperately tried raising a free hand to grab a line, yet each time the ship swayed port, he missed.

Loggins leaned over and yelled, "Hold on, hold on." He knelt, stuck his head between two lines while grasping the top, lowered himself, and extended his wounded arm as far as possible, attempting to grab Bearden's free hand. He shouted, "Don't worry, I'll get ya, I'll get ya." He grimaced, as pain increased from the wound, while his bloody arm dripped, like a faucet on the struggling sailors' head, a few feet below him.

As the ship rolled starboard, Tim winced an stretched his arm, touching Bearden's fingers. He yelled, "Grab my hand now, Walt." Gasping for breath, Bearden reached and clutched his hand as Log shouted. "Ok, I gotcha."

He began pulling as the struggling man looked at him. Bearden grinned while displaying a confident show of relief, but suddenly, a violent six-foot, rogue wave unexpectedly swept over his torso with such intensity its force separated the victim from his rescuer and the line. He let out a blood-curdling scream as he plunged head first into the sea and was swallowed by the vessel's wake. Walter Bearden descended into the abyss, sank and ceased to exist.

Exhausted, Tim looked aft for signs of life, but only Satterfield's constant wake and the sea remained. He sat, took out a handkerchief, pressing it against the three-inch long wound, stopping the blood flow. Tears quickly formed, and he thought. "Damn it, he shouldn't have tried killing me. I tried saving him. He was evil, but there must have been some good in him."

He staggered back toward radio when a sharp pain slammed into his chest, like a boxer's fist. He thought, "I've felt this way before, but never this bad. I'd better reach sick bay." He grimaced while struggling for breath.

Seconds after walking through a hatch into a passageway, dizziness enveloped him. Suddenly, he became disorientated. His heart pounded, as he stumbled like a drunken man trying to focus on the large black letters "Sick Bay"above a hatch. He thought, this is it, I need help. Muscles ached as his fist struck the steel entrance four times, then he collapsed against the door.

The Chief Corpsman slowly opened his sleepy eyes after hearing a knock and gasping sound. He leaped out of bed, turned on a light, and opened the hatch as Tim's large head and arms fell across the knee knocker.The stocky corpsman pulled him through, quickly grabbed a wrist and checked the pulse of the unconscious man. Loggins had suffered a severe heart attack.

He grabbed a syringe and quickly inserted solution into his veins, then slid a pillow under Tim's head, and lowered his ear against his chest. He thought, "My God, this guy's going fast. I'd better contact the bridge." The petty officer grabbed a black internal communications phone off the wall and dialed. A seaman answered. "Bridge, aye."

In a desperate tone, he yelled, "Listen, this is the duty corpsman. Get me the O.O.D., right now."

"What's going on back there, Chief?" the lieutenant inquired.

"Sir, Loggins from radio just had a bad heart attack. I gave him a shot and I think he's coming around, but it doesn't look good."

"Ok, Chief, I'm sending a messenger back there to help you. Do you need any other assistance or another corpsman?"

"No, sir"

"All right, keep me posted on his condition."

A tall, nineteen year old tanned seaman ran back and asked, "How can I help?"

"You pick up his shoulders, and I'll get the legs." They placed him on a gurney, and then he gave an order. "Listen, run back to the radio shack and let those guys know what happened."

Just before he departed, Tim came around, murmuring. The corpsman quickly lowered an ear over his face. "Please g g get J, J, Jimmy, n n eed h, h, him."

"Loggins, Jimmy who?"

He struggled for breath gasping, "H, h, Hickey."

As the messenger left, he shouted. "Hey, first get down to berthing and bring Hickey in here quick."

"Ok, doc, will do." The seaman, holding a flashlight, rushed down as several men slept in semi-darkness.

Meanwhile, Mac rose, took a few steps toward the other two and remarked. "Damn, he's been gone a while now. I wonder if he's all right."

Squeeks remarked, "Aw, he's probably still out there chewing on his cigar thinking. He likes doing that, ya know."

McGovern turned and looked at him. "I don't like it. Maybe my mind's playing tricks on me, but I think theres something wrong."

The messenger walked between rows of bunks whispering. "Hickey, Hickey. Where are you? Where are you?"

Mike woke and asked, "Who is it?"

"Hey, I gotta find Hickey. Where's his rack?"

He raised his head and pointed, "Right there, now let me sleep."

The young man turned the flashlight directly on his face, shocking him. "What the hell ya doing? I'm trying to sleep. This better be important, damn it."

The messenger's nervous, scared disposition caught Jim off guard. "I'm sorry Hickey. The chief corpsman told me ta wake ya because Loggin's is in bad shape and asking for ya."

He rose, rubbed his eyes and asked, "Where is he?"

"He's in sick bay, but you better get there quick."

Jim leaped out, put on dungaree trousers and quickly ran into sick bay. The sight of his friend lying, gasping for breath was overwhelming. He lowered his head inches from Tim's face. "I'm here Log, I'm here. What happened?"

His eyes slowly opened, gazing at Jim, but struggled murmuring words. "Ah, ah, ah, Jim, glad you're here. Bearden tried ta, ta, kill me with a knife. Ya won't have to worry about him anymore. He, he, went over the side. I, I, tried saving him, but couldn't. I'm not gonna make it. T, t, tell the men I'm proud s, s, serving w, w, with em'." Tears trickled down Jim's face.

Jim shouted, pleading, "Log, Log, hang on, hang on, don't go." Tim's hand slowly rose, settling on Jim's head as Jim eyed his dying mate. Tim's eyes gleamed as he stared and grinned at him with a slight grin.

"Worry not for me. I'm done suffering. Ya see, I'm go, go, going to a better place. I love ya Jimmy." The hand suddenly dropped to Tim's side, the eyes closed, the chest expanded as he breathed his last, and Timothy Loggins entered eternity.

Hickey threw his arms around him, cried, hugged Tim and shouted. "No, no, no, not now." The corpsman gently pulled him back as Hickey wiped away tears.

"I'm sorry about your shipmate, Hickey. He must have been a special man."

Jim looked down at the body, and nodded. "The best. He was the older brother I never had. Ya couldn't ask for a better leader. I'm kinda in shock because it's so sudden. Damn it. This is like a bad dream ya know. I don't know what to think now." He took a deep breath, exhaled, never taking his eyes off him, then at the corpsman saying, "I've gotta leave, and try and get some sleep if I can."

The chief blocked his exit. "Hickey, I only caught a little of what he said. What happened out there?" He closed his eyes a few seconds, and then stared at his departed buddy.

"Looks like Bearden tried killing him with a knife. There must have been a fight."

The chief remarked, "Yeah, I saw that nasty slice on his arm."

"He said he tried saving him, but he went over the side. I think ya should call the bridge and let em' know about it. I've gotta go."

The corpsman quickly grabbed a phone and called the bridge informing the O.O.D. what occured. After a messenger woke Kowalski in his stateroom, he ordered the helmsman to turn the ship 180 degrees to search for the missing man. Six lookouts were posted on weather decks with high-powered binoculars, yet in darkness it was almost impossible spotting anything. Flashlights and smoking were prohibited on weather decks at night because of the wartime conditions in the combat zones.

Meanwhile, the messenger knocked on the radio hatch. After hearing of Loggins' demise, McGovern's jaw dropped in astonishment, but the men in radio were unaware of Bearden's fate.

Mac closed the door, turned and sat behind the desk burying his head in his hands. "What's wrong?" Warden asked.

"Log had a heart attack and died." Gates looked befuddled, but his expression suddenly changed to a slight gleam. He thought, "Good, Bearden must be glad, no sweat, and no more problems."

Mark looked at them, calmly stating, "Listen, both of you, I'm just as shocked as you are.

Damn it, he was ok in my book." He shook his head. "I don't know what's going to happen now.

When Badass relieves us in a few hours, I'll let him know. There's not much going on now. I'm not waking Stewart; I guess he'll know soon enough in a few hours."

Two sailors carried his body, placing it below, inside a steel reefer where boxes of frozen meats and perishables were stored. After Kowalski was alerted, he entered the bridge, grabbed a phone and called radio. "Radio, petty officer McGovern speaking."

"McGovern, this is the captain. Listen, get a secret dispatch quick to COMSEVENTHFLT, COMCRUDESPAC, MACV, and Da Nang."

"Aye, aye, sir" He grabbed an eight by ten pad and wrote as the skipper dictated the classified message.

At 0:340, 10 Sep. 72' as *Satterfield* steamed vicinity Chu Lai, one enlisted deceased, cause, heart failure, one enlisted missing, presumed lost at sea. Conducting search, informed via TBS, ships in vicinity. Will advise results of search and subsequent inquiry.

Leland Kowalski, C.O.

Mac turned and looked at Gates. "Send this on the wireless now." He walked, sat, placing a black headset over his ears and quickly pounded out code, then Warden typed on perforated tape and sent it over a covered teletype orderwire circuit. Mark reflected, "We sent it both ways. They should get it fast because the frequencies are good tonight. I wonder who the missing guy is."

Jim returned and lay on his rack, thinking. "We're leaderless, other than Thomas. The only reason Log would leave watch a few minutes would be to make a head call." He surmised, "They must have had a meeting. Even though I hated Badass, I hope he made his peace with God before dying." A tear dripped down his cheek. "I miss Log already. Man, I loved that guy." He prayed. "God rest Tim and Lord be merciful to him."

By 0:900, Kowalski sent another TBS message to other vessels calling off the search, ordered a ninety-degree turn, and called Stewart to the bridge before he finished breakfast. "Good morning, sir," greeted the lieutenant.

Kowalski was somber. "I suppose in the officer's mess you heard what happened. Mister, two senior petty officers from your department are dead. I want a full report in my stateroom by noon today, understand?"

"Yes, sir"

He saluted, turned and started leaving when Kowalski called him back. "Ya know somethin' Bob? We're not feeling too good now. I'm upset this happened and understand they were both good men, even though not compatible with each other."

"Ah, Captain, did Pursell tell you about information I got from Loggins regarding Bearden and a possible conspiracy against a sailor that happened before you took command?"

"No, why? Should he have?"

"Yes, captain, I believe so because it could possibly have a direct bearing on what happened this morning."

Lee lowered his head, pondering, and back at him. "The corpsman is writing his report and I'll get his take on it, and then speak with Pursell. Take care, Bob."

Stewart told a messenger to contact everyone in radio on or off watch, having them assemble in radio central. Shortly thereafter, they all congregated in the space. Word quickly spread throughout the ship of Loggin's death and the missing man's identity.

In radio, the silence was deafening as worried and pensive men milled about. After hearing about Bearden, all eyes focused on Gates. He was silent, almost maudlin as he lowered his head staring at the deck.

Stewart entered, cleared his throat and spoke softly. "I'm sure all of you are surprised and saddened as I am after hearing what happened early this morning. They were good sailors and leaders. It'll take some time for this to heal, but though it's tough, we gotta move on with our duties." He at Mike and announced, "Thomas, your now leading petty officer.

McGovern and Reemer will be the other two section supervisors. If anyone has information regarding how and why this tragic event happened, write it down now. The captain needs a full report before noon."

After he departed, there was dead silence, as each man at one another. Everyone wrote statements, everyone but Gates who swiftly departed into berthing.

Mike walked over, placing an arm around teary eyed Jim. "I feel for ya buddy. I know ya were close to him."

Jim hung his head. "This place here seems empty without him and sort of strange in a way. Log was like a father to us, a pillar of strength against Badass. Now, he's gone." He buried his head in his hands and exclaimed, "God, I can't believe this happened. It's like something out of a nightmare. All we can do is hang in there."

Sid finished writing, walked over and remarked, "Guys, isn't it weird? Man, they were just here." He was despondent, struggling with words as tears streamed down his cheeks. "I think we shouldn't take people for granted every day. I'm sure gonna miss him. Shit, I haven't cried like this since I got my ass spanked as a kid. Guys, those idiots who say you're not a man if ya cry don't know what the hell they're talkin' bout."

Sid wiped a tear and raised his voice, "It's tough going through this, but ya know, Log would want us to remember him like he was and do our duty."

Jim patted his muscular back and remarked, "Sid, you're right. I think those are all our sentiments."

Mike turned and looked at Jim, "Well, the old man's taking us east ta Subic, far from war, then home, and you're gonna see your girl once more. That's good news."

Jim grinned slightly, but stress lines quickly appeared on his forehead. "Yeah, I can't wait. Damn, I'm sure gonna miss him. I was just thinking. A man like Tim with his charisma doesn't come around too often in life. We'll have some good memories. Despite his problems, he supported, inspired, gave us hope and confidence."

Jim took a deep breath and stared at them. "Log found out what happened back in Subic."

"No kidding?" Duff asked.

"Yup. I'm running down ta engineering and getting statements from the two guys Badass conned."

He walked toward the hatch as Mike hollered, "I wouldn't wanna be in Gates shoes, now."

Hickey bounded into engineering and received permission from a Chief to speak with Kirby and Spencer. Each gave written statements about the affair, and Jim handed them to Mike. "Here, the lieutenant and skipper should find these interesting." By 1100, Stewart collected all the data into a file folder for Kowalski's possession in his stateroom.

The captain called the personnel department, ordering a yeoman to retrieve Loggin's personal belongings from his locker and sea bag. While placing uniforms, clothing and other items into a large box for shipment, something caught his eyes. Inside a five-by-seven Bible was an envelope with the words "For the captain in the event of my death."

After the yeoman carried the box into personnel, a lieutenant perused and retrieved a small note-book-sized diary. He looked at the petty officer. "It's a journal and against Navy regs, but the Captain should see this and the note. Get these up there as soon as possible."

"Yes, sir."

Donald Gates lay in bed, a troubled man, examining his conscience, wondering about his fate. "I'll miss Bearden. We had good times together, but in a way I'm glad he's gone. It was stupid going along with his plan screwing Hickey, but Badass scared me half to death. I should have gone to Larson and Stewart, but I figured they wouldn't believe me anyway. Shit, this hurts getting caught. I was selfish, seeking extra time off to drink and make love ta women in exchange for being his spy. Damn, it wasn't worth it. I don't know what's going to happen." Sleep was difficult for the stooge.

*Satterfield* steamed east at fifteen knots on a calm sea as normal work routines continued. While Pursell assumed O.O.D. watch on the bridge, a Filipino steward attired in a white jacket poured a second cup of black coffee for Leland, sitting at a desk in his stateroom, reading the reports.

He lit a Marlboro, reached and opened an envelope withdrawing two neatly printed sheets.

His jaw dropped, as his eyes widened, almost incredulous at reading the words detailing Bearden's behavior, conspiracy and subsequent cover up. He focused on poignant sentences.

In addition to information contained in the diary, Bearden with CPO Larson covering up, was also directly responsible for one former sailor being forced out of the service under less than honorable conditions despite a clean record and medical situation beyond his control. A second young man in Dept. committed suicide after weeks of harassment by RM1 Bearden. I was aware of all the facts and cover up, but I offered little support to the men before, during investigations and Captain's Mast due to Bearden and Larson's persuasion. I feared vindication and chose compatibility. I now realize I was wrong and decided to amend past my behavior by finding the truth regarding the unfair treatment of Petty Officer (now Seaman) Hickey and the injustice displayed, not only by Stewart (I know he feared Bearden), who should have investigated further, but also by X.O. Pursell. He was aware of declining morale after the suicide and of Hickey's situation, but did nothing. Former C.O. Harrison's intransigence was appalling, refusing to listen to Hickey's entire statement during Captain's Mast. Lies and deceptions occurred without logical actions or solutions. Though against Navy regulations, I had no recourse, but to initiate a diary four months ago regarding the principles behaviors, actions and facts. Hickey should be exonerated and did nothing wrong, been a credit to our division, is a morale builder, and is compatible with shipmates. I desire to have a good legacy Captain, and to go to my grave manifesting these facts before you and God. I hope and trust you will see justice done with appropriate and action. Finally, should something happen to me, I request burial at sea at your earliest convenience. I have been very proud serving under you.

Thanks and God bless you. Timothy Loggins, RMC, USN

Stunned, his mouth opened. The letter slipped out of his hand as his forehead slowly lowered, touching the desk. After spending an hour reading various statements by enlisted and Stewart, he reflected, "My God! This sounds like a bad dream. I've never heard or experienced anything like this since I've been in. Gates will have Captain's Mast in Subic, and I'll speak with Pursell and Stewart. It's outrageous what happened."

Needing reflection to gather his thoughts, Jim walked outside on a hot, bright day, leaned against lifelines and gazed at the horizon. His soul felt empty as if someone had snatched part of his being. He saw a figure suddenly approach from the corner of his left eye. It was Tom. "Jimmy, I heard what happened and am real sorry for ya buddy. Are you all right?"

He choked back tears as Tom strained, listening to his low tone in responding. "I'm hurting deep inside, pal. Ya know something? He was a great leader, had class, inspired us and we enjoyed working under him. I never thought this would happen. I was there when he went. Before he died, he mentioned Bearden tried killing him. He slashed one of his arms. A bunch of us wrote statements for the old man, and the truth's coming out, buddy."

"I feel for ya. I liked him too." He put an arm around his shoulder. "Well, despite everything happening, we survived this cruise and in a couple weeks we'll be back home."

"That'll be nice. I was just thinking of Tim's folks on that farm in Iowa. You know, they're retired and certainly have paid their dues working hard. He was their youngest, and soon they're gonna get that dreaded Western Union telegram saying he's dead. God, I feel sorry for 'em. He often spoke bout 'em. His slutty wife's also gonna get one too in San Diego, but who knows or cares what her reaction will be. I'm glad he changed his beneficiary, now his folks will get the bucks."

Tom gazed outward, turned and sought to change Jim's disposition. "Betcha can't wait to see her, eh?"

"Yeah, if I could, I'd smuggle her aboard and take her back to the states." Tom chuckled.

"What's so funny?"

"Reminds me of something I read a few years ago in *Stars And Stripes* bout a sailor who fell in love with some Aussie babe when his ship visited Sydney. He got her hair cut military style, but not too short, put her in dress whites, showed her how to salute and what to say when boarding and brought her aboard his cruiser."

"Are you kidding me?"

He shook his head. "No, actually happened. A few of his buddies covered for him, brought her chow and watched her, but finally some lifer or officer discovered the stowaway's hiding place when the ship reached Pearl. They flew her back to kangaroo country and I'm sure they threw the book at him, but apparently the guy was the first to try it."

"Wow, that's something. Listen, thanks for letting me bend your ear. Let's grab chow."

At 1600 the bridge watch changed and Pursell dined in the officer's mess. Lee declined, but called Stewart into his stateroom. After arriving, the lieutenant saw a stern expression on the Captain's face. "Sit down, mister. I've spent some time going over these reports, the diary Loggins secretly kept and a final letter regarding background details of two former crewmen, one of whom committed suicide, before I assumed command."

Stewart interrupted and uncomfortably shifted. "That was very unfortunate."

"I read Loggins diary with interest, the enlisted statements, yours and two from men in engineering."Stewart swallowed, nervously twitching his fingers while his eyes shifted away.

Lee moved his chair within three feet, paused, and stared. "Did you like Bearden?"

"Ah, ah, yes, sir. I did. He was very smart and trained men well. If I had a problem or question, he'd solve or produce a correct answer. He was extremely intelligent and I never worried about communication problems while he and Larson were in charge. Loggins was also good."

"Lieutenant, were you apprehensive or did you fear the man they called Badass?"

Stewart's face immediately turned red as he at the ship's photo on a wall, thinking.

"Well, it's a simple question." The captain's voice raised, "Answer."

"Ah, yes sir, I was. I didn't wanna ruffle his feathers or upset him. He'd been in for several years, and here I was at twenty six a j.g.(junior grade lieutenant) with limited knowledge and four years' service. At times he seemed strange. His eyes sort of penetrated me, and I didn't feel comfortable sometimes around him. I let him run the department after Larson departed."

He lit a cigarette, never taking eyes off the subordinate. "You were cognizant of the poor morale and the rift between Bearden and Loggins.

You didn't fully investigate the Hickey affair, nor the two other unfortunate sailor's situations. You knew Bearden's attitude and conduct toward some men and choose the easy route, rather than taking responsibility for the well being of your men."

The skipper's eyes narrowed as he raised his voice and continued to admonish. "Mister, in less than two years, three men died while you were communications officer. You shirked your duties as an officer." Stewart quickly interrupted.

"Excuse me, Captain, but I tried approaching the X.O. with information I got from Loggins about the Hickey conspiracy."

"That's interesting despite the fact you acted as if Loggins was disturbing you, and you really didn't wanna give him time to explain everything. The petty officer recorded it here in his diary on my desk." He turned, picked it up, and waved it in front of the lieutenant. "Would you like to read it?"

Stewart swallowed and lowered his head. "Captain, Loggins was right. I should have listened. I tried speaking with Pursell about Log's statements, but he said the matter was over months ago and wasn't important. Pursell refused hearing anymore, suggesting I see Bearden. Bearden said Loggins was vindictive and thought he was losing it because of personal problems. That's the truth, sir."

Lee turned away, thinking a few minutes, then moved within a foot and glared. "Mister, Log stated you seldom entered radio, maintaining a passive role. Instead of being proactive, it seems you were primarily inactive." His eyes squinted as he raised his voice. "Listen, you've never been an enlisted as I have. I know how they think and behave. You're responsible for their welfare just as Larson and Bearden should have been. You should have written both up, especially that unbalanced man. He was a poor excuse supervising others." Stewart sat immobile, gazed at the deck, humbled, looking like a school boy being scolded.

"Quite frankly, I'm surprised the radiomen performed well during our combat period, despite his erratic behavior. I admire their courage and am ashamed of you, Stewart. I'm sending a message today to COMSEVENTHFLT and BUPERS requesting you be transferred at the earliest convenience after we get to Subic. Understand?"

Stewart's eyes teared. He pleaded, "Give me another chance."

Kowalski rose, looked down and retorted. "You've had many chances and opportunities for two years and blew it, mister. There's a tiny window for error for officers aboard this warship." He quickly became irate and shouted, "Now, get out of my sight." Stewart exited, a broken man.

The skipper lowered his head, placed both hands over his face and pondered, "It's amazing none of those sailors in radio cracked up because of that unstable man. I can't comprehend what I would have done and I don't relish the action I'm about to take, but it must be done."

The wall phone rang on the officer's mess bulkhead. A Filipino steward answered, and replied, "Yes, sir." Pursell scooped the last piece of chocolate cake and laughed after hearing a joke from a junior officer.

"Who was it, steward?" asked Pursell.

"Ah, sir, Captain tell me he want you in stateroom immediately."

"Ok, thanks. He rose and addressed the six officers finishing dessert. "I wonder what it's about? Probably last night's incident." He grinned, "See you later, fellas."

Lee sat, pondering the matter of conveyance and decision regarding his exec when he heard a knock. "Captain, it's Chad."

"Enter. How was chow tonight?"

He smiled. "Excellent. We missed you."

"Well, I had more important matters on my plate. Sit down." He sat with a puzzled expression on a small couch, folded his hands and stared.

"You look exhausted, Lee." The skipper rose from a desk and sat near him. Stress lines were clearly evident on his forehead.

"Mentally, I am after what occurred." He paused, studying the man a few seconds, unnerving Pursell.

"Is there anything I can do to help, Lee?"

He took a deep breath and glared, "No, I believe you've done enough damage, mister." Wrinkles quickly appeared on the X.O.'s forehead as a worried expression came over him. Pursell shimmied away a few inches clearly unnerved.

"I don't understand. What do you mean?"

"You've been aboard about two years. Is that right?"

"Yes."

"Do you like sea duty, Chad?"

His head lowered while cupping his right hand to his chin. "It's all right, I guess, but I'd rather have a shore assignment."

"That's good, because you're being transferred." Pursell's eyes expanded. He grinned, anticipating choice stateside duty.

"Where, Captain?"

The skipper gazed at him and took a breath "Shortly after we arrive in Subic, you'll be transferred to Naval Communication Station, Adak, Alaska."

Pursell's mouth opened and his eyes bulged, like a man who'd just received a divorce notice from his wife. He blurted, "Why that's way up in the Aleution Islands and isolated duty. I, I, don't understand."

"A few weeks ago, I requested you be assigned after a billet recently became available there. It's a small base, and perhaps you'll employ better relations with junior officers and enlisted, but quite frankly, you're not fit for sea duty, not aboard this ship." The X.O. lowered his head between his palms, dejected.

"I just finished completing officer's quarterly fitness reports, including yours and Stewarts'. What do you think yours are, Chad?"

Pursell cleared his throat. "Well, Captain, I believe I performed well in coordinating various functions within all departments and kept excellent records of personnel and ship's logs."

"Yes, you did, but you failed in the human element. I gave you 3.5's for those responsibilities, but 2.0 in welfare, discipline and morale. That's inexcusable mister. I've carefully observed your behavior since taking command. You've been haughty, arrogant and complacent at times." He raised his voice and berated the officer. "Your behavior and attitude toward others was suspect before and after I took command, particularly in Hickey's situation. Hell, this man risked his life helping Alden fight those damn fires after we were hit."

He looked down at the couch as he continued reprimanding him. "Damn it, mister. A major responsibility is the morale and welfare of the crew. I don't mean officers and senior NCO's; I mean everyone. You knew of problems between the two dead men. You were cognizant of declining morale after Hickey was set up and unfairly busted. You knew, or should have known, how Bearden treated some of the men, and of Gates' racial bias. You were complacent and apathetic, instead of being involved." Pursell folded his arms and looked away. "Stewart tried explaining about Loggin's investigation, but you refused inquiring saying it was over and insignificant."

Pursell looked at him. "Ah, sir, how did you know?"

He picked up the journal, flashing it inches below Pursell's face and glared. "It's all here, and I've got Loggin's final statements explaining just about everything. Do you care to read it?" The X.O.'s eyes shifted as he took a deep breath. Lee's eyes squinted while asking. "Why didn't you inform me about Loggin's request for special Captain's Mast? We've had several daily and weekly conferences, and not once did you manifest what was happening. On occasion I asked how the men were, and if there were problems I should be aware of. You responded everything was normal." He shouted, "Didn't you?"

Pursell ran his fingers through his hair and slowly nodded. "You're right, Lee."

Irate, the skipper snapped, "Forget the Lee, it's sir or Captain, mister."

"Yes, sir"

Lee glared, raised a forefinger and stated, "Listen damn it. A ship is like a family. There's gotta be harmony, cohesion and good morale. The family's the basic unit of society, and when there's a cancer like a Bearden or Gates, responsible men must contribute to eradicate the disease. Both should have been written up and given dishonorable discharges. You know that." He leaned closer. "Pursell, you failed miserably not performing that important responsibility."

Despondent, Pursell looked at him. "I'm sorry, captain."

Lee rose, placing his hands against his hips and stared as Pursell gazed up.

"Sorry, doesn't cut it, Chad. You're finished here. Quite frankly, I wish you'd never been aboard. Captains before me took *Satterfield* into battle in two previous wars and never had three non-combat deaths as we've had during the period you've been X.O. Of course, I bear responsibility for the last two, but your conduct has been unbecoming an executive officer. Don't you understand that a ship's only as efficient as its crew?"

"Yes, sir"

"In war, a destroyer's the first in combat. This is the real Navy." He shouted, "Damn it! Wake up." Silence permeated the room. Lee walked over, sat at the desk, took a deep breath, and lowered his voice "Tomorrow, we're burying Loggins at sea. Make sure the Master at Arms knows. Its appropriate men from radio are casket bearers. Now Chad, I hope you rectify your past mistakes because if not, you'll never command a ship or be an effective leader even on shore. You should understand that sea service for enlisted men are tougher than cake shore duty. You're dismissed."

He turned dejected, avoiding eye contact and walked toward the hatch as the skipper rose to make a final statement. "Listen, a few months ago I requested Silver and Bronze Star medals be awarded to Alden and Hickey for their actions during the battle. Follow up on it."

"Yes, sir" He quickly left and walked into his room, collecting thoughts.

At 0:900, *Satterfield* steamed east 100 miles southeast of the Paracell Islands on a bright steamy day. Kowalski ordered the ship's engines stopped as the entire crew in dress whites assembled on weather decks for Loggins' funeral.

Burial at sea accompanied by religious ceremony is one of the oldest naval traditions. The solemn act was repeated numerous times during the Second World War.

A boatswain's mate announced over the 1MC. "Now all hands prepare for burial detail." A twelve-man honor squad, bugler, Master at Arms, X.O., C.O., six body bearers comprised of Thomas, Smith, Reemer, Hickey, Duff and McGovern, and a seven-man firing squad formed on the quarterdeck. The colors were lowered to half-staff. The M. A. A. ordered the firing squad to fall in near lifelines and everyone assumed parade rest.

For additional weight, a five-inch diameter 50-pound shell was put inside next to the remains before the white canvas bag coffin was stitched, then placed on a six-by-three flat board. The men carried their

**Map of South China Sea**

leader between the saluting honor guards over to lifelines. The flag was placed over the head as his legs faced the water.

The firing squad was positioned a few feet from the body as Purcell and Kowalski stood six feet behind the casket. The captain's uniform was impeccable with five rows of ribbons adorning his upper right chest. Each bearer raised the board so the feet portion rested on the top lifeline. All sailors remained covered.

The skipper, carrying the Bible, stepped near the remains, opened and read from one of the Psalms. "The Lord is my shepherd. I shall not want. He leadeth me to lie down in green pastures......" He closed the book, looked down, moved behind a microphone, took a deep breath and spoke.

Chief Radioman Timothy Loggins was an inspiration. He exhibited great leadership with a unique charisma and personality, motivating others. In my years of naval service, he was indeed one of the best sailors I've had the pleasure to command. He loved his men, ultimately sacrificing himself for them. God only knows where we get such men, for they do not pass this way often. Speaking for myself and our crew, we will miss him. We lost a good shipmate. Let's carry his example with us always.

Jim, holding the board near Mike quickly raised his left hand wiping tears while somber men heard the poignant words. Lee handed the Bible to Pursell and received the Naval manual.

The M. A. A. shouted. "Firing party, present arms." Immediately in unison M-14 pieces were raised in front of each member's chest. The captain thumbed a few pages, stopped, took another deep breath, repressing tears. Still at parade rest, each sailor bowed his head as the captain read the prayer.

We therefore commit this body to the deep, to be turned into corruption, looking for the resurrection of the body when the sea shall give up her dead, and the life of the world to come through our Lord Jesus Christ who at his coming shall change our vile body, that it may be like his glorious body according to the mighty working whereby he is able to subdue all things unto himself. Amen

They tilted the board, and Timothy Loggin's body swiftly plunged into 2,600 fathoms of ocean to the bottom. Sam Powers' prophesy was fulfilled. The M.A.A. Barked, "Firing party, order arms, parade rest. All hands bow heads."

After 30 seconds of silence he announced, "Ships company, attention, hand salute. Firing party, attention. Firing party, port arms. Firing party fire three volleys." The honor squad assumed hand salute. "Ready, aim, fire; aim, fire, aim fire." The cracking sounds of rifle fire echoed above the tranquil sea. The party remained at firing position.

A young crew-cut Seaman holding a bugle, walked to a point behind the party and played Taps. As sailors stood at attention with hand salute, tears streamed down several cheeks while the last few notes were blown. Two other sailors held the colors, then another smartly folded it into the traditional diamond shape showing the white stars on a blue background, and handed it to Kowalski while slowly saluting.

The M. A. A. ordered everyone dismissed. The six strolled, leaned over lifelines almost transfixed, staring at the location of body entry. No one spoke. On the saddest day of their lives, part of them died.

Jim murmured, "He was the best, the very best, like a father to us. God, take care of him." He turned, stared at his buddies and softly murmured, "We will never be the same."

Sid, Mike and Smitty rubbed their eyes and followed Jim down below. Two shafts turned screws churning saltwater, halting the vessel's drift and *Satterfield* steamed toward Subic.

# 17

## "A FIGHT, A MONKEY AND HOME"

The next morning, *Satterfield* tied up in Subic astern of another destroyer. Stewart bid adieu to fellow officers after spending a few minutes shaking hands with radiomen on watch. Few words were exchanged.

McDonald, Duff, Warden and Hickey stood on deck looking down as he walked off the forward brow carrying a large suitcase. 'Buddha' looked at them and informed. "Saw a message the other day that he's being sent ta Midway Island. Shit, that speck of land is only two miles long and a mile wide with only a few hundred guys stationed there. Man, its 1,200 miles from Hawaii and nothin'around, but thousands of stupid gooney birds."

"Yeah, good, couldn't happen to a nicer guy. I'm glad he's gone", Jim remarked.

Duff quickly exclaimed, "Hey, we just sent a message for the skipper to the Admiral in charge of the Twelfth Naval District in Frisco where Larson's stationed. Their initiating an inquiry stateside about his involvement in the whole matter and the other two guys. They got plenty of evidence thanks to Log's statement. Man, I hope his ass is grass and they nail him."

Mac snapped, "Yeah, I couldn't agree more." He lit a cigarette, smiled and at them. "We're only here for two days and then heading home. Well mates, there's some serious drinkin' and lovin' ta do cause we're not coming back."

As a humid tropical breeze increased, Jim scanned swaying palms nearby. He thought, "I hope she's working at her aunt's club. I'm off tomorrow and gotta see her." Time was short.

Before evening watch, Kowalski sent a messenger ordering Alden and Hickey to dress in tropical whites and assemble in the officer's wardroom. After entering, the captain and X.O. wearing khakis, and a yeoman in whites stood in front of the ship's large black and white framed photo on a bulkhead.

Pursell ordered, "Alden, Hickey, front and center." Tom advanced two paces, standing at attention as Jim remained behind. The captain read.

On 19 April, 1972 Damage Control Man Second Class Thomas Alden aboard destroyer USS *Satterfield*, without regard for his own safety, removed injured sailors from the destroyed area after enemy bombing attack and led damage control men into a dangerous space with live ammunition present against almost impossible odds as the vessel sank in Tonkin Gulf waters. Despite volatile and hazardous conditions, he fought blazes for hours until they were extinguished. You are hereby awarded this Bronze Star Medal for your actions and devotion to duty, which are in keeping with the highest traditions of the U. S. Naval Service.

Vice Admiral William F. Peterson, Commander U.S. Seventh Fleet

A yeoman handed a small box to Kowalski. He took out a shiny bronze medal and looked at Tom. While leaning and pinning the device on his right chest, a tear formed in Lee's eye. He murmured, "You saved the ship. I recommended you for a higher medal but was overruled.

Congratulations, Alden. He smiled, shook his hand as Tom grinned and reciprocated.

"Thank you, sir, but there were others who deserved medals."

Lee stared and grinned, "I understand exactly how you feel." He turned, looked at Jim and read a statement.

On 19 April 1972, Seaman James Hickey assisted Petty Officer Thomas Alden aboard the destroyer USS *Satterfield*, fighting fires in a volatile area after an enemy bombing attack. Despite extreme conditions, live ammunition and burning fires, he maintained position holding a powerful spraying hose while backing Alden, the lead O.B.A. man. You are hereby awarded this commendation letter for your actions and devotion to duty which are in keeping with the highest traditions of the U.S. Naval Service.

Vice Admiral William F. Peterson, Commander U.S. Seventh Fleet

He received an eight-by-ten gold-framed glass-encased letter with the words below an impressive yellow and blue U. S. Navy emblem signed by the admiral. The captain smiled, shook his hand and remarked, "Congratulations, Hickey, I'm proud of you. I recommended the Bronze Star for you, but my request was vetoed."

"I appreciate that, sir, and thank you."

Lee gazed at the three Seaman stripes on his upper left arm and stated, "Hickey, I've investigated the events of last January before I assumed command, the injustice by my predecessor, two officers and the conspiracy against you. Today, you're hereby reinstated Petty Officer Third Class with full retroactive back pay."

He leaned within a foot of the surprised sailor and whispered, "Hickey, I'm sorry this happened and have taken the appropriate actions."

Jim smiled, "Ah, I really don't know what to say, but thank you, sir.

Lee stepped back and grinned, "No, sailor, thank you. I'm proud having dedicated men aboard. I know you and Loggins were close. You're mourning his loss as we all are, but I believe he's got it made in Heaven. Take comfort knowing that. You're both dismissed." Tom and Jim about faced, and marched out.

Lee gazed at Chad and remarked, "It pleases me having loyal men aboard this old bucket. Now, you'd better pack your belongings and get going. You'll be here in Subic for a few days until a flight out of Clark can be arranged." Pursell lowered his head, a dejected man. "I hope you've learned Chad. Maybe someday you'll make a better officer. Good luck, mister." He saluted, frowned and departed.

Jim and Tom walked near the stern gazing at the bay. Tom turned, and looked at his friend. "Know something Jimmy? I wish some of the other guys would've gotten medals. Your commendation letter looks impressive.

"Thanks, and that medal on your chest really stands out. I'm looking forward to having my crow sewed back on and wearing civvies again on liberty."

"That's right, you deserved it."

Tom took a drag on a cigarette. "Did ya hear where Pursell's being transferrred?"

"No."

He grinned, "I heard they're sending him to Adak, Alaska. Shit, there's nothin' up there. For many years the joke's been that there's a girl behind every tree there, but ya see, there's no trees.""They chuckled.

Tom's expression suddenly turned sad. "What's wrong, buddy?"

"I was just thinking. Log should have gotten a medal for what he did. I'll miss him too. Man, we actually survived all that crap. I remember reading Churchill's quote when the Germans were bombing the shit out of London. He said something like never, never, never, never give up. Well, shipmate, we never did, and now we're going home. I can't wait. By the way, tomorrow you might see Linda. Give her a hug for me. She's a doll." He smiled.

The following morning, Captain's Mast was convened on the quarter deck. Donald Gates was reduced to the lowest rank, Seaman Recruit and given a dishonorable discharge for conspiracy, deception, defamation of character, and conduct unbecoming a sailor in the U.S. Navy.

For the record, Kowalski ordered a yeoman to include honorable and dishonorable posthumous discharges respectively in Loggins and Bearden's personnel files. Loggins' flag and belongings were specially wrapped, placed in a box, and shipped to Iowa according to protocol.

Shortly before 1300, Jim grabbed lunch, showered, changed into civilian attire and walked on deck to joining Sid, Mike and Smitty. Sid down at the pier and exclaimed, "Hey, look fellas. It's Gates, leaving." As they stared, Gates carried a sea bag on the dock looking stoic. He stopped, looked up and waved. They refused returning the gesture and merely watched as he faded into the base.

Mike looked at the others, "You know somethin'? In a way, I feel for him. It'll be tough finding a decent job with his discharge, but I hope he makes it and has a good life because there has to be some good in everyone."

Smitty remarked, "Yeah man, even though he's a bigot, ya gotta hope he changes because ya only get one chance in life, right?"

Jim replied, "You said it." He smiled. "By the way, I got my crow back. The old man restored it, and I'm getting 360 bucks back pay."

Sid slid over, put an arm around him and smiled. "Well, hi there my man. Ya know, I'm your buddy and I'll even let ya buy us a few rounds of suds tonight." They laughed.

"Hey pals, I haven't got it yet, just twenty bucks on me, but when I do, I'll treat ya."

Mike said, "Ok, Jim, we're gonna hold ya ta yer promise."

Jim backed away. "I gotta run. You guys going on liberty today?"

Sid replied, "Yeah, probably later, and we might have a couple in the club your girl works in. See ya later, Jimmy."

By 1400, he walked through the main gate and across "Shit River" tossing a few quarters to destitute kids begging in a craft. The main street teamed with numerous sailors and Marines entering and leaving establishments. Noisy jeepneys packed with military, and locals honked and sped by. The steamy air whipped paper and dust from old sidewalks flanking the avenue.

Wearing white trousers and a light blue tropical shirt sprinkled with tiny white palm trees, Jim entered Maria's Place, a little bar crammed with several sailors. Nineteenth Century Spanish paintings of Seville and castles adorned three walls behind circular wooden tables. A six-foot long counter with a cash register sat above a large sliding glass door displaying cigarettes, cigars, candy bars and gum.

A half dozen mini-skirted young women buzzed around tables hustling drinks, a few sitting on the laps of drunken men. Top hits *Brandy, You're a Fine Girl* and *American Pie* blared from a corner juke box while couples danced and embraced.

He prayed, "God, let her be here." He walked behind a large stationary sailor and peeked.

There she was! He was elated. Drink orders were brought and placed on the counter. She operated an old cash register, six feet in front of a large green curtain reaching the floor, separating a small back office.

Intending surprise, he snaked around dancing couples and sat at a table near a rear window forty feet away. Business boomed after the giant carrier USS *Constellation* with 5,000 sailors nestled, tying up at Cubi Point Naval Air Station across the bay.

A cute petite mini-skirted girl with heavy makeup, long black hair and a round nose swiftly walked over and smiled. "Hi, Joe, you buy me dink?"

He shook his head. "Nah, honey, my name's Jim, not Joe." He tossed a peso on the table. "You can get me a San Miguel though, ok?" Chagrined, she grabbed the coin and returned with the beer.

He studied Linda, exchanging Tagalog with waitresses and bar girls. Her short middle-aged aunt walked out from behind the curtain and grabbed a stack of receipts. The bags under her eyes bore evidence of years managing the establishment.

His girl wore little make up above a short yellow dress decorated with attractive botanical designs a few inches above her knees. He took a large gulp while staring and reflected, "She's so beautiful and a real lady." The beer refreshed him as air conditioning circulated tobacco smoke.

She stood behind the register scanning the club. Suddenly, her face brightened with an instant smile as their eyes locked. He rose as she ran around the counter and leaped into his outstretched arms. Tears of joy flowed down her brown cheeks while he planted a long kiss on her receptive lips. "Oh Jeem, you supise me. I so happy."

He put his arms around her waist and hugged her, "Can you sit with me?"

"Yes, only little while."

His lips pressed together while lowering his head. "What wong, honey?"

He moved closer and murmured, "Well, we're leaving tomorrow morning for the States. We don't have much time, angel. When do ya get off?"

Sadness crept over her. He gently wiped a tear off her cheek. "I off seven o'clock, but maybe wok late." Linda gave him the location of her aunt's house, agreeing to rendezvous shortly thereafter. "Jeem, I go back now, honey." He rose, placing his right hand just above her lower back, gently pulled her close and kissed her.

Meanwhile, three inebriated, uniformed sailors sitting nearby gawked, making off-color remarks as she walked toward the counter. A lanky six-foot-one foul-mouthed goon sitting between his two cronies quickly shifted his eyes and examined her like a dentist gazing into a patient's opened mouth.

Suddenly, he rose, walked and grabbed her waist, pulling the surprised girl toward him. "Come here, baby, I'm loaded. What's your price?" She quickly shook him off as others laughed.

Linda blurted, "I don't do dos tings. Only take money, wok regista. You talk to odda gils." The drunk grabbed her arm and leaned, attempting to kiss her as she struggled.

"Oh, honey, you're special." He looked at his buddies. "Hey fellas, I like the hard ta get ones. They're more fun. Come on, you little Flip, let's go ta bed."

She screamed, "Let me go, let me go."

Others shouted, "Get her sailor, get her." Customers ceased dancing and stared.

Seconds after she left his table, Jim, took a swig and gazed out a window marveling at white tropical birds resting near a nearby palm tree when he heard a ruckus. Enraged, he leaped off the chair, ran and shoved the perpetrator away and shouted, "Damn it, leave her alone." He turned. "Are you all right, honey?" Still fearful, she nodded. "Listen, there's gonna be trouble. You'd better get behind the counter." She ran as her aunt popped out from behind the curtain, observing the disturbance.

As the lurch staggered toward him, one of his cronies hollered, "All right, brave little man, let's see ya take on Kenny and whoever wins gets her for the night. How bout it?" One of his chums threw five bucks on the table in a bet and looked at Jim. "You win, you get the babe and the bucks."

Jim thought, "I don't need any more fighting and trouble." He turned and started walking away when the man blindsided him with a sucker punch to his neck knocking him a few feet against the side of an occupied table. Intense pain shot through his head and veins. Jim winced and put his hand against his neck, somewhat easing the tingling sensation.

Temporarily stunned, he took a deep breath, turned around and ducked as his opponent swung wildly. His friends shouted, "Deck 'em Kenny, deck 'em."

Jim spread his legs, raised his hands in front of his face, glared and shouted, "You bastard! Ya got me with a cheap shot, but messed with the wrong girl this time. Ya like picking on little people cause of your size. Well, let's go, asshole." Rock music continued playing, but every eye was glued on the unfolding action.

The perpetrator clenched a fist and lunged as he swung his right arm toward Jim's jaw, but his timing was perfect. Remembering a judo move, he quickly lowered his body, grabbed the opponent's arm with both hands while buffering himself against his waist, and threw him on to the floor. Stunned, his face shook while gazing up as Jim backed away. Jim spread his legs apart, ready for another assault. The man rose slowly, glared, wiped blood oozing from his nose onto a black mustache and shouted, "You're gonna get it now."

Kenny thrust, wildly swinging both fists. The frustrations, anxiety, hatred of Bearden, and Log's death bubbled and surfaced within Jim, exploding in furious rage like an erupting volcano. Jim quickly moved ducked a blow, and lunged, torpedoing a swift right fist into the goon's chest and sent the 180-pound brute between his pals on top of a table, scattering glasses and bottles. The two down at their chum spread eagle on the table as their eyes bulged in astonishment. Jim pounced, and raised his fist, inches above the man's face, ready to strike when her aunt shouted, "Stop, stop." She grabbed a phone and dialed the base requesting shore patrol assistance.

While the instigator laid on the table, his eyes rolled. He looked up as Jim hovered over him clenching a fist. He looked down and shouted, "You ever do that again I'll kill ya, understand creep?" He'd never been this irate in his life.

He turned, walked toward the counter, checking on her when the two rose, and one boasted, "All right, now you're gonna deal with both of us." Jim raised his hands backing away when suddenly two figures in civilian attire walked in, eyed the situation and surrounded the would-be attackers.

Jim grinned, "You're just in time, Mike and Sid."

Mike glared at one stocky man three feet away and shouted, "Now it's a fair fight. Come on bird farm boys. Let's see what ya got." Muscular Sid quickly reached and grabbed the other medium-built guy by the throat with both hands, lifting him a foot off the floor as the terrified man gasped for breath.

"Put, put, put me down, please." He released the grip and lowered the frightened man.

Mike stared and exclaimed, "I really don't think you wanna go a round with us, do ya? You two squirrels thought it would be cool taking on our buddy, eh? Well now, it's even odds. What are you gonna do about it, huh?"

They looked down at their friend on the table as Kenny shook his head and slowly rose. One crony chirped. "Come on, let's beat it." They tossed pesos on the table, glared, and quickly hustled their drunken sidekick outside.

Sid smiled, "Hey, nice job, Jim. Looks like ya got 'em good. Let's get a beer."

"I think they might have wasted me if you guys hadn't shown up." He described what occurred as a waitress brought three cold beers.

Patrons resumed their partying activities. Five minutes later, two tall helmeted shore patrolmen in whites entered with night sticks hanging from duty belts and armed with holstered .45 caliber pistols.

Linda ran over and Jim introduced her. His buddies smiled, eyeing her countenance as her aunt spoke to the military police while pointing toward Jim. They approached as Linda pleaded, "Jeem not at fault. He help me and good guy. Bad saila ty get me and he dunk."

Hickey interrupted and retorted, "Honey, just sit down, and I"ll explain everything." Shortly after giving a statement and describing the men, he suggested. "Ya know, if you guys leave now you might catch them because the more sober two are probably holding up the drunken jerk somewhere out there.

They turned and started leaving, but one spun around, gave a stern look while pointing the night stick at him and warned, "Listen, sailor. Based on what you, the girl and her aunt said, we're letting ya off this time, but if it happens again we'll throw ya in the brig. Understand?" He nodded.

She enjoyed the company of Jim's friends and Mike ordered another round. After a short spell, more swabbies filtered in as her aunt motioned Linda for help behind the counter. They drank a few suds while singing the popular song *Horse With no Name* by the group America which blared from the juke box. Sid stopped and gazed, "Wow, Jim, she's some knockout. I like the way she carries herself. Like ya said, she's a real lady. I'm happy for ya pal."

Mike agreed. "Yeah, ya know a lot of guys come here, get suckered into marrying bar girls or hookers, then after reaching the States as citizens, they forget the G.I., leave and file for divorce. I know it's happened a lot. Ya, know, there are exceptions. Some stay married, and that's a good thing. She may be just be the one, pal.

"Yeah, ya never know for sure. He looked at them. "Thanks for showing up and getting me out of a jam."

Sid took a swig and remarked, "Sure, anytime buddy. Linda's decent, got class and isn't loose like a lot of these babes."

Mike nudged him, "Look, speaking of babes. Check out that one over there; she sure has a nice stern." An eighteen-year old, small-breasted and attractive mini-skirted girl sat on a sailor's lap, kissing him.

"Hey, Mike, I think the hops and barley's kicking in for ya, guys", Jim observed.

Shortly thereafter, they both rose after refusing several solicitations from women. Mike looked down and asked. "You wanna go steamin' with us, Jimmy?"

He thought and replied, "Thanks anyway, but it's our last night here and I'm gonna meet her after she gets off cause we've only got a few hours, ya know."

"Ah, that's ok, we understand. Hey face it, you're in love and it's a good thing. See ya back aboard. Remember Jimmy, we're sailin' at 0800 tomorrow." He watched them depart as they waved at Linda and her aunt. Nursing a beer, he thought, "Those guys are ok in my book. I'm blessed having good friends.

As a precaution, he waited, in the eventuality of someone else hitting on her. In late afternoon, he walked toward the entrance, blew a kiss and waved at her. She smiled. He desired a tranquil little place to unwind, dine and think.

In late afternoon, more servicemen flooded the downtown area as music resounded from clubs. He desired peace. After walking a quarter mile, he spotted an inconspicuous small diner on a side street off the main avenue. A large old wooden sign barely visible, hung by a rope over the main door of a one-story gray bricked structure.

He stood in front, looking up at a sign, bearing the name Cruz Diner, Delicious Home Cooking, and then peered through a window viewing an unlit, almost dark area where six dined. He thought, "This place looks gaudy, but it's probably inexpensive. Why not give it a try?"

Just after entering over a creaky wooden floor, he scanned. Six circular tables were strewn a few feet from a long metal counter. Three large ceiling fans provided little comfort in the non-air conditioned restaurant. A few dusty paintings of mountains and islands hung on two dull yellow painted walls.

A short, hairless chubby faced 60-year-old Filipino, wearing an apron stood frying fish near a grill behind the counter. The cook turned, smiled, and hurried, greeting the stranger. Jim smiled at his enthusiastic demeanor, as words shot out of his mouth like a machine gun. "Hi, Joe, hi Joe, I Jose Cruz. Come, come, you sit over here."

Cruz grabbed a napkin on a wooden table wiping off dust before Jim sat and then shoved a little menu in front of his face. "Here menu, all food good. I make myself, you know." The man retreated behind the counter and continued his culinary duties as Jim perused twenty items, primarily Philippine cuisine, including lumpia, pansit, pork, vegetables, rice, baluut and fried rice.

Intrinsically a happy man, Cruz scampered back, smiled, hovered over him, and asked in a high squeaky voice. "You like beer? I ga ice col San Miguel."

He thought, "I've had enough. How bout a Coke and shrimp fried rice?"

The owner quickly giggled nodding, "Ok, ok G. I. I bing and you like. A small radio on the counter played soothing Filipino guitar music as Jim scanned the patrons.

Four locals conversed in a corner wolfing down pansit consisting of noodles, vegetables and pork. An aged Filipino sat alone near a window sipping tea, gazing out; then he spotted a middle- aged American 40 feet away, sitting at a table against a wall, facing him.

While drinking a soda, Jim's eyes beheld a little creature sitting on a table a couple feet from the gentleman. A monkey! He thought, "Wow! Cruz probably lets cats, dogs and other varmits in here too."

Jose whipped around the counter, smiled and brought the hot Asian meal. "Lookie, good, good G.I., you ty now." After putting on a little soy sauce, he took a large bite as Cruz continued hovering, inches away, unnerving him. "It good, you like, you like?" He giggled, nodded and ran back to fry chicken. It was delicious with the shrimp not under cooked. It was habitual eating quick aboard ship, and in less than ten minutes he finished most of the dinner.

After lighting a smoke he turned, seeing the little critter staring and yipping at him. The American looked, smiled, rose and walked toward him holding a short rope attached to the pet.

"May I sit down?"

"Sure, be my guest." As the man sat two feet away, the creature hopped up, resting a few inches from the plate in front of his master. He had short brown hair, and no higher than ten inches with a cute little face, a pug nose and one-inch sharp claws.

The man laughed, exclaiming, "Ha, ha. Buster's just eye ballin' ya, lad. Don't be afraid. Just don't make any fast moves in my direction because he'll think you're threatening me. Ya see? He's my protector and buddy." He smiled. "Oh, by the way, I'm Jerry Grow, retired Chief Signalman from Sarasota. I've been living here for ten years since I left the Navy." His voice and demeanor were pleasant as they shook hands.

His salt and pepper hair receded above a tanned six foot medium frame. He wore old khaki trousers and a short-sleeve yellow shirt decorated with miniature blue anchors. A large conspicuous black tattoo of an old sailing vessel adorned his right forearm. Below hazel eyes and a curvy nose, the end of his jaw uncommonly jutted, reminiscent of renowned Hollywood actor Kirk Douglas.

Jim at Buster, and grinned, "How'd ya pick up this little guy?"

"Well, I think it was a few years back. I went on the base to see a buddy who had access to an old jeep. We rode around, way over near the perimeter where the jungle is, and then I saw him hopping around. I leaped out, took off my shirt, ran, jumped and captured him. Ya, see, they have small, razor sharp teeth and I wasn't about gettin' bit."

"What happened next?"

"Well Jim, it took time training him in the little two-bedroom house I was renting because they're pretty messy and wild ya know, but I did it and we've been friends ever since. Shit, he even sleeps and eats with me."

He looked at the pet, "Wow, that's something. I'll bet ya must live like a king over here. Ya know, with the exchange rate and low cost a living."

Grow smiled, "Ya took the words right outta my mouth. Yeah, it's been real nice. Here I am living on a 1,000 a month pension at the great age of fifty and don't have a care in the world. I've even got a young girlfriend who visits and cleans the place."

His expression turned serious as he gazed at Jim while asking, "Ah, by the way sailor, how are the States these days? I haven't been back in eleven years. I read the English version of the *Manila Times* and *Stars and Stripes*, but tell me, has it changed much?"

Jim told him about pop culture including radical Hippies, a few current movies, sports, civil rights, changes in clothing styles and few snippets about his family and ship. After ten minutes, he raised his hand and interrupted. "Say, you mentioned Satterfield. I read in *Stars and Stripes* what happened to you poor guys. It's a miracle you all survived."

Jim lowered his head thinking, and remarked, "Yup, I agree. A fearless buddy won the Bronze Star fighting those damn fires and I was right behind him."

He smiled, "Well, that's what shipmates are for, right? We fight for each other."

"Yup, absolutely, pal."

Grow eyed a quarter sized peso, sitting near the plate. "Hey, ya wanna see something?"

"Sure, why not?"

"Now, pick up the coin and put it in his mouth."

His eyes opened wide while exclaiming, "Ya gotta be kiddin' me. Heck, he knows you. Why don't ya do it? He's got sharp teeth and I value my fingers."

He laughed, "You're right, I'll tell him to do it." Grow picked up the coin, holding it in front of the creature's mouth. Buster quickly grabbed and placed it inside. Grow smiled and at Jim and Buster, "Ok now, Buster, open up buddy, open up." The creature's mouth opened. "Now, look inside. Do ya see anything?"

He leaned forward, gazed and replied, "Nah, nothing."

"Now, move a little closer." Grow reached into a pocket, retrieving a three inch long flashlight and shined it near his mouth. "Look way back there." Beyond two rows of small canines was a two-inch skin like sack near the back jaw where the coin rested. "See it now?"

"Yeah, there it is. Well, I'll be. I've never seen anything like that before."

Grow ordered the pet to return the peso, which tumbled onto the table. "You see monkeys are like squirrels. They store all kinds of things back there like nuts and stuff."

Fascinated, Jim shook his hand and thanked him. The man rose and smiled as Buster leaped into his arms. "Well, good luck, Jim. It's been nice talking with ya. Have a safe voyage back and kiss the States for me, will ya?"

"Sure will Jerry. Take it easy." He stared and thought, "What a nice man." Shortly thereafter, he left, hopped aboard a jeepney and walked a few blocks to her aunt's home. It was a three bedroom quaint little place with two banana trees flanking a rear entrance near an alley.

Mentally tired, he laid on a comfortable brown couch and closed his eyes. Now in the days of September, time was becoming precious for James Hickey. He reflected, as the waning sun's rays pierced above him through a window. Snippets of past events flashed through his mind, the rapidity of such coupled with emotional stress was almost overwhelming—the storm, shipboard turmoil, months of combat—Bearden's irrational behavior, conspiracy resulting in demotion, loss of pride—balancing himself as seawater rushed against his body in an explosive fiery space, the shocking, unexpected death of mentor, hero and friend Tim Loggins—defending Linda.

A pounding headache suddenly came. He took a deep breath and thought, "Home, I miss it." He reflected about the wonderful family in Michigan and California he left behind, of three women on the coast, visiting exotic ports of call, knowing a decent Filipino girl who brought him joy, love and relief from the evil clutches of Bearden, yet she too was temporary—another chapter in his life—for earthly pleasures are fleeting, but unlike the sea, there is one permanent element that never changed—the love exemplified by dedicated and unselfish men aboard Satterfield, who sacrificed for each other, saving the ship. He smiled, consoling himself, cognizant of personal victory. He had conquered fear. The sailor rolled over on his side and slept.

Later, a soft voice whispered near his ear, "Jeem, Jeem, wake up honey." He opened his eyes seeing Linda's smiling face.

He pulled her gently near him, kissed her lips, and whispered, "Is this a dream?"

She giggled like a little girl and smiled, "Oh no. I really here for you." She nuzzled near his side while her head rested on his chest.

"Hey, what time is it?"

"It nine o'clock. I sorry, work exta time."

He rose, hugged her and looked into her eyes. "We only have a couple hours left before I've gotta be back. Go change and we'll take a taxi over to White Rock Beach." She smiled and went into a bedroom to change.

Linda slipped into pink shorts and matching tank top. They walked, hailed a cab and sped two miles toward the vacant beach. A light refreshing wind blew from the South China Sea across the bay swaying palm trees above. No words were exchanged as they walked hand in hand along the shore listening to intermittent little ripples of water striking the beach. It was serene as the full moon's light reflected on the bay.

They returned near the small thatched-roof wooden hut where months before he snapped photos while she smiled, posing. They sat and he put his arm around and gazed into her beautiful sparkling eyes. He looked at her. "Honey, this is really a bittersweet time."

Puzzled, she asked, "I no undastand Jeem."

He at the water, thirty feet away, then turned and looked at her. "It means it's a happy, but sad time." She nodded in her usual reserved manner. "I'm glad you're with me. My folks and your letters gave me confidence. Every time reading about your activities, how you felt about us, your cheerful attitude, and prayers gave me hope, and hope is a good thing because each day brought me closer to you."

Jim leaned within inches, paused and looked into her eyes. "Now it's a sad time for us because I'm leaving and sailing 8,000 miles back to California." His lips pressed together as he gazed down at the sand. "Damn, I wish I could stay here longer." Tears quickly formed in his eyes as she planted a long kiss on his lips.

"I undastand. Happy and sad time."

"Right, honey."

The couple gazed at the moon and thousands of stars sprinkled the heavens. Jim poured his heart and soul out to the girl and softly murmured as he moved within inches of her. "Linda, this time, this place and these moments will never be repeated for us. Let's cherish the time and never forget it." He wiped her soft teary cheeks, then kissed her again and took a deep breath. "Wow it's hard to believe the summer flew by so fast."

Slowly, she pulled away with a serious expression. "When you get out of navy, Jeem?"

"About six months after we get back. Why?"

"I get out nursing school in year, save many pesos and come to States and see you."

He looked and grinned, "You are such a sweet angel." He stood, looked at the sky and exclaimed."Thank you God for bringing me this wonderful girl who I love."

She stood and wept as her head rested against his chest. "Oh my Jeem, you have good way with word, but make me cry again. I sorry."

His hand smoothed the top of her dark hair as he replied, "Don't be. I'm just a romantic, speaking from my heart." Suddenly, he broke out singing *The Shadow of Your Smile*, an old standard popularized by singer Andy Williams. After finishing, she grabbed him tightly, hugging the sailor, again weeping.

"You have nice voice."

He rose, looked at her, reached into a pocket and handed her a little box. "Open it, angel." She smiled as her eyes beamed, looking at a two inch wide heart-shaped watch surrounded by a pink trim attached to a 20 carat silver necklace.

She quickly hugged him. He grabbed the watch, set the correct time, securing the gift around her neck so it nestled comfortably just above her breasts. "Now, sweetheart, this is a reminder when you wanna know the time, you'll think of me."

"Oh, Jeem, this is best gift anyone give me. I don't know what to say, but salamat." (thank you)

She pulled him close as he gazed at the watch and grinned saying, "Sure looks good on you. I wish I could be here seeing you wearing it on a nice dress."

She smiled, "I send photo."

Suddenly, he jumped up nervous, slapped his forehead and shouted, "Wait a minute! I just realized something. I don't have to be back aboard till 7:45 tomorrow at the latest. What was I thinking? I thought we had Cinderella liberty tonight, but don't. That's good news honey, eh?"

Linda rose, smiled, threw her arms around and kissed him. "Oh, that make me happy, Jeem. You stay with me at auntie's house tonight."

He grinned, "I can't think of a better place sweetheart. Excitedly, he suggested, "I'll take you on the base and you can see me off."

She smiled, "Of course I will and then I must take bus to Manila because classes begin soon."

They took another walk along the placid shore until midnight as the moon drifted west. Her aunt retired before they arrived. He embraced, kissed her goodnight, took off his shoes and jumped on the couch. She turned around, slipped off her shoes and lay beside him. He gazed at her smooth short legs and warm body. Linda's eyes closed as her cheek clung against his while her hand rested on his chest. He whispered, "Linda, I'd be lying if I said I didn't wanna make love with you tonight, but maybe we'd lose respect for each other; besides it's wrong and you've never known a man, and wanna wait till you're married. Is that right, honey?"

"Yes, Jeem, I want be with you all night. You good man." A tear slowly dripped down her cheek. Her fingers gently massaged his hair. "Oh my Jeem, I love you so much and do spect you, but I will know man after marry and hope it you my dear." Tears formed in his eyes. Her head rested on his chest. They were content with the moments and sleep came easy.

"Jeem, Jeem, hurry, wake up, it late." He rubbed his eyes as sunlight poured through living room windows. She stood over, looked down, and shook him. "We must go now."

"Ah, ah, what time is it?" he asked while sitting on the edge of the couch.

While changing into a revealing yellow and green dress, she exclaimed, "Hurry, it 7:30. Let's go."

He yelled, "Oh my God, gotta buzz." He sprang off the couch. He put shoes on. then quickly escorted her into a cab and shouted to the diminutive driver, "Get us to the main gate quick and get extra pesos."

The taxi driver back and smiled, "Ok, Joe, ok, Joe."

After exiting, they ran across the smelly creek where an imposing large white sign with bold black letters greeted them. U. S. Naval Station, Subic Bay, R. P. A well-built tanned Marine gate guard, attired in uniformed royal blue trousers, short-sleeve khaki shirt, and wearing a pistol suspiciously eyed them as they halted, catching their breath.

Jim whispered, "Don't say anything, I'll do the talking." He approached the entrance and produced a liberty card and military I.D.

A stern expression came over the lance corporal. "Who's the girl? She can't come in here sailor."

"Look, she's my guest and has been here before pal."

He pressed his lips together and stared at the couple. "Ok, let's see some I. D." She retrieved a student I. D. with a photo from her purse, handing it to the inquisitive guard who perused, looked at her, and then addressed him. "Listen, you'll have to sign her in as a guest, and you're responsible for the lady."

Jim nodded and thought, "Let's get this over with, my ship's leaving in ten minutes."

After quickly scribbling his name, he grabbed her hand, "Come on sweety, we gotta run." Her little legs tried keeping up with him, but after 500 yards she abruptly stopped to catch her breath. He put his arm around her saying, "Don't worry Linda, I'll slow down." A few gray Navy jeeps and little Toyota cars motored about as they sprinted past the club where they danced months before.

Jim halted against a palm tree and placed his hands on his knees, and bent down as his chest heaved. He looked 200 yards beyond seeing black smoke billowing from two stacks of a ship. His eyes bulged, while excitedly pointing and exclaiming, "There she is honey, that's her. Come on, we gotta make it."

Hand in hand they scampered between scattered banana and palm trees through a small park While moving, he reflected, "Boy, here I go again tryin' to catch my ship like in Frisco. Damn it, I can't miss her."

Several enlisted attired in short sleeve dungaree shirts and tropical whites, walked along the pier as they reached the dock. He moved near Linda as her chest heaved and asked, "Are you ok sweetheart?" She nodded, wiping sweat off her forehead.

Approaching, he yelled toward the vessel, "Wait for me, wait for me." His eyes widened as the lines had already been cast off. She slowly moved away! He stopped near the pier's edge, quickly retrieved all his money, handed it to her and kissed her. "Here angel, you'll need this for bus fare and food."

Most of the crew stood at parade rest in tropical whites on weather decks. As the ship drifted further, an officer on the quarterdeck stared, at a Chief and asked, "Who's that?"

"Well sir, if he's one of our guys, he's in deep trouble."

The destroyer was now twenty yards away and still backing into the bay. He shouted, "Hey, this is my ship. Throw me a line now."

A burly chief stared and bellowed, "You snooze, you lose sailor."

He quickly slipped off his white loafers, turned, kissed her lips, and lovingly stared. "I will miss you until I see you again, and if not, may we meet in Heaven, Linda. I love you." She teared, but was aghast seeing him dive into the oil-spotted water taking long quick strokes.

Linda shouted, "Jeem, Jeem what are you doing? Be careful. I love you."

He'd gathered an audience as one sailor at another on the dock, "That guy's crazy."

*Satterfield* was now 50 yards from the dock as he vainly tried reaching her. He'd never swam faster. The O. O. D. motioned to Kowalski standing on the bridge, "Captain, I don't believe what I'm seeing. Looks like a civilian swimming toward us." The skipper walked out on the quarterdeck, , doing a double take with his eyes.

"Now I've seen everything. It's some kid. Why is he swimming toward us?" Sailors on stationary vessels as well as Filipino dock and shipyard workers in the immediate vicinity ceased activities, looked, stunned at seeing a man in the water.

A few hollered encouraging words. "Go sailor, go."

Tired, he quit stroking, raised an arm and shouted, "Stop, stop, please stop. It's me, Hickey, Hickey. Treading water, he waved his arms back and forth like a windshield wiper.

Sid, Mike, Smitty and four others looked down, incredulous seeing the sailor 150 yards away.

Reemer shouted, "Oh my God, it's Jimmy!"

"Ya gotta be shitting me," exclaimed Smitty.

"I'm gonna see the old man", Mike said.

"Are ya crazy or somethin'? We're at departure stations," snapped Reemer.

Mike broke ranks, ran into the bridge, and saluted Kowalski. "Excuse me captain." He pointed to starboard exclaiming, "Sorry for breaking ranks sir, but that's one of our guys out there trying to catch us and board."

"Well, as far as I'm concerned he's over the hill and will be written up. Do you know who he is?"

"Yes sir, it's Hickey. Ah Captain, with all due respect sir, couldn't we stop and toss him a line?"

He stared at the petty officer, and then glared, "Thomas, do you know long it takes this ship to build up enough steam?"

He shook his head, "Ah, no sir."

Kowalski lowered his head resting a fist under his chin, thought a few seconds and responded. "You know something Thomas, if it was anyone other than Alden or Hickey I would've kept steaming, but I'll say this much, he sure had guts in April and guts now." He looked at the O.O.D. and helmsman and ordered, "All stop."

"All stop, aye. "

He motioned Thomas with a forefinger to follow him outside. The two shafts ceased revolutions after the engines stopped as *Satterfield* now drifted further, 300 yards from land. Mike looked down and waved as Jim swam faster and neared starboard. The captain gazed down and muttered, "Crazy kid."

The O.O.D. barked down to a boatswain mate standing near a lifeline, "Lower a Jacob's ladder." The exhausted sailor reached, grabbed it with both hands, slowly climbed aboard and collapsed on deck. One man extended an arm, grabbed and pulled him up.

The seaman laughed and looked at Hickey, "Wow, this is something I'll never forget."

Sid, Mac, and others looked down, smiled and clapped as Smitty hollered, "Hey, Jimmy, you made it. Way to go buddy." A corpsman ran into sick bay, retrieved a large brown blanket and placed it over his drenched body.

Cognizant he was safely aboard, Kowalski ordered the ship to steam at six knots. As water dripped from his civilian clothing, Jim leaned against the lifelines gazing at the pier. She hadn't moved, but waved and blew a kiss. He reciprocated, never taking his eyes off her. The vessel sailed away as he watched her image slowly fade into a tiny speck, vanishing into the landscape. His eyes moistened with tears and he thought, "God, she's so good. I already miss her and wonder if I'll ever see her."

Shortly after breaching the bay's entrance, an announcement came, "Secure from special sea and anchor detail. Deck section one commence duties. The smoking lamp is lit. Petty Officer Hickey report to the bridge on the double." He thought, "Oh no, here I go again getting into trouble. The shit's gonna hit the fan, and the captain's probably gonna write me up."

After wiping as much water off as possible, he walked into the bridge as four enlisted, the O.O.D. and Kowalski stood watching. He gazed at the sailor's dejected expression. Jim took a deep breath, swallowed and meekly apologized, "Ah, sir, thanks for helping me get back aboard.

I'm sorry for what happened out there, but I had to get back. I love the *Satterfield,* Captain, and am willing to accept the consequences, sir." He studied him, pondered and moved within two feet, addressing him.

"Hickey, you understand you were to be aboard for muster before we got underway, didn't you?"

"Yes, sir."

"Well, explain yourself, sailor."

He looked at the deck, thought and replied, "Ah, well sir, I met this decent college girl some months ago and fell in love." A lanky nineteen-year-old helmsman, grasping the wheel near the quartermaster chuckled to himself. "Last night we walked along a beach, and talked then we fell asleep on her couch, but overslept."

Lee slightly nodded and inquired, "Oh, I see. Was that her on the pier waving to you?"

"Yes, sir"

The Captain repressed his amusement between the exchanges and replied, "Well, I'll make this as brief as possible." He grinned. "I can't say I blame you. She's a real looker. You have fortitude, perseverance, tenacity, Hickey and are an asset aboard." Lee smiled. "In all my years of sea service, I've never seen anything like what you just did. I admired Alden and your performance after we were hit." His tone lowered to conciliatory. "Don't worry, son. I'm not throwing the book at you, but don't let it happen again, understand?"

He grinned, "Yes, sir."

Kowalski placed his hand on Jim's shoulder and smiled, "Now, if I were you, I'd get below, take those wet civvies off and jump into the shower. You're dismissed."

"Ah, yes, sir and thank you, sir." He smiled and departed.

The skipper at the lieutenant, shook his head and laughed, "Ha, ha, I'm telling ya mister, this one's for the books. I'm gonna enjoy entering the log this evening. You know, I'm glad we have men like Hickey aboard. I don't think we'll have any more problems or incidents sailing back home."

The officer turned, and grinned, "I agree. I think it'll be smooth steaming."

Jim clambered down the ladder seeing Mike, Smitty, Sid and three others changing into work uniforms. Smitty smiled, approached, and gave him a hug. "Man, Jim, we thought you went A. W.O.L or somethin', and then we see this crazy guy in civvies swimming fast toward us. Shit, we didn't know who it was till we seen ya waving and shouting."

As Jim stripped off his clothes and wrapped a towel around his waist, Mike sat on his rack, laughed and exclaimed, "Ha, ha, it could only happen ta Jimmy after all you've been through. Man, ya got balls, but I'm glad ya made it back buddy. You must have had a good time with her last night, eh?"

"Yeah, but fellas, it's not what you're thinking. We just fell asleep on her aunt's couch and cuddled. I talked her into going on base and seeing me off."

Sid buttoned his shirt, and grinned, "Yeah, she saw you off all right when ya jumped into the water. She must have thought you were losing it, leaping in and swimming like some nut trying to catch us. Ha, ha. Buddy, this is something I'm gonna tell my grandchildren."

Jim exclaimed, "I'm glad the captain let me off. Man, I sure was nervous. He at Thomas and asked, "Hey, Mike, do I have duty later?"

"Yup, in my section. Well, we're getting outta here just before typhoon season starts and I got a feeling it's gonna be a good voyage back." Home was two weeks away.

Satterfield repeated her January course, traversing southeast around several islands before entering the Philippine Sea, then steamed east past the Marianas. Six days later, she moved into the channel at Pearl Harbor. Liberty was granted after customs officials inspected the vessel including required claim forms completed by those who purchased any foreign item(s).

Jim and his three buddies congregated and enjoyed a relaxing few hours at Shipwreck Kelly's in Waikiki Beach, their late shipmate's favorite club. Memories of "Log" dominated the conversation while they listened to enchanting Hawaiian music.

Two days later she departed on her final leg of ocean. The trip was uneventful with anticipation running high on calm waters while steaming thirty knots toward the U.S. mainland.

At 0:800, on 1 October, lookouts spotted a low hovering mist, extending miles north and south. As the destroyer sailed closer, a long stretch of slightly visible brown coastline suddenly came into focus on a cloudless, bright morning. California! "Now, make all preparations for entering port. Set the special sea and anchor detail. The smoking lamp is out."

Excited, Tom's heart beat faster. He thought, "I can't wait to see my family." Jim and mates changed into dress whites.

Smitty, standing near Hickey, chuckled and hollered, "Hey fellas, after what we've been through, I wonder if they're gonna give us a parade this morning."

Jim giggled and remarked, "As my dad used to say, yeah sure, plan on it, but don't count on it."

As they approached within a few miles of the channel buoys, Kowalski ordered speed reduced to six knots. Standing on the bridge he flipped a switch under the 1MC speaker and addressed the crew, his voice resounded throughout, as radiomen sat on their bunks.

Good morning men. This is the captain speaking. Soon we'll be home and reunited with family and friends. We've been through a lot during these last nine months, but by the grace of God survived, thanks to your fine efforts and devotion to duty. I'm satisfied and happy to have commanded such a fine crew and proud of each and every one of you. Enjoy your liberty and leave. God bless you. That is all

Mike remarked, "Wow! That was some speech the captain gave." He at teary eyed Jim nearby. "Hey, what's wrong buddy?" A half dozen others turned and looked.

He wiped his eyes, "Ah, it's just the Irish in me coming out I guess. I got emotional hearing the skipper's address." Jim paused, took a deep breath and continued. "Man, we have the best captain in the navy. He'd do anything for us cause he's a good man. His burden of command is great and I can't fathom what I'd do. You know, he spoke from the heart and loves us."

Sid rose, stood near Jim's rack and endorsed, "Jimmy, I couldn't have said it any better. Man, I'm proud we've got him as our skipper."

Mac sat, finished polishing his shoes and yelled, "Man, I'd go to hell and back for that guy."

They turned and quickly looked at him. Jim pulled a white jumper down over his shoulders and chuckled. Mac asked, "What's so funny?"

Jim remarked, "Hey fellas, I think Mac's drift factor's needle is shaking at ninety-nine percent and can't go any further." He looked at Mark. "Hey, where ya been? I think we just did overseas." Everyone laughed.

Mike endorsed and ordered, "That's for sure. Come on, let's go topside and fall in."

Unbeknown to Kowalski and crew, 600 people had congregated on pier two anticipating her arrival at the naval base. Among the throng of families, relatives and friends were a Congressman, several officers, a Rear Admiral, the mayor, local, national media, photographers, on lookers and the Navy band.

*Satterfield* entered the channel as most of the crew stood on weather decks at parade rest. Standing near Mike on the portside, Jim murmured, "Its melancholy."

"What do ya mean?" he whispered.

"Seems like yesterday when we first entered here after sailing from Seattle two summers ago. Log stood right next to me and now he's gone. He'd want us to be happy and enjoy this time."

"Yeah, I agree."

The ship turned, rounding the naval air station where two carriers nestled, moved past downtown then under the Coronado Bay Bridge, when the shipyard came into view. A small harbor tug greeted the vessel, nudging her close near the pier.

Kowalski, standing on the bridge exclaimed to the O.O.D., "My God, I don't understand. Look at all those people down there. I never expected this lieutenant."

"Nor I, skipper."

She stopped as lines were tossed toward sailors securing her against the dock. Suddenly, the Navy band struck up the inspiring *This Is My Country*. Several men wept looking at the throng gazing up, shouting names and waving. Numerous individuals held white signs above their heads. Welcome back George, Tom, Kevin, Dennis, Patrick, Mike, Paul and others.

The announcement came, "Secure from special sea and anchor detail. The officer of the deck is shifting his colors from the bridge to the quarterdeck. The smoking lamp is lit. Liberty commences immediately."

Sailors rushed against lifelines and stood searching for love ones waving. Sid, Mike, Smitty and Jim congregated, gazing at the crowd as the band continued. A few feet from musicians, twelve sailors unfurled a large fifty foot white banner with the words "WELCOME BACK *SATTERFIELD*, THE SHIP THAT WOULDN'T DIE."

Jim smiled and hollered, "Wow, this is great. Look at all those people and brass waiting for us down there. I've never seen anything like it."

Tom departed, ran and scanned, attempting to locate his family. Jim looked at his buddies. "See ya later."

He hurried near Tom who turned and remarked, "There's so many down there. I don't see em' Jimmy."

Suddenly, Jim's eyes widened, catching sight of his wife Janet, holding Shannon. Excitedly, he pointed, "I see em' Tom. Look over there behind those two guys."

Tears streamed down his face as he jumped up, down waving and smiling, "Oh man, Jim. I dreamed of this day. Look at them, aren't they beautiful?" She smiled, lifted Shannon and jumped up, and down, waving.

"Yeah, buddy. This is what it's all about. You sure appreciate this great land and family after being where we were."

Tom placed his hand on Jim's shoulder and grinned, "I couldn't have said it any better.

Dock sailors placed and secured wooden forward and after brows to the main deck. Sailors bounded off running into loved one's arms, hugging and kissing. Two men dropped and kissed the pier as photographers snapped away. The joyous occasion was a scene repeated numerous times after men returned from World War Two.

Several members of the media surrounded Lee and the officers shortly after debarking as cameras rolled. He saluted an admiral, who smiled and shook his hand. Lee's eyes quickly beheld his short blond wife who ran into his arms and embraced the happy warrior. A reporter, holding a microphone, rudely attempted interrupting with a question. He kissed his wife, and retorted, "Not now." The reporter backed away, seeking another sailor.

Tom looked at his buddy, and smiled. "See you later, Jimmy. I'm going down. What a homecoming."

Tom ran off as Shannon's little legs pumped toward him, hollering, "Daddy, daddy."

He picked her up, held and kissed her.

With outstretched arms, Janet followed, yelling "Tommy, Tommy." She slammed into him embracing her man as tears flowed.

"Oh my, God, you're here, and that's all that matters," he said. Holding his little girl, he planted a long kiss on his wife's anticipating lips.

She wiped her cheeks, remarking, "We missed you so much and worried after we heard about what happened. I love you and am so happy. I don't know what to say, honey."

"Darling, ya don't have to say anything. I'm the happiest man in the world right now cause I'm back and we're together again on God's good earth."

The band struck up *Anchors Aweigh* while Jim scanned for relatives. Still aboard, he wondered, Well, Pete and Jean are probably working now, but I wonder if Mim and Pop are here. Seconds later, his eyes focused on a tall senior with a little blond haired blue eyed girl, sitting on his shoulders standing near a diminutive, elderly lady holding a sign which read "Welcome home Jimmy." Gloria, standing near Mim saw him. Exited, she jumped up and down, smiled and screamed, "There he is."

Sid rushed over as Jim excitedly pointed, saying, "There they are Sid. There they are." He jumped up and waved.

He slapped his back, ordering, "Get going and have a blast tonight on liberty, buddy." Jim walked down, shimmied between several people, ran and hugged them.

After reuniting with his family, for some inexplicable reason, the sailor turned around. Fifty yards behind, an elderly couple stood somber, holding a folded American flag, observing the joyful arrival as several people strolled, departing down the pier, oblivious of the two.

"Excuse me. I'll be right back," Jim announced. He walked away and slowly approached two people standing in the background. He reflected, "They look like they're from some way out rural area and could be Tim's folks. I wonder what they're doing here.

The man wore a short-sleeve, dark blue shirt under suspenders, holding up baggy light green trousers. Above large cheeks and a protruding stomach was a full head of disheveled gray hair. The shoulders were broad and muscular below a weather-beaten face, and a six foot frame. His petite wife's black-rimmed glasses rested on a pug nose above an old fashioned polka-dot white dress, reaching below the knees.

He stopped, stood a few feet away, smiled and asked, "Are you Tim's folks?"

"Yes. Who are you?" the man asked in a broken crusty voice.

"James Hickey." Jim shook his hand. Both hands were tough with callouses, evidence of years toiling on a farm. His wife's voice was sweet and gentle, almost childlike.

She asked, "Did you know our son?"

"Yes, I was proud knowing him pretty well. He was our leader, and like a father or older brother, but most of all, I'm proud saying he was my friend who sacrificed himself out there for us." He looked at both and asked, "Ah, why did ya come all this way?"

Mr. Loggins toward the ship at some lingering sailors and curiosity seekers. "I wanted to see the ship he served on. We were hoping to meet a few men who knew him. I'm glad you took an interest."

Jim looked down thought, and responded, "I'm very sorry for your loss, Mr. and Mrs. Loggins. We loved your son. He was an unselfish, caring and good man. I just want ya to know that no finer man ever served or wore the uniform of the U. S. Navy better than your son, Tim. All of us really miss him." He moved closer, widened his arms, placing them on their shoulders.

She quickly reached into a little black purse, retrieved a handkerchief and wiped tears. Her husband wept while placing an arm around her. Jim stepped back and wiped a tear.

"You raised a great son who inspired and kept us together, despite all our problems. I see why he was such a man because of good parents like you."

She looked up and nodded, "Thank you Jim. It means a lot to us. We received a nice letter of consolation from the captain explaining his death."

Mr. Loggins lowered his head pressing his lips together and asked, "Where they bury him?"

"He requested an at sea funeral and rests on the bottom of the South China Sea."

His mother remarked, "Well, we'll have some fond memories of him. Ya know, his son isn't taking it too good after we got the telegram, but time heals all they say."

"Well, I have to get back. I'll pray for you. I'm glad I met you. God bless you."

Mr. Loggins placed an arm around her, turned and slowly walked down the pier toward a nearby parking lot. He watched until they faded among the departing throng, and then wiped a little tear and thought, "God, I feel so sorry for them."

James Hickey looked as an assemblage of screeching gulls dipped their wings above, surrounding the destroyer while a small white cloud drifted, and hovered over her. Silent to mortal ears, Heliena Satterfield's soft, angelic voice from heaven resounded throughout the vessel.

My spirit guided you through the years, you my sons who fought so bravely in this war and never gave up, just as I never gave up, fighting against that terrible epidemic so long ago. Without you they couldn't sink this fine ship which bears my name. I love all of you who proudly honored with your service. Well done sailors.

At our nation's capitol, the old man struggled rising, stood back, wiped tears while gazing at the name Timothy Loggins and saluted the Vietnam Memorial. The family drew near and surrounded him.

His wife inquired, "Honey, are you all right?"

He gazed into her eyes, took a deep breath, tightly embraced her as his daughters and grand- children surrounded and hugged him. Jim wiped another tear, grinned and looked at his wife.

"Yes I am, dear. Now, Linda, let's go home."

# ABOUT THE AUTHOR

James Layton is a freelance writer, speaker and consultant. He served six years in the U.S. Navy as a Petty Officer holding a top secret clearance working in Communications aboard two ships in war zones off Vietnam in 1968 and 1971 including duties on a Rear Admiral's staff.

After an honorable discharge, he majored in history and psychology in college, was a business owner and consultant. Specializing on the Vietnam War, on occasion has lectured at community colleges; been a key note speaker at the U.B.S. Financial Services annual shareholders dinner, and monthly Rotary Club meetings. His human interest and war veteran articles have been featured in the Heritage Newspapers. He is currently writing a non-fiction book, A Yank in the Pacific, a chronology of Naval service to be published in 2017.

Contact: jameslytn@yahoo.com.

www.ingramcontent.com/pod-product-compliance
Lightning Source LLC
Chambersburg PA
CBHW051236260626
47162CB00002B/460